No Cure for Murder

Lawrence W. Gold, M.D.

No Cure for Murder 2011© by Lawrence W. Gold, M.D.

A Grass Valley Publishing Production
To order additional copies of this book, e-mail
grassvalleypublishing@gmail.com

Cover Art©2011 by Dawne Dominique
Edited by Diana Rubino

SBN-13: 978-0615575070
ISBN-10: 0615575072
Second print edition December 2011

Printed in the United States of America

Dedication

To my wife, Dorlis, for incredible dedication and support.

In memory of Charles M. Gold
(1908-2008)
He loved life, his family, and taught us not to fear aging.

Acknowledgments

Donna Eastman, a great editor who made this possible.

Joseph Barron, a true renaissance man, my writing buddy. Gone but not forgotten.

Writers groups on both coasts. WOW in Palm Coast, Florida and Sierra Writers in Grass Valley.

Other Works By Lawrence W. Gold, M.D.

Fiction Brier Hospital Series:

First, Do No Harm

No Cure for Murder

The Sixth Sense

Tortured Memory

The Plague Within

Trapped

Hybrid

Never Too Late

State of Mind

The Doctors' Lounge

Other Novels:

For the Love of God

Rage

Deadly Passage

A Simple Cure

Non-Fiction:

Talking To Your Physician, a lighthearted look at the doctor/patient relationship

All available in print, Kindle, and most as audiobooks.

Chapter One

Julie Kramer pulled off her sweat-soaked green surgical cap as she entered the recovery room at Brier Hospital. "Where is Mrs. Hogan?"

The recovery nurse checked her clipboard. "She's in bed one, Doctor."

Julie walked to the gurney and placed her hand on Shannon's cheek. "Are you awake?"

Shannon Hogan drew the thin sheet up to her neck. "I think so. It's freezing in here."

Julie brought a heated blanket to Shannon and reviewed the results of the colonoscopy just completed.

Shannon heard the cold words and felt Julie's warm hand on her shoulder. "I'm sorry, what did you say?"

"I wish there were other words than tumor or cancer...they spark our primal fear like shouting 'fire!' in a crowded theater."

Shannon held her face between both hands and cried.

Half listening to Julie's explanation, Shannon tried to absorb the surgeon's meaning. Like a drowning woman, she fought for the surface and gulped for the essence of life just in time to hear the reassuring words. "Thirty years ago, cancer was a death sentence. Not anymore."

Julie grasped Shannon's hands. "We found it early, that means you're going to be around for a long time."

Shannon and Peter Hogan were deeply religious people and had their faith tested through a lifetime of loss. First came the tragic death of their six-year-old daughter

Mandy to leukemia. Then the business failures, the loss of their home in the Berkeley Hills fires of 1991, Peter's heart attack and bypass surgery, and Shannon's cranky, stubborn mother who lived with them for twenty years, proving that misery, indeed, loved company. With her mother gone, the kids settled and Pete's retirement in sight, Shannon made a tragic error; she forgot that providence had not lost its special interest in her.

With retirement a year away, Pete came home one night with a pile of brochures.

Shannon scanned the colorful photos. "Mexico! We can't move to Mexico."

"South of the border, we can live like royalty. They have everything we'll ever need."

After several trips, they settled on San Miguel de Allende for their retirement. It had perfect weather, a large American community, and cultural richness...their dream come true. They'd sell their home and be on their way.

So much for that, Shannon thought one morning, three weeks before they were to leave. It began with non-stop cramps in her abdomen, followed by the shocking bright red blood in the toilet. Colonoscopy and the dreadful diagnosis followed, bad news delivered with blinding speed.

Peter walked alongside the gurney as they wheeled Shannon toward the elevator and surgery. "You must get her through this, Julie."

Julie placed her hand on his shoulder. "Don't worry, Pete, Shannon will be just fine."

After the fourth hour, Julie came into the surgical waiting room. Her smiling face was the most beautiful thing Pete had seen in his lifetime.

Naturally, that wasn't the end of it. Weeks of complications followed. Cycles of desperation and relief, then more despair, and finally the answer to their prayers, Shannon was nearing discharge.

As I enter 502, Shannon Hogan's room, I see my hazy outline cast against the wall from the subdued indirect lighting. I blend with the shadows and move in silence to her bedside.

Her face reflects the peace of untroubled sleep, a few moments of respite from her pain. She's caught in a dream, ignorant of the futility of it all, as if her denial could stem the inevitability of the final release—the ultimate freedom to a life everlasting.

I smile in anticipation, feeling the force of my will over her existence, a power reserved to the few.

When I reach into the pocket of my white coat, I feel the syringe. It's warm from my body heat. It's 30ccs of a milky fluid—my special gift.

Sterile syringe...what a joke.

It's time.

I withdraw the syringe, rub it against my cheek, and then caress it as if it were a chess piece, a captured queen. The clear plastic IV line is within my reach as I find the intravenous injection port. The pink cover over the hypodermic slides off exposing the shiny stainless steel needle. It sparkles gaily as its razor sharp tip pierces the rubber stopper of Shannon's IV line.

I look up, staring at the heavens through the two floors above and say my silent prayer.

I grasp Shannon's sleep-warmed hand, giving it a gentle squeeze. Her eyes flutter then open. Shannon looks around and tries to focus on my silhouette. With the light behind, I know that all she can see is my outline.

"What..." she begins, but I silence her with a whisper. "It's going to be all right. He is with us tonight."

Shannon trembles. I'm certain she's not sure if this is a nightmare.

I feel warm as I push the plunger slowly, inexorably down the barrel toward the syringe's base. Shannon grimaces as the fluid burns the veins of her arm. Then her lips part to scream. I quickly cover her mouth with my leather-gloved hand. She grasps my arm trying to escape, but I hold her still with my other hand. She's remarkably strong until the medication forces her muscles to relax, to twitch, then they refuse to respond to her commands to contract. Finally, the muscles surrender to the potent power of the paralyzing potion.

She's awake, I can tell, a silent witness to her death, but she's unable to move a muscle.

Her pupils widen in panic.

Her heart pounds.

She tries to breathe...smothering...gasping in her mind, but frozen.

Shannon's conscious brain cries, please...please...no...no...Pete...Mandy...My God, no... no...no!

I take a serene sigh of satisfaction, raise the sheet to her neck, and caress her face. A single small tear streaks over her cheeks from the corners of her pleading eyes.

My work done, I stroll to her door and depart.

Chapter Two

Ginny Harrison stared at the clock—just minutes left to make a final dash through her assigned patients before morning report. Although exhausted from a busy, understaffed night shift, she felt satisfied. She'd handled each curve ball pitched by her difficult patients during the eight-hour inning.

When Ginny reached Shannon Hogan's room, she sensed it at once.

Something is wrong.

She pushed the door open, rushed to the bedside, touched Shannon's cold hand, and felt the throbbing terror pass through her abdomen. She flipped on the overhead light. Shannon's rosy face had turned an ashen purple-blue in the bright fluorescence. Ginny's hand hovered over the Code Blue button at the head of the bed...

Is it too late? she thought.

She pushed the button.

Code Blue 5th Floor, Code Blue 5th Floor, Code Blue 5th Floor, screamed the PA system throughout the hospital.

Ginny applied her mouth to Shannon's cold lips, gave three quick deep breaths, then placed both hands, one above the other, on the lower part of the breastbone and began cardiac compressions. She felt Shannon's sternum groan under her pressure. She counted each compression...one, one thousand, two, one thousand, three, one thousand. In moments, the room filled with members of the Code Blue team.

Too late, Ginny thought. Shannon's gone.

"Jack!" Ginny shouted, as Dr. Jack Byrnes entered the room followed by Ahmad Kadir, his resident from UC San Francisco. "She was fine just two hours ago."

Jack Byrnes had consulted on Shannon's case and as the medical director of the Intensive Care Unit, he supervised the code. When he placed the defibrillator paddles on her chest, the monitor traced a listless line across the screen. The cooling body, fixed and dilated pupils told it all. He turned to Ahmad. "Let's call it. We're too late."

Ginny clutched Jack's arm. "No...please."

Jack's head swung in a pendulum of hopelessness.

The team's reaction to Jack's announcement was like opening a beautifully wrapped gift box and finding it empty. Their energy and enthusiasm, like that of the disappointed child, evaporated in an instant.

Jack looked across the room. "Has anyone called Dr. Weizman?"

"No," said Ginny.

Jack dreaded the need to awaken the old-timer so early in the morning. "I'll do it."

"Get me Dr. Weizman," Jack asked the hospital operator. Seconds later, he heard the phone click.

"Dr. Spelling here."

Zoe Spelling had joined Jacob in Family Practice two years ago.

"Oh, Zoe, I was trying to reach Jacob."

"I'm on call tonight. Can I help you?"

"It's about Shannon Hogan. The nurses found her dead this morning."

"My God. What happened?"

"Don't know."

"I'll have the answering service put you through to Jacob. He's cared for that family for years. He'll want to know."

Jack waited on hold for several seconds, when the phone clicked. "Dr. Weizman, here. So what's so important it can't wait a little longer?" came the words with a hint of an Austrian accent.

"Jacob, it's Jack Byrnes. I have bad news for you."

"Say it."

"Shannon Hogan's dead. Her nurse found her thirty minutes ago. It was too late to try to resuscitate her."

"My God...the expected, I can deal with, but surprises like this, I hate. Have you called her husband Pete?"

"No. I'll do it now."

"I'll be right in."

"That really isn't necessary, Jacob. I'll deal with him."

"Thanks for the thought, Jack, but after sixty years of practice, I know my responsibilities. I may be old, but that I remember."

Jack smiled. "I'll have the orderly meet you at Brier's front door with your walker."

"For a nice guy, Jack, you can be a real...what's the technical term...oh yes, a schmuck."

Jack laughed. "I'll see you when you get here."

Jack thought his interchange with Jacob reflected an interesting phenomenon. They had jumped seamlessly from the somber gloom of death, worse because it was unexpected, to the light-hearted banter of physicians working under the double whammy of stress and disappointment.

Shrinks call humor of this type a defense mechanism. Jack wasn't so sure. When Jack first experienced this type of humor during his internship, it smacked of indifference, like a doc at the end of a failed code blue, announcing, "Well, that sure made me hungry. Who wants pizza?"

Now that he was part of this brotherhood, Jack understood that anguish endured alone, like pain at night, was always worse. Humor, like the cool strength of gravity that binds our solar system, draws people together by its warmth.

Of all the senior physicians at Brier Hospital, it was only Jacob Weizman's calm congeniality that allowed Jack to treat the eighty-eight-year-old esteemed physician as he would a contemporary.

Jacob Weizman and his wife Lola were Holocaust survivors. Jacob came to New York City after the Second World War and ran a General Practice for several years before moving to Berkeley.

Jacob graduated from the University of Vienna Medical School two years before Hitler's invasion of Austria. He accepted a teaching position at that venerable institute, well known for a faculty that included some big names in the history of medicine, including Semmilweis and Billroth, among others. Jacob's father, a senior officer at the Bank of Vienna, shared his pride in Jacob's achievements with anyone who'd listen.

The Nazi invasion of Austria began on March 12, 1938. By mid-March, 138,000 Jews came under the control of German troops. The Germans immediately disseminated anti-semitic hate propaganda in newspapers and magazines and destroyed Jewish businesses. In a matter of weeks, they removed all Jewish professors and instructors from Austrian universities. The Nazi SS captured and sent Jacob and his entire family to Auschwitz concentration camp. Jacob was the sole survivor. He never talked about his dark days at Auschwitz, except to recall for his children the icy Saturday, January 27, 1945 when Soviet forces liberated the camp. That day, Jacob and Lola Ophir, another survivor, left together. She was to become his wife of fifty-eight years.

Jack Byrnes had, on occasion, caught a glimpse of the tattooed numbers on Jacob's forearm, the inky image of a world gone mad and the symbol that cried, "Never Again."

Jack's thoughts returned to Shannon. What the hell happened?

Shannon Hogan, age sixty, had been through a horrendous hospital course. She spent three weeks in the ICU recovering from complications of surgery for a bowel obstruction secondary to colon cancer. Jack hated to characterize anyone with cancer as fortunate, but the bowel obstruction had revealed the tumor early, and without evidence of local or distant spread, her prognosis was good. Even someone in this business who sees death on an almost daily basis, never really gets used to it, especially when the end arrives without notice.

Jack grabbed Shannon's chart, found her home number and dialed to reach Pete, her husband.

The sleep-distorted voice answered. "Hello. Who's calling?"

"Pete, it's Jack Byrnes..."

"What's wrong?" came his alarmed reaction.

"It's Shannon. You'd better get down here in a hurry."

"What is it?"

"Just get here right away."

Is this small deception an act of kindness or of cowardice? Jack thought.

Pete lived only four blocks from Brier Hospital. A few minutes of anxiety for Pete, and a moment of mental preparation for both of them.

Ten minutes later, Jacob Weizman walked up to Jack as he was making his final note on Shannon's chart.

Jack looked up.

While Jacob knew the term degenerative change accurately described the physical affects of aging, the word degenerate, its cognate, had a sardonic appeal for him. Something about the term 'dirty old man' made him smile. Hardly the giant at five feet six inches, Jacob couldn't deny the recent measurements showing that he'd become even more vertically challenged—two more inches gone. He looked a bit like Sigmund Freud with a white beard and a matching full head of hair combed straight back. He wore a cream-colored Harris Tweed sport coat, a matching vest and bow tie.

Jacob looked around. "Is he here yet?"

"He should be here any moment."

Jacob turned to Ahmad, extended his hand. "Jacob Weizman."

"I'm sorry, Jacob. Ahmad Kadir is with me on an intensive care rotation. He's a resident at UC."

Ahmad, dark-skinned and heavily bearded, looked Middle Eastern. "Nice to meet you, sir," said Ahmad with a subtle Palestinian accent. He hesitated a second before accepting Jacob's extended hand.

Jacob turned back to Jack. "What happened?"

"Don't have the slightest. She was recovering well. It's a shocking loss."

Jacob stroked his beard. "We're going to need an autopsy."

Ten minutes later, the door of the elevator opened and a red-faced and anxious Peter Hogan stepped out. As he rushed toward Shannon's room, Jack moved from the nursing station and stepped in his path. "I'm so sorry, Pete. It's too late."

He paled. "Too late? What are you talking about?"

"We tried everything, but she died in her sleep."

Peter clenched his jaw and reddened. "Died? What the hell are you talking about? She was getting better. She was going home in a few days. We were moving to Mexico..."

Jacob walked up to them. "I'm so sorry, Peter. She was sleeping...she didn't suffer."

Pete tried to push past them into her room. Jack held him back for a moment, and then felt Pete sag in his arms. They sat him into a wheelchair. He leaned forward and wept.

After a few minutes, Pete raised his head. "What happened, Jacob?"

"I don't know. We sure didn't expect this. Maybe it was a heart attack or a stroke." Jacob hesitated for a moment. "I'd like to get an autopsy. Then we'll know."

"My God. Hasn't she been through enough? I can't stand the thought of her being cut open like that."

Jacob placed his hand on Pete's shoulder. "It's not that way. It's more like surgery."

Asking a grieving family for permission to perform an autopsy felt like hitting a person when they were down, but Jacob tried to get one on his patients when the cause of death was unclear.

In many ways, the postmortem examination is a character test for physicians and sometimes a Pandora's Box. Through the autopsy, physicians expose themselves to the revelation of a mistake, a missed critical diagnosis, or the chance that they injured the patient with their treatments.

"Can I see her?"

"Of course, but let me see if she's ready."

He stared at Jacob oddly. "Ready?"

"The nurses like to straighten up and make her presentable."

"Presentable?"

With Pete standing before them, Jacob slowly pushed the swinging door open and they followed him into his wife's now dim and silent room.

Ginny Harrison had remade the bed and just pulled the sheet over Shannon's face.

The white-sheeted body is iconic of death. The image draws immediate attention, the respectful pause, the turned head, and the questioning glance.

Pete stood by her bedside, looking down in silence. After a moment, he stared at Jacob and nodded.

Jacob grasped the top of the sheet. With solemnity, he slid it down to expose Shannon's face.

Pete stared at the bloodless, lifeless wax figure of what was once his wife, his life. His eyes widened and his legs weakened. He grasped the bed for support.

Jacob held Pete's shoulders for a moment until he regained control.

Pete placed his hand on Shannon's cheek. When he touched her cold lifeless skin, he reflexively retracted his hand with the reality of death. He stared at the woman who'd shared his life, then bent over and placed a kiss on her lips.

"Get me the papers to sign, Jacob. I need to know what happened."

Chapter Three

Jacob Weizman slipped out of Brier Hospital at 8:00 a.m. and walked, head down, toward the parking garage. A few deep breaths and the salty scent of the San Francisco Bay, just three miles to the west, cleared his sleep-deprived head.

When he reached the bright fluorescent entranceway, Angel Hernandez, the night attendant, waved. "Don't tell me you worked all night, Doc."

"No, Ángel," said Jacob, using the Spanish pronunciation, "just a sad beginning to another day."

"Sorry, Doc. Hope the rest of your day is better, and say hello to Mrs. Weizman for me. Ella esta La Pistola."

"Lola, a pistol...fair enough."

Jacob stared at his 1970 black Volvo 122. He brushed away the light coating of dust blurring his wrinkled image in the mirror-like hood finish and recalled the day he and Lola purchased the car new from the Berkeley showroom floor. Growing old together, he and the Volvo remained sturdy, a bit outdated, but far from useless, he prayed.

Jacob climbed in. He sank in the well-worn driver's seat, and drove through the ground fog up the steep wet streets to their modest home nestled in the Arlington section of the Berkeley hills.

When he cracked open the front door, the smell of freshly ground coffee and baking blueberry scones set his mouth watering.

Lola bent before the oven, holding the door ajar and checking on her creations. The kitchen table held a stack of newspapers, including the San Francisco Chronicle, the Oakland Tribune, and the New York Times. They shared these papers each morning and fought over the crossword puzzles, especially the Times. Jacob was faster, but Lola was better, and she delighted in looking over his shoulder and kibitzing—more like tormenting him over missed clues. More than once, he fended off her pencil-poised-hand that loomed over his empty squares.

Lola was three years his junior. She stood at five feet two inches and weighed 98 pounds. She looked and sounded like a skinny Dr. Ruth Westheimer. Her pruned face reflected the calendar and the years of heavy smoking. Her brown-stained second and index fingers said that in spite of Jacob's admonitions, she remained a slave to the deadly habit.

"If it hasn't killed me yet, it never will."

Jacob sagged into his kitchen chair and rolled to his place before the east-facing window. The rising sun finally broke through the morning fog and shined brightly through white sheer curtains.

Lola pushed the button on their Senseo coffee maker for a second cup. The machine growled, forcing pressurized hot water through the Colombia Supremo blend.

As she zipped across the room, Jacob smiled. Lola still had the graceful movement of a much younger woman, a talent hard earned in the ballet she studied in Vienna so long ago.

"Shannon Hogan's gone."

Lola froze for a moment, then carried Jacob's mug to the table and added three teaspoons of raw sugar.

"What happened?"

Jacob yawned. "We don't know."

"Come on, Jacob. You must have some idea."

"She went through so much. I could have accepted her death at any time during the initial part of her hospital stay, especially in the ICU when she was so sick, but to die suddenly when she was getting better, when she was getting ready for discharge, I'm getting too old for that kind of disappointment."

"Maybe it was her time."

"Her time?"

"It amazes me that after all we've seen, all we've endured, you still see the world in black and white."

Jacob placed his mug heavily on the table, splashing coffee on the crossword puzzle. "The camps left no room for God, Lola. Where was He when so many suffered and died?"

"I'm not talking God or religion. I can't remember the last time we went to temple...a wedding, I think. I believe we survive for some purpose, and maybe we die for reasons we can't understand."

"You're getting spiritual in your old age."

"Maybe. Our survival is a miracle. Perhaps we're still here for a reason."

"Stubbornness."

Jacob inhaled the sweet scone scent, and then took a bite, washing it down with coffee. "If you're looking for miracles, start with your coffee and scones."

"That poor woman, and Pete. I can't imagine how he's going to cope with her loss. They had a great marriage."

"What choice does he have?"

Jacob took another sip then looked up. "You're going to court today?"

Lola studied her feet. "Yes, Jacob, love of my life."

"It's not funny, Lola. They'll pull your license one of these days. It's your third speeding ticket this year."

"I'm not counting."

"This isn't Florida, where senior power prevails. In California, they'll pull the license of any octogenarian for looking the wrong way. With you, they don't have to look so far."

Lola drove a bright red Honda S2000, literally a red flag for the CHP who knew Lola by name and by reputation as the car with its headless driver sped along.

"Don't worry, sweetheart, if they convict me again, I'll go back to traffic school."

"They won't let you get away with that forever."

"Don't be concerned, Jacob." She winked. "I have a way with judges."

After breakfast, Jacob put aside the papers and incomplete puzzle. "I'll stop at the Zimmerman's on my way to the office. Got to check on Hazel Pincus."

"Eighty-eight years old and still making house calls. The medical staff's going to put out a contract on you."

"I should worry." He smiled and kissed Lola on the lips.

She held him tight for a moment. "I love you, Jacob."

"I love you too, old woman. See you tonight." He hesitated and grasped her hand. "And, do me a favor."

She caressed his cheek. "Anything for my sweetheart."

"Don't get a speeding ticket on the way to court."

Chapter Four

For the first twenty years of medical practice, Jacob Weizman used the small office attached to their home. He enjoyed stepping from his kitchen into his waiting room. Even in those days, his practice was considered outmoded by most physicians who dissociated work from life. Jacob never made the distinction. If it weren't for his success, the need for additional space, and the licensing requirements of a medical office, he'd still be living and working at home.

In the fall of 1965, Jacob purchased a Victorian just two blocks from Brier Hospital. The large first floor served his practice. He rented the second floor to a psychiatrist, Ross Cohen, and a speech pathologist.

As he drove toward his office, Jacob passed by the Brier Hospital complex, a study in contrasts. Bernard Brier, heir to the Brier Mines near Nevada City, California, lived in a Victorian mansion in the hills above Berkeley. Next to the mansion, he built a convalescent home that became a sanitarium, and finally a private, not for profit community hospital. The modern six-story hospital dwarfed the original Brier Mansion, now on the list of historic California sites.

Jacob parked in the space labeled, Jacob L. Weizman, M.D., General Practice and entered the house through a side door.

Margaret Cohen, his office manager smiled at Jacob. "Good morning, Dr. Weizman."

Margaret was only his second office manager, having replaced Lola who threatened to kill Jacob if they worked together one more day. Margaret was in her late 60s and widowed. She had grown old with Jacob and the practice.

"Good morning Maggie, you're looking particularly fetching this morning."

She blushed, pushing back a lock of gray hair from her forehead. It was amazing that at her age, with three children and eight grandchildren, Jacob still made her blush.

"Let me introduce myself, Dr. Weizman, I think you're getting forgetful. The name's Margaret or Marge or Margie."

"I could use a little forgetfulness. Did you hear about Shannon Hogan?"

Margaret nodded. "She was a wonderful woman. I'll miss her. Why do all the good ones go so soon?"

"Don't know, but at least you and I have nothing to worry about."

"How's Pete?"

Jacob shook his head slowly. "Devastated."

"What happened?"

"Don't know. They're doing an autopsy at noon. Just get me out of here on time for a change."

"If you stop flapping your gums, you'll get out of here, no problem."

"Flapping my gums...how charming an image, Maggie."

"You'd better start flapping your wings, Old Man. You have a busy morning."

"Busy. Why do you always keep me busy?"

"You're the one who says I shouldn't turn anyone away...just squeeze them in."

"Start noodging me at eleven. If I'm not out of here before noon, then..."

She slapped a chart into his hands. "It'll be my pleasure, Dr. Weizman."

Jacob finished with his last patient at 11:50. "You're a good girl, Margaret. Thanks."

"Just be back by two, Doctor."

Jacob walked under the midday sun to Brier Hospital. He entered through the enormous sliding glass doors into an ornate lobby decorated with paintings and sculptures. Plaques recognizing major contributors lined one entire wall. He took the elevator to the basement and walked into the morgue.

In his sixty years of practicing medicine, the smell of a morgue—decaying human tissue and formaldehyde, never changed.

Mark Whitson was a man in his mid fifties, Brier's chief of Pathology. He looked up as Jacob entered. "You're on time. I'm just getting started. Is anyone else coming?"

"Jack Byrnes said he'd be here."

"I read the chart. You didn't expect this death, did you?"

"I never expect my patients to die, Mark, but they keep disappointing me."

"Should I look for anything specific?"

"Just the usual. Anything that explains a sudden death."

Mark wore a green scrub suit, a large white plastic apron, and protective goggles. "Do you want a brain exam too?"

Jacob nodded.

Billy Bliss, the diener, or morgue attendant, was as thin and pale as many of their clients and looked like he just came out of the corpse refrigerator himself. He wore the same uniform as the pathologist and stood at the head of the stainless steel table holding a Stryker vibrating saw used to open the skull. Whitson made the classical Y-incision from each shoulder, meeting at the lower ribs and extending to the mid-groin. Jacob watched the diener roll back Shannon Hogan's scalp and begin cutting. The room resounded with the coarse vibrations of the electric saw. Fine puffs of bony powder billowed from the saw's rapidly moving blades. Beyond the incisions, the foul aromas, and the lifelessness of the corpse, opening the skull with this coarse instrument reflected, more than anything else, the vulgarity of death.

Whitson spoke into the microphone hanging over the autopsy table. "The body is a middle-aged woman, measuring 162 centimeters and weighing 63 kilograms." He went on to describe, in vivid detail, his findings as he dissected each major organ system and examined them with care.

Halfway through, Jack Byrnes and Ahmad Kadir arrived. "Anything yet, Jacob?"

"Nothing."

Billy Bliss sneered at Ahmad. "What's that damn Arab doing here?"

Ahmad reddened.

Jack stared at Billy with disgust. "Dr. Kadir is a resident from UC San Francisco. He's working with me. Do you have a problem?"

Billy turned his face down in silence.

Jack shook his head at Mark who raised his palms in the what can I do gesture.

Ignorant and malicious, a great combination, Jack thought.

After about 45 minutes, Mark Whitson had examined the heart, brain, and major organs. He turned to Jack and Jacob. "Sorry, guys. Can't find anything on gross examination. Maybe the microscopic will show something."

Jack shook his head. "I hate this."

Jacob had seen more autopsies than he cared to remember. "It happens. It may have been a lethal heart irregularity. We'll just have to wait for the detail to follow."

Mark smiled at Jacob. "Do you remember your first autopsy?"

Jacob shook his head. "That would be Moses, of course. Do you remember yours?"

Mark nodded. "Who could forget."

Jacob's eyes moved up and to the right. "I can still see the large amphitheater in Vienna. Two hundred medical students and doctors in training. I threw up...three times. Very embarrassing...undignified, in those days. You know, Mark, except for the fancy tables, the modern plumbing, the bright lights, the digital scales, and the electric saws, the procedure hasn't changed in my professional lifetime."

Jack looked around the room. "I guess death hasn't changed much either."

Jacob shook his head. "No, Jack. Death used to be simple...not anymore."

As they left the morgue, Ahmad stroked his black beard. "That wasn't necessary, Dr. Byrnes, but I thank you anyway."

"Ignorance and bigotry must be carried on the same set of genes."

"That was nothing. It was tough being an Arab in the U.S. before 9/11, now it's impossible."

Jacob Weizman entered Brier Hospital at seven the next morning to begin his rounds. After seeing his medical patients, he took the stairs to the fifth floor orthopedic unit. His patient, Lillian Brown, an 81-year-old woman, was entering her second day post op. She'd had her hip replaced by Harrison Baldwin, a new orthopedic surgeon. Lillian had been Jacob's patient for thirty years.

As Jacob walked toward her room, he saw the Code Blue cart parked by the door to her room. He picked up his pace and entered.

Jacob turned to the charge nurse. "What's going on here?"

The nurse was a woman in her early twenties. She turned to Jacob. "Mrs. Brown's sodium level in her blood is extremely low and Dr. Baldwin is about to give her a concentrated salt solution."

"Why didn't you call me?"

"Dr. Baldwin said not to disturb you. He'd take care of it."

Jacob felt his pulse rise and his face redden. He walked to the bedside. "Wait a minute, Harrison. What are you doing?"

"Hi, Jacob. Her sodium is down to 127 and she's a little confused. I'm giving her some salt to fix it."

Jacob pulled Harrison aside. "Don't give her anything. She's been on water pills, diuretics, for years and her sodium level tends to be on the low side."

Harrison gritted his teeth. "Like hell I won't. It's going to be my ass if she has a convulsion and dies."

"Did anyone see her have a seizure or any sign she might?"

"I'm not waiting for that to happen, Jacob. Now, with all due respect, let me take care of my patient."

Jacob faced the nurse. "Nurse, I'm giving you a direct order not to give that salt solution, it's dangerous."

The nurse looked first at the youthful surgeon, recently completing his training, and then at the wrinkled octogenarian, trained before WW II. "I'm sorry, Dr. Weizman, but Mrs. Brown is on Dr. Baldwin's service. I must follow his orders."

"Listen, Harrison, and you too nurse. You're about to make a grave mistake. If you raise her sodium level too quickly, you could kill her."

"I know what I'm doing, Weizman. I'd appreciate it if you'd butt out."

Jacob looked up in dismay. "First of all, Doctor, Mrs. Brown is my patient and has been for many years."

"I'm sorry, Doctor, but she's on my service, and I'm responsible for her care."

"How many emergency cases of low sodium have you treated, Dr. Baldwin?"

"That's none of your business."

"Tell me what you know about central pontine myelenolysis or CPM, Doctor Baldwin."

"Central pontine what?"

"As I thought. After you give that salt solution and Mrs. Brown has seizures or winds up paralyzed in all her extremities, you'll be pleased to know." He pointed at the surgeon and the nurse, "that I'll be the prize witness for the plaintiff when they sue you both. Keep this little fact in mind, this won't merely be a malpractice case, this will be felony assault and if she dies, manslaughter."

Harrison paled.

The nurse looked at Jacob with a new level of respect. "Tell me what I should do, Dr. Weizman."

Jacob smiled, and then looked at the IV bag of fluid and at Harrison. "First stop this IV. It's only making her situation worse. I'm writing new IV orders and a series of blood tests for the next six hours. I'm making additional adjustments as I see how she's correcting her sodium level."

Harrison turned away from the bed and shuffled toward the door.

Jacob followed behind. "I thought I was arrogant in my youth, but compared to you, sir, I was humble."

"Fuck off, old man."

Jacob laughed. "Some time soon, you'll recognize that I just saved your ass. Do me a favor, please."

"What?"

"Don't thank me."

Chapter Five

At 4 a.m., the indirect lighting on the fifth floor medical unit was on its lowest setting in Brier Hospital's silent hallways. Carol Fox, the ward clerk, sat at her desk organizing patient charts and adding the lab and other diagnostic reports.

Carol looked up over the raised nursing station counter and saw Tommy Wells's smiling face.

"Don't you ever get to go home, Tommy?"

He winced at her use of Tommy, but smiled. "It's Thomas, please."

"I'm sorry."

"That's okay. The lab ran out of technicians again, so I volunteered to do a second shift. I really wish the laboratory administration would get its act together."

Thomas was five feet four inches and looked a bit like a fifteen-year-old Michael J. Fox, although he recently celebrated his twenty-fifth birthday. Always small for his age, Tommy took crap from the first day he entered intermediate school. He complained to his brothers, one a sophomore and the other a senior in high school. "I'm tired of being pushed around."

His oldest brother Stan wasn't sympathetic. "Keep away from them."

"I can't."

"Then, you better stand up. If you let them get away with it, they'll never stop."

"They're going to kill me, Stan."

"You want me to have a word with them?"

Tommy's first thought was damn yes, and then he changed his mind. "No. That will only make things worse."

The next day when Mitchell Davis, his main tormenter, knocked the books out of Tommy's hands saying, "Watch where you're going, shorty," Tommy surprised him by landing a punch squarely on Mitchell's nose, his face erupting with a spurt of blood.

Mitchell held his nose. "You fucking punk. I'm going to kill you."

As Mitchell charged toward Tommy, the principal approached the group. "What's going on here?"

"Nothing, Sir. I just tripped and banged my nose."

The principal took one look at it. "Have the school nurse check it out."

Mitchell turned to leave then leaned over to Tommy and snarled, "I'll see you after school."

After school, Tommy was beaten so badly, he was hospitalized and swore he'd never let this happen again.

He took karate lessons and was more than ready when, at eighteen, he joined the Marines and trained as a medical corpsman. After his discharge from the Marines, he took a job at Brier, working in the lab drawing blood. He had fantasies of becoming a physician, but his grades were poor. Who wanted to spend most of his life studying? Tommy thought about nursing, made some inquiries, but in spite of the college counselor's enthusiasm, he knew he didn't have the discipline or the patience for five more years of education.

As he worked each day with physicians and nurses, Tommy was less than impressed with their skill and intelligence.

They're no smarter than me, he thought.

Finally, he concluded that his long-term goal was to be an Emergency Medical Technician. That would give him some degree of independence and he would no longer be at other people's disposal.

Tommy's friendly attitude and helpfulness made him popular among most of the nursing staff. He often stopped at the local Krispy Kreme on his way to work bringing doughnuts for the staff. He dated several nurses, but had yet to sustain a relationship.

Tommy leaned over the counter. "What have you got for me, Carol?"

"Mrs. Hanson in room 512 needs a clotting time."

"No problemo. I'll get right to it."

Tommy hesitated a moment, then smiled at Carol. "Why don't you join me for breakfast after the shift? We can go to Spenger's. They have great seafood omelets."

"I'd love to, Tom...I mean Thomas, but my boyfriend is picking me up this morning. Maybe some other time."

Right.

It was a quiet night except for Sylvia Brockman, an eighty-one-year-old patient of Jacob Weizman. This was the third time she activated the nurse call button.

"I can't sleep," she cried. "They're keeping me awake, get me something to sleep."

Carol, the ward clerk pushed the talk button. "Who's keeping you awake?"

"The rats. They're here. I can hear them chewing."

"Just a minute, Sylvia. I'll get your nurse."

Carol turned to Marion Krupp, Sylvia's nurse, who sat nearby writing chart notes. "You heard, Marion?"

"Yes goddamn it. I'm sick of her complaints and of her physician too. Get Weizman for me, please."

"Dr. Weizman, this is Brier fifth floor. I have Marion Krupp for you about your patient Sylvia Brockman."

"What can I do for you?" said the sleepy voice.

"It's Sylvia again. She's driving us crazy. You must prescribe something for her."

"I'm sorry, Marion. She's only sundowning, getting confused at night. Anything I give her can only make things worse."

"Listen, Doctor, I have five other patients to care for. I can't spend my time holding her hand."

"Get a sitter."

"I don't know if one's available at this time of day. Just give her a mild sedative, please."

"What's mild for you or for many of your younger patients can be dangerous and possibly life-threatening for Sylvia. If you can't get a sitter, call her family and have someone come in. Her hip's much better and she should go home today or tomorrow at the latest."

Marion's face reddened. "You're not helping us, Doctor. This isn't the first time either. I'm reporting this to nursing administration."

"Do whatever you think best, Marion. I've been treating the elderly for a little while, and I know what's best for them."

"We'll see."

"Yes, we will, nurse. Goodnight."

Marion Krupp, now in her mid fifties, was a grouch. Appearance matching personality, she looked like a linebacker in drag. A few senior nurses at Brier had worked with her years ago when she was a practical nurse and equally cranky. After she completed her Associate in Arts degree, she obtained her RN license and continued to work at Brier.

She was an equal opportunity malcontent. Few took Marion's griping personally. She applied her animus to patients, staff, her husband but not to Abigail, her only child. Abby, age eight, was Marion's oasis in the desert of her discontent and could do no wrong.

When Marion's complaining had escalated into vitriolic attack, she found herself before Judy Hoffman, the Director of Nursing.

"You're a good nurse, Marion, but you're so angry."

"I know. I'll do better."

"What's going on?"

"We go way back, Judy. Each year, being a nurse is more difficult and frustrating. I guess I haven't mellowed over the years."

Judy laughed. "I'm not asking for mellowness, Marion, but a little civility would go a long way. When doctors, patients and others on the staff make note of your grim disposition, we have a problem."

"I'll do better, I promise."

"We have resources available from counseling to anger management programs. Think about it before this escalates out of control."

"I will."

Several staffers had known Marion from early childhood. She grew up in Berkeley near the Oakland border. Even with a neglectful mother and an alcoholic father, Marion, to the casual observer, appeared to have a normal happy childhood.

All that changed when her mother died unexpectedly shortly before Marion entered Berkeley High School. She retreated into a shell, refusing the help of friends, relatives, or counselors.

Lola, now awake, turned to Jacob. "What was that?"

"Just another nurse, too lazy or too overworked to sit with an old lady for a minute. Drug them; that's the way out for too many of them these days."

"Put yourself in their place, Old Man. You know how inadequate staffing is at even a good hospital like Brier."

"I'm sorry, Sweetie. To sedate or tranquilize a confused old lady only increases the chances that she'll never go home. I won't do it."

"You're going to get yourself in trouble with the nurses."

"It won't be the first time."

Jacob's brain had a built-in time clock. His eyes popped open regularly at 5:30 a.m., except if something had disturbed his sleep pattern overnight as it had last night. This morning, Lola shook him at 6:15. "Get moving, Old Man. Time's a wastin." One look at the clock and Jacob sprung out of bed and headed to the bathroom.

After they finished breakfast, Lola pointed at the calendar. "Don't forget Saturday. It's Donald's birthday."

"Not again."

"I can't believe we have a son eligible for Medicare. Think how old that makes us."

Jacob smiled. "Can I sedate myself?"

"I can't believe that our three have produced ten."

"I'd substitute quality for quantity."

"You're so full of shit, Jacob. You love your grandchildren."

"I love them when they're asleep. What are you up to today?"

"I'm working at the clinic."

The Berkeley Women's Mental Health Clinic had the support of the city's Department of Health. Lola, a practicing psychotherapist during their early days in Berkeley, was a founder and advisor. She worked closely with younger women, particularly teens, who recognized in Lola a kindred free spirit. She'd done it so long, each generation had its own lexicon that she thought she'd earned a degree in Adolonics, the teenage linguistic lexicon.

Each time she brought one or more of her girls home, Jacob made notes of their peculiarities of speech like the substitution of 'go' for 'said', and the use of chillin', crusin', kickin', 'tights', and 'whatevers'.

Lola smiled as Jacob engaged them in conversation, understanding their syntax and meaning, yet responding with the King's English, albeit with an Austrian accent.

Lola smiled at her husband. "I love how you're able to talk with them. Worlds and decades apart."

"My mind's like a parachute, it functions only when it's open. I only hope they grow out of it. The jargon, Adolonics in this case, is a poor substitute for the precision of the English language for communication of ideas, and it announces to the world that the purveyor is, pardon the expression, a slacker. Three pins short of a strike."

Lola smiled indulgently at Jacob. "You're a very disturbed man."

During their early days, Lola kept up her psychotherapy practice and managed Jacob's office, but soon tired of the intractable despair, frustrating narcissism, and interminable banal neuroses. She found herself caught in a web of mental fatigue, empty and drained of energy. Convinced she couldn't help, she opted to save herself and her marriage. The clinic gave her the opportunity to help young women and maintain her sanity.

Chapter Six

Two and a half years ago, while Jacob was finishing up for the day, Margaret Cohen came into his office. "I have a Dr. Bernard Spelinsky on the phone. He says he's an old friend."

Jacob's mind flashed back to his early days on the lower east side of Manhattan where two young immigrants began the practice of medicine.

"Spelinsky, you old fart, you're still alive."

"I said I'd outlive you, and I meant it."

"What are you doing with yourself? I heard that the New York Post printed banner headlines the day you retired: FINALLY, THE CITY IS SAFE!"

"So, you're still at it. Haven't you done enough damage?"

"I'm hanging on as a community service. Somebody's got to keep these young doctors honest." He paused for a moment. "I was so sorry to hear about Rebecca. She was a gem."

"You and I got better than we deserved when we married. The worst part, Jacob, is the loneliness. Living with someone you loved for so many years then, in a moment, she's gone. How's Lola?"

"Too mean to die."

"I'll be coming to the bay area in the fall. My granddaughter Zoe is moving to Berkeley this summer. Her husband's accepted a position at the University of California." He hesitated. "That's why I called. I'd like you to meet with Zoe and give her some perspective on medical practice in Berkeley. She just completed her residency in Family Practice at Columbia. If you're not too senile, Jacob, you'll convince her to join you in practice."

"I'll meet her, Bernie, but I've practiced alone for too many years. Change at my advanced age may be difficult. Partnerships are like marriage...and they're tough enough."

"Speaking of marriage, meet Zoe. You'll love her. In many ways, she's a modern version of Lola."

"I'm getting chest pain, Bernie. I barely survived Lola as a young man."

"I'll ask her to call you. Her name is Zoe Spelling."

"Spelling? You must be kidding."

"Don't ask me. She changed it for professional reasons."

"Professional reasons?"

"What can I say? She's young."

"Well, Bernie, I'll meet her, but denying her heritage equals strike one."

Three weeks later, Margaret Cohen came into Jacob's office smiling. "Dr. Zoe Spelling is here to see you."

"What are you so happy about?"

"Nothing." She smiled again.

Jacob rose from his desk and walked toward the door to greet Dr. Spelling. Before he could utter a word, a beautiful and very tall woman looking like a fashion model embraced him.

She kissed him on the cheek. "Dr. Weizman, finally we meet. The way grandpa talks about you, I feel like I've known you my whole life."

Zoe paused, then sniffed Jacob's cheek. "You smell like grandpa...that tangy-spicy cologne, what is it?"

"It's Pinaud. You smell it in most barbershops. It's older than your grandfather and me."

Jacob was a little shocked by her informality. He straightened his bow tie then looked up into her dark brown eyes. "It's nice to meet you too."

She had chestnut hair to her shoulders and pulled back over her ears to reveal multiple earrings. Her teeth were so bright, he felt himself squinting from their reflection. She wore a form-fitting sundress with spaghetti straps that accentuated her well-toned arms and shoulders. She had a small tattoo of a hummingbird over her left upper arm.

Jacob absorbed her appearance and felt himself reddening. Thank God I haven't lost my appreciation for a beautiful woman, he thought.

Zoe caught him staring and laughed. "It's okay, Jacob." She hesitated. "Can I call you Jacob?"

"Of course, Zoe."

"I mean that I'm used to it...men staring at me...and not just the young ones."

"I didn't mean anything improper, Zoe, and anyway, I choose not to spend what's left of my life on an analyst's couch."

"It means you're alive, Jacob. Don't apologize. I like when men look at me...at least some men...when they're gentlemen."

Jacob blushed again. "What can I do for you, Zoe?"

"Give me a job. Teach me what it's like to practice today and preserve the old values, then if we like each other and you think my work's good enough, make me your partner."

"Have you picked out your furniture and wall coverings?"

She smiled. "Grandpa said you liked straight talk."

"I do. You just expressed in one sentence what it might take hours of conversation and reading between the lines to elicit."

"So, how about it?"

"You're sure that you want to get into bed with me," he smiled, "metaphorically speaking, that is, and my old values?"

Zoe smiled seductively. "You want me, you got me. I don't like to brag...well maybe a little, but I have high academic scores, great recommendations from the program directors, and I even won Resident of the Year."

"How can I possibly reject the Resident of the Year?"

"When can I meet Lola? I hear she's something else."

"That's one way of expressing it."

Jacob watched as Lola raced around the house with her feathered dust mop. "Enough already."

"Don't tell me what's enough, Old Man. The house has got to look good for company."

"For a brilliant, eighty-five-year-old psychotherapist, don't you think it strange that you're acting like our mothers and grandmothers, women whose entire worth depended on their domestic skills?"

She smiled while caressing Jacob's cheek. "That's crap and you know it. Those women gave so much more. You're a product of their domesticity."

Jacob was suddenly quiet. "If only they'd lived to see the fruits of their labor."

He gazed out the window to their view of the San Francisco Bay while his mind relived the horrors of a painful past.

Lola walked through their living room. "This is ritual, I know, but it makes me feel good to see a clean house ready for visitors. It says something about us, our values, and how we feel about our guests."

When the doorbell rang, Lola scanned the room once more then took a last look in the mirror, straightening her hair.

"Welcome," said Jacob as Zoe Spelling and Byron Harwood entered.

Zoe kissed Jacob on the cheek. "This is my husband, Professor Byron Harwood."

"Professor, it's great to meet you. I've heard so much about you from Zoe."

"Please, Jacob. It's Byron."

They're an odd-looking couple, Jacob thought. She's tall and elegant, and with heels, she stands an inch or two taller. He's rail thin with an Ichabod Crane physique and Adam's apple.

While Jacob backed into the room, Zoe looked at Lola, and then rushed to hug the tiny woman. "I'm so happy to meet you finally. I feel I've known you all my life."

Lola disengaged herself from Zoe's embrace, and then studied her face. "I can see it...it's definitely there."

"What?"

Lola took Zoe's hand and walked her to a wall-mounted photo collection. She pointed to a sepia photograph of two young women. "Look here."

"My God, is that her? I haven't seen that one before."

"Yes. It's Rebecca. I see her in you, a younger, larger version to be sure, but Rebecca nonetheless."

Zoe grasped Lola's hand. "That's so sweet. I loved her so much."

"When I get the chance, I'll make you a copy."

Zoe turned to Byron. "Take my coat and give Jacob the package."

"Of course," said Byron, handing Jacob the ornate cedar wine box.

Zoe beamed. "It's a Cabernet Sauvignon we have made for us and our friends. It's a bit pretentious, but fun."

Byron smiled. "I think you'll like it."

Jacob studied the box. "I hope it's not too expensive. Fine wine is wasted on my palate."

Lola thought she saw pain flash across Zoe's face.

"Something smells delicious," said Byron. "What is it?"

Lola opened the oven and sampled the aroma. "It's Jacob's old world pot roast. It's an old...very old family recipe."

"It's the only thing I can cook," said Jacob. "For Bernie's granddaughter, it seemed appropriate."

The evening passed quickly. Jacob and Lola shared stories of their early days in New York with Bernie and Rebecca.

Zoe glowed when she described her affection for her grandparents. "It nearly killed him when Rebecca died."

Lola caressed Jacob's hand. "We understand. If we could arrange it, we'd go together."

"Don't go anywhere yet," said Byron. "You two provide inspiration for us all."

Afterward, Jacob turned to Lola. "What did you think of Zoe?"

"From what you describe, sweetie, Zoe's more representative of her grandparents than her mother and father."

Jacob smiled. "That's great. Maybe that way our grandkids still have a chance."

Chapter Seven

Jack Byrnes sat at the utilitarian metallic desk in his small office adjacent to the ICU.

"Come in," Jack said to the knock on the door.

Arnie Roth, a family practitioner and chairman of the Quality Assurance Committee, came in and sat next to the desk.

"Hey, Arnie. What's up?"

"It's Jacob Weizman. We must talk about him."

"Give me a break."

"This is more than a little awkward..."

"That's not the word I'd use. I'd use the word ridiculous."

"If you think I want any part of this Jack, you're nuts, but I chair QA and we have complaints."

"Jacob Weizman may be the best physician Berkeley has ever known. Sure, he's a bit of a therapeutic nihilist, but I for one wouldn't like to debate him about that philosophy."

"It's one thing to be skeptical about medication. It's another to make his patients and our staff suffer from his refusal to use them when appropriate."

"When appropriate...that's the phrase that's going to get you into trouble, Arnie."

"Listen, Jack. Jacob's not a kid anymore. He must be in his early eighties."

"He's eighty-eight, Arnie. I can't believe you'd raise his age as an issue."

"You're overreacting. What would you have me do with complaints from the nursing staff? Ignore them?"

"Maybe you're right. I know Jacob, and love him like a grandfather. We live in a world that embraces the young and dismisses the venerable. I won't take part in anything that smacks of such bias at Brier."

"Easy, Jack. Let's just look into the details."

"Be careful, Arnie. Don't screw this up. Looking into something can take on a life of its own, especially when you deal with a committee, its biases, and its hidden agendas."

Carleton Dix had worked as chaplain at Brier Hospital for the last five years. Following his graduation from the American Healthcare Chaplain's Association's program, he had a ministry in Rapid City, South Dakota. Although he engaged everyone in extensive conversation about virtually anything, he said little of his ministry days.

When Jacob Weizman entered Greta Schwartz's room, he saw the chaplain's broad shoulders and the thick mane of hair facing his patient. Carleton was in his early fifties and always wore a freshly pressed ministerial shirt and collar under his white coat with the word Chaplain embroidered on the breast pocket. He constantly licked his lips and adjusted his collar to remind people of his ecclesiastical status.

One morning, while Jacob sat with Dr. Warren Davidson, the chief of medicine, he said, "I never liked the man. I didn't know why at first, my reaction was so visceral. Finally, I concluded that this was because the chaplain is too fixed in his beliefs. I don't like to paraphrase a philosopher, but I agree with him that: Fanatical belief means not wanting to know what is true."

"I agree with you, Jacob, the man's a little ripe for me, but overall, I think he helps many patients. Moreover, he's a good man and demonstrates extraordinary concern for our patients' welfare."

"Maybe so, but when I think back on that most unpleasant part of my youth, I agree with Jonathan Swift: We have just enough religion to make us hate, but not enough to make us love one another."

"Don't you think you're a little old to be crusading against organized religion?"

"Crusade is a word you might wish to avoid these days. I'd be the last one to join such a movement. I saw how religion helped in the camps and how it provided peace for so many in times of trouble. However, if you weigh the deeds done in the name of religion, not the rhetoric, I'm not sure if the good outweighs the evil."

"When that philosophy comes from someone your age, with your experiences, and your intelligence, maybe I should pay attention."

"Bullshit knows no age limitation, Warren. Make up your own mind."

Jacob also hated how the chaplain expressed his beliefs with thoughtless glib platitudes delivered as pronouncements from above. The other thing that bothered Jacob was the chaplain's willingness—probably more than that, an obsession—to foist his beliefs on others whether Christian, Jew, Muslim, or atheist.

"Good morning, chaplain," said Jacob. "How goes it in the Kingdom of Heaven?"

"God is very present with those who are suffering."

"He was AWOL at Auschwitz."

"We can't know His way."

"To paraphrase a philosopher: In religion, neither morality nor belief comes in contact with reality at any point."

"Thank you, Doctor. I recognize the quote, Nietzsche about Christianity. Imagine a Jew quoting that anti-Semite."

"Nietzsche hated all religions, chaplain, but remember what Maimonides said: You must accept the truth from whatever source it comes."

Jacob approached the bedside, grasped Greta's wrinkled hand. "If you'll excuse us now, chaplain."

"Of course, Doctor," he said as he rose to leave. "Have a good day, Mrs. Schwartz."

Greta took Jacob's hand. "He's such a nice man."

Jacob shook his head in disgust, but said nothing. He listened to her heart and lungs, examined her abdomen and extremities. "If you're ready, Greta, you can go home today."

"Isn't it too soon, Doctor?"

"No, Greta. Hospitals are dangerous places. The sooner I get you out, the better."

Jacob returned to the nurse's station and wrote discharge and medication orders for Mrs. Schwartz. When he handed the chart to her nurse, she quickly looked at the orders. "Isn't it a little early to be sending her home, Doctor?"

Jacob shook his head. "No, it's not," then turned and departed.

Chapter Eight

As they drove back in the blowing rain from another old friend's funeral, Lola grasped Jacob's hand. "They're all disappearing. Soon, we'll be the only ones left."

Jacob sighed. "Our young lives started with death. In reality, or by metaphor, it will end the same way. What's left are the crumbs of a life rich in joy and friendship. If it wasn't for your attraction to youth, I wouldn't recognize the names of today's celebrities."

Lola pulled up before Jacob's office. She turned to him and whispered, "Don't leave me, Jacob. I couldn't go on without you."

"Too many funerals, sweetheart. It's depressing."

"Promise you won't leave me."

He leaned over the tight bucket seats in her sports car and kissed her. "I'm not going anywhere...as long as I can help it."

She looked into his eyes. "I'm not letting you go, Old Man."

They understood death and dying, and their solemn vows to each other that when death came, they'd meet it with dignity and on their own terms.

Jacob entered his office at 10 a.m.

Margaret Cohen stuck her head into Jacob's office. "Dr. Spelling wants to see you. It's important. She just finished examining P.J. Manning."

"How much time do I have before my next patient?"

"You have time."

One day, six months after Zoe joined his practice, Jacob got a call from Bernie Spelinsky. "How's it going with Zoe?"

"I love Zoe, but she's too damn serious."

"She hasn't had it easy, Jacob. I love my son Maury, but he's a prick."

"That's a great way to talk about your own son."

"Maybe putz is a better word...it's less angry, and judgment impaired is more accurate than evil."

"Oh well, that's better."

"He spoiled Zoe, doting on her, treating her like a little princess. Nothing she could do was wrong. It's amazing she turned out so well."

Zoe Spelling grew up in the elite Kings Point area of Long Island and had a mixed reaction when she reached Great Neck High School. She was smart, pretty, and popular, an affirmation to an ego already overdeveloped by parental indulgence.

"I'm bored to death, Daddy. The schoolwork's too easy."

Great Neck High was one of the top school systems in the country. Maury didn't understand why they were unable to provide challenging material to his daughter. After several contentious meetings with school officials, Maury sat with the principal. "Gifted students are equally entitled to assistance as the learning disabled. Zoe isn't getting the enrichment she needs."

The principal shook his head. "You're joking. We have more advanced placement classes, arts and clubs supporting a multiplicity of interests than any school in the nation. If Zoe's unable to find intellectual stimulation at Great Neck High, she's not looking."

After two semesters at Higgins Academy, an upstate prep school, Zoe came to Maury. "Get me out of here, Daddy. Great Neck High is a paradise by comparison."

Maury was a bit surprised when the headmaster at Higgins supported her decision. "That may be the best choice for Zoe. Don't worry, we'll keep her records sealed."

"What are you talking about?"

"Ask your daughter."

When he did, Zoe was ready. "They don't get it, Daddy. They may call this a prep school, but to my way of thinking, it's more like a military school. I, for one, won't put up with their crappy rules and regulations."

When Zoe returned to Great Neck, she fell into the swing of high school life, becoming class president, editor of the yearbook, and homecoming queen. With SAT scores through the roof, several prestigious universities expressed an interest, but she'd already selected Hunter College in the heart of Manhattan. She graduated Summa Cum Laude and gave a speech at the commencement held at Radio City Music Hall.

She attended medical school at Columbia and during her training in Family Practice, she volunteered several nights a week at the Free Clinic. The year before completing her training, she met and fell in love with Byron Harwood, a professor of applied statistics at the university.

"The Waldorf-Astoria, isn't that a bit much, Daddy?"

She didn't try to change his mind.

"That's the price when you're my only daughter. You...I mean, we, deserve a gala affair."

During their six-week honeymoon in Europe, Byron received the offer to join the mathematics department at the University of California, Berkeley.

Jacob knocked on Zoe's door, and then entered.

"Oh, Jacob. I need to talk with you about P.J." She paused then continued, "I'm sorry to hear about your old friend."

"They're all dying off, Zoe. What's wrong with P.J.?"

"Since you were away this morning, I saw him. Let me describe what's happened, and then you tell me."

"Shoot."

Jacob delivered Paul Joseph (P.J.) Manning forty-five years ago at Brier Hospital. His father Chester Manning, a former professional football player, was coach for The Golden Bears, and Chester's wife Phyllis was the head librarian. Jacob had cared for the entire family for decades.

P.J., like his father, became an All-American at UC, then played eight years as a wide receiver for the San Francisco 49'ers, retiring after a knee injury.

P.J. married his college sweetheart, Julie, and they settled into a comfortable life in Orinda just east of Berkeley. He had several remunerative offers, but chose instead to accept a position as Director of Athletics at Diablo Valley College in Concord.

They had three girls, the light of their father's eyes.

P.J. and Julie rode their bikes together on the large complex of east bay paths and P.J. played over-thirty basketball two nights a week.

Zoe held P.J.'s chart. "P.J. noticed fasciculations, twitches in his shoulder muscles. At first, they occurred about once a month then increased in frequency to several times a week. Although basketball wasn't his primary sport, P.J.'s jump shot had an accuracy of nearly eighty percent. In the last month, that declined to half that figure. He and Julie became more alarmed when his speech began to thicken and weaken."

Jacob paled. "Shit! Sounds like ALS or Lou Gehrig's Disease."

"Right. He's already showing weakness and atrophy of his hand muscles and fasciculations of his thigh muscles."

"Does he know?"

"No, but he knows it's something serious. You'd better talk with him."

P.J. wore jeans and a denim shirt. He sat on the examining table when Jacob and Zoe entered the room.

"Hey, Jacob. I missed you this morning. You sure hired a cute one in Dr. Spelling."

"And a good one, too."

P.J. looked into the serious faces and grew quiet. "You're making me nervous, Jacob. What's up?"

"We don't know for sure, P.J., but I don't like these symptoms and findings. It suggests neurologic disease of some kind. We need to do some testing."

"Come on, Jacob. You have some idea. How bad can it be?"

Zoe turned her eyes away from P.J.

"We think it might be ALS, Lou Gehrig's Disease. You've heard of it?"

"Heard of it! Years before I joined the 49ers, two players died of ALS, Matt Hazeltine and Gary Lewis. Hazeltine died within two years of the diagnosis."

"I'm not making that diagnosis. We must run some tests."

"There's got to be some other explanation, Jacob. This will kill Julie and the girls."

Chapter Nine

Marilyn and Robert Hughes had difficulty believing in their good fortune. Robert served as medical director of Brier Emergency, and the Coldwell-Banker office in Lafayette had named Marilyn Real Estate Agent of the Year with over twenty million dollars in sales. They planned carefully and Sarah Hughes dutifully complied by choosing to be born just as Marilyn celebrated her thirty-ninth birthday.

The attractive couple lived in the Piedmont section of Oakland. He was tall and athletic, but had added a few too many inches to his girth over the years. She, like most of the women in her family, looked years younger than the calendar suggested. She kept her blonde hair short and always looked great, especially when she dressed for work.

Sarah was a beautiful baby at eight pounds nine ounces. She had her mother's love and her daddy's adoration.

They tried to fulfill their master plan by having a son, but in spite of many attempts, including in-vitro fertilization, Marilyn was never again pregnant. They accepted the fact that Sarah was their one and only.

By the age of ten, Sarah was the perfect little girl. She had short chestnut hair worn back with barrettes or bows. She loved the expensive dresses Marilyn purchased for her. She dutifully attended art, ballet, and girls' soccer, having little time left for anything but homework.

"She's the sweetest thing," said Robert, "but she's too neat, too organized, and too restrained."

"Wait until she reaches her teens, honey. You'll be begging for the good-ole-days."

Sarah had one close friend, Kelly Cowan, who lived three houses away. The two spent long hours in each other's rooms doing homework and surfing the Internet.

One day, when Sarah was thirteen, Marilyn returned home early. When she ignored the Do Not Disturb sign on Sarah's door, all their lives, in a moment, changed forever. Marilyn heard the Rolling Stones blasting from the room, and when she opened the door, both girls were dancing before the web camera in bra and panties.

Marilyn froze at the sight. "What's going on here?"

Sarah gasped, and then reached for the computer keyboard blanking the screen at once. "It's nothing, Mother. We're just having fun."

"Don't lie to me, Sarah. I'll have your father here in ten minutes. He'll find out what you're up to."

Kelly looked at Marilyn. "I'd better get home."

"You wait right here, young lady. Do your parents know about this?"

Kelly rolled her eyes and smirked. "There's nothing to know."

Marilyn picked up the computer and locked it in her closet. "Have it your way."

Later, with the help of monitoring software, Marilyn and Robert discovered the streaming videos, the emails, and the trail of payments to the girls over the Internet.

Marilyn shook her head in disgust, as they watched the videos.

Who had been paying for and watching their daughter? she thought.

"Turn it off."

Robert opened Sarah's ledger book. "Look at Sarah's record keeping. They're in incredible detail and show an income of $500 to $1000 dollars a week."

The reality shattered the Hughes's image of Sarah's sweet innocence. More alarming was Sarah's attitude, the combination of dismissing the significance of what she'd done and her indifference to its effect on herself and her parents.

The next year brought more changes in Sarah, most of them unpleasant. She rarely talked with her parents except to argue. She sabotaged each intervention by counselors and psychiatrists.

"You can't control me anymore, Mother. I don't care how many shrinks you bring around."

By her fifteenth birthday, she completed her transformation. Sarah knew how to reach her parents, especially Marilyn, and flaunted her independence with multiple piercings in both ears, the side of her nose, and her tongue. She rejected the refined tattoos, the flowers, or hearts, for the vulgar violent and bloody ones that decorated her neck and ankles. Worse, she adopted the Goth theme; black nail polish, hair, eyeliner, and black clothes with studs and zippers. Her clothes reeked of marijuana and she returned home drunk on several occasions.

Sarah gave her usual response to Marilyn's 'where are you going' question, "Out," as she left the house one evening.

Robert and Marilyn sat in the kitchen. He shook his head. "I don't know her anymore. More than that, I hate her appearance. I detest the word revulsion, but it's close to how I feel about my own daughter."

"That's exactly the effect she desires, and it's working. I hate it too, but it's only a symptom of an underlying problem."

"For the moment, we have an uneasy truce. It's the carrot and the stick approach...not a philosophy I thought we'd ever embrace."

"Can she talk with anyone at the hospital?"

"Not really. She's rejected the shrinks and social workers." He hesitated a moment, then said, "Carleton Dix, the hospital chaplain, maybe he's a possibility."

"You must be kidding. From what I've heard of him, his rigid orthodoxy is all wrong for Sarah."

"I agree, but the chaplain directs a teen group. Don't underestimate the power of peer pressure on even someone like Sarah, look what it's done to her so far."

Chapter Ten

P.J. Manning shuffled through Jacob's parking lot to his car. He gazed up, feeling the warm midday sun and bathing in the soft westerly breeze carrying the salty smell of the San Francisco Bay. Days like this made P.J. reflect on how great it felt to be alive. Today, he couldn't escape the irony.

Julie Manning seared the pork loin and the kitchen filled with the hearty aroma of roasting meat. She turned as the front door opened. "Is that you, P.J.?"

When she heard no reply, she walked to the family room and found her husband sitting on the sofa, head down. She stared at him, finding it difficult to breathe. "What's wrong? What did Jacob say?"

P.J. looked up at his wife. His eyes were moist with tears. "They don't know for sure, but it's bad."

"Bad...what are you talking about?"

"Jacob and Dr. Spelling ordered some nerve tests...something's going on in my nervous system."

"They must have some idea," she said as her voice moved up an octave.

"They do..."

"P.J., don't do this to me. I'm your wife and I love you. Whatever it is, we'll deal with it."

His dry mouth felt like paste. "Have you heard of ALS or Lou Gehrig's Disease?"

"I've heard the name, but I don't know anything about it."

"I've known Jacob all my life, and I've never seen him so upset as when he said this was most likely ALS. Jacob's seen a lot in life, and if he's upset..."

"You're still young. You're the strongest man, the most determined man I've ever known. We'll beat this, whatever it is."

P.J. pulled Julie beside him on the sofa. He grasped her hands, and in a near whisper said, "If it's ALS, medicine has no effective treatment." He hesitated, then continued, "Did I ever tell you about Matt Hazeltine and Gary Lewis?"

"No, I don't think so."

"Both young. Both healthy, perfectly conditioned athletes for the 49'ers who died of ALS in the 80s. Few live more than five years. Matt Hazeltine died in two."

"That's a long time ago. They must have learned something about this disease by now."

"They've learned a lot, except how to treat it. They have a few new drugs, but nothing works for long."

"Something must be useful..."

"I don't know how much we should get into this until they confirm the diagnosis, but... "

"What?"

P.J. struggled with the words. "It's a horrible, debilitating disease. Eventually you can't walk, talk, dress, or bathe yourself. You may not be able to swallow. It's awful...just awful, Julie. I thought I could face anything, but this..."

"Does it affect your mind?"

"Oh, if you have a perverse perspective on life, that's the good news. Your mind remains perfectly intact. I'll have a ringside seat to my own destruction."

A week later, nerve and muscle testing established the diagnosis. Jacob referred P.J. to Michael Brader, the Chief of Neurology at U.C. Medical Center in San Francisco. His examination and review of the testing confirmed the diagnosis.

Julie leaned forward. "Don't you have anything that works?"

"I've talked to Jacob about treatment. We have a few drugs that might help, but I won't mislead you; so far nothing has had a permanent effect on halting the progression of the disease."

Robert Hughes took the elevator to Brier Hospital's fifth floor. He knocked on Carleton Dix's door.

"Come in, Doc."

"Do you have a moment?"

"Of course, Bob. Moments like this make up my daily life. What can I do for you?"

"I'd like information about your teen group." He hesitated. "We're having a tough time with Sarah."

"I know."

"You know?"

"This isn't that large a community. I work with teenage girls who attend Piedmont High with Sarah."

"We're in trouble with her. We've tried everything but a nunnery, and I'd consider that too, if I believed it would work. This is way beyond mere teenage rebellion. Her behavior is destructive and we're ready to admit that we can't handle her anymore."

"I'd like to help you Bob, but...let me be honest. I've heard a lot about Sarah from the other girls, none of it good.

It isn't that I avoid the tough cases, you should see what we've had in the past. But for the sake of my girls, I avoid taking on anyone who may adversely affect the dynamic of the group."

"I understand, and to be completely candid, I can't blame you. Do you have any other recommendations?"

The chaplain thought a moment then licked his lips. "Why don't I sit for a few minutes with Sarah. Maybe we can work something out."

Chapter Eleven

After dinner the next night, Robert Hughes paraphrased his conversation with the chaplain.

Sarah stood. "Carleton Dix! The chaplain? Are you out of your fucking minds?"

Robert stared at his daughter. "Use that language with your friends, if you will. It doesn't impress me."

Marilyn's eyes were red from crying. "We're trying to help you before it's too late."

"You want me to join with those dorks, those slackers who are only in that group because they got busted."

Marilyn shook her head. "That's not true. They discuss things that are important to girls your age. Kelly Cowan is in the group and her mother says she loves it."

"Keep it real, Mother. I don't hang with Kelly since she got back from the loony bin."

Robert tightened his jaw. "Make it hard or make it easy, but go you will."

"You people will never learn." Sarah ran to her room and slammed the door.

Marilyn turned to Robert. "This may be a mistake. If she doesn't respect the man, I don't think he'll get anywhere."

"How much worse can it get? One day soon, if we can't get to her, she's going to leave."

The YMCA on Allston Way in Berkeley donated a room each Wednesday night for Carleton Dix and his TeenTalk group.

Sarah Hughes sat on the sofa in the foyer outside the meeting room picking at her fingernails. She wore a short black skirt and a blue tank top.

Kelly Cowan smiled as she arrived for the meeting. "What are you doing here?"

"What do you think?"

Kelly sat next to Sarah. "I think you're seeking spiritual enlightenment."

"Right."

"I don't know what happened, Sarah. We were tight."

"Until you went all lame on me. That loony bin did something to your mind."

Kelly looked at her feet. "It was bad, Sarah. I went bonkers. They helped me see that I was giving away my future. For what? In many ways, I feel more in control of myself than I ever did with the drugs and the booze."

"I have a flash for you, Kelly; it's all a load of shit, the easy way out. You really want to be like them?"

"Them?"

"Your 'rents?"

"At least my mom and dad have done something with their lives. You and me, girlfriend, we were heading for the big crash. I'm out of that life, and I'm staying out."

Just then, Carleton Dix arrived. "Go in, Kelly. I'll join you in a minute."

He turned to Sarah. "I know you're not exactly stoked being here, but why not give it a try?"

Stoked? Sarah thought. Who's he kidding?

"I'm not into this, but to make peace, I'll sit in just this one time."

"Sit in. Don't sit in. It's all up to you."

"I don't like anyone preaching to me, chaplain...is that what I should call you?"

"That's okay or reverend or Carleton, and I don't preach here, I moderate. The girls do the talking, that is those who have the guts to do so. If you want preaching, I can send you to any number of churches."

Afterward, Kelly approached Sarah. "What do you think?"

"Lame...it sounded pretty lame to me. I got enough problems without listening to a bunch of whining preps."

"Come on, Sarah. It wasn't so bad. At least they speak a language you can understand, and don't tell me their problems are totally foreign to you. Why don't you come over for a while. We can catch up."

"Sorry, Kelly. I got a date."

Chapter Twelve

Nothing prepared P.J., Julie, or their girls for the reality of ALS.

Six months after fighting it with all his strength, P.J. found himself confined to a wheelchair. The family sat at the dinner table with a roast chicken in the center.

It smells great, P.J. thought as he looked down at his bowl filled with an unidentifiable gruel. Pureed and soft foods were all he could handle.

He reached for the plastic cup of orange juice, raised it with difficulty to his lips with trembling hands and sipped. He choked and coughed as fluid entered his windpipe and his lungs.

P.J. reddened as tears streaked down his face. He continued to cough, then shook his head. "Get me out of here, Julie. I can't stand this."

His weight declined from 160 to 130 lbs. Speaking had become more problematic, an especially difficult loss as the house was always full of strong vibrant voices. Julie pushed the wheelchair into the family room.

"Please sit with me, Julie, I need to talk with you while I can."

"Of course," she replied sitting next to him on the sofa. She watched the movement of his mouth as he tried to control his speech and saw the twitching, the fasciculations, on his tongue.

"You must make me a promise."

"Anything."

"When I reach the end...when they say, if we don't put him on the ventilator, he'll die, I want you to say no, and I want you to say no to resuscitation. I want a DNR, Do Not Resuscitate order in my medical records."

Julie placed her hand across her mouth. Tears rolled down her cheeks. "You don't have to worry. You've signed all the documents, the living will and the advanced directive for medical care. That should do it."

"That doesn't mean shit, Julie," he choked over the words. "In the end, the hospital and Jacob will accede to your wishes. I want your promise."

"I don't know if I can..."

"Julie...it's what I want. Let me die in peace. It's bad enough for the girls to see me this way, let's not make it worse."

"What about the hospital? At some point, you'll need to be admitted...we may not be able to take care..."

"No, that's fine. I understand. It's a miracle you've done so much."

"I can only think of one miracle, sweetheart."

"I know."

Julie Manning hugged Jacob as he arrived after office hours to visit. "You don't have to do this. I feel guilty taking up so much of your time."

Jacob came three to four times each week, staying long enough to see how P.J. was doing and offering support and grandfatherly wisdom.

"Time...time? Let me introduce myself to you, Jacob Weizman, P.J.'s doctor."

Julie smiled then came again into his arms, her head lying on his shoulder as she sobbed.

"It's horrible, Jacob...watching him struggle this way...brave, loving, and always worrying about me and the kids instead of himself. One minute I'm heartbroken, the next I'm in awe of the best and most courageous man I ever knew."

"I have a forty-six-year investment in P.J., Julie. I remember the day I delivered him. He nearly slipped through my hands as he wriggled for freedom at birth, and you know something; he never did stop struggling."

"I don't know how you do it, Jacob. After all these years, here you are."

Jacob sat next to Julie on the sofa, holding her hands. "The death of a son or daughter is devastating. Parents can't comprehend the possibility that they'd survive their child. That's the way I feel about P.J. and all the others I've outlived. I've had a long life. I'm reasonably intelligent, yet I find no sense to any of it. It's the one place where faith, if you have it, offers the solace denied to reason."

She squeezed his hands. "We're so lucky to have had you all these years, Jacob."

"Don't think of me as a saint, I'm not. I don't think I need to be one. It doesn't take much to show the love I have for my patients...well, most of my patients. If they know I really care, if they respect my judgment and experience, and if they trust me to suggest what's best, the amount of time I spend isn't an issue. I can't move into your home, that's the surest way to destroy your fantasies about my sainthood, but you can reach me any time, day or night. I consider it an honor to see this through with you."

"P.J.'s care is becoming more difficult, Jacob. I don't know how much longer I can keep him at home."

"I'll make sure you get whatever support you need so he can remain here as long as possible, but a time will come..."

"You know how we feel about hospitals and end of life care. You'll make sure they follow P.J.'s wishes?"

"Julie, honey, that's the last thing you need to worry about."

One month later, P.J. lay in his hospital bed on Brier's fifth floor. A large Do Not Resuscitate sign hung on the door and over his bed. Julie and the girls just left for the day.

P.J. felt his nose itching, but couldn't raise his hand to scratch or push the nurse call button. Something about paralysis sharpens the other senses, he thought. He remained fully aware of his world, every sight, sound, smell, and touch...all mind and no body.

Ginny Harrison turned to Marion Krupp as they began the morning shift. "I have five patients already. You'd better take P.J. Manning."

Marion picked up P.J.'s admission sheet and scanned it. "Why did they bother putting him in the hospital? He's practically dead already."

"My God, Marion. How can you be so cruel?"

"Well, I'm sorry, but Jacob Weizman just can't make up his mind. First, he pushes his patients toward an early grave and here, where he can do nothing, he wastes our time and the hospital's resources. I'm tired of Weizman's shit."

Ginny had heard it all before.

How can they keep such a woman on staff? We can't need nurses that badly, she thought, shaking her head.

Marion paused a moment, then grabbed Ginny by her upper arm and whispered, "If you take him, I'll take two of your patients...that's a good deal."

Ginny wondered why Marion wanted to be off P.J.'s case so badly.

It must be Weizman she's avoiding.

Ginny hated having Marion care for any of her patients, but how could she force her to care for a patient she couldn't or wouldn't help? It was about time the administration did something about her.

"Okay, Marion. Just this once."

P.J. heard the door open. He struggled to move his eyes that saw two shadows approaching his bed. "I'm seeing double again."

I shake my head in sorrow over this once powerful man.

The DNR sign says it all.

Your sojourn is almost over, I think and smile...no illusions remain.

I bend over and whisper, "So good to see you, P.J...Paul Joseph."

He turns his eyes to see me but the soft light at the entrance to the room leaves me in black silhouette.

"It's time," I say holding the clear fluid-filled syringe before his eyes. His pupils widen. "Oh, excuse me," I say. "I'm sure you want to know the instrument of your death...it's insulin; life to most; a quick peaceful death for you, P.J. My gift."

P.J. tried to speak, but the weakened and uncoordinated musculature of his mouth and tongue kept him silent. I want to say goodbye. My last vision of Julie and my girls. Don't rob me of that.

I bend over P.J.'s body and whisper again into his ear, "Don't be afraid. You'll be with Him soon. You'll be what you were...healthy...intact, an eternal journey of peace."

No! No, P.J.'s mind screamed.

"Don't fight it," I say as I insert the sharp needle into the rubber stopper of the intravenous line placed into P.J.'s vein for IV fluids and medication. I flush the contents of the syringe, a lethal dose of Insulin into P.J., and smile.

P.J. felt suddenly hungry. His body began to tremble, then all turned black as his body began to convulse.

When I reach the staff parking section, the lot's lamp casts dim lights over my car's shiny trunk. I stare at the back bumper's faded sticker: No Jesus, No Peace; Know Jesus; Know Peace, and smile. It's a good sticker, and it's been a good day.

Thirty minutes later, beginning routine afternoon rounds, the nurse entered P.J.'s room. She knew at once.

Thank God, she thought.

When the phone rang and Julie heard Jacob's voice, she knew.

"I'm so sorry. You meet many people in a lifetime. P.J. was the best. I'll never forget P.J. We'll all miss him."

Tears streaked down Julie's cheeks. "Thanks for everything, Jacob. I don't think we could have made it without you and Zoe. You two are the best of what medicine has to offer. Please thank Zoe for me. You got it right when you chose her for your practice."

Chapter Thirteen

When the phone rang during dinner, Lola turned to Jacob. "Don't pick it up, it's probably a damned telemarketer."

Jacob rose. "We should monitor these calls or subscribe to the phone company's screening service."

"Don't...you'll be sorry."

Jacob set down his glass of wine and picked up the receiver. "Dr. Weizman speaking."

"Sorry to bother you at home, Doctor, but Dr. Vincent is convening an emergency ethics committee meeting tonight. It's at seven-thirty, can you make it, Doctor?"

Jacob shook his head and looked at Lola. "I'll be there." He replaced the receiver. "An emergency ethics committee meeting."

"What kind of ethical problem can't wait for a decent time of day?"

"You know better, sweetie. You served on our committee for years."

"I enjoyed those meetings and the gritty exchanges of ideas on real life and death issues."

"It's still that way, but lately it only serves to rubber stamp decisions made by patients, families or physicians themselves. We're in a position to help, to explore important issues, not to justify actions which belong to physicians and their patients. It's just another example of physician domestication."

"Nobody's domesticated you."

"And they never will."

Jacob picked up the phone and dialed Zoe.

"Hi, Jacob. What's up?"

"Can you cover for me from about seven-thirty to maybe ten tonight?"

"Sure, what's up?"

"I have an emergency ethics committee meeting."

"That sounds exciting. Do you know what they're discussing?"

"Not a clue," he replied.

"Use your influence for me, Jacob. I'd love to serve on that committee."

"It's very popular, Zoe. Everyone wants that committee."

"You'll do what you can, won't you?"

"I'll try, Zoe. Promise."

The committee met in Brier's boardroom, with its long, highly polished oak table. Stern-faced portraits of the hospital's historic figures, former CEO's, Presidents of the Medical Staff, and Chairmen of the Board of Trustees decorated the walls. Even the more recent pictures followed the tradition that a small grin would somehow offend convention. The kitchen placed carafes of coffee, tea, and ice water on the table with plates of cookies. In spite of the interruption of their evening, members were relaxed and in good humor.

Jaime Vincent, an internist and social activist, chaired the meeting. His lanky physique was that of the long distance runner. He pushed his salt and pepper hair back and began.

"Sorry for dragging you out tonight, but neither time nor ethics waits for man."

Warren Davidson, the chief of medicine stared at Jaime. "This better be good. If I could find my assistant chief to take my place, I'd be at the Warrior game."

Jaime smiled. "Thanks, Warren. We appreciate your sacrifice."

The medical staff bylaws designed the ethics committee with a majority of non-physicians. It had representatives from nursing, social services, pastoral care, hospital administration, and several community representatives who were not hospital employees. The hospital attorney, Alan David, sat as an ex-officio member.

"Arnie Roth, a family practitioner, has asked for our assistance tonight," said Jaime. He turned to Arnie. "Let's have it."

Arnie placed a thick hospital chart before him. "Don't worry, I won't read it all."

"Helen Ashley, of the Piedmont Ashleys, has been my patient for fifteen years. At the age of eighty-two and with the presumptive diagnosis of early Alzheimer's disease, her tests showed that she had advanced kidney failure and needed dialysis."

Jacob shook his head. "She doesn't sound like the best candidate for dialysis."

"You're right and that prospect led to much discussion involving her husband and daughters. Helen, though a little slow, was competent and her decision, dialysis rather than death, was unequivocal.

"Initially, she did well, though the treatments were exhausting. She required about twenty-four hours to reconstitute her energy level. After six months, things deteriorated. First, it was the failure of her vascular access needed to perform dialysis. She had three procedures in two months, each one taking a toll on her cognitive function and her mood."

Warren raised his hand. "Had she signed an advanced directive for health care or a living will specifying her wishes under these circumstances?"

"She did, and that's where the plot thickens for two reasons: First, we know from experience that decisions made in the abstract about terminal care can be different when death arrives on your doorstep. Then, we have the family. Her husband and two daughters living in the Bay Area, all agree with some limitation on how far we should continue treatment. Her estranged daughter Patricia just flew in from Tulsa and entered the picture. As you might expect, she has a completely different perspective."

Carleton Dix, the chaplain, raised his hand. "These are all chronic problems, Jaime. Why the emergency meeting?"

"Helen's vascular access clotted again, and she hasn't had a dialysis treatment for three days. She needs one tonight or it's unlikely she'll make it to morning."

"What's her mental status right now?" asked Sharon Brickman, Chief of Cardiology.

Arnie looked around the room. "You guys like complex ethical issues, here's a big one." He paused, and then continued, "She's semicomatose, probably in part from a lack of dialysis treatments, and therefore she can't assist in this decision."

"Let me get this straight," said Jacob. "The woman's condition has deteriorated over time. She's previously expressed a desire that her physicians not prolong her life, and allow her to die with dignity. Her family, who knows her best, agrees with stopping treatment, and finally, even if we do everything, what will be left? I don't see the issue. Let the woman die in peace."

"Any way you cut it, it's suicide or worse!" Carleton Dix spit out each word. "And this comes with the tacit support of family, physicians, and Brier Hospital. Suicide is a violation of divine law, and in a Christian nation like America, it's fundamentally immoral."

Jacob boiled. "That's the typical response from a cleric who can't accept that in this country, so far, we have a separation between church and state. Why is it that some religions are all too happy to impose their moral values on others?"

Carleton leered at Jacob and shook his head in disgust. "Your life is not your own, but a gift from God. Nobody has the right to take her life before its natural time, and to take someone else's life...well you've heard the phrase, Thou shalt not kill."

"Excuse me, but the phrase is Thou shalt not murder...a chaplain should know that. In any case, aren't you the same cleric who justifies violence against abortion providers? Haven't you publically glorified Eric Rudolph, the so-called Olympic Park Bomber, who killed three and injured one hundred fifty in his campaign against abortion?"

"It saddens me that the deaths of the innocent push the faithful to those extremes."

Jacob reddened. "Your anguish is misplaced, chaplain. Another thing, only an ignorant ideologue like you has the chutzpah to talk with me about life and death. I know it in a way, if you lived ten lifetimes, you'll never understand."

"I'm getting sick of the moral superiority of Holocaust survivors," said Carleton.

The room went silent.

Carleton reddened, then coughed his reply, "I just mean that other views can be equally valid, Dr. Weizman."

Jacob rose. "I think you said exactly what you mean..."

Jaime interrupted. "We're getting off track here, gentlemen. I have reason to believe that both sides are showing good faith on these sensitive ethical issues."

"Let me lay out the facts on which we can agree," said Warren Davidson. "Mrs. Ashley will die if she doesn't receive a dialysis treatment; she's expressed her desire verbally and has executed documents that she wants no heroic end of life treatments. Those family members close to her concur in her decision. An estranged daughter, new to the situation, wants her treated. Her physicians think that intervention will only prolong her suffering on the pathway to her death."

"For God's sake," said Jacob, "let the woman die in peace."

The discussion moved around the room. The consensus followed the theme that a person has the right to decide whether she wants to live or die.

"How can you be absolutely sure you know, right now, that's what she wants?" Carleton asked. "She's semicomatose. If we are to make a mistake, it must always be on the side of life."

"You mean," Jacob asked, "that if you knew with moral certainty that she wanted no further treatment, you'd be okay with her choice?"

"Well..." Carleton hesitated, "that decision is contrary to my belief."

Jacob shook his head in dismay. "So, you'd have all of us live and die by your set of beliefs?"

Alan David, the hospital's attorney, raised his hand. "I don't have a vote on this committee, but you need to understand that your decision and the action of Mrs. Ashley's physicians could leave us liable for wrongful death charges. Clearly, we're interested in avoiding such involvement."

Warren Davidson stared at the attorney. "Are you saying that Brier Hospital administration will superimpose its will on physicians' decisions just to avoid litigation?"

"Hold onto your shorts, Warren," said David. "We live and die by the medical staff's policies and decisions. I wouldn't have it any other way...I may be a patient here some day."

"I call the question," said Jaime. "All those supporting Mrs. Ashley and her family's decision to terminate care, vote yes, those opposed, vote no."

When Jaime counted hands, one abstention and two no's. "Thank you, ladies and gentlemen."

Carleton Dix, stone faced, rose, and then stretched his hand, pointing around the room. "Physicians who took the Hippocratic Oath promised to do no harm, that's plain and simple. Killing Mrs. Ashley is doing harm any way you phrase it. I'm ashamed to be part of this institution."

In an audible whisper, Jacob, said, "Does that mean he'll resign in protest?"

Chapter Fourteen

When Lola Weizman entered the Berkeley Woman's Health Clinic on Channing Way, the receptionist, Elena Ordoñez smiled. "Good morning, Lola. How's it goin'?"

"Slow Elena, very slow. Is Kathy in yet?"

"Just got here. She's in her office."

Kathy Bingham directed the clinic. She was a MSW., a psychotherapist, and family counselor who came up through the county mental health system and had the scars to prove it. Kathy was a large black woman and could move from compassionate supporter to vitriolic attacker in a heartbeat.

Lola had persuaded the city to replace the program's previous director. After twenty years, he was out of touch with the clinic's clients and staff. Lola interviewed dozens of qualified applicants, looking for a rare constellation of talents: psychotherapeutic skills combined with street smarts and the toughness to deal with a frustrating bureaucracy. Lola remembered Kathy's interview.

Kathy looked down at the diminutive Lola Weizman who shook her hand and, spoke with a precise Austrian accent. "Please be so kind as to have a seat."

"Thank you."

Kathy, nobody's fool, knew a great deal about this unique Viennese psychotherapist, her personal and professional life, and her role in establishing the clinic.

"Tell me something." Lola, smiled and met Kathy's eyes, an action perfected by years of therapeutic encounters. Lola's face carried the wrinkles of age, cigarette smoking, and the smile lines of a lifetime. They codified her joy in helping others.

"Let me tell you what I've done and what I'd like to do with the clinic."

"I read your resume. Tell me something I don't know."

"Where's the couch?"

"I don't use a couch. I do better looking at people, don't you?"

"I don't know what you want, Dr. Weizman."

"Call me Lola. Everyone does." She locked on Kathy's eyes, and then shook her head. "Don't fail me. I'm too old for disappointment, and I have great hope for you."

My own analyst never made me this nervous, Kathy thought as she peered into Lola's soft brown eyes.

"I'm good with the sort of people you see in the program, Lola. One way or the other, they're me. We understand each other and I have the skills to help them. In addition, I have a low tolerance for bullshit. I've been bullshitted by the best, and that includes patients, colleagues, and functionaries of every description."

"Why teenage girls? They're not easy."

"Tell me about it. I have two of my own."

Kathy stared at Lola who remained silent. "These girls…they have no idea about the unconscious factors that motivate them, but they're young enough to learn and become better at dealing with the realities of adult life."

Lola rolled up the sleeve of her blouse to reveal the blurred letters of the tattoo she received at Auschwitz. "What do you feel when you see this?"

Kathy's eyes welled with tears as she stared. "Rage and despair."

"Good answer."

Sarah Hughes, under constant pressure from her father, continued to attend TeenTalk meetings. She coped with the repetitive banal whining on one hand, and the religious affirmations on the other, by shutting most of it out.

Before the next meeting, Carleton Dix pulled Sarah aside.

His smile makes me want to puke, she thought.

"I'm glad you're coming to our meetings, Sarah. Maybe it's not so bad after all."

Sarah said nothing.

He approached and sat on the sofa by her side.

Without thought, she slid away.

He moved closer, placed his hand on her shoulder, and stared into her eyes.

Sarah felt repulsed at once.

His eyes...his touch...he's interested in something else, she thought.

Shuddering, she shifted her body away from his hand. "Don't touch me. Don't ever touch me. I'm doing this because I have no choice."

Afterward, at the meeting, Carleton leered at Sarah. "You've been with us several times, Sarah, maybe it's time to share your feelings."

"No thanks, Padre."

"Are you afraid? It takes courage to stand up in public, to speak your mind."

"All this blabbering is crap. It accomplishes nothing. And the religious dogma...you can keep it."

Several girls gasped.

Carleton reddened. "How does a girl your age reject two thousand years of truth that's engaged the best of humanities' minds?"

"I'm not rejecting anything. I just need a reason to believe, and so far, I haven't discovered one."

"If you don't believe in the revealed word of our Lord and Savior...then you're lost."

Sarah bit her lip. "Lost? I don't think so. Anyway, I don't want to get into a philosophical debate with a man who has committed his life to a fantasy."

"A fantasy?"

"I only have one question, Padre, and then I'll let it go. If God is all-powerful, all knowing, and perfectly good, how can evil and suffering exist in your world? I don't get it."

"God allows what we consider pointless suffering for reasons we can't comprehend."

Sarah sneered. "Right. A typical bullshit answer. I think I'll pass."

Evolution must explain it, Jacob Weizman thought as he wheeled Gabriella Sago through the hallway at Brier. Men, and women too, stopped and stared at this well-proportioned, blond, blue-eyed beauty, a showgirl at the Bellagio in Las Vegas.

Mary Oakes turned to one of her nurses. "It's as if she's an alien species, like those air-touched models in magazines. When I look at her, I think, what's the use...I might as well shoot myself."

As they passed the nursing station, Jacob turned to Mary. "Give me a hand, will you?"

They wheeled Gabby to the bedside. Jacob held her arm. "Just support your weight on your good leg, Gabby, and then we'll get you into bed."

Mary supported Gabby's shoulders while Jacob lifted her thickened, shiny red left leg and placed it on two pillows.

After Gabby got settled, Jacob turned to her. "This is Mary Oakes. She may be the best nurse we have around Brier."

"It's great to meet you, Mrs. Oakes."

"Please call me Mary. How long have you known Dr. Weizman?"

Gabby smiled and winked. "He was the first, but not the last to smack me on the ass, thank God. He delivered me. Once Jacob delivers someone, he takes it as a lifelong obligation."

"Get her vital signs for me, Mary, and admit her. She has a nasty infection in her leg veins, phlebitis. I'm writing the orders and starting her on anticoagulants."

After Jacob left the room, Mary took Gabby's temperature, pulse and blood pressure. The left leg was angry red and swollen twice normal.

Mary shook her head. "That's nasty looking, Gabby."

"I'm so stupid. I should have gotten on it a week ago, but you know me...Wonder Woman."

"Don't tell me you danced on that leg?"

"Well, it wasn't that bad at the time...and with my costume, if you can call it that, I don't think many people were looking at my leg."

"You'll be back on your feet in no time."

"If it wasn't so painful, I wouldn't mind. I could use the downtime. I have so much to catch up, especially my reading."

"You sure draw a lot of attention, Gabby."

"I know, and I'm not complaining. It's an occupational hazard. I don't want to appear snobbish...I'm not, but can you do anything to protect my privacy?"

"Of course. I'll deal with it. Meanwhile, make yourself comfortable. I'll be back with the moist heat pad. Slip into this." Mary handed Gabby the hospital gown.

Gabby pulled out a simple cotton lace-trimmed gown. "Is it all right if I wear this?"

"Sure, but I can hear the sighs of disappointment already."

"They'll survive."

After changing, Gabby lay in bed trying to find a comfortable position when she heard a knock on the door.

"Come in."

Tommy Wells entered pushing his lab cart. "I'm Thomas Wells." Smiling with a Dracula accent, he said, "I come for your blood."

Gabby winced. She hated to have her blood drawn. They always had difficulty finding a vein and it often left a large black and blue mark.

Seeing her discomfort, Tommy smiled. "Not to worry. I'm the best."

While he tied the rubber tourniquet around her upper arm, Tommy looked up into her eyes.

God, she's gorgeous, he thought.

Gabby had seen that look thousands of times. She smiled politely, closed her eyes, then felt a tiny pinprick and it was over.

"Thanks, Thomas. That wasn't bad at all."

He held the site for several minutes. Way too long.

Thomas drew her blood twice each day, each time asking more personal questions until she stopped him. "Please, Thomas. You seem like a sweet man, but I'm only interested in getting well."

Tommy reddened, and then stomped away.

When Tommy returned the next morning, he said nothing. He placed the tourniquet around her arm. Suddenly she felt the agonizing pain as he probed for a vein.

"Get out of here!" She clutched her burning arm. Tears ran down her cheeks, as her arm began swelling, and turning black and blue.

When Jacob saw the arm and heard her story, he found Tommy sitting in the coffee room. "Keep your damn hands off my patients...what's the matter with you?"

"If you don't like it, Weizman, take it up with my boss."

"You can be sure I will."

When he left, Tommy mumbled under his breath, "Fucking kike."

"What did you say?" said Jacob as Tommy walked away.

Tommy turned. "Don't mess with me, old man. You'll regret it."

Chapter Fifteen

Jack Byrnes listened as the Quality Assurance Committee (QA) discussed the complaints against Jacob Weizman. "I don't like this one bit."

The clock showed 12:20 p.m. The committee members finished lunch and began their meeting. The east-facing windows showed pedestrians walking to and from Brier Hospital in the bright midday sun.

"I don't like it either," said Warren Davidson, the chief of medicine, "but we can't ignore the complaints lodged by the nurses and some physicians."

Ernie Banks was a family practitioner in his early 70s. "These complaints reek of ageism. I've had to deal with it myself, and if you don't mind, I hate it."

"Age discrimination in the People's Republic of Berkeley," said Warren, "impossible."

"Berkeley's progressive, but I can't say the same for Brier Hospital," said Arnie Roth, the chairman of QA. "All this is beside the point. The complaints are here and we must deal with them."

Arnie grabbed a manila folder. "This is the most recent complaint. It's from Marion Krupp..."

"Christ," Jack interjected. "Marion Krupp is a bitter, angry woman...you're going to listen to her gripes?"

"This is just an example. I have several others, all with the same theme: Jacob's reluctance to prescribe medication and his passion to get people out of the hospital as quickly as possible."

Jack smiled. "That should make him the poster-boy for the HMO."

"Please, Jack," said Arnie. "We're here to deal with practice issues only." He paused a moment, then continued, "I asked Jacob to join us to discuss these problems."

Jack smiled. "It's your funeral, Arnie."

Arnie walked to the door. "Jacob. Why don't you join us?"

Jacob smiled and strolled to the head of the table.

The witness stand, he thought.

Jacob looked around the room. He knew these physicians well. He'd delivered a few and cared for several others and their families.

Arnie read the complaint from Marion Krupp.

"She'd have me sedate an old lady for her convenience. I won't do it. It's bad practice."

"We see a pattern here, Jacob. Everyone knows you're a therapeutic nihilist, that you resist using medication to help your patients."

"Therapeutic nihilist...ha! You use the term as a pejorative. As I define it, it's a compliment...thanks."

Jacob looked around the room. "When you reach my age, and lived through the claims of wonder drug after wonder drug, eventually it forces any thoughtful physician to question our entire body of knowledge about the therapeutic properties of medications. That's what Oliver Wendell Holmes, Sr. said in 1860: I believe that if the whole Materia Medica as now used, could be sunk to the bottom of the sea, it would be all the better for mankind, and all the worse for the fishes."

"You're kidding," said Warren Davidson, "Eighteen sixty?"

"More than any of you, I appreciate the benefits of modern medications. I treated pneumonia without antibiotics, cancer without chemotherapy, and heart failure without powerful diuretics, and all of them with prayer. I recall how great we felt with each so-called advance in the treatment of pneumonia that included knowing the precise time during the course of pneumonia to open or close the windows. Imagine, treating a severe infection by the manipulation of windows!"

Jacob bit his lower lip. His eyes filled. "Don't dare tell me I don't appreciate modern therapeutics. Do you think I'll ever forget standing helpless at the bedside of child after child dying with acute lymphocytic leukemia? Today, 85 percent plus, survive.

"I remember when you came to Brier, Warren, and the many problems that came with each highly touted drug. I know our intentions were honorable, but then I remember George Bernard Shaw: 'The way to hell is paved with good intentions.'"

Jacob paused, and then continued, "The original therapeutic nihilists were early 19th-century French clinicians who decided that the therapies available then were worse than useless. Since their treatments included bleeding, purging, puking, and the use of toxic substances such as arsenic and mercury; they're surely looking good now."

"How can you equate what we do now with those outmoded practices?" asked Arnie Roth.

"Practices are deemed outmoded only in retrospect, Arnie. Just like us, they thought they were practicing medicine at the highest level."

"Times have changed," said Warren.

"You think so. Let me cite just a few statistics: Pharmaceutical drugs kill more people than die in traffic accidents each year in the United States. Studies in the late 90s show that more than two million hospitalized Americans suffered an adverse drug reaction in the study year and over one hundred thousand died as the result. That didn't include one hundred thousand deaths from overdosage and errors in administration."

"We know the horror stories, Jacob," said Warren. "That's why we have QA and pharmacy review committees."

Jacob scanned the room. "Let me give you one more statistic, and then I'll shut up. Public health researchers have concluded that adverse drug reactions are now the fourth leading cause of death in the United States after heart disease, cancer, and stroke."

Jack looked around the silent room and smiled. "Therapeutic nihilists, line up on the right."

Jacob stood beside his patient while the nurse brought in a syringe filled with clear fluid and prepared to inject it intravenously. "What's that?"

"It's Tobramycin, sir."

"I wrote antibiotic orders for Gentamycin, not Tobramycin."

She opened the chart. "Let me check the orders, Dr. Weizman."

She flipped to the order sheets. "Dr. Spelling changed the order, sir."

Why? Jacob thought. For this patient they're equally effective and Gentamycin's less expensive.

This was another minor modification of his orders by Zoe of late. He also noted that on several occasions, Zoe wrote orders for diagnostic tests that he'd already written.

Alteration of my orders, minor changes in dosing and writing for tests, he thought. She doesn't trust me.

After they finished in the office later that day, Jacob sat before Zoe's desk.

She read his discomfort. "What is it, Jacob?"

"I don't mind if you change my orders, Zoe, especially if I make a mistake or if our patients will benefit, that is if you have good reason."

Zoe paled. "I'm so sorry, Jacob. I was just trying too hard to help, and…" she hesitated, "to prove myself to you. Please forgive me."

"You don't have to prove anything to me, Zoe. You're a great doc and I expect to benefit from your recent training. Maybe I'm getting too sensitive in my old age or perhaps I've practiced alone too long."

"God no, Jacob. You're the best. I'll do better. I promise."

Chapter Sixteen

Ahmad Kadir came from Nablus on the West Bank. His father Habib taught history and his mother Jasmine was a bank officer.

The family had originally lived in Gaza where Ahmad Kadir's father thought his son had avoided the infectious militancy of the Palestinian youth that spread over the Gaza community in the years before its overt expression in the intifada.

Ahmad confronted his father. "How can you work with them? They're killing us. It's every Palestinian's obligation to wage war to the death against the Zionists."

"It saddens me to think that after all I've taught you that you choose to absorb the shallow, destructive beliefs of the ignorant jihadists. You're a Christian, not a Muslim. How do you think they feel about you?"

Ahmad's face turned red. He stared at his feet, and in the tradition of this patriarchal culture, said nothing.

"The struggle against aggressive Zionism is legitimate, but our means are worlds apart."

In the months to come, Habib resigned his position at Al-Athar University and moved his family to Nablus where he accepted a new position at Al Najah University. He had few illusions about his son and his beliefs or Ahmad's frequent unexplained absences, as militancy abided no geographic limits in the occupied territories.

After medical school at Yale, Ahmad planned to return to the Middle East to complete his training, but the ongoing intifada made him decide to remain in the states. The Kadir family was among the 1.6 percent of Palestinians who were Christians and suffered as Arabs in the west and as Christians among the Islamists. The entire family eventually fled to the U.S.

Ahmad noted the discomfort among his classmates to his Arabic appearance, but this became insignificant compared to the reaction to him after 9/11.

Ahmad sat with his roommate, Jerry Towns. "It's getting impossible. Some people cross to the other side of the street when they see me coming. They stare at me in public places like I'm carrying a bomb."

Jerry smirked. "What did you expect? America's shock came with faces like yours."

"What's worse, several patients took one look, and refused to see me as their physician."

"It'll pass."

"I love this country, Jerry, but I can't stand how it treats Arabs and how it blindly supports the Jews over the Palestinians."

"Be smart, Ahmad, don't say Jews, say Israelis. You can get into this with your close friends, but otherwise, I'd keep my mouth shut."

When an opportunity in the internal medicine program at UC San Francisco arose, Ahmad decided to move to the more tolerant bay area. Once in the program, Ahmad became fascinated with the excitement of intensive care. He was fortunate to discover an opening in their intensivist program.

Marion Krupp knocked on her nursing care coordinator's door.

"Come in," said Gail Sergeant. "Marion, what can I..."

"I demand an answer to my complaint against Weizman," she interrupted.

"If you think rude behavior will get you anywhere with me, Marion, you're nuts. If you can't be civil, then get the hell out of my office."

Marion paled as she took the chair beside Gail's desk. "I'm sorry."

"For an intelligent, experienced nurse, you're amazingly self-destructive. Your anger will get you nowhere."

"It's an ongoing problem with several physicians, but Weizman's the worst. I try to avoid his patients whenever possible."

"I'm afraid I don't have good news for you, Marion."

"That doesn't surprise me. These damned doctors always stick together."

"I talked with Arnie Roth, the chairman of the QA committee. They discussed your complaints and dismissed them. Physicians remain responsible for prescribing medication and most health professionals don't deny the risk in sedating an elderly hospitalized patient. Absent some adverse effect from prescribing or not prescribing medication, they'll always come down on the side of the doctor's autonomy."

"Weizman...look at the old guy. He doesn't know what he's doing half the time. They're allowing him to practice at Brier...ridiculous."

Gail stared at Marion and saw the glassy-eyed stare of the true believer. "I don't know where all that's coming from, Marion. Jacob may be old, but his mind is twice as quick as yours and mine put together. He has his own way of doing things, but if I or anyone in my family was sick, Jacob Weizman is near the top of my list for a physician."

"I think your friendship with Weizman is blinding you."

"Your position at Brier is already tenuous, Marion. Nobody wants to work with you. I've had several patient complaints. You may be a good nurse, but you're so disruptive that I may have to let you go."

Marion rose, sneering at Gail. "Should I call my union rep?"

Gail reddened. "Your union rep? Do as you damn well please. Now get out."

Chapter Seventeen

Ginny Harrison was just about to enter the medication room
on the fifth floor medical ward when Thomas Wells closed
the door behind him. "Tommy, what are you doing in there?"

"Oh, hi, Ginny," he replied, eyes narrowing, "I just
needed some alcohol wipes for my tray. I need to draw Mrs.
Cohen in 512."

"The supply cart in the utility room has a ton of
wipes, Tommy. You shouldn't be in here."

Tommy reddened. "No big deal. Check the
medication cabinet. It's still locked. I didn't take anything,
and I resent your implication."

"I'm not implying anything, Tommy. The medication
room is off limits to anyone but physicians and nurses. You
know that."

"I'm sorry. It was just more convenient. I won't do it
again...all right?"

"I'm sorry too, Tommy. Nursing administration is
paranoid about medication theft at Brier. I have a stack of
memos to prove it. Let's just forget about it."

"Thanks Ginny. I'm not looking for trouble. It won't
happen again."

As Tommy turned to walk away, he reached into his
pocket, felt the key to the medication cabinet, and smiled.

When Ginny entered the room, she scanned its
contents and checked the doors on the medication cabinet.
They were all locked. If anything's missing, Ginny thought,

it would show up in the medication count done at the beginning of each shift.

Sarah Hughes and her most recent boyfriend, Kevin Meeks, were parked in his family's Land Cruiser on Grizzly Peak in the Berkeley Hills. They were so busy groping each other they didn't notice the car, headlights off, approaching from the rear.

The rapping of something hard against the steam-covered driver's seat window brought them back to reality. "Open up. Berkeley Police."

Kevin tucked his shirt back into his pants and rolled down the window. "What can I do for you, officer?"

The patrolman smelled the marijuana at once and turned to his partner. "I'll take care of him. You get the girl."

The officer stood back from the door. "Raise your hands where I can see them, then step out of the car."

When Kevin exited, the patrolman grabbed and pushed him against the car and applied handcuffs.

Sarah fought against the patrolman as he pulled her roughly from the car. "Leave him alone! We weren't doing anything wrong."

"Cuff her too."

When the phone rang at 11:30 that night, Marilyn Hughes picked up the handset at once. Sarah had again defied curfew. "Mrs. Hughes? This is Sergeant Peterson, Berkeley P.D. We have your daughter Sarah under arrest for an open container violation and possession of marijuana."

"We'll be right down."

"Don't bother. She'll be visiting with us overnight."

Marilyn turned to Robert. "Your daughter's in jail. We can't get her until tomorrow."

Robert managed a slight smile. "Maybe this time, she'll learn."

After they bailed her out the next morning, their sullen and angry daughter sat in silence, arms crossed, in the back seat as they drove home.

"Don't say anything," Sarah suddenly shouted. "This is bullshit. We weren't doing anything wrong."

"Good," said Robert, "Then you can handle this yourself."

Then Robert Hughes hired an attorney and he got the court to agree to refer Sarah to the Berkeley Woman's Mental Health Clinic for evaluation and treatment in lieu of prosecution.

On their way out of court, Robert turned to his daughter. "Please, Sarah, try to do something constructive with this opportunity."

"Some great opportunity. I don't know how much more of this crap I can take."

Chapter Eighteen

Lola sat with Jacob at breakfast. "What's happening to Joshua Friedman?"

Jacob stared through their west-facing window. Dark clouds drifted toward the city, covering the Marin highlands, and blanketing San Francisco Bay. He shook his head. "His family couldn't handle him at home. He's back at Brier."

Josh Friedman was one of Jacob's first patients. They had grown old together.

When they first met, Josh worked as a park ranger. He lived in Berkeley, but spent weeks at a time in the Sierras. He'd been a vigorous, athletic man who stood six feet four inches and weighed a solid two hundred forty pounds.

He retired as regional director and lectured locally at all levels from elementary school to the university. Eighteen months ago, he came to see Jacob complaining of trouble swallowing. He pointed to the lower edge of his breastbone. "Whatever I eat stops here."

"Is it everything, or just solid food?"

"Just solids, like a chunk of steak or a piece of chicken."

Jacob was alarmed at once by the often-deadly symptom. "We're going to need some tests."

"What is it, Jacob?"

"I don't know for sure, but I'm concerned."

"Don't tell me it's cancer."

"It could be any number of things, most of them benign."

"Well, let's get to it."

Three days later, Margaret Cohen came into Jacob's office. "I have the radiologist on line two."

Jacob's hand hesitated over the handset.

"I'm so sorry, Jacob. Mr. Friedman has advanced carcinoma that involves a good part of the lower third of his esophagus."

"There's no possibility...?"

"None."

I'm so sick of this, Jacob thought. Sixty years of small victories and big disappointments...swimming the currents of hope only to drown in a senseless sea of savagery...God's negligence or nature's cruelty...a distinction without a difference.

Josh and his wife Joanie sat across from Jacob's desk. When Josh heard Jacob's words, he paled and withdrew into silence. Joanie sobbed softly.

Joanie blew her nose. When she regained control, she stared at Jacob. "Today, with modern medicine, there must be something we can do."

"I'm not saying that we won't try to treat this. It's just that our best falls terribly short. We'll try chemotherapy and radiation and we have techniques to ameliorate problems caused by the tumor."

Josh studied his old friend. "You're omitting something, Jacob."

"I know."

"What is it?" asked Joanie.

"Cure...Jacob hasn't used the word cure."

Two months after completion and recovery from radiation and chemotherapy, Josh felt much better. "At least I've survived the treatment, Jacob. What's next?"

"Watchful waiting. Enjoy your life, Josh. None of us really knows how long we have."

"Right," Josh responded. He paused and stared at Jacob. "I've signed an advanced directive for health care and a living will. I'll sign or etch anything into my skull so that when the time comes, I can die in peace."

"That should do it. It helps if you and Joanie are on the same page with this."

"We made vows to each other, promises we intend to fulfill." Josh reached over to his friend and physician. "We put our lives in your hands, Jacob. Now, I'm placing my death there, too. Don't let me down."

"Never."

When Jacob entered Brier 515, Josh Friedman's room, a sour-faced Marion Krupp followed. Joanie sat next to Josh's bed, her head resting against his arm.

The once powerful man was skeletal. His weight had declined to 120 lbs. The tumor had recurred, completely blocking his esophagus, and forcing Jacob to place a tube above the mass, to remove Josh's normal salivary secretions.

Jacob turned to Marion. "Why do you have his arms in restraints?"

"I was afraid he'd pull at his tube or his IV."

"Take them off."

"But, Doctor..."

"Damn it, I said, take them off."

Marion sneered. "Yes, Doctor."

When Jacob leaned over, Josh felt his presence and opened his eyes. His mouth formed a gentle smile. His lips were encrusted and dry, teeth stained with blood.

"When did he have his mouth care?"

"I was just about to do it," said Marion.

Josh lifted his hand, making a come here gesture. When Jacob leaned over him, he whispered, "It's time, Jacob. I can't take any more of this...it's time."

"Is it the pain?"

Josh smiled. "It's pain or coma. I can't find anything between. Tubes, IV's, restraints, spit running out of my mouth, and my own smell...I reek of death. I can't stand it. Let me go, Jacob. I'm ready."

Jacob turned to Joanie. "Joanie?"

She trembled. "Don't ask me this, Jacob. I know what I want...what he wants...please don't ask me."

Jacob turned to Marion. "Let me have a word with you, outside."

They stood in the corridor. Marion folded her arms firmly across her chest.

"I want you to replace the 50 fentanyl narcotic patch with the 100. How much morphine is he taking?"

"I'm giving him 50mg every three to four hours."

"I'm amending the orders so that you can titrate his morphine dose up to 100mg every three to four hours. We have no reason to let him suffer."

Marion reddened. "Absolutely not! I won't be a party to your desire to kill Mr. Friedman."

"I have no such intention. He's suffering, don't you think he's entitled to relief?"

Marion placed her hands on her hips. "Don't take me for a fool, Doctor. I've been around here long enough to recognize orders that will kill a patient. Those large doses of morphine will stop him from breathing...I won't take part in that...it's immoral."

"If this disease isn't frustrating enough, I have to deal with..." Jacob counted to ten. "Show me one study where a patient treated with high dose morphine for control of pain showed depression of respiration...you can't...it doesn't."

Marion placed her hands on her hips. "I won't do it. Get someone else."

It's later that evening when I arrive. I planned this timing with care, knowing that the night shift had just begun. They'll be busy for at least fifteen minutes giving report. I walk down the hall looking over my shoulder then enter room 515.

How peaceful Josh looks.

He's right on the edge.

Just a small step away.

This is too easy, I think, as I pull the syringe and insert the needle into Josh's IV port.

Josh awakens. His eyes wander as if still dreaming then they fix on me.

He looks at the syringe then back at me.

"What are you doing here?"

"It's okay," I say. "It'll be over in a moment."

I watch his eyes widen as the syringe empties into his vein and he says, "No...no, it can't be."

As he closes his eyes, I lift his lids and watch as his pupils contract to the point of a pin and his breathing stops. You're free now!

When the night nurse entered Josh's room, she knew. She touched his icy hand, listened to his chest, and shined her penlight into his dilated and fixed pupils. She dialed Dr. Weizman's answering service. They told her that Dr. Spelling was on call.

Moments later, Zoe was on the phone. "Mr. Friedman's gone. Do you want me to call the ER doctor to pronounce him?"

"No, it's all right. I'm nearby. I'll come up and do it."

When Marion Krupp arrived for her shift the next morning, and heard of Josh Friedman's death, she went at once to Gail Sergeant, the charge nurse. "I demand an investigation of Mr. Friedman's death."

"What are you talking about?"

"You may call it physician assisted suicide or euthanasia, or any damn thing you please, but I call it murder. You think that the staff doesn't know what goes on at those ethics meetings. Somehow, the good Dr. Weizman always sides with death. I'll see to it that your esteemed Jacob Weizman doesn't get away with it this time."

Chapter Nineteen

"Dr. Byrnes, Dr. Jack Byrnes, call ER stat," blared the Brier Hospital speaker system.

Jack grabbed the nearest phone. "Dr. Byrnes, here. What's up?"

"Dr. Hughes says it's urgent. I'll get him for you."

Robert Hughes, director of the Emergency Department at Brier, trained in emergency medicine at UC with Jack and frequently referred patients to him.

"Sorry to do this to you, pal, but I have a Mrs. Mavis Smith down here that has overdosed."

"What did she take and how bad is she?"

"She's semicomatose. We have the empty prescription bottles, Valium, Theophylline, and a variety of antidepressants. I can't tell yet whether her drug levels are rising or falling. You'd better come down."

Jack turned to Ahmad Kadir. "Let's go. We have an OD in the ER."

When they arrived, the nurse pointed them to room two. Mrs. Smith was an obese female, age fifty-eight. She lay on the hospital gurney wearing a faded housedress. When they stimulated her to measure the depth of coma, all they got was a groan.

After a quick assessment, Jack observed as Ahmad inserted a tube into her stomach. Jack ordered charcoal instilled into her gastrointestinal tract to absorb whatever she swallowed then ordered IVs and diagnostic tests in preparation for her transfer to ICU.

Jack turned to the nurse. "Does she have any family?"

"A husband and two grown children."

"Ask them to come in."

Two minutes later, the door opened and her husband Horace entered with their adult children Randy and Lucille.

Horace wore dirty jeans, a plaid shirt, and a black leather jacket. He stared at Ahmad and pointed his finger. "What in hell is he doing here?"

"My name is Dr. Byrnes. I'm the medical director of the Intensive Care Unit. This is my assistant, Dr. Kadir. We'll be taking care of Mrs. Smith."

"Like hell he will," said Randy. "We ain't having no fuck'n A-Rab lay his murdering hands on my mother."

Ahmad paled, but remained silent.

"I'm sorry you feel that way. Dr. Kadir is a skilled ICU physician, and I need his assistance in the care of your mother."

"I don't give a goddamn..." started Horace, stopped by Jack's raised hand.

"Here are your choices," said Jack. "As long as she's under my care, I will treat her in any way I see fit and use the assistance of any physician I think helpful. You can fire me, find some other physician, or transfer to another hospital. You can choose to do that, but her condition is unstable. I don't advise such an action." Jack scanned the family's faces and saw Lucille jerk her head diagonally. She wanted to talk. "If you'll excuse me a moment."

When Jack left the room with Ahmad, Lucille followed. "I'm so sorry, Dr. Byrnes. Just last week we received notification that Jesse, our baby brother, was killed in Iraq. It's what set mother off. Of course I know that Dr. Kadir had nothing to do with this, but..."

"Dr. Kadir is a Palestinian, not from Iraq or Iran. You have no beef with him."

"Please do what you can for mother. I'll deal with Horace and Randy."

When they wheeled Mavis away to the ICU, Lucille remained in heated conversation with her father and brother. The ICU nurses settled Mavis into bed five, right across from the nursing station.

Jack was completing his admission note when Ahmad approached. "Her blood levels are falling. If we can control any heart irregularities, I think she'll do well."

Jack nodded in agreement. "We'll need to watch her closely. Check her mental status every thirty minutes."

At 9 p.m., the family asked to see her.

"Only two at a time," said the nurse.

Lucille and her tattoo-covered brother Randy stood by the bedside holding their mother's hand.

Randy squeezed her hand. "Mom...mom...it's me and Lucille. We're here. You'll be fine."

Mavis groaned.

Ahmad approached the bed for his next thirty-minute check.

Randy tensed. "What are you doing to her?"

"Nothing," said Ahmad, "I just need to check her pupils and her mental state."

As Ahmad shined his penlight into her pupils, he felt himself jerked backwards by a strong arm and thrown against the wall, his head crashing with a blinding thump. He collapsed as the fist smashed into the pit of his stomach and felt the blinding pain as his nose exploded in agony.

Moments later, through blood-blurred eyes, Ahmad saw Brier security guards pulling Randy Smith away. Ahmad's mind screamed with rage.

Mavis Smith recovered without incident.

Ahmad refused to press charges.

Chapter Twenty

Lola Weizman, after many years of rewarding but exhausting work as a psychotherapist, finally donated her tear-stained couch to The Salvation Army. She missed the best times and the closeness with her patients as well as the intellectual stimulation of the psychotherapeutic process. But being human after all, Lola found herself, on occasion, responding like the computer program Psyche: the 'I sees', the 'what do you thinks', and her all time favorite, the 'tell me mores'.

"At least I still have the Berkeley Woman's Mental Health Clinic to indulge myself and see patients," she said to Jacob over breakfast.

"Don't let this go to your head, but you were the smartest, most compassionate therapist I ever knew. They're lucky to have you, even part-time."

Lola met Elena, the clinic's receptionist, with her favorite behaviorist greeting, "You're fine; how am I?"

Elena smiled, not from the joke, she'd heard it a thousand times before, but from Lola's warmth—her charisma.

"I've never heard that one before, Doctor. You're getting to be like our Alzheimer's patients, making new friends every day."

"That's an awful cruel thing to say to an old lady."

Elena smiled. "Report me. She's waiting for you."

"Who's waiting?"

"Sarah Hughes."

"If I don't come out in an hour, call the cops."

Lola approached her tiny consultation room and saw Sarah picking at her black fingernails. She was an image in black: boots, miniskirt, and leather jacket.

"I'm Lola. Come into the office."

When Sarah looked up, Lola read her defiance—more black, thick eyeliner, lipstick, and multiple piercings.

Lola wondered...where else is she pierced?

Lola faced Sarah, extending her warmth, and then smiled. "I love your earrings, and that diamond in your nose. Is it real?"

"No, it's faux...it looks real, doesn't it?"

"Yes," Lola said as they entered the room with a small metal desk and two easy chairs facing each other, a small coffee table between them, and a La-Z-Boy in the corner.

"Where's your couch?"

"At home. It's real simple here, Sarah. We just talk."

"Talking's going to change me?"

"Do you want to change something?"

Sarah smiled. "That's a real shrink question if I ever heard one."

Lola smiled in return. "You've talked with a counselor before?"

"Counselors, psychiatrists, psychologists, and even a chaplain. It's all a lot of crap." Sarah paused for a moment, staring at Lola. "How old are you? You look like a hundred."

"Almost, I'm eighty-five. How old are you?"

"Fifteen," said Sarah as she walked around the room. She stopped at the wall behind Lola's desk, looking at the framed certificates. She pointed to several ornate diplomas. "I can't read these. What language are they?"

"They're German."

"You must be pretty smart to have so many diplomas."

"If you live long enough and you keep your eyes and mind open, you can learn a few things."

"I think this psychiatry stuff is so much bullshit."

"You mean a smart woman like me has been wasting all these years on bullshit?"

Sarah stared at Lola, then returned to her chair and inspected her nails again. "You wouldn't be the first. Anyway, you know I'm not here by choice. It was either get shrunk or go to jail. I don't know which is worse."

Lola laughed. "I know what you mean, but you and I know that forcing somebody into therapy guarantees its failure...I have two strikes against me before I begin."

Sarah felt herself smiling back. "Well, what do we do?"

"Let me ask you a few simple questions: Are you happy? Are you satisfied with the way your life is going? Are you optimistic about the future?"

"No, no, and no...and neither of us can do a damned thing about it."

"You're wrong, Sarah. We can accomplish a lot together if you'll give me a hand."

Sarah lowered her head into her hands and began to cry.

She looks like a little girl, Lola thought. She rose from her chair, stood beside Sarah, caressed her hair, and handed her a tissue.

When Sarah regained control, Lola faced the girl. "You hate bullshit, so you won't hear any from me. When we meet, this will be the one place you can talk about anything, and I mean anything. What we say here, stays here. That's called patient-physician confidentiality. I've never broken it. I never will. Moreover, I've been at this a long time and I doubt you'll tell me anything I haven't heard before."

"How is this supposed to help me?"

"Getting feelings off your chest will help a little, but it's just the foundation for what I hope to accomplish with you."

"And that is?"

"You're a smart girl. I can give you objective advice if you want it, but what I really want to do, is help you understand yourself and change."

"Change what?"

"I don't know yet. We'll need to work that out together."

Sarah stared at her hands.

"Once you do that, you'll be the one in charge and you can deal with most anything. When you take control of your life, anything's possible, including happiness." Lola stood. "Think it over. We'll talk about it next week."

Chapter Twenty-One

When Zoe Spelling entered the house at nine that evening, Byron was sitting in his leather lounge chair reading. Zoe hung her coat on the rack near the front door. "I'm sorry I missed dinner. I had another emergency."

"Jacob's on call tonight. I thought we'd have a pleasant evening together."

"I couldn't help it. I couldn't walk away from my patient. It's part of how I practice medicine. You, of all people, should know that by now."

"Look Zoe, we agreed to try for a semblance of a normal life...I don't see much effort on your part."

She sampled the air. "Something smells good. Is anything left over from dinner? I'm famished."

Byron stared at her with disbelief. He sat across the table watching as she ate.

When Zoe finished, she looked up at Byron. "That was really good. Thanks for saving some for me."

"Can we talk?"

"I'm tired. Can't it wait?"

"You're always finding excuses for not paying attention to me. Do you know what's going on in my life? Do you know or even care whether I'm happy or depressed, satisfied or unfulfilled with my work?"

"Damn it, Byron, you're not a child, don't act like one. I work long hours and carry incredible amounts of responsibility...I really don't need this shit!"

Byron turned away. When he turned back, she had moved to his side. She held his face between her hands, and then kissed him.

"I'm so sorry, sweetheart," she said. "Forgive me. I'm way behind in my sleep. I'm working too hard. I love you, and I don't know what I'd do without you beside me."

He grasped her waist and held his face against her breasts. "I love you too. Let's see if we can get some time off together. Maybe we can go down to Big Sur for a few days."

"That's a great idea. Let me check my schedule." She paused. "Come to bed with me. I'll bet I can think of something that you can do to relax me and help me sleep."

The next day at noon, Jack Byrnes and Warren Davidson sat in the doctor's lounge drinking coffee.

Warren put his cup on the table. "Marion Krupp was in my office this morning. That woman's a swift pain in my ass."

"She's a malcontent who loves to share her misery with others. What's she up to now?"

"She's always been hostile to Jacob...God knows why. Now she's accusing him of killing his patient, Joshua Friedman."

"The woman's out to lunch."

"They went to war again over the care of Jacob's terminal patient. I have fought with her over the same issue, and to tell you the truth, I'm sick of it."

"Jacob may be the most compassionate physician I've ever known, Warren. He doesn't believe in letting his patients suffer as they die. Neither do I."

"She's alleging that when she refused his orders for high dose morphine, he gave it himself."

"Does she have proof?"

"Why? Would that stop her? I'm meeting with the director of nursing. Maybe it's time Marion Krupp and Brier Hospital parted company."

Jack smiled. "She'll love that."

Just before breaking for lunch, Zoe joined Jacob in his office. Zoe patted Jacob's shoulder. "I heard about Josh Friedman. I know you two were close, but his death was a blessing. He suffered enough."

"I agree, but each death of late carries with it an extra element of grief. It's great to live a long life, but it's tough to watch the characters in your play move off stage for good. I'm outliving my patients, my colleagues and the public figures, some of whom enriched my life."

"You're in a philosophical mood this morning."

"When you reach my age, that's all you have left."

"Don't be ridiculous, Jacob. You're more alive, more involved, and more in touch with life than anyone I know. You and Lola bring hope for all of us."

Chapter Twenty-Two

Warren Davidson, the chief of medicine, stretched back in his leather desk chair after his last patient of the day. Following a night interrupted by phone calls, naturally he'd have a busy day.

His office manager, Stacey, stuck her head into the office. "I have Marion Krupp on the line, Warren."

Shit! "Tell her I'm with a patient, or better, tell her I died."

Stacey stood, hands on hips, awaiting a response.

Warren shook his head. "All right, get her number and tell her I'll get back to her as soon as I can."

"She says it's urgent."

"Everything's urgent with that woman."

Warren shook his head and picked up the phone. "Marion, it's Dr. Davidson. What can I do for you?"

"I tried to talk with the director of nursing, but she won't listen to me."

"Yes."

"I know you think I'm just a complainer..." she paused. "It's about time the medical staff did something about Jacob Weizman. He's too old to practice. His ideas are out of date..."

"I heard it all before, Marion. I know Jacob and I assure you, he's among the most competent of our docs. I don't know what's going on between you two, but I'm getting a little sick of it. Maybe it's time for you to move on."

Marion let out a long sigh. "You guys always stick together. If you only knew..."

"Knew what?"

"I can't prove it, but I suspect Dr. Weizman in the death of one of his patients, Joshua Friedman."

"Are you prepared to give me specific written evidence to back up such a charge? This is serious business."

"No, but..."

"I think you're a very disturbed woman. I'll be discussing this with nursing administration."

Marion hung up.

Warren called Jacob. They agreed to meet the next morning.

Jacob groaned as he plopped himself in the doctors' lounge easy chair next to Warren Davidson.

"You're moving kinda slow this morning, old feller."

"Wait until you're eighty-eight."

"Odds are, I'll never make it."

Jacob smiled. "Of the myriad benefits that accrue with age, one tickles me."

"I'm waiting. Remember that I'm not that far behind you."

"Only twenty years or so, Warren."

"I'm still waiting."

Jacob scratched his head. "What was I talking about?"

"You're a truly evil man, Jacob."

"Oh. I remember. As a young man, I wasn't what you'd call a catch. Not tall, not dark, and not handsome, but short, pale, and with an entirely forgettable face. At eighty-eight, I still recall the pain of girls' rejections...crazy, isn't it, after all these years?

"It's a good thing I'm happily married, or maybe it's the threat of Lola in her Honda S2000 rolling over my body, but I always enjoyed just flirting with women. It was benign and fun, but always I perceived an element of reticence in women...a built-in evolutionary constraint that protects them from predators. It was rare with women who knew me, but common with casual contacts.

"Now, at eighty-eight, and looking it, I can approach and talk with women I don't know and they're perfectly comfortable with me. It's like I'm wearing a sign around my neck that says, not to worry...he's safe, he couldn't get it up if he tried."

Warren laughed. "And that tickles you?"

"Nature has her way. Each time I lose one thing, she replaces it with something else. In my case, it's mostly humor. You wanted to see me, Warren?"

"I'm sorry to have to bring this up, but Marion Krupp's at it again."

"It's time to do something about her."

"It's funny, Jacob, but she used the same exact words about you."

"Look, Warren, I know she's obsessed with me, but I'm not the only one."

Warren smiled. "Well, it will please you to hear that she thinks you're special."

"Of course. I remember a number of Krupps...prison guards at Auschwitz. I think she may have a special affection for Jews."

"Don't be paranoid. She can be obnoxious without being an anti-Semite."

"You're right, of course, but don't accuse me of paranoia...with my history, I don't think that's possible."

"It's the Josh Friedman case. I know you two fought over end-of-life care, specifically morphine dosing, but now she's suggesting you had something to do with his death."

Jacob smiled, his 'when-does-it-ever-end' smile. "I figured that living long enough would put me beyond banal human pettiness. I guess you're never too old to learn."

"We've all eased the way for patients, Jacob...you and I agree that it's part of our responsibility, but it is possible to go too far. You haven't been shy about expressing your opinion. Everyone understands your position on the care of terminal patients."

"Even if I were inclined to act aggressively, Josh Friedman was so close to the end that it wasn't necessary. Look over his hospital chart. Josh died without my assistance."

"I know, Jacob. Times don't allow me to deal with these problems out of hand. I hope you understand."

"I do, but not to worry. When I decide to do one of my patients in, nobody will suspect it or be able to prove it. My first and last loyalty is to my patients...nothing will subvert that."

What a stiff-necked, stubborn old man, Warren thought. God bless him!

I smile at the name, Rory Calhoun. This can't be the cowboy, the movie star Rory Calhoun. He died in 1999 from complications of diabetes. That Rory was a handsome heartthrob of the fifties. This one's the scum of the earth.

I managed to read his chart. Rory, age seventy, was admitted for treatment of a non-healing foot ulcer. He has a thirty-year history of heroin addiction...thirty years...unbelievable. Then twenty years on Methadone maintenance. The drug addict somehow managed to work steadily and he actually remarried eight years ago.

I watch as he sleeps fitfully, thrashing his arms and legs around the bed and pulling against groaning leather bed restraints.

The sight of Rory draws me to his bedside. I raise his arms, one at a time. It sickens me to see the dark pigmented tracks, the dead labyrinth of veins, the portals for his ecstasy that cover his lower and upper arms.

Disgusting.

I look at the central line placed just below the clavicle, the only choice they had for IV fluids and antibiotics in a man who spent a lifetime destroying his own veins.

He opens his eyes. I quickly place my gloved hand over his mouth.

"I have something for you," I say, holding up a 20 cc syringe filled with a clear fluid. "It's something you're going to enjoy...an old friend."

I grasp the injection port on the IV line and inject 100mg of morphine.

There it is, thought Rory, the old familiar rush.

Rory smiles.

I smile back. This is such an appropriate ending for a wasted life.

Rory feels his dry lips.

His arms and legs are heavy.
He feels himself nodding off.
Where have you been all these years?
Enjoy the ride, I say, then walk to the sink and wash
my hands of his contamination.

When Ginny Harrison entered Rory's room twenty minutes
later, she found him asleep. She took his blood pressure,
100/60—much lower than normal for this man, and measured
his respirations, four per minute. His skin looked flushed and
when she shined a light into his pupils were pinpoint.

Low blood pressure, flushing, reduced respiration,
and pinpoint pupils screamed narcotic overdosage. She
pushed the Code Blue button, and in seconds, the room filled
with members of the resuscitation team.

Ginny stood wide-eyed clutching her stethoscope. "I
think he OD'd...I think he shot up with heroin!" Jack Byrnes
approached the bedside. "That would be some trick. He's in
restraints."

One minute later, after Jack injected an ampule of
Narcan, a specific narcotic antidote, Rory started moaning
and pulling at his restraints. After another minute, he
slumped back into a coma.

They moved Rory to the ICU.

Jack turned to the ward clerk. "Draw a toxicology
panel. I want to repeat it every hour until we know that he's
safe. We could be dealing with anything, multiple drugs,
contaminants and who knows what."

Each time Jack administered the Narcan, Rory
surfaced only to sink back into coma. At the end of the
second hour, Rory's nurse, Carla Watts, frowned. "His

respirations are up to 40 per minute and he's looking a little blue."

"Get another set of blood gasses and give him more Narcan."

Five minutes later, Jack looked at the arterial blood gasses results. Rory's oxygen saturation had dropped markedly and the acid in his blood had increased as well.

"He's going out." Carla pulled the pillow from under Rory's head and shoved a resuscitation board under his back.

"Push the button, Carla," said Jack with a calm voice, "then break out the intubation tray."

As the ICU resounded with the pulsating beat of the Code Blue alarm and the room filled with members of the team, Jack stood at the head of the bed with the stainless steel laryngoscope in his hand. Like a street thug with his switchblade knife, he jerked his wrist and the curved blade flipped out.

"Hurry up, Jack. He's purple and his pulse is up to 180 beats per minute."

Jack inserted the blade under Rory's tongue, lifting the tissues and trying to visualize his vocal cords. The entire area filled with blood-tinged foam obscuring all landmarks.

"Get me the suction," Jack yelled. "I can't see a damn thing."

Carla passed the clear plastic suction tube to Jack who began sucking away the foam. With fewer bubbles, Jack tried again to see the vocal cords when the area again filled with foam and bloody mucous. Pulmonary edema...his lungs filled with fluid. Jack suctioned again, and then turned toward Carla. "When I tell you to, push down on his thyroid cartilage, his Adam's Apple. Hold it until I say stop."

Jack strained for the v-shaped slit, the vocal cords, a drowning man reaching for a lifeline. He needed to pass this breathing tube through them, but again he saw nothing. "Push now, Carla!"

When she pushed down, the vocal cords, those beautiful vocal cords, descended into view. Jack pushed the tube through the cords, and then inflated the balloon cuff around the tube to fix it in place. He then listened to the chest as they inflated Rory's lungs with a resuscitation bag.

"We're in," he said with relief. "Get a stat portable film and give him 40 mg of Lasix intravenously."

Lasix, a powerful diuretic, would help remove the excess fluid in Rory's lungs. The chest x-ray showed massive amounts of fluid, making his lungs look white on the films.

Jack had to repeat the Narcan twenty times in the next six hours with additional doses of Lasix until Rory's condition stabilized.

That was one hell of a narcotic overdosage, Jack thought. What happened?

Chapter Twenty-Three

While Mark Whitson, the chief of pathology, loved the medical aspects of his job, he hated the business part.

I must hire an administrative assistant, especially for the dirty work, he thought.

Mark turned to the small tray behind his desk containing his fly-fishing tools. He placed his newest idea, a small fly for Bass, in the vice, put it under the magnifying glass, and began his complex tying.

"It relaxes me," Mark always said when caught in the act.

Few made the mistake of asking Mark about his hobby unless they had hours to spare.

Mark's secretary interrupted his intense concentration. "Tommy's here."

"Show him in."

Tommy Wells's face remained impassive as he sat in Mark's eight-by-ten office before a large oak desk covered with piles of charts and reports. On Mark's light blue painted walls were diplomas and board certifications, plus perhaps a hundred specialty licensing documents for a whole range of diagnostic equipment and testing.

"I'm sorry to have to bring you in here again, Tommy, but I'm getting more complaints."

"What the hell is it now?"

"That's part of it, Tommy. Your short fuse."

Thomas took a deep breath. "Who did I piss off now?"

"Jacob Weizman and his patient Gabriella Sago are two. They claim that you made inappropriate advances and when she rejected them, you deliberately hurt her."

"What a load of crap that is. She had shitty veins. I can't help it if I can't get blood the first time, every time. As far as advances, have you seen her? She's a gorgeous showgirl and I think it's gotten to her head. Did I flirt with her…sure a little, but nothing out of line."

"This whole thing comes close to assault. I really had to talk Jacob down."

Whitson looked at the papers within the manila folder. "Look, Tommy, you're an intelligent guy. You may mean well by involving yourself in ward activities, but the nurses especially don't like it. Initially, they thought you were trying to be friendly and helpful, but many see you as interfering."

"I'm sorry, Dr. Whitson, but for the moment, I spend most of my waking hours here. I have friends here. I meet women here. What's wrong with that?"

"I don't have the formula to make sure you don't cross the boundaries of impropriety, but according to several nurses, you've done just that. In addition, this was the third time you've been warned away from the medication room. In this drug crazed culture, the nurses are paranoid about anyone pilfering medications."

"I needed a few simple supplies. Now I'm stealing drugs? Where's the proof? Show it to me."

"Wait a second, Tommy. I'm not here to fire you. I hope that won't become necessary. I'm trying to help. I owe it to your father. He was a dear friend."

"Whatever I do…it turns out wrong. I hate being the lowest man on the totem pole, taking crap from everyone, but I understand that's where I am for the moment. Once I complete my EMT training, I'm out of here."

"Nobody's asking you to take abuse from anyone. You come to me if that happens. Meanwhile, take the advice of someone who wants to see you succeed. Do your job. Be careful with your attempts at friendship with the staff. They may misinterpret it. And, Tommy…" he paused.

"What?"

"Keep the hell out of the medication room."

Zoe sat with Margaret in the office after hours. "Look, Margaret, if the staff has some sort of problem with me, let them bring it to my attention rather than talking behind my back. I'm a reasonable person. We can work it out."

"I'm sorry, Dr. Spelling, I don't know what you're talking about."

"That's another thing. I've asked you to call me Zoe when we're out of the range of patients. Why do you insist on the formality?"

"I'm sorry Dr…I mean Zoe. It's just a habit."

"You have no problem calling Dr. Weizman 'Jacob'."

"Oh, but I did. It took nearly twenty years until I got that one right."

"Maybe I'm too sensitive, pushing for the informality that only comes with time."

"About the staff, they talk about everyone, but it's totally benign. I haven't heard a mean word from anyone about you. To Jacob and me, these people are family, but unlike a real family, we can get rid of the malicious gossipers."

"I heard someone say that I didn't know what I was doing...that pissed me off at first, then, in retrospect, it hurt my feelings."

"I don't know what you think you heard, Zoe, but the staff has taken to you. That's a heck of an accomplishment when they naturally compare you with Jacob."

"Nobody can compare with Jacob. If they try, I lose. He's simply the best." Zoe stood. "I'm sorry. I want people to like me. I don't want Jacob to think he made a mistake when he allowed me to join his practice."

"I think that you'd blush if you heard all the nice things that Jacob has said about you, Zoe. You're doing fine. Relax. Lighten up."

That evening, after dinner, Jacob and Lola sat at the kitchen table sipping their Decaf.

Jacob put down his cup. "This isn't bad. Sorry we can't have the real stuff."

"If you want to be awake all night, I'll brew you a cup of the real thing."

"No thanks. My sleep is poor enough."

"I saw Sarah Hughes in the office today."

Jacob took another sip. "How did it go?"

"She's angry and confused."

"Just like us?"

Lola smiled. "No. She's both those things and dysfunctional as well. I think I can help her, but it's hard to get beyond the popular stereotypes of psychiatrists...they don't exactly encourage confidence."

"Look at the competition, Lola: Richard Gere in Final Analysis, Robin Williams in Good Will Hunting, and the psychiatrists' favorite, Judd Hirsch in Ordinary People. Let's not forget Dr. Melfi in The Sopranos, and our all time favorite, Cannibal Lector."

Lola smiled. "I love the line from Professor Glen Gabbard. He's the author of Psychiatry in Cinema who said: I've checked the American Psychiatry Association regulations, and I have to tell you, they have no rule against eating your patients."

Jacob laughed. "I love it."

"Psychotherapy is tough enough without preconceptions. Some of them may be appalling enough to keep patients away...that's tragic. When you add the Scientology plot against psychiatry and especially psychiatric medication, and their use of celebrities, like Tom Cruise, you see the problem."

"Want to hear my favorite psychiatry joke?"

"Okay, but I've probably heard all your jokes by now."

"Well, at our ages, if I don't remember telling it, you may not remember hearing it. Ronnie Shakes, the comedian, said: After twelve years of therapy, my psychiatrist said something that brought tears to my eyes. He said, 'No hablo inglés.'"

Chapter Twenty-Four

By the next morning when Jack Byrnes entered ICU, Rory Calhoun was sitting up in his bed laughing as he watched television.

Jack grabbed his chart and made himself comfortable at the nurse's station. Ross Cohen, one of Brier's senior psychiatrists, and Rory's shrink, pulled up a chair.

"What the hell happened last night, Jack?"

"Somehow, Rory got a massive overdose of a potent narcotic...heroin, I'd guess. If he wasn't an addict with a high tolerance for drugs, and especially if he wasn't on Methadone maintenance, he wouldn't have made it."

"How did he get it?"

"Don't have a clue, but since he was in restraints, it came with someone's help. Does he have any enemies?"

"Just himself."

"Could he have arranged for someone to give it to him, and they screwed up?"

"I don't see that," said Ross. "On Methadone, he didn't need anything to control withdrawal symptoms. Was he seeking a high? You can never be sure with an addict."

They walked over to the bedside. Rory stared at Ross. "Hey, Dr. Cohen, what in hell am I doing in this damned place?"

Ross turned and pointed to Jack. "This is Dr. Byrnes. He saved your sorry ass last night."

"Thanks, Doc. That must a been one hell of a ride. I haven't felt a high like that in years, maybe never have."

"Do you remember what happened?"

Rory smiled. "Someone gave me the rush of my lifetime...who can I thank? That was some great shit."

"That stuff would have killed a normal person, Rory," said Ross. "Your tolerance after all the years of dope and the Methadone, saved your life."

"You mean something good came from my bad habits?"

"Who gave it to you?" asked Jack.

"Haven't the slightest..."

"Don't hold back on me now, Rory," said Ross Cohen. "We just want to know what happened."

"Me too, Doc. All I saw was a dark shadow and a glint of a white coat. When I saw that needle entering my IV line, I thought I'd had it, then the all time high...shit, I really miss that."

They found nothing new on examination, so Ross wrote transfer orders returning Rory to the ward.

"I think we have a reportable problem here, Jack."

"I know."

"By intention or by mistake, this could have killed Rory."

"I'll talk with Brier's CEO and with risk management, today. They'll begin an investigation."

"Can we get blood levels to find out what he received and how much?" asked Ross.

"I think police forensics can do that. I have a series of blood tubes drawn for analysis. Once we know the drug and can measure the blood levels over time, we can calculate the original dose."

Jack called Warren Davidson, and together they met with Bruce Bryant, Brier's CEO.

"Shit," Bruce said. "That's all we need now. I know Ira Green, the chief of the Berkeley P.D., we play tennis. Maybe he can get into this before the media does."

"Maybe," said Warren. "All the same, it's time for us to take a hard look at hospital security."

Ira Green looked more like an accountant than Chief of Police After meeting with Bruce Bryant, and Al David, Brier's attorney, Ira met with Jack and Ross.

"Deliberate O.D. or a mistake?" he asked.

Ross stared at Ira. "You've dealt with addicts as much as I. It's a culture that I still find difficult to understand. Nothing they do surprises me."

"Has the hospital experienced any other unusual or unexpected deaths or injuries lately?"

"We always have deaths," said Jack. "Some unanticipated, but nothing that's raised suspicion. Have other hospitals in the area reported any type of suspicious activities, chief?"

"Not a thing. I'm assigning one of my best plainclothes detectives, Shelly Kahn, to the case. I'd like her to work with your risk management people so she can keep a low profile. She was a nurse, so she knows how to fit in. Any other suggestions?"

"Once the blood levels return, we can extrapolate backwards," said Jack. "Then, we'll know what someone gave him, and what dose. That should put us in a better position to tell if this was an accident."

Ira looked at the group. "This was no accident."

Chapter Twenty-Five

Jacob had bad patients in sixty years of practice, but Justine Howard was in a category of her own. He used all the considerable tricks in his bag attempting to control her obesity related diabetes.

"I ain't takin' no shots," was her first salvo ten years ago, then after the family interventions, she finally agreed.

Then it was, "I ain't stickin' myself for them damn sugar tests four times a day...no way in hell."

Ever the rational man, Jacob didn't understand why she rejected all his efforts on her behalf.

"It's that damn pride of yours, sweetheart," said Lola. "How many years does it take before you understand that you can't live your patients' lives for them?"

"Look, I have no illusions that patients follow all my instructions to a T. The medical literature is clear on how poor compliance is for medication, diet, etc. Justine, however, is deteriorating right before my eyes, and I know that with a modicum of cooperation, I can reverse it."

"I've been a shrink for a while, and I tell you, you can't help anyone who won't help themselves."

Over the years, Justine's condition deteriorated. Her recent hospitalization at Brier was the worst.

Justine called one afternoon. "I got this terrible pain in my belly, doc. I been putting a heating pad on it for days, but it ain't helped it none."

"How's your sugar?" Jacob asked.

"Hell if I know."

"Do you have any fever?"

"Ain't got no thermometer, but I'm hot and sweaty."

"Come in to Brier Emergency. I'll see you there."

"No thanks, Doc, I'm sticking with it for a while."

"This could be serious."

"Everything's serious with you, Doc. I'll call you back if'n it don't get better."

"But," he shouted into the dial tone.

I had better get the visiting nurse out to see her ASAP, Jacob thought, or I'll be hearing from her in the middle of the night.

At three a.m., Jacob's phone rang.

"This is Brier Emergency, Dr. Weizman. You should see what we've got for you."

"Just don't tell me it's Justine Howard."

"You're a mind reader, doc."

It was nearly 4 a.m. when Jacob entered the ER.

The ER nurse pointed to the door to her right. "She's in treatment room II. How long has she had that hernia?"

"What hernia?"

Jacob and the nurse gave their heads the knowing shake of those who tried and lost in the care of the pig-headed patient.

Justine held her hands on her abdomen. "Hey, Doc. This thing is really killing me. Fix it up and let me get out of here."

Before Jacob lifted Justine's hospital gown, he smelled it, the stench of decaying tissue, gangrene. He stared in disbelief as he exposed her abdomen, reeling from the full force of the foul odor and feeling his stomach churn.

He recalled a case from medical school...his first days working with the living. The thirty-five-year-old woman came into the Vienna clinic with a grapefruit-sized tumor of her left breast. She'd had it for three years. How could someone let this go on for so long?

Now he looked at Justine's abdomen and saw an enormous hernia, a ballooning out of her intestine through an old C-section abdominal incision. The thin white scar over the hernia had a dark spot in its center.

"My God, Justine! How long has it been this way?"

"A couple of months Doc. I used to push it back in, but lately the damn thing won't go in. Then it started to hurt a lot."

Jacob palpated the melon-sized mass. It was firm, tender, and he dared not reduce it... push it back into the abdominal cavity.

"Hey, take it easy Doc...that kills."

"That's an incarcerated hernia, Justine. It's gangrene. You need surgery, and I mean right now."

"In car sir what?" she asked.

"Incarcerated hernia. It's stuck in that swelling and that dark spot means the tissue is dead or dying."

After a protracted argument, Justine finally agreed to surgery. Jacob called a general surgeon and he repaired the hernia by 9 a.m. that morning.

In the recovery room, Jacob talked with Justine. "I want you in bed for the next 24 hours. Give us a few days to let this heal a bit, keep your sugar under control, and make sure that you don't develop an infection, and I'll get you out of here."

"Make it quick, Doc, this place gives me the willies."

Just as Jacob finished his afternoon office hours, the hospital called. "You'd better get over here to see Justine."

What now? When he arrived, three nurses were at Justine's bedside. Two holding her arms, one pressing on her abdomen.

"We told her not to get up, but we found her grunting on the toilet. When we got her back to bed," the nurse said, pulling away the abdominal dressings, "this is what we found."

Jacob knew before he looked, but seeing the open incision with small intestines protruding . . . an evisceration was the technical name, was still a shock.

Jacob shook his head at Justine.

"Don't blame me, Doc. I had to take a crap. I ain't usin' no bed pan."

Jacob held the earpiece of the phone away from his ear as the surgeon vented his anger. Justine was back in surgery within an hour. He repaired the wound and closed it over with thick stainless steel sutures. The real risk now was another evisceration due to weakened tissue and infection.

For the next two days, with sedation, physical restraints, and the equivalent of a whalebone corset, they were able to keep Justine in bed. The angry wound was swollen, but showed no signs of infection...a small miracle.

On day three, Jacob came into Justine's room and smelled two distinct aromas...the ones best known in medicine: the Juicy Fruit aroma of uncontrolled diabetes and the distinctive stench of a Pseudomonas bacterial wound infection.

When Jacob thought what more could go wrong? Marion Krupp entered the room. Oh...no!

"Marion, do you have this morning's lab?"

She handed him the laboratory printout. "Yes, Doctor."

They were as he anticipated, but the magnitude of the uncontrolled diabetes (diabetic ketoacidosis, DKA) and the signs of infection were alarming.

"Nurse Krupp, we're going to need an ICU bed for her ASAP. In the meanwhile, I'm ordering IV's, insulin, bicarbonate and antibiotics. We've got to get on this before it's too late." He grabbed her chart, wrote the orders, and handed them to Marion.

She scanned his orders and frowned. "Are you sure you want this much insulin, Doctor?"

"Of course I'm sure. This is a sick woman with severe DKA and infection. She needs aggressive treatment."

Marion smirked. "I'm sorry, Dr. Weizman. I'll need to check these orders with my head nurse...I don't think they're appropriate."

"Are you out of your mind? We don't have time for this, Marion. Any delay could kill her."

"I'm sorry, Doctor. I'm responsible and cannot follow orders which are questionable."

Jacob looked up and shook his head. "Questionable? Give me the keys to the medicine cabinet!"

"I can't do that, Doctor."

After finally finding Mary Oakes, the ward's head nurse, and having her berate Marion for obstructing the doctor's perfectly appropriate orders, getting the insulin, the bicarbonate, and the IV's, they returned to Justine's room to find her unresponsive.

Jacob listened to her heart, checked her pupils. "She's dead."

He turned to Mary Oakes, pointed to Marion Krupp. "Get her out of here and never let her set foot again in this hospital."

Marion reddened, and without a word, departed.

Chapter Twenty-Six

Instead of his leisurely breakfast ritual, reading the papers and doing the crossword puzzles, Jacob gobbled down his lox, eggs, and onions.

"What's the rush this morning?" asked Lola.

"Sunshine Manor called me to see a new patient. With five patients in the hospital and a full office, I need an early start."

"Can't the nursing home patient wait a few days?"

"She's been waiting. Every doctor the family called refused to come to the home. Finally, all they had left was old doc Weizman...some testimonial. It's been a week now, and someone has to see her."

"Getting sensitive in your old age?"

"Not the esteemed Jacob Weizman."

Sunshine Manor, a modern one-story glass and redwood building, sat on the outskirts of town. Its broad decks and large skylights created a bright and cheery atmosphere. The glass automatic doors whooshed open as Jacob approached. When he entered the lobby, Marcia Katz, the nursing supervisor, came from behind the nurse's station to greet him.

Marcia hugged Jacob. "Thanks for coming. We're finding it nearly impossible to get physicians in to see our patients. I don't know what we'd do without you."

"I'm not going to live forever, Marcia. Maybe if the home puts a physician on salary and pays him or her enough that will solve your problem."

"Sure, Jacob. I can just see the board of directors signing up for that. They're constantly complaining that they can't make it as things are now."

"Where is my patient?"

"I'll introduce you."

"No, that's okay. What room?"

"Room 1247. Her name is Mildred Kaysen. Her daughter Paige is with her." She bent over to whisper, "I'd watch out for that one."

As Jacob walked through the quiet corridors, he looked at the photos, art reproductions, and craft work of some residents that decorated the off-white walls. Some inmates shuffled, hands on walkers, vacant eyes down. Some remained fixed by an umbilical cord, the tether, to an attendant immediately behind. Others, also head down, were wheelchair-bound, literally tied into the seat by a broad canvas waistband around their torsos. Diapers protruded from trousers and hospital gowns. The stench of disinfectant, Desitin, and excrement defiled the air.

Jacob, all too familiar with this display of degradation, felt embarrassed as if he was somehow responsible. This was a disgrace and a dishonor to lives once valued. To this group, Sunshine Manor was the warehouse for the unwanted, the decrepit, and the useless—the last train station on the route to nothingness.

Jacob and Lola had survived one holocaust. He thanked the fates for their luck, so far, in avoiding this one. He knocked on the door marked 1247 and entered.

A well-dressed middle-aged woman stood next to the bed. She stared at Jacob. "I'm so sorry. I'll call the nurse. She can show you back to your room."

Jacob reddened, and then laughed.

The woman watched Jacob as if he were a lunatic. "Please, I'm sorry. This is a private room. No guests."

"I'm sorry too, but I can't help the way I look. I'm Dr. Weizman. I'm here to see Mrs. Kaysen."

"Oh, excuse me, Doctor. I'm Paige Sims, Mildred's daughter. I wasn't expecting someone so...." she hesitated.

"Old," said Jacob with a laugh. "You're not the first one to confuse me with a resident of Sunshine Manor. Once, they forced me to sit down to play games with the group. A nurse who knew me, set me free...too bad, I was about to yell 'Bingo'."

Jacob spent twenty minutes examining Mildred and obtaining a brief history.

Mildred was a sweet, intelligent woman, a year younger than her new doctor. "Thank you, Doctor. It's great, for a change, to see a doc who doesn't have pimples."

Jacob laughed. He turned to Paige. "If we don't have all her old medical records, we'll request them. After I have a chance to review it all, we'll meet again to discuss the treatment plan with you and your mother. For the moment, I'll keep everything the same."

Paige offered a cool hand. "Thank you, Doctor."

When Jacob began to leave, Mildred smiled and winked. "Do you need help finding your way out, Doctor?"

Jacob laughed. "No thanks, Mildred. I left a trail of breadcrumbs behind. I'll find my way."

I really like Mildred Kaysen, he thought.

After Jacob departed, Mildred turned to her daughter. "I like Dr. Weizman. The nurses say he's one of the best physicians in the community."

"Mother. He's even older than you."

"I love that...older than me."

A week later, Jacob returned. "I've reviewed all your medical records, Mildred. I have but one suggestion."

"What is it?" asked Paige.

"The digoxin. You've been on it for twenty years, yet I can't find a good indication for its use."

"Her internist said it was for mother's heart. He's on the staff at Columbia University in New York."

"Whatever. Without a legitimate indication, I'm recommending that we gradually stop it. When you age, pardon the expression, Mildred, and as your kidney function slows down, the drug poses a real possibility of danger. If I felt we have a good reason for its use, I'd leave it alone, but I can't find justification for digoxin in your chart or on your examination."

Mildred looked at Paige, and then turned back to Jacob. "If you think that's the thing to do, then sign me on."

"Mother," said Paige, alarmed.

"If you like, I can ask one of our cardiologists at Brier Hospital to consult with your mother for a second opinion about the digoxin."

"That won't be necessary," said Mildred, staring at her daughter.

Paige's lips pressed together as she stared at Jacob.

Chapter Twenty-Seven

Sherrie Lotts, a new graduate nurse, and just two weeks on the job, watched as Jacob meandered down the hallway. "Who is that?"

Mary Oakes, the head nurse, stared down the hallway. "That's Dr. Jacob Weizman. He's an institution around here."

"That's Weizman? He looks like he ought to be in an institution. How old is he?"

Mary rolled her eyes. "Jacob will be eighty-nine in the fall, I think."

"Isn't he a little old to be practicing medicine?"

"You'll find out when you work with him and you'll get your chance today. Alice Kramer is Dr. Weizman's patient."

While Jacob sat at the nursing station reviewing Alice's chart, Mary and Sherrie approached.

"Jacob, I'd like you to meet Sherrie Lotts. She's a new grad and she's taking care of Alice today."

Jacob stood, bowed slightly, and extended his wrinkled hand to Sherrie, whose tentative touch suggested she was shaking hands with a Leper.

"Nice to meet you Doctor," Sherrie shouted.

Jacob stared at Mary as they communicated as by telepathy…give the girl another chance, Jacob.

"Come, let's make rounds," Jacob said.

"Can I carry the chart for you Dr. Weizman?" Sherrie shouted.

"I ain't deaf, young lady," said Jacob warming to his task.

Sherrie turned to Mary. "I thought he was hard of hearing. I didn't mean anything."

"Why are you telling that to me? Dr. Weizman's standing right here."

Jacob held the chart. "Come with me, nurse Watts," said Jacob looking back at Mary who was shaking her head. "We'll take a look at Alice."

"It's Lotts, not Watts, Dr. Weizman." Sherrie bit her lip in frustration.

They walked to Alice's room and when they entered, Jacob turned to Sherrie. "How's her vital signs, nurse Watts?"

"They're fine, except for a little fever."

Jacob turned to Sherrie. "A beaver? What in hell is she doing with a little beaver? They don't allow beavers in the hospital."

Sherrie turned red. "A little fever...I said she had a little fever."

"Whatever," said Jacob.

Jacob listened to Alice's heart, and then turned to Sherrie. "Maybe she needs to see a heart doctor."

"You mean a cardiologist?"

"Yes. Why don't you see if William Harvey is available? He knows a lot about the circulation."

After ten minutes checking the Brier Hospital directory of physicians, Sherrie entered Mary Oakes's office.

"Dr. Weizman wants a Dr. William Harvey to see Mrs. Kramer, but I can't find him."

Mary began laughing uncontrollably as Sherrie stared in wonder.

When Jacob poked his head into the office, Mary was still laughing. "You're a mean old man, Jacob, very mean."

"What's this all about," said Sherrie.

"Dr. Weizman was having a bit of fun at your expense, Sherrie."

"Fun?"

"Did you get her name wrong, Jacob?"

He nodded. "Twice."

"You didn't do a word substitution?"

"A little one. Beaver for fever. That was quite creative. I also liked the William Harvey consult…we'd have to go back to 1657 to dig up the man who first described the circulatory system." Jacob sat beside Sherrie. "I'm really sorry, but the devil made me do it." He stroked his beard and continued, "I can't remember who said it, but the first thing I do when I wake up in the morning is to breathe on a mirror and hope it fogs."

Sherrie smiled.

Jacob looked at Sherrie. "Can you define ageism for me, Sherrie?"

"It's prejudice against old people."

"You're right, but let me make it clearer. Ageism is when you, I, or anyone else uses the age of a person to define them. That happens through words, gestures or actions and the net effect implies that the person is less worthy and of less value."

"I certainly didn't mean to do that, Dr. Weizman."

"Please, call me Jacob. Everyone does. I don't know why I picked on you when middle aged and seniors themselves are the worst perpetrators…well, I do know. Please don't be offended, but when we know better, we do better. I know, as my grandmother used to say, that I'm no spring chicken, but please wait before you assume that I'm deaf or need physical assistance. Furthermore, you can skip my all-time favorite, talking about me in the third person while I'm present. That one sends me through the roof."

Mary patted Jacob's shoulder. "You're too damned sensitive."

"Wait a few years, and then talk to me about it."

Jacob stood and shook Sherrie's hand. "Friends?"

She smiled, and then nodded.

Jacob rose to leave then turned back into the room. "Got to get home early enough to hear President Nixon's speech."

Mary shook her head and laughed.

When Jacob entered the office after lunch, he looked down at the worn appointment book and reviewed the list of patients scheduled for the day.

"I see Nathan Seigel's first, Maggie. Put him in the examining room."

"Dr. Spelling is with him now. He asked us if it was okay if he saw her today. That's all right, isn't it?"

"Of course. What's the use of having a smart and beautiful doc in the practice, if we're not going to use all her assets."

It's stupid, Jacob thought, but it hurts when patients choose to see another doc…stupid and painful!

Margaret placed her hand on Jacob's shoulder. "Don't give it a thought, Old Man, patients, especially men, are human after all."

"I promised to write a consultation request for Nathan Seigel. He's scheduled to see Sharon Brickman, the cardiologist, again."

"Dr. Spelling said she'd do it."

Two weeks later, Margaret approached Jacob. "Dr. Brickman called. She hasn't received the consultation request for Nathan Seigel. His insurance won't pay her unless they get a formal request for consultation."

"I thought Zoe was doing that. Find out, and let me know."

Margaret knocked on Zoe's door between patients. "Dr. Spelling, have you dictated the consultation request for Mr. Seigel?"

"Of course. I did it on his last visit. Can't you find it?"

"No. Did you use a new tape? Maybe we missed it."

"Missed it? Don't tell me I have to dictate it again, damn it."

"Did you check all the tapes?" asked Margaret of the office transcriptionist.

"I checked them all. I found her patient before Mr. Seigel, her office visit with him, and then the next patient, but no letter of referral. I don't know what happened, but it's not here."

Margaret told the story to Jacob. "It's just a mistake. No big deal. I'll dictate the referral letter right now."

Later that day, Jack Byrnes and Warren Davidson received calls from Mark Whitson. "Can you come over after work for a quick meeting?"

"What's it about?" asked Warren.

"Morphine."

When Jack entered Mark's office, Warren was chatting with him.

"Have a seat, Jack. I have some information about the Rory Calhoun case."

"Let's have it," said Warren.

"I have no doubt that Mr. Calhoun suffered a narcotic overdose...clinically that was obvious. The problem is with the laboratory evaluation."

"What problem?" asked Jack.

"Morphine levels were extremely high...that we expected. The problem is that injected heroin is immediately converted in the blood to morphine. It takes about nine minutes."

Warren looked at the report. "You can't tell us whether he got heroin or morphine."

"Not yet. We'll have to go back to examine other tissues for heroin before we'll know for sure."

"How long will that take?" asked Jack.

"Six to eight weeks."

"Have you told Chief of Police, Green?" asked Jack. "Maybe he can help speed up the analysis."

"He's my next call," said Mark.

Shelly Kahn, thirty-four, looked half her age. She stood five feet two inches and with shoulder length straight black hair, she'd pass for the average university student seen walking down College Avenue.

Her two brothers were police officers, as was her grandfather and father, but she rejected family tradition by going to nursing school. All that changed when her oldest brother was killed on the job.

She'd been one of the Berkeley P.D.'s best undercover officers, but success had brought with it the notoriety that made undercover work impossible.

Shelly sat with Mary Oakes, the nursing care coordinator of the fifth floor medical unit.

"You know why I'm here?"

"The Rory Calhoun case."

"Right. Have you noticed any other unusual deaths or complications on your ward?"

"Medicine is full of the unexpected, but something suspicious...no, I don't think so."

"Brier's not real big on security, is it?"

"It's like most hospitals. The pediatric care units have the most security, and surveillance is pretty good at night after hours, but otherwise, people have more or less free access."

"So, it's unlikely you'd notice strangers on the ward."

Mary smiled. "We'd probably notice the Grim Reaper, detective."

"Please call me Shelly."

"Here's the truth, Shelly. Most of our wards have free public access. If a person doesn't cross in front of the nurse's station or is not noticed by the staff, and nobody sees a trail of blood, he can come and go as he pleases. Anyone wearing a white coat or green scrubs is virtually invisible in a hospital."

"On the subject of staff," said Shelly, "do you suspect anyone...I mean by personality or behavior, that might raise a question?"

"We have all types. Hospital work is stressful and with cutbacks, it's only the saintly that haven't had a few nasty things to say. I include myself in that category. But, someone who'd deliberately injure a patient...nobody comes to mind."

"With your permission, I'll hang around for a few days. I'm not going undercover here . . . that's too obvious and takes too much time. Once we're sure what we're up against, maybe it will come to that. For the moment, just tell your staff that it's okay to talk with me."

"Good luck. Let me know if I can help in any way. Brier's a good hospital, as good a hospital as you can get these days. I hate to see its reputation tarnished."

Chapter Twenty-Eight

At the Hughes's home, an uneasy truce hung over the battle lines after Sarah began seeing Lola Weizman at the Mental Health Clinic.

Sarah met her father's none-so-subtle questions about the sessions with, "It's private."

Brusque answers are a hell of a lot better that the mayhem we had, Marilyn thought.

They sat in the breakfast alcove with the bright morning sun streaming through the white-curtained windows. Robert read the paper while Marilyn and Sarah watched Saturday's version of the Today Show.

At a commercial break, Robert looked up from his paper. "What's on your schedule today, Sarah?"

Sarah stared at her father, her lips drawn tight.

Robert raised his hands in surrender. "It's not an accusation, Sarah, it's just a simple question."

"I'm sorry, Daddy...old habits die slowly. The Pro-Life people have organized a demonstration at the Emeryville Woman's clinic. I'm going there with a few friends to add an element of sanity."

Marilyn stared at her daughter. "I can't believe you're going to a Pro-Life demonstration. I thought we were all on the Pro-Choice page."

"Hello Mother. Earth calling Marilyn Hughes. I have a flash: We are Pro-Choice, but keepin' it real means doing something about it, not just talking."

Marilyn stared at her daughter. "This isn't going to upset you, is it? You're doing so much better lately."

Sarah smiled. "Mother, that's so lame. This is important to me, and to my friends. Don't worry, I'm not fragile, I won't break."

At first, Sarah thought the Saturday demonstrations would be all show—getting the faithful out on their day off. Later, she understood that many working women used their weekends for abortion services.

Sarah was appalled her first time. How was it possible that so much vitriol could spew forth through the fangs of people professing to be Christians? What affected her the most were the attacks on the most vulnerable, those young women forced to make the most private of personal decisions in full public view and under relentless vicious verbiage. With dark sunglasses, their heads down or covered by newspapers, young women marched like felons in a perp walk through the gauntlet of zealots eager to force-feed their faith on others.

Although Sarah's convictions drew her to the cause of a woman's right to choose, it was Betsy Brown's tragedy that converted her from spiritless supporter to passionate partisan.

Betsy came to the woman's clinic on one such Saturday with two girlfriends. Telling her two close friends about her six-week pregnancy was a snap compared to the revelation that her father and the baby's father were the same. "I'm so scared. I shake just thinking about going to the clinic."

"We'll be with you all the way."

As they walked between the screaming demonstrators, one friend on each arm for support, Betsy turned back to the street just as a rotten tomato hit her in the face. She wiped off the red foul pulp, vomited and ran back to the street to the applause of the true believers.

Two mornings later, her mother found Betsy dead in a pool of blood, the victim of a botched back-alley abortion.

The Emeryville Police, veterans of many demonstrations, drew the lines of battle, and roped off areas for the combatants. With signs and posters held high, the armies jeered at each other across the trenches while the innocent, or the damned, depending on your point of view, scurried through the neutral zone between opposing armies, trying to avoid verbal hand grenades from the smug and faithful.

After the demonstration, Sarah packed the back of the family's Lincoln Navigator with the Pro-Choice signage. She was closing the tailgate when Carleton Dix approached with several girls from his TeenTalk group, including Kelly Cowan.

Shit!

The chaplain slid his tongue over his lips. "I thought it was you, Sarah. It disappointed me greatly to see you so willing to disregard the claims of innocent lives."

Kelly Cowan turned red. "They're baby killers...murderers, Sarah. How can you be with them?"

The chaplain raised his arms to the sky. "Judgment has come to this nation...innocent lives are lost every day. Judgment is already here. September eleventh proved that, don't you see?"

I don't want any part of this, thought Sarah. She pulled her keys from the tailgate and walked toward the driver's door.

Carleton Dix moved to block her way.

Sarah tried to move around him. "Excuse me, Padre."

When the minister grabbed her by the arm, holding her in place and staring into her eyes, Sarah felt her heart racing. She felt dizzy and placed her hand on the car to steady herself.

Don't let him do this to you.

"We just want to talk with you," said Kelly.

Suddenly enraged, Sarah shouted, "This isn't the first time he's laid his dirty hands on me, but it's going to be the last."

Like the frozen frame of a feature film, time stopped. Sarah looked around and saw the wide eyes of the crowd. She pulled her arm away. Carleton Dix paled and dropped his hands to his side.

"You little whore!" He raised his hand to strike Sarah.

"No...no..." cried a chorus of teenage voices...don't..."

Carleton Dix slowly lowered his hand, stepped away from Sarah, then reddened with shame at his emotional outburst and loss of control.

Sarah stepped close to the minister and whispered, "I told you never to touch me, Padre. Be smart, quit while you're ahead. I promise you won't like my next step."

She opened the driver's door, started the car, and drove away.

The TeenTalk girls stared at Carleton Dix through questioning eyes, then lowered them and walked away.

Chapter Twenty-Nine

The cardiac step-down unit occupied parallel corridors adjacent to the Cardiac Care Unit (CCU) and was a mirror image of the ICU on the opposite side of the building. It served as an intermediate stop on the route between CCU and the general medical ward for those recovering from heart attacks and other serious heart problems.

They moved Nathan Seigel from CCU to the step-down unit after his fifth visit in four months. Each time he returned, the staff greeted him like a long lost friend. Nathan was an alcoholic who had failed to control his drinking in spite of repeated attempts by his family, his physicians, AA, and several drug and alcohol rehab programs, including the famous Betty Ford Center.

Nathan was the paradigm for the intractability of alcoholism. Beyond the destructive effects of drinking on his professional and personal life, he developed heart muscle damage that Jacob, his doctor, and Sharon Brickman, his cardiologist, called alcoholic cardiomyopathy. The disease weakened his heart and forced its rhythm into chaotic and dangerous irregularities.

Kate Planchette, an experienced CCU nurse, greeted him. "We always enjoy your visits, Nathan, but aren't you getting a little tired of this?"

"Katy, sweetheart, I only do it as an excuse to see you and the girls."

Kate Planchette had never taken her good fortune for granted. She had so much, great parents, material comfort, and intelligence that she felt an obligation to make her life meaningful. She considered medical school, but chose nursing instead.

Kate married her college sweetheart, Benjamin Planchette, and within six years had three daughters. Although Ben wanted a son, they agreed that three was enough. She worked part-time during the preschool years and returned to full-time nursing two years ago.

In retrospect, her problems had been going on for years. Symptoms, so vague and fleeting, and their lives so busy, she never gave them more that a moment's thought.

"Everybody has unexplained symptoms, Ben. Doctors don't evaluate unless they are more serious or persistent."

"Still," said Ben, "you had the numbness before the last two pregnancies, and then you had the vertigo."

"They went away each time. I feel fine."

Ben shook his head, and then caressed her cheek. "You're not fine, sweetheart. Something's wrong. You're having difficulty with the morning Sudoku puzzle."

She stared at him. A tear ran down her cheek, then she whispered, "I know. I'm frightened. When you're a medical professional and you live with disease each day, you wonder why you're the lucky one. Maybe I've run out of luck."

"Don't do this to yourself. Make an appointment to see Arnie Roth."

The rest happened in a flash. Blood tests, MRI, neurology consultation, spinal tap and finally Arnie's diagnosis. "You have relapsing-remitting Multiple Sclerosis."

Kate felt dizzy as her intestines contracted in shock.

She took a deep breath. "Me and the West Wing president."

"Right, except the writer's need for drama made things worse than it's likely to be for you."

"I've cared for MS patients, Arnie. I know what that disease can do."

"Of course. I understand, but remember, you only see the sickest of the sick. The ones who need hospitalization. I see the good part of it, MS patients who are doing well, and I'm telling you that after many years in practice, odds are in your favor to have a normal life."

"I can't say the diagnosis surprises me. I don't know if we have an increased incidence of MS or if it's more in the public's consciousness because of magazines and television."

"We'll start you on interferon. You'll give yourself an injection once a week." He hesitated and stared at Kate. "MS isn't a reportable disease, Kate, but we need to consider its effects on your work."

"My mind is fine, Arnie, but I'll notify nursing administration."

"That's smart, and responsible. I'm sure they won't have a problem. I'll support you in any way possible."

She leaned over and kissed him on the cheek. "Thanks, Arnie. You're the best."

While experienced medical personnel eventually tired of the frustration in dealing with chronic alcoholics, the lies, excuses, and destruction of the individual and their families, the staff at Brier never abandoned hope for Nathan Seigel. He maintained a great sense of humor, treated the staff with respect, and blamed only himself for his problems.

When Nathan appeared in Brier Emergency three days ago, Jacob Weizman admitted him and called Sharon Brickman for a consultation. Jacob tried to handle most problems himself, but Nathan's heart irregularities had proved difficult to impossible to control on prior occasions.

Sharon shook her head in disgust. "I'm going to keep him on Lidocaine to control his irregular heart rhythm, but one of these days we'll be too late."

Jacob shared her frustration. "Tell me something I don't know already."

Patients in the step-down unit had their hearts monitored by telemetry. Each patient's heart tracing appeared on a central station where computers and a trained technician scanned the screen for abnormalities.

I check my watch as I enter Nathan Siegel's room. It's 3:15 p.m., the perfect hour for my visit.

How much time, energy, and dollars have we spent on a man determined to kill himself with alcohol?

As he sleeps, I see that rosy, vein-streaked face and that bulbous nose and hear his soft snore.

The nurses have mounted the sophisticated infusion pump on an IV pole next to the bed. I check the label on the plastic infusion bag. It reads: Lidocaine, Do Not Exceed 50 mg per minute.

The bag is about half full...perfect.

I study the drop as it grows in the drip chamber then falls into the fluid level about one drop every two seconds.

I smile as my gloved hand reaches for the infusion rate entry keys and push them repeatedly until they read 999, the maximal setting. The slow drip becomes a fatal fluid flow.

Nathan stirs momentarily, and turns in bed trying to find a comfortable position. My pulse races with excitement.

When the fluid in the bag is almost gone, I pull a 250 cc bag of saline from my Adidas pouch, attach the infusion tubing, a needle at its tip, and restore the original volume in the Lidocaine bag. As my final step, I restore the pump to its initial setting.

His will be done.

I smile then roll up my empty bag and its tubing and place it back into the athletic bag.

I look back at Nathan then move to the door. I peek out, look both ways, toss the athletic bag over my shoulder, smile, and depart.

Another job well done.

The monitor tech turned to Kate. "Something's wrong with Nathan Seigel. His tracing shows widening complexes like he's having slow conduction of electrical flow through the heart."

Kate Planchette stared at the monitor. Alarmed at once, she rushed to his bedside. Nathan looked like he was asleep, and when she shook him, he opened his eyes and slurred his words. "Whasup, Katey?"

Oh my God, she thought. He's drunk. Won't you ever learn, Nathan?

She could barely understand his speech. "I'm feeling sick, Katey. I have a metal taste in my mouth."

"How could you do this, Nathan? Now, where is it?"

Nathan failed to respond. Suddenly, Kate noticed his right eye twitching. Then came the contractions of the entire right side of his face and the right side of his body. In seconds, Nathan's bed rattled as he convulsed rhythmically. Kate shoved a padded wooden tongue depressor between his teeth then pushed the Code Blue button. She removed Nathan's pillow, listened for breathing and felt for a pulse. Finding neither, she gave him three quick mouth-to-mouth breaths and began external cardiac massage.

In moments, the room filled with the Code Blue Team, the respiratory therapist, and several physicians who had been nearby. Kate continued external massage while they placed a mask over Nathan's mouth to ventilate his lungs. The monitor on the defibrillator showed a flat line, no electrical activity at all as Sharon Brickman entered, followed by Ahmad Kadir who ran from ICU.

At that moment, Sharon was all business. "What's happening?" she shouted. "Someone get hold of Jacob Weizman."

"The tracings widened," Kate said, "and when I got in here, he sounded drunk. I don't know how he got alcohol in here. Then he had facial twitching that quickly progressed to a generalized convulsion. His heart tracing showed no electrical activity, a flat line."

Sharon stared at the tracings, examined his heart. "Continue CPR and set up an Isuprel drip while I prepare the pacemaker."

Moments later, Sharon, with the help of Ahmad, inserted a long catheter into a large vein in Nathan's groin and passed it up to the heart. When she started the pacemaker, she was pleased to see the resumption of the heart's electrical activity, but in moments, she found her hopes dashed. His heart muscle contractions were so feeble, they failed to support a blood pressure.

Jacob Weizman entered the room. He looked at Sharon who shook her head. "I'm so sorry, Jacob. We did everything possible. Nathan finally ran out of luck."

The nurses gathered the resuscitation supplies and straightened the room. Kate prepared Nathan's body for the morgue.

Jacob stood with Kate. "What in hell happened?"

Kate reddened, and then turned away.

Jacob turned to the cardiologist. "Sharon?"

She hesitated a moment. "Don't know, Jacob. I'd say a lethal cardiac irregularity, but the tracings look funny to me and I can't explain the seizures."

"Has anyone called the family?" Jacob asked.

"No. I'll call if you like."

"Thanks, Sharon. I'll do it. In spite of all his close calls, this is going to kill his daughters."

"I think we need a postmortem examination."

"No question. I'll get the family to sign the permit and I'll notify pathology."

"Something's not right about this, Jacob."

"I know."

Chapter Thirty

Margaret Cohen tapped on Zoe's door Friday morning. "Brenda Gomez is ready, Dr. Spelling. She's in examining room three."

Zoe frowned. "Why is she here? She isn't due back for two or three months."

"You know Brenda...it's always something."

Zoe grabbed Brenda's chart from the door rack and entered.

Brenda, age forty-five, and single, sat on the table, lost in an examining gown three sizes too large. Her body language was a paradox; thin arms crossed her chest said, 'keep away', wide, teary eyes pleaded for help.

Brenda smiled. "Hi, Dr. Spelling."

"What is it now?"

Brenda fumbled with her purse, rummaged through, and then produced five pages of handwritten notes.

"Put those away and tell me what's bothering you the most."

"I don't feel good."

"Please, Brenda. You must give me more than that."

Grasping her notes again, Brenda began paging through.

"I told you to put those away. I don't have all day to waste on every little problem."

Brenda's eyes filled. "I need some tests...something's wrong with me. Please, Dr. Spelling, help me."

"We've run out of tests, Brenda." Zoe pulled the stethoscope from her lab coat and began her examination. After Zoe finished, she opened the examining room door and stood with Brenda's chart. "You're as healthy as a horse, Brenda. Let me see you again in six months."

"You're not finished seeing me, are you? You must give me something."

"You don't need anything. You're fine."

Brenda clutched her wrinkled list. "I don't feel good. I wrote it all down. Let me tell you a few things."

Zoe shook her head in disgust. "Give me that." She grabbed Brenda's list and placed it in her pocket. "I'll look them over as soon as I can."

"Thanks, Doctor. I'll hear from you soon?"

"Sure."

While Brenda headed for the front desk, Zoe returned to the examining room. She reached into her pocket grabbed the list, crushed it in her hand, and tossed it into the trashcan.

Margaret Cohen watched from her desk. Brenda may be difficult, but this...?

Three emergency office visits, late patients, and doctors delayed on rounds kept Jacob's office in a frenzy throughout the day. Finally, it was over. Fridays were bad, this was ridiculous.

Margaret sat in the lounge with Betty Kaufman, the office receptionist, and Trudy Sims, their bookkeeper. She'd retrieved three cans of soda from the refrigerator.

Betty took a sip. "I'm glad this day's over. If Jacob asks me to squeeze one more patient into the schedule, I'm going to squeeze him."

Margaret smiled. "He can't help it. It's in his soul. How do you think Zoe's doing?"

"I think she's great," said Betty. "She's so smart and beautiful. I think she's a real asset to the practice."

"She's a little distant with some patients," said Margaret. "Don't you think?"

"Well, Margaret," said Betty, "we have a few that try the souls of any man or woman. Brenda Gomez is a good example."

Margaret faced Betty. "You don't think Brenda deserves our attention?"

"It's not that, it's just that she's so needy...so impossible to deal with, that I understand Zoe's difficulty with her. Unfortunately, the world produces few saints like Jacob."

Margaret shook her head. "Jacob's no saint. He has had his moments, like all of us, but he never takes it out on our patients.

"What do you think, Trudy?"

"She's charming for sure, but I keep having to remind her to complete the office visit forms for billing and letters that we need to appeal disallowed services...that's a real headache. I have one other thing..."

"What?" asked Margaret.

Trudy looked back over her shoulder. "Well, technically, Zoe's an employee, I guess. Nobody's told me anything else, yet she's demanding details about all our billing practices, income, and receivables. It's awkward for me. I feel uncomfortable talking about those things with her. I wish you or Jacob would clarify the situation for me."

"I'm sorry," said Margaret. "In the craziness of daily life, Jacob and Zoe have never formalized their relationship, although I know he wants her to be a full partner." She took another sip of soda. "Maybe I've been a one man office manager too long. I want things to go well for us and for Zoe too."

When Robert Hughes picked up the phone at home, he heard, "Bob, it's Lola Weizman."

"Lola, it's great to hear from you. How's Jacob?"

"Old."

"None of us are getting any younger."

"Don't remind me...every time I move, my body complains."

"What's up?"

"I wanted to talk with you about Sarah."

"Should I sit down first?"

"Come on, Bob...give the girl a break. She's doing well, so well, in fact, that I'd like to invite her for dinner. Is that okay with you and Marilyn? We thought of inviting all of you, but that should wait a while longer."

"Of course it's okay. Things have really improved since you began seeing her. Maybe you should take on Marilyn and me?"

"I'm good, Bob, but I'm not a miracle worker. Don't be surprised if everything improves at home."

Shortly after noon Saturday, Jacob returned from hospital rounds to find Lola in the kitchen making a salad. He removed his coat and hat and sat at the kitchen table, grabbing a pencil and a crossword puzzle.

"How were rounds today?"

"Too smooth. I get suspicious when things appear to be going well. It's like waiting for fate to slip us a fast one."

Lola carried the salad bowls to the table. "You're getting paranoid in your old age, sweetie."

"Ordinarily, I believe the esteemed psychotherapist in residence, but our lives make it difficult to be paranoid."

Lola laughed. "I think you're full of shit."

"Is that a psychoanalytic term?"

"It means, my love that I see a world of difference between what you say and how you live. I can't call you irascible, you have too good a sense of humor...maybe you relish your dark side out of habit?"

"Don't shrink me, Lola. Time and gravity are doing enough of that. When's Sarah coming over?"

"About three."

"For dinner?"

"I'm not giving her a free ride. She's helping me prepare dinner, an ethnic one, chopped liver, matzo ball soup, and stuffed cabbage."

"Where's the Milk of Magnesia?"

"You've survived my cooking. You'll survive this."

Jacob slept in his La-Z-Boy chair with a book across his chest. He was snoring softly when Lola brought Sarah into the kitchen.

Sarah spoke in a whisper, "Thanks for having me, Lola. This is a real treat."

"Why are you whispering?"

"Dr. Weizman's asleep."

"Call him Jacob. A supersonic transport couldn't awaken him now."

They worked for an hour and a half before Jacob sat up and shook his head. "Why didn't you tell me company was here?"

"You needed your sleep, Old Man."

Jacob rocked back and forth in the chair, then grabbed the footrest lever and jerked to the sitting position. He approached Sarah, extending his hand.

"We're pleased you decided to come. I hope you can tolerate a little time with the old folks."

"You guys are great . . . especially Lola," she whispered.

"I heard that," said Lola, "I'm old, but not deaf."

Jacob walked to the kitchen table. "Why don't you join me, Sarah. I speak adolonics."

Sarah looked at Jacob with questioning eyes.

"It's Jacob, Sarah, call me Jacob. Adolonics...teen talk...you know: chillin', peeps, tight...I know most of the lingo, thanks to Lola."

Sarah laughed. "You're almost as funny as Lola..." she paused, staring at Lola. "I mean that in a good way."

Lola flapped her hand forward in a 'forget it' gesture.

"You can help me with the crossword puzzle, Sarah. It's the modern culture stuff that stumps me."

Sarah rolled her chair next to Jacob, staring at the almost completed New York Times crossword puzzle.

"Here's one. Five letters, ending in an 'a'. Marge's twin. I don't have the slightest."

"Don't you watch The Simpsons?"

"The cartoon?"

"It's not a cartoon. It's an animated sitcom, a satirical parody of the American lifestyle."

Jacob looked at Lola. "You heard that? Satirical...parody...she's a middle-aged person in disguise."

Sarah blushed.

Jacob smiled.

Lola glowed.

"Anyway Dr...., I mean, Jacob, the answer is 'Selma'."

"Selma?"

"Marge Simpson's twin sister is Selma."

Jacob entered the four other letters, and then completed the puzzle in a flash.

After a pleasant dinner and light conversation, all three stood at the sink. Jacob washed, Sarah dried, and Lola put things away. They moved into the family room.

"I don't want to spoil a pleasant evening," said Lola, "but the Carleton Dix thing is all around town."

"I was going to bring that up with you at our next session, should I...?"

"No, Sarah. We'll get into it Monday. Jacob's had his own problems with the chaplain, and I thought you should know that you're not alone in your disdain for the man."

"I love Einstein's quote," said Jacob. "The difference between genius and stupidity is that genius has its limits. The chaplain is a stupid man, and a dangerous one."

"Don't, Jacob," said Lola. "He's not stupid, and don't make the mistake of underestimating him."

"I won't, but how can I respect the chaplain, a man of God, who perverts the beauty of his religion to his own ends?"

Sarah stared at Jacob, then at Lola. "Thanks, Jacob. It's great not to be alone, but Lola, I have much more..."

Lola reached for Sarah's hand. "I know. We'll get into it Monday."

Chapter Thirty-One

When Kate Planchette arrived home, her husband Ben had his worksheets spread across the dining room table. The kids sat before the blaring television in the family room.

"How was…?" he hesitated as Kate's face said something was wrong.

She leaned over Ben, wrapped her arms around his shoulders and began sobbing. "What happened?"

"It was terrible…I don't know what happened…I feel like I might have done something wrong."

"Have a seat, take a deep breath, and tell me what this is all about."

"You remember Nathan Seigel, Jacob Weizman's patient?"

"The alcoholic with heart problems of some sort. The guy who had a season pass into CCU."

"That's the one, but the man is so much more. I enjoyed taking care of him. You know how attached I can get to some patients."

"What happened?"

"He died late this afternoon. I feel awful. Something happened. Neither Sharon Brickman nor Jacob understands what caused his death. He looked drunk, had a seizure, then his heart stopped."

"You said he was fortunate to have lived this long considering his alcoholism and his heart problems. You can only be so lucky."

"I know, sweetheart, but on my watch, in the hospital, and on a heart monitor and he died anyway." Kate hesitated. "I think they were staring at me."

"Don't do this, Kate. You're not responsible for everything that happens in the world."

"But…"

"No buts, Kate. Did you do anything wrong?"

"I don't think so…"

"Kate?"

"Everything was routine, I think. Maybe I made a mistake. My mind's been clear, but sometimes I can't tell when I'm having an exacerbation of the MS."

"You're not. I haven't seen the slightest evidence of the MS in a year. Don't do this to yourself."

"You're right…but…"

"Go see Dr. Roth, if you need reassurance."

"I'll think about it."

Kate tossed and turned through the night, unable to quiet her misgivings. She decided to take the next day off.

When she returned to work, everything seemed normal…or was it?

Mark Whitson was sweating under the bright autopsy lights. He looked up from his dissection as Jacob Weizman pushed open the heavy morgue door.

"We've got to stop meeting like this, Jacob. People will talk."

"That's what comes from living too long and having your patients' age with you."

"Not this one. Nathan Seigel was only fifty-four."

"A hard living fifty-four years you'll see if you review his medical records."

Just then, Sharon Brickman entered. "Let's get to the heart of the matter."

"Remember, Sharon," said Mark, "the body contains other organs."

"Merely appendages to the heart, gentlemen."

Mark lifted his scalpel. "As a courtesy to a lady, we'll examine the heart first."

"Don't use the 'L' word on me, Mark, people may be ready to believe many things about me, but you'll never sell me as a lady."

The room resounded with the coarse vibrations of the electric Stryker saw, its pitch increasing each time the stainless-steel teeth bit into bone. Mark completed the last cut through the chest wall and elevated the incised rib cage and breastplate.

Mark dissected the heart away from the major vessels and surrounding tissue, and then placed it on the digital scale. "Five hundred eighty four grams, nearly twice the weight of a normal heart."

He next placed the heart on the dissecting board and with scissors and scalpel examined the valves, heart muscle, and the coronary blood vessels. He next sliced through the heart muscle with a razor-sharp chef's knife as if he were carving a London Broil. "A big flabby heart, consistent with his alcoholic heart disease but I see no evidence of any major coronary event to explain his death. Maybe when I do the microscopic examination, we'll get more information about why he died."

Sharon shook her head. "I really hate autopsies that tell us nothing."

"We always learn something," said Jacob.

"Just not why he died."

"You're pretty fussy, Sharon."

They stood by as Mark completed his gross anatomic examination of Nathan's major organs. His liver showed the characteristic signs of alcoholic cirrhosis but the pathologist saw no other obvious abnormalities. "If nothing shows on the microscopic, we're stuck without a diagnosis."

"Can you think of any reason for toxicology studies?" said Jacob. "I always think of the arcane when I can't explain a death."

Mark picked up the toxicology request form. "We can easily do a broad toxicology screen."

Sharon pointed to the form. "Add a Lidocaine blood level. Maybe this is an unusual form of Lidocaine toxicity."

Chapter Thirty-Two

For some reason, it was rare to find an empty seat at Zoe's table at noon in the doctor's dining room. Her charm, intelligence, and self-effacing sense of humor made her a big hit with Brier's medical staff. In addition, the female physicians embraced Zoe as a welcome asset in their battle with the vestiges of sexism in the medical community.

When Jacob pulled up a seat at the table, Ernie Banks, a family practitioner, turned to him. "Hey, Jacob, I have a patient up at Lake Tahoe who needs a house call. Can you make it?"

"Very funny, Ernie. I always wonder why you guys find my making house calls so threatening."

Jack Byrnes scanned the table. "It makes them look bad, Jacob, even if you weren't eighty-eight."

Ernie scowled. "Well said, by an ICU specialist who never leaves the hospital."

Jacob shook his head. "You have it all wrong. I'm no saint, although compared to some docs in this community…"

"Don't get him started," said Ernie.

"Many of my patients are my age or older. Either they can't get in or the process of traveling to my office is too difficult or stressful. On a busy day, I'm in and out of a home in ten minutes and can handle 98 percent of their problems. It also keeps me moving. Keep moving, gentlemen, and you'll keep living."

After Jacob gobbled his bag lunch and excused himself, Edith Keller, an infectious disease expert, turned to Zoe. "When's Jacob going to retire?"

Sharon Brickman laughed. "Are you kidding? Jacob's never going to stop on his own...we'll have to carry him off the field."

Edith stared at Sharon. "You're not saying that you see some reason that he should retire?"

"No. Of course not. Jacob's as smart and as opinionated as ever."

Edith turned to Zoe. "You haven't noted anything, have you, Zoe?"

"No, but I don't see any of us getting sharper as we age."

"Well," said Sharon, "Jacob and I don't always agree, but if I had to debate him in public, I'd be up studying the night before."

Sharon finished chewing another bite of her sandwich. "Jacob doesn't believe that it's age alone that results in cognitive impairment, and I think...or I hope that he's right. It's the three D's: disease, disuse, and disinterest that are the villains. Jacob's mind works out on a treadmill of stimulation: work, puzzles, interaction with the world around him, and his perverse desire to be right all the time."

"Well, sooner or later," said Zoe, "like the rest of us, he's got to face the calendar. I just hope that it's on his own terms."

After lunch, Zoe had one patient to see in the hospital before she returned to the office. Sylvia Brockman was Jacob's eighty-one-year-old patient with recurrent congestive heart failure. In the last year, she was in and out of the hospital, staying two to three days at a time for a 'tune-up'.

When Zoe entered room 513, she found Sylvia sound asleep. Zoe shook her several times in an attempt to arouse her, but all she got was groaning.

Zoe pushed the call button. "Can you ask Mrs. Brockman's nurse to come in here for a moment?"

"Certainly, Doctor," said the ward clerk.

While she waited, Zoe performed a careful neurological examination, but other than lethargy, she found nothing. Zoe was scanning the chart when her nurse arrived. "How long has she been this way?"

"She slept through my assessment when I came on this morning."

"I see the night nurse, Marion Krupp, gave her Haldol at 2 a.m., but the chart doesn't say why." Zoe paused a moment. "Why is Marion Krupp still working at Brier? I thought they fired her?"

"From what I understand, Marion is fighting her dismissal through her union representative. She's still around. Getting back to your question, Doctor, during morning report Marion said that Sylvia was confused and belligerent, and that she needed sedation, so she gave her the Haldol as prescribed."

Zoe pointed to the chart. "The notes don't reflect any such thing, and everyone knows how Dr. Weizman feels about sedating such a patient. This is disturbing."

"But," said the nurse, "you left orders for sedation as needed…Marion thought she needed this, Doctor."

"Don't make excuses for Marion's poor judgment," said Zoe. She pointed to Sylvia. "This is what happens when nurses don't listen and substitute their convenience for good patient care. Your head nurse will be hearing from Dr. Weizman…bet on it. He's going to go ballistic when he hears it's Marion Krupp again."

Tommy Wells sat in the shadowed booth at the rear of Kelly's, a noisy bar in downtown Oakland, near the Alameda County Superior Courthouse.

As he filled his frosted mug from the icy beer pitcher, Morgan Ferris slid into the opposite seat. In his gray Armani suit, he looked just like what he was, a successful criminal defense attorney.

"I don't like meeting here, Tommy…too many damned lawyers."

"That's why you fit in. Me, I'm just a client."

"Do you have it?"

"Have I ever failed you?"

Tommy reached into his pocket and palmed the small brown envelope holding it close to his chest. "This is 10, 40mg Oxycontin pills…that's $450."

"Shit, Tommy, that's highway robbery."

"For stuff like this, 100 percent reliable, no contaminants, a little over $1/mg is a fair price."

Morgan peeled off four hundreds and a fifty, and in an orchestrated ballet, they traded their passions.

"It's always great doing business with you, Morgan. If you want something interesting, I've got the real thing, ampules of Morphine Sulfate."

"I'm in enough trouble as it is, Tommy, and I hate needles. I'll pass."

Morgan slipped the envelope into his suit coat pocket. "How do you get away with it? Don't they count pills?"

"I'm careful, for sure, but it's the Internet that makes it all possible. I buy phony oxy pills from Malaysia. They look like the real thing. It's easy. If cancer patients or anyone else with severe pain gets a pill that doesn't work, they just give them another or up the dose."

"Well, be careful, Tommy."

"I will, but you'll always be around for me if I get busted."

Chapter Thirty-Three

The anxiety of that all-too-public conflict with Sarah Hughes encircled Carleton Dix like a wet neurosis. He recalled the eyes of the TeenTalk girls as they caught the vile implications of Sarah's words; their doubt and his inability to hold their gazes. In his business, a hint of scandal was lethal.

One girl failed to show for her counseling session. Another gave a weak excuse. Carleton worked through the first part of the week at Brier, busy as usual, but his mind remained focused on the upcoming Wednesday night TeenTalk meeting.

It was after rush hour on Shattuck Avenue in downtown Berkeley, yet the streets remained crowded with traffic slowed by heavy rain. Red brake lights reflected off the shiny pavement.

Carleton Dix finally turned onto Allston Way, but was unable to find a parking space near the YMCA. After ten frustrating minutes, he decided to use municipal parking three blocks away. He rummaged through the back seat and the trunk...Goddamn it, no umbrella.

He rushed through the rain holding his attaché case over his head. By the time he arrived at the YMCA, his feet squished as he climbed the stairs. He entered the men's room, peeled off his coat, then dried off with paper towels and the hot air hand dryer.

Kelly Cowan sat in the foyer outside the meeting room. "I'm so sorry, chaplain. It's so unfair."

"What do you mean?"

"Those ridiculous charges by Sarah Hughes...she's lost it."

He moved toward the door. "I think we'd better get in."

"Chaplain..."

"What is it?"

Kelly began crying. "I'm so sorry..."

"Please, Kelly, what's wrong?"

"Only half the girls are here tonight. They...they just assumed that you did something wrong. I know that's not possible."

That damned Sarah Hughes...not again, Carleton thought. I might as well be guilty if I'm going to take the blame.

He walked to the front of the room and turned to face their doubts. "I'm sorry you had to be a witness to that sorry demonstration with Sarah Hughes. She's a disturbed young woman and I'm loath to say, an evil one too."

Several girls raised their heads. Others still failed to meet his eyes.

"Let me assure you that my conflict with Sarah Hughes is religious, philosophical, and yes, political too. You and I have certain strongly held beliefs...Sarah rejects them. Initially, I thought she was simply a confused young woman. Now, I'm not so sure."

Carleton arranged the chairs in a circle as usual, but after twenty minutes of his best attempts at promoting conversation and the exchange of feelings, he knew it was useless. "We're not getting anywhere. Let's call it a night."

"But chaplain..." said Kelly.

"I'm sorry too, Kelly. I hope that we can rebuild the intimacy we've shared in the past. Without it, what we do in group is a waste of everyone's time. We'll try again next week. Remember Proverbs 3:29-30: Do not accuse a man for no reason–when he has done you no harm."

Each day when detective Shelly Kahn entered Brier Hospital, the sights, the sounds and especially the smells, evoked memories of her days as a nurse. Except for the effects of losing her brother, Shelly wasn't sure why she gave it up...she loved nursing. Maybe police work was in her genes...a true calling.

The one skill that made Shelly a great undercover agent was the comfort she felt with people and they with her. After a few days, she became one of them, entrusted with the coin of the realm—gossip.

Shelly separated the trivial, who was doing what to whom, the affairs, and the petty infighting from the substantive. The latter included deeply held conflicts between members of the staff, between staff and administration, and anyone whose behavior suggested that they might be capable of a criminal act.

She met with Ira Green, her chief, one morning a week after beginning this assignment.

"Ask me anything about the daytime soap opera that is Brier Hospital. I have it all."

"I'm too busy for that crap, Shelly...just give me the facts, ma'am."

"Skipping over the petty personality problems," she smiled as she talked, "Brier Hospital has its own set of real problems. They're what you'd expect in any large institution that functions under stress."

"Have you got anything or not, Shelly?"

"Hold your horses, boss. I'm getting there. First, I looked into those who left Brier involuntarily; those fired for cause or those terminated under the pressure of downsizing. Nothing there. Then I looked for the oddballs, the personality problems, and especially the drug users. As you might expect in an institution the size of Brier, there's quite a bit of recreational drug use, but nothing big time. Many staff talk about an interesting conflict between an elderly physician, Jacob Weizman and a number of nurses and physicians."

"Jacob Weizman? He's our family doctor...I think he's everyone's doctor."

"With Weizman, it all seems personality based. I detect a hint of ageism as well. Thomas Wells, a lab technician, may be of interest. He's had his run-ins with nurses, and finally, we have a nurse, Marion Krupp, who has had run-ins with just about everyone."

"What about the ancillary staff?"

"It's more difficult to get information about support personnel, but nothing stands out. Then we have professionals who come to the hospital to provide specific services, like the chaplain, psychologists, music therapists, etc. By the way, your doctor and the chaplain; they don't get along at all."

"If I know Jacob, he has a good reason. What about the medical staff?"

"You remember the Blue Wall that cops use to protect each other. That's nothing compared with the White Wall used by docs. If you want me to get into that, I'll need to talk with the Chief of Staff."

Ira stood, indicating the meeting was at an end. "Look a little harder at the possible drug connections. With what happened to Rory Calhoun, that looks like the best way to proceed."

Chapter Thirty-Four

"I have Dr. Brickman on line two," said Margaret Cohen as Jacob entered the office at 8:30 a.m.

Jacob picked up the phone. "What's up, Sharon?"

"Mark Whitson called. He needs to see us. It's important, he said."

"What is it?"

"Don't know, but it's about Nathan Seigel. Can you meet me at Mark's office at noon?"

"I'll be there."

I hate when they do that.

When Jacob exited his office just before noon, he felt a light rain. He jammed his Bugsy Siegel fedora on his head and walked the two blocks to Brier. He kept his head down, trying to avoid the puddles of the earlier downpour. Water dripped over the brim of his hat. He swiped his card in the security reader at the hospital's back door and entered a corridor by the pathology department.

Sharon paced before Mark Whitson's office.

That woman's driven, Jacob thought, but one hell of a physician.

"It's about time you dragged that old carcass here, Jacob."

"It's good to see you too, Sharon. Accept an old man's advice and take it down a notch or two. You'll live longer."

"If I follow your advice, it will only seem longer. I'm intense. I was born intense, and I'll die that way."

Just then, the door opened and Mark Whitson stuck his head out. "Come on in." He shuffled through a pile of reports. "Have a seat. We have a big problem."

"Cut the drama, Mark," said Sharon. "What do you have?"

"Always the soul of patience, Sharon," he said, finally finding the reports he was seeking. "I'm talking to you guys first as a courtesy, but I'm reporting this to administration and to risk assessment."

"Enough already," said Jacob.

"The Lidocaine levels in Mr. Seigel were through the roof, specifically 23 micrograms per milliliter."

Sharon leaned forward. "Bullshit! That's impossible. Our dosing protocol, adjusted for the weight of the patient, should have produced a therapeutic level of 1.5 to 5. The level of 23 is twice the lethal dose. It must be a mistake."

"No mistake, Sharon. I drew the postmortem blood myself from the veins in the lower abdomen and directly from the heart. When I saw the levels, I had the same reaction; it's a mistake. I sent the blood to two other reference labs who confirmed these findings."

Jacob paled. "My God! How is this possible?"

"Logically, I can think of only two possibilities," said Sharon. "He got too much Lidocaine or his body was unable to get rid of it for some reason."

Jacob scratched his head. "He was on medication that might make him more sensitive to the Lidocaine, like a beta blocker or a stomach acid reducer, but these levels are just too high to be anything but a mistake in administration."

"Not so fast, you two," said Sharon. "Our CCU nurses make up dozens of Lidocaine infusions each day. It's cookbook. I can't believe anyone could make such an error."

"If it's not an error," said Mark, "then it's deliberate. You want to consider that possibility for a moment?"

"Ridiculous," said Sharon.

"I'm open to suggestions, doctors."

Sharon stood. "I'll meet with everyone involved. I'll get to the bottom of this."

"Make it quick. I'm going to administration with this."

"I know."

The digital clock just flashed to 6:04 p.m. when Bruce Bryant, Brier's CEO, admitted the group to his office. Following the call from Mark Whitson, Bruce had called Warren Davidson, Jack Byrnes, Al David, the hospital attorney, and Ira Green. Ira asked Shelly Kahn to join them as well.

As they settled into place, Bruce looked out his street level window spattered with rain, the plants, and trees swaying in the strong wind gusts. He made the introductions, and then scanned the group. "We've got a problem...maybe more than one. Mark called today with disturbing findings."

Mark reviewed the circumstances surrounding Nathan Seigel's death and the lethal Lidocaine levels. "Sharon Brickman thinks it might be a mistake. I'm not buying it. Our worst nurses or pharmacists couldn't have provided this lethal dose by error. I think death was the result of a deliberate action, a premeditated murder."

The room remained silent until Ira Green said, "Hold on for a second. Only the Medical Examiner can make such a designation."

"I'm not talking legalities here, chief," said Mark. "I'm giving you my medical opinion. Sharon Brickman's trying to see if it was an error of some sort, but she's kidding herself."

"We're already dealing with the massive narcotic overdose in the Rory Calhoun case," said Ira. "Shelly Kahn's investigating. Tell them what you've discovered so far."

Shelly grabbed her notes. "We have no doubt that Mr. Calhoun received an overdose of a narcotic that would have killed a normal person. His long history of narcotic abuse and the Methadone maintenance saved his life. We're still not sure if he got heroin or something else."

"Have you identified any suspects?" asked Warren.

"No," said Ira, "but this Lidocaine overdosage puts the investigation on another level." He paused to scan the faces, then continued, "My mind keeps asking the same questions: do we have other unexplained deaths, and is Brier Hospital dealing with a serial killer?"

Bruce slumped back in his chair. "My God!"

"My God is right," said Ira. "Is it possible to write-off deaths as natural when they were anything but?"

"Of course it's possible," said Warren. "Since the managed care, HMO era, our patients are older and sicker than ever before. Absent anything suspicious, death in this group of patients is considered natural or the result of their underlying medical condition."

"I'm referring the Nathan Seigel case to the Medical Examiner," said Ira. "Shelly will continue her investigation, and Mr. Bryant, I'm requesting that Brier Hospital conduct its own review of all hospital deaths in the last 18 months. God help us, if our suspicions prove accurate."

The next day, when Jacob looked at Kate Planchette, she reddened and looked away.

"I want to talk with you a moment, Kate."

"I have to give some meds." She started to walk away.

"Kate..."

She stopped and looked at her feet.

"I'll wait for you in the dictation room."

When Kate finally arrived, she stood across from Jacob with the expression of a prisoner awaiting execution.

"Sit, please. Put it out of your mind."

"Put what?"

"You didn't do anything wrong. It's not your fault."

"Are you sure, Dr. Weizman?"

"The Lidocaine levels were through the roof. An accidental overdose is impossible. Someone murdered Nathan."

"I kept thinking that it was my fault...that maybe the MS allowed me to make a mistake."

"How is your MS?"

"Dr. Roth says I'm still in remission, although I guess I really can't ever leave it behind."

"You're doing great. In my experience, when you've had a benign course for as long as you have, the odds are overwhelming that you'll be fine."

Kate walked up to Jacob, kissed him on his cheek, and gave him a hug.

She took her first deep breath in a while. "They're right,"

"Who's right?"

"Whatever it is that makes people trust you, derive comfort from you, Jacob, you have it."

Chapter Thirty-Five

"Shit," Byron said when the phone rang for the fifth time that evening.

"You know I'm on call tonight," said Zoe. "Grow up!"

"We have Sunshine Manor on the line, Dr. Spelling. They say it's an emergency."

"Put them through."

"It's Mildred Kaysen, Doctor. She's in severe respiratory distress, turning blue, and sitting upright. It looks like heart failure to us, Doctor."

"What happened?"

"Nothing. She just awakened and couldn't breathe. We put an oxygen mask on her, but that didn't do much."

"Give her a shot of morphine sulfate and call 911. I'm on my way into Brier Emergency."

Zoe arrived just as the ambulance pulled up to the ER entrance. She followed Mildred into Treatment Room One and began her assessment. Mildred was still sitting upright and struggling to breathe. She had a bluish tinge around her mouth and in her nail beds. Her respirations were 40/minute.

The EMT looked up from his clipboard. "She's much better since getting the morphine, Doctor."

Zoe turned to Mildred. "I'm Doctor Spelling, Dr. Weizman's partner. We're going to get this thing under control."

Mildred looked up at Zoe. "You're a very beautiful woman."

Zoe smiled, and when she placed her stethoscope on Mildred's back, she jumped.

"Oh...that's cold," she gasped.

Zoe smiled. "It's not easy to keep it that cold."

Mildred took Zoe's hand and gave it a firm squeeze.

Zoe moved the head of her stethoscope over Mildred's back and front of her chest, hearing the coarse bubbling sounds of fluid in her lungs. When she listened to Mildred's heart, she heard the telltale sounds of the struggling, overburdened, and failing heart.

The portable x-ray machine banged against the door to enter the room. Paige Sims, Mildred's daughter, followed behind.

"What going on here?" she yelled. She stared at Zoe. "And who the hell are you?"

"I'm Dr. Spelling, Dr. Weizman's associate."

"I told mother not to listen to that old man...now see what's happened."

"I'm sorry, Mrs. or is it Ms. Sims..."

"It's Mrs."

"I'm afraid I don't know what you're talking about...listen about what?"

"Mother...Mother," Paige cried. She hugged Mildred. "It's Paige...are you all right?"

"I'm just a little winded, sweetheart," Mildred gasped. "I'll be fine. I don't know what the whole fuss is about."

Paige formed her mouth into a tight sneer, and then turned to Zoe. "I told her it was a mistake...now see what you've done."

"I still don't know what you're talking about, Mrs. Sims."

"Twenty years on digoxin and never a problem. Then Weizman stops it. Why? Look what happened."

"If Dr. Weizman stopped digoxin, he had a good reason."

"Stop making excuses for that old man. I don't want him touching my mother ever again. I demand that you call a heart specialist."

Zoe lowered her voice. "Please. You're upsetting yourself and your mother for nothing. It's not necessary to demand anything. All you need do is ask that we get a cardiologist to evaluate your mother."

"Don't play word games with me, Doctor." Paige burst into tears. "I want to file a formal complaint against Weizman...I'll make sure he doesn't hurt another patient."

What have you done, Jacob? Zoe thought.

"Oh, by the way," said Paige. "I love your dress."

Zoe gave Mildred a powerful diuretic and within two hours, she was breathing easily. Sharon Brickman consulted and they agreed to place Mildred in the cardiac step-down unit for observation.

"What do you think?" asked Zoe.

"The cardiogram doesn't show any acute changes, Zoe. I'm getting an echocardiogram . . . maybe that will help pin down the cause of her heart failure."

"Her daughter Paige...she's got it in for Jacob for some reason," said Zoe. "What do you think about Jacob stopping the digoxin?"

"Medically, he made the right decision. Knowing this patient and especially her demanding daughter, I might have kept it up just not to rock the boat. After all those years, I doubt that the digoxin would have hurt her."

"You know Jacob, and how he feels about the risks of medication. He's always looking for an excuse to stop useless or potentially dangerous meds. He calls himself a therapeutic nihilist, skeptical about all medications. Maybe, as a purist, he's right, but this case and several others have caused people to question his judgment."

"Can you talk with him, Zoe? Will he listen to you?"

"I'll try, but I don't think it's an argument I can win."

Sharon nodded. "He's headed for a fall, Zoe. It's cases like this, his therapeutic bias, and his outspoken position on right-to-die issues that's undercutting a lifetime of excellence and achievement. I'll do anything to make sure that doesn't happen."

When Zoe entered the office the next morning, she walked into Jacob's office. "I had to admit Mildred Kaysen last night."

"What happened?"

"Don't know for sure, but when I arrived, she was in heart failure."

"I should get up to see her."

"That's a problem, Jacob," Zoe said as she sat next to his desk.

"Problem?"

"It's Mildred's daughter Paige. She blames you for her mother's condition. She doesn't want you on her mother's case."

"What about Mildred? What does she want?"

"I don't know, but perhaps it would be best if I took care of her with Sharon Brickman as a consultant."

"Best for whom?"

"Please, Jacob, don't make an issue out of this now. Paige is an angry woman. She has a problem with you. Let it go."

"She can't dismiss me like that, Zoe. Mildred's my patient...if she refuses to see me..."

"It's no reflection on you. You must have dealt with angry patients and relatives."

"Listen for a minute, would you. In sixty years of practice, patients have rejected me for all sorts of reasons...many completely irrational. Do I like it? Hell no.

"If I screwed up, it wouldn't be the first time, and it won't be the last. "

"Did I do something wrong with Mildred? I doubt it. I'm going to let this go for a while or at least until Sharon completes her evaluation, but I'm not going to abandon Mildred to the ministrations of a controlling and misguided daughter...count on it."

"Why in hell is the hospital administration sticking their noses into the QA process?" asked Warren Davidson, the chief of medicine as he sat with Arnie Roth in the QA office the next morning.

"You know why, Warren," said Arnie, Chairman of the QA Committee. "They don't want a repeat of the situation we had with that psychopath, Joe Polk, or with several other physicians who we discovered, too late, I might add, to have psychiatric illness or Alzheimer's. We all share a degree of responsibility when patients are injured under those circumstances."

"So specifically, what do they want?"

"Physical examinations on all physicians over age fifty."

"That's window dressing. They want to cover their asses by saying that they have a physician surveillance program. That kind of assessment won't show a damn thing."

"Look, Warren, we have only two choices: Just go along with the farce or decide to make physician evaluation meaningful like looking at the nuts and bolts of how docs practice."

"I don't like patting ourselves on the back too much, Arnie, but we have a pretty good QA program as it is. We see the reports every week and when we have a doc whose work is beginning to slide, we know it. Everything we do at Brier is under the scrutiny of someone, especially nurses and other docs. That's the best way to pick up problems from dementia, to psychiatric, and to my all-time favorite, staff who just don't give a damn."

"That's doing nothing, Warren. It's the status quo."

"If you tell me that we're going to do psychiatric evaluations, cognitive function tests, tests of physical skills, especially fine motor skills and dexterity, and if you're going to do them on everyone, fifty and over, who works at Brier Hospital, professional, administrative, and all others, I'll go along."

"That's not going to happen."

"Then, I'll pass," said Warren.

"We still have to talk about Jacob Weizman."

"I don't want to hear it," said Warren.

"You think I like this? Jacob, just like the rest of us, is answerable for his actions. We have too many complaints. If we don't deal with them, someone else will. I'm calling a special meeting of QA to discuss our options in dealing with Jacob Weizman."

Chapter Thirty-Six

Monday morning. They hadn't seen their first patient when Betty Kaufman, the receptionist at Jacob's office turned to Margaret. "Lydia Barns wantS a word with you."

"Send her in."

Lydia was one of their newest patients, and a professor of economics at UC Berkeley. "Margaret, thank you for speaking with me."

"Of course, Lydia. What is it?"

"Can you find someplace private?"

"Sure. Come into Jacob's office. He's still on rounds."

"The main reason I moved my care to this practice was Dr. Weizman. I guess I'm a little old-fashioned, but I really like the hands-on, and if you'll excuse the term, old-fashioned type of medicine."

"You sure picked the right place."

"It disturbed me a little when instead of seeing Dr. Weizman, you assigned me to Dr. Spelling, but I assumed, wrongly I'm sad to say, that she practiced like he did."

"Jacob is so busy, and he's not a kid anymore. That's why we brought Dr. Spelling on board."

"Believe me, I understand perfectly. I not saying that I'm prepared to leave the practice, but Dr. Spelling, while she has all the moves, the charisma, and the intelligence, doesn't have it."

"It'?"

"The patients who sent me here said that Dr. Weizman is smart, compassionate, and when he works with his patients, they have his full attention. Moreover, they know that he cares about them. Dr. Spelling's mind is all over the place. She feigns caring, but she can't sell it to me. I think someone should talk with her, perhaps Dr. Weizman."

"I will. Thank you for being so forthright. Too often we discover we've screwed up when a patient sends us a nasty letter or transfers to another physician."

"One thing more. Please don't use my name. I hope to work this out."

When Lola arrived at the clinic Monday morning, Elena pulled her aside. "She was waiting at the front door when I arrived."

"Who?"

"Sarah Hughes. It looks like you have your work cut out for you today."

As Lola approached her office, Sarah stood and stared at her through reddened eyes. She looked at the floor and began chewing on her fingernails. "I'm real upset, Lola, I..."

"Hold your horses, Sarah. Let me get my coat off. Would you like some tea?"

"No thanks, but I could use a strong cup of coffee."

Lola buzzed Elena. "Are you doing a Starbuck's run this morning?"

"Sure, what would you like?"

"A double cappuccino," whispered Sarah. She paced the room while Lola shuffled papers around her desk and pulled out a note pad. Dust motes danced in the sunlight streaking through the blinds and illuminating Lola's still-messy desk.

Lola watched Sarah's fitful actions. "I can't work on a moving target. Have a seat."

Sarah marched to the La-Z-Boy chair, but continued to fidget in place.

"I want you to do something for me, Sarah."

"Okay."

"I need you to relax. Let's take a minute, then we'll start."

"I am relaxed."

"Sure. If you were any more relaxed, I'd need to put you in a straightjacket."

Sarah clenched her arms across her chest.

"This will take just five minutes. First, lie back on the La-Z-Boy letting your weight fall into the cushions, then close your eyes and slowly inhale and exhale. As you breathe in, say to yourself, 'I AM'; as you breathe out, say 'RELAXED.'"

Sarah sat up. "You're kidding."

Lola smiled, and then gently guided Sarah back into the reclining position. "Just do it."

After ten minutes, the soft knock on the door ended her relaxation as Elena handed Lola the paper cup with the Starbuck's logo. Sarah sat, opened the lid, and added five packs of Splenda.

"That was good. Don't you feel better now?"

"Yes, Doctor." Sarah smiled.

"How's it going?"

Sarah studied the carpet. "You heard about the anti-abortion demonstration in Emeryville?"

"It's a small town, Sarah. I talk with many girls, and to answer your question; yes, I heard about your meeting with the chaplain. I know you want to talk about it."

"It wasn't just that we're on different sides of that issue, it's..."

"What is it?"

"The chaplain, Carleton Dix...he creeps me out, and the demonstration was not the first time. You believe in body language...I mean reading a person by movement, gesture and look. The man licks his lips...can you imagine...he licks his lips?"

"Of course. Often body language tells me more than words. It's essential in my work and it's crucial in understanding how people relate to me and to each other."

"The chaplain touched me before and he did it again at the demonstration...it made me feel sick...it grossed me out. Is it me? Am I overreacting?"

"He touched you sexually?"

"That's it, Lola. I'm not sure. I only know that he did it once and I told him never to touch me again, but he did it anyway and I went ballistic. I said things that maybe I shouldn't have."

"If you have something to tell me, it's all right, you know."

"About the chaplain?"

"Anything."

"I left the impression that he tried something sexual but I'm not sure it did happen, yet..."

"Jacob's a pretty good judge of character, Sarah. He's had many run-ins with the chaplain. He thinks something's not kosher with that man. Maybe what you're feeling is more accurate than you know."

"But, what if I'm wrong? What if he was just trying to help? Even a hint of molestation can ruin a man."

"Maybe you need to talk about this with him. Maybe a meeting would clear the air."

"I can't, Lola. I can barely stand to look at him."

"You're holding something back from me, Sarah. What is it?"

"It's nothing...I mean nothing happened."

"Don't be ashamed. If something's happening to you at home or anywhere else, I can help. Please let me help. If it's about your mother or father, I can..."

"Oh, God...no...no. They'd never... He'd never. If anything's wrong, it's with me."

This is all wrong, Lola thought. Too much...too soon...too little control.

Lola moved to Sarah's side. "I've been at this for a long time. Nothing you say can shock me. I've heard it before. We'll work our way through this, I promise."

Sarah sobbed in Lola's arms. "I'm so sorry...so sorry."

A soft knock at the door interrupted their session.

"I'm sorry, but we must stop. I think we did a lot today. I'll see you Thursday."

When Sarah reached home that evening, it was pouring. She saw Kelly Cowan's Honda Civic parked in the driveway, with her wipers on and the windows fogged.

She's been there a while. What is it now?

She exited the car. Kelly approached her saying, "I'm so sorry, Sarah. Those girls killing their babies...it's just too much for me."

"What are you talking about?"

"The protest at the abortion clinic. I just wanted to apologize."

"I'd almost forgotten that pathetic demonstration. Go away. I've had enough of you and that sick chaplain."

"He didn't mean anything. He's too emotional about the issue, and for reasons beyond me, he finds it particularly frustrating when he deals with you."

"That's an easy one to solve, tell him to keep the hell away from me."

Kelly took two steps closer to Sarah, and looked down. "I want us to be friends again. We were so close. We had so much fun together...I don't want this stuff to keep us apart."

"It's not going to happen, Kelly. I've moved on. I'm in a new and better place. I'm not going backward."

"But, we were so close..."

"You're a sweet girl, but we live in different worlds."

"Please, Sarah."

"Don't make me say something I'll regret."

"Don't do this..."

"I have a flash for you Kelly, go home." Sarah turned and started for the front steps.

Suddenly, Kelly grabbed Sarah's upper arm and spun her so they were face-to-face.

She reddened, her nostrils flaring. "You can't diss me that way and get away with it. Don't screw with me, Sarah or you'll regret it."

Suddenly calm, Sarah faced Kelly. "You just proved to me how right I was. Now get the hell out of here."

Chapter Thirty-Seven

Ahmad Kadir joined his family for dinner in their small apartment in Berkeley. This was the first time in three weeks that he found the chance to eat at home.

"We never see you anymore," said his mother Jasmine as she left the tiny kitchen and placed a large casserole dish on the dining room table. The aroma of spiced lamb and onions filled the room. "Habib. Come, it's ready."

His father Habib came to the table, placed his textbook to the side, and stroked his black curly beard. "You look too thin, Ahmad."

"How are things at Brier Hospital?" asked Jasmine. "I love that place. I volunteered for a while."

Ahmad put down his fork. "They hate us. Everywhere I turn, they hate us!"

"They don't all hate us, Ahmad," said Habib.

"Please, father. You teach at the university, a fantasy world. I deal with reality, the average American, and that group…well, let's say that they're not the most enlightened."

"It took me nearly a year after 9/11," Ahmad continued, "before I had to stop watching the news on television. It makes me sick, and every time the media reports a new Islamic atrocity, people look at me as if I were responsible."

Habib put down his fork. "Terrorism is the last resort of the oppressed who have no options."

"Respectfully, father, you know that's only a small part. It's powerlessness, the ignorance of people living in the distant past, and an intolerance of the beliefs of others. We're not Muslim, nor did we know of any Arab, Muslim, or Christian who would carry out such vile acts."

"You've lived in the U.S. too long. Have you forgotten your days in Gaza and in Nablus? We both know many such individuals."

"Nevertheless, father, just like the mortification of American Jews over the Rosenberg case, the reaction of the Italians to The Sopranos, or the embarrassment of the Irish over the vicious acts of the IRA, we're Arabs and we're tainted by the acts of our brethren…the savagery of an archaic culture inflicting mayhem on itself and everything it touches."

Ahmad took a drink of ice water. "You should see how they look at me…how they stare. Some refuse to have me as their physician. I can't stand it. I thought we had a life here, but now, I'm not so sure."

"It will pass," said Jasmine. "Americans carry the pain of 9/11 and the daily losses from the action of Islamic extremists. To them, an Arab is an Arab."

"Nobody cares that we're Christian. That we've been Christian for generations. Turn the other cheek…I don't think so mother."

"This is a wonderful country," said Habib, "but not one without its faults. You're going to hate this, Ahmad, but as a Palestinian Christian, unwanted by our Muslim brothers, I have a taste of what it's been like to be a Jew in the world: homeless, reviled, and oppressed."

"Abba, you don't understand. How would you like to hear, 'Get that fucking A-rab away from me'? Who knows what they're saying behind my back? I'm torn between my oath as a physician and my dignity as a man...an Arab man."

Ever since her confrontation with Tommy Wells, Ginny Harrison noted a change in his behavior. He was extraordinarily polite in his interaction with her and the other nurses and several times, she caught him staring.

Ginny sat with Mary Oakes, her nursing director. "I hate the way he looks at me, it's freaky."

"Are you sure you're not reading too much into this? Maybe you're feeling a little guilt for reporting him."

"No way. I gave him ample warning, yet he refused to listen. I was doing my job, Mary, and I'd do it again."

"I always attributed his behavior to the small-man syndrome...his need to ingratiate himself with the nurses and to increase his standing, pardon the pun. I don't think more is going on, Ginny, do you?"

"I don't know, except the hospital's and nursing administration's preoccupation with drug security has succeeded in making me uncomfortable when I enter that room. It's reached the point when a simple mistake, a counting error, a broken vial, can become a career ender."

"I know, but I've lived through a DEA investigation of drug pilfering. You get to know what a hamburger feels like on the grill."

Ginny saw Tommy several times that evening as he pushed his laboratory supply cart around the ward drawing blood. She looked at the wall clock that read 10:45 p.m. Only 15 minutes to go.

Nurses' report, and I'm out of here.

Ginny turned toward the nurse's station when she saw a white-coated man leaving room 545, the room farthest away from the nursing station and near the stairwell. The man started her way, and then suddenly headed toward the stairwell.

"Wait...wait!" Ginny shouted as she ran down the corridor.

At the sound of her voice, the figure stopped moving and turned to face her. It was Tommy Wells.

She approached him asking, "What were you doing in 545? Where's your equipment cart? What's going on?"

"I was just..."

"You were just what?"

"Damn it, Ginny. If you let me talk, I can explain."

"Explain what? I'm sick and tired of your lame explanations. You'd better tell me right now. What you were doing in Mr. Soto's room, and it better be good."

Tommy's hands, balled into fists, hung at his side as he leaned toward Ginny.

Suddenly frightened, Ginny backed away. "Don't," she cried.

"Don't what? Haven't you done enough to screw me at Brier?"

He's not going to intimidate me, Ginny thought.

"I asked you a simple question, Tommy. Should I repeat it?"

"I came here at the end of my shift because Mr. Soto asked me to. I saw him earlier tonight. We got to talking, and he asked me to come back if I could."

Ginny said nothing.

"If you don't believe me, ask him."

Ginny entered the room. Mr. Soto, a 70-year-old Japanese man with multiple myeloma, a painful malignancy of his bone marrow, sat propped up on three pillows, watching TV.

"Hey, Ginny. Isn't it about time for you to leave?"

Ginny inspected the room to see if anything was amiss. "Just about. How are you feeling?"

"You know...I feel like crap. I don't like to talk about it. I was just about to take my pain pills and try for some sleep."

Soto looked past Ginny, saw Tommy. "Shouldn't you be going home too, Tommy?" He paused a moment, turned toward Ginny. "You have a good man in Tommy. The hospital's fortunate to have him. He was kind enough to keep an old man company. I really appreciate that, in fact I plan to write to the hospital to thank them for the likes of Tommy and your nurses. They've been great."

Tommy smirked and left the room.

When Sharon Brickman returned to Mildred Kaysen's room the next morning, Paige Sims stood with her hands on her hips, demanding, "Well, what did you find?"

"Nothing so far. Her cardiogram's okay, but we need to run some other tests to find out why your mother went into heart failure."

Paige sneered. "Isn't it obvious? Weizman did it when he stopped her medication. Don't tell me otherwise."

Sharon stared at the woman. "Eight times out of ten, when I bet against Jacob Weizman, he comes out ahead. He's a great doc."

"I'm sick and tired of everyone defending that old man."

Mildred grabbed Sharon's arm and led her down the corridor. As she looked back at her room, she whispered, "Don't listen to her. She's an unhappy spiteful woman."

"I had another word in mind."

Mildred leaned close to Sharon's ear. "You mean the 'B' word."

Sharon smiled and nodded, then walked back to the room. "I'm ordering a heart scan. We'll take a look at your mother's heart and its blood supply."

"Do what you need to, Doctor. Just keep Weizman away."

The next afternoon, Sharon sat with Mildred and Paige. "The scan shows the strong likelihood of coronary artery disease. We need to do an angiogram and maybe an angioplasty."

"An angio what?" asked Mildred.

"It's a fancy word that means if we find narrow parts of the arteries to your heart, we'll open them one way or another."

In the recovery room the next day, Sharon stood next to Mildred's gurney. Paige held her mother's hand.

"You had a major narrowing of one main vessel and two smaller ones, Mildred. We were able to open them. You should be fine."

"Thank you, Doctor," said Paige. "We're so grateful. Does this explain what happened to Mom?"

"It's likely that her heart failure started when the heart muscle didn't get enough blood, and she had a mild heart attack."

"That damned Weizman. I knew he did this."

Sharon turned to face Paige Sims. She had to control her hands that contracted repeatedly in choking moves as she imagined them around Paige Sims' throat.

"You're a disturbed person, Mrs. Sims," said Sharon. "You're a bigot and an idiotic one at that!"

"Well, I never..." Paige gasped, turning red.

"You believe that aging makes one stupid, incompetent, or both. We call that 'ageism' and it's just as deadly as any form of racism or anti-Semitism. Jacob Weizman, he's too good for the likes of you, Mrs. Sims, and just for the record, if your mother's heart attack happened when she was on digoxin, it would have made things worse. Maybe, thanks to that 'incompetent old man' your mother is still alive."

Mildred applauded. "I love it," she laughed. "That's the best thing I've heard in years. Come over here, Sharon, and give an old lady a kiss."

Chapter Thirty-Eight

When Lola entered Jacob's small staff lounge, she wrinkled her nose at the acrid burnt coffee smell. She quickly removed the brown-bottomed carafe from the coffee maker and turned off the power. She settled into the aged sofa once the centerpiece of their family room. Lola stretched out on the cracked leather to read The New Yorker while waiting for Jacob to take her to lunch.

Lola was well into an article by Seymour Hersh when the door opened. Zoe came in and plopped herself in Jacob's lounge chair.

Zoe looked up. "Lola. How nice to see you. I didn't notice you when I came in."

"You look tired."

"I am. I had to go in again last night. Don't know how Jacob did it all these years."

"Jacob has one trick that served him well, he can fall into deep sleep in an instant and get its restorative benefits. I call him the grandfather of the Power Nap."

"The call schedule is rough on a marriage," said Zoe. "Byron hates when I have to leave our bed in the middle of the night to go to work. How did you handle it?"

"You know Jacob. He loves his work and I think he thrives on those nighttime emergencies when his patients need him the most. I love Jacob and if that's what it takes to keep him happy, it's a small price."

Lola caught herself. Don't be a shrink. "I hope this isn't a serious problem for your marriage, Zoe."

"I think all marriages are a compromise, don't you?" Without waiting for a response, Zoe continued. "...Except, of course, you and Jacob. You guys have it together."

"People imagine we have an ideal relationship, but nobody outside really knows what's going on. Don't you agree that's how it is in a marriage?"

"I guess so, but I'm afraid my expectations were too high. I mean Byron is a great guy, but we don't have much in common."

"Having a lot in common is overrated, I think, especially if you two make the best of the time you have together. Do you go to temple?"

"That's a laugh, Lola. Byron wasn't even Bar Mitzvahed and for a while, I was a member of Jews for Jesus...that became a joke. I even dabbled in Kabbalah...me and Madonna."

"Your family must have loved that."

"They didn't give a damn except for my grandfather Bernie...he went crazy...he lost it. It surprised me. I didn't know what the big deal was about." Zoe stretched and ran her fingers through her hair. "It really bothered me. He was my biggest fan then..."

"Why did that surprise you?"

"I don't know. The whole Jews for Jesus thing didn't mean much to me, except for the idea of Jesus. Even non-Christians must recognize his unique appeal."

"Come on, Zoe. You're an intelligent woman. You know Bernie's past history. He's a holocaust survivor. Religion had little or nothing to do with his reaction. Just like

Jacob, it's his cultural identification as a Jew and all the paranoia that goes with it."

"I guess I should have known. It was no big deal."

No big deal? Lola thought.

"Bernard Spelinsky loves you, Zoe. He would have done anything for you. Joining Jews for Jesus was an act of betrayal for your grandfather."

"Well, it didn't last long. I got caught in the mystique, but when religious doctrine became dogma, and I realized they were fanatics, that was enough."

"You lost your interest in religion?" asked Lola.

"No. Just in zealots."

"Bernie must have been relieved."

"He was, but things were never quite the same."

Zoe hesitated a moment. "Jacob's been having problems with some nurses and physicians."

"From what I hear, he always has."

"It's getting serious. People are talking about his age and his methods. I know you don't like to hear it, but complaints have a way of escalating into formal inquiries. I don't think we want any part of that."

Lola reddened. "Let me be clear, Zoe. I know Jacob. He has more intelligence, more compassion, and more integrity than the whole lot of those small-minded people at Brier Hospital who suddenly find him wanting. If you don't know that...well, I'm disappointed."

Zoe's face hardened, then her eyes filled. "Oh no, Lola. I love Jacob. I'm his biggest fan. I owe him so much. I'd never do anything to harm him."

Suddenly, the door opened and Jacob entered. "I'm sorry to be late, sweetie. No consideration, these patients." Turning to Zoe, he asked, "Can you join us for lunch?"

Zoe checked her watch. "Sorry, Jacob. I'm late for a meeting."

At Classico, an outdoor café near the Rockridge Bart station, Jacob and Lola sat under a multicolored umbrella that protected them from the noon sunlight.

"That looked like more than a casual conversation," said Jacob. "Is everything okay?"

"It's hard to break old habits. You can take the shrink out of psychotherapy, but can you take psychotherapy out of the shrink?"

"Get real, Lola. You can't separate the therapist from the person. In either role, you're smart, perceptive, and have a little experience."

"Get real? You sound like one of my teenagers."

"You mean I'm not too old to learn?"

"How is Zoe doing?" Lola asked.

Jacob raised his hand until he finished chewing on a wedge of sourdough bread. "She's smart, beautiful, well-trained, and with my sage advice, how could she go wrong?"

"If you don't want to get into it, say so. I'll understand."

"Easy there, Grandma. What did she say that got you so concerned?"

"Not so much what she said, but how she said it."

"What does that mean?"

"You know the expression, 'too good to be true', well that's how I feel about Zoe. Maybe I'm getting cynical in my old age, but something's missing from that pretty picture. Don't tell me you haven't noticed anything."

"No, not really."

"I don't know. Maybe it's generational. I prefer individuals who embrace the people in their lives with passion. I don't feel that with Zoe, especially when she talks about Byron, her grandfather, and even you, Jacob. It's an ambivalence or a vague sense of discomfort...I don't really know."

"I'm not looking for trouble, and I don't see any."

"How does Margaret feel about Zoe? She's a good judge of character."

"I don't know, but that's a good question."

Carleton Dix stared at the sleeping form as he entered the room. She looks so peaceful. He slipped his hand into the pocket of his white coast, but pulled it back as she stirred. Sensing an intruder, she raised her wrinkled lids, the pupils of her bright blue eyes dilating with fear.

"I'm so sorry to disturb you. I'm Reverend Dix, Mrs. Charles. I'm the chaplain for Brier Hospital."

Edna Charles sighed in relief, although her pulse still raced. Edna was an eighty-one-year-old retired high school principal. She was one of Jacob Weizman's patients from the first day he opened his doors and Lola's oldest friend. Four days in the hospital for a fractured hip became three days too many for Edna. Each extra day at Brier rendered her more testy. Her reputation as a sweet old lady was in jeopardy.

"I'm sorry, reverend, but did Dr. Weizman ask you to call on me?"

"No. I stop in on almost everybody just to see if I can help in any way."

"That's sweet of you, chaplain, but I'm not much into religion."

Carleton laughed. "It's nondenominational help of course. I make my services available to anyone, regardless of religious affiliation. We all are children of God, aren't we?"

What's Lola's favorite word? Edna thought. Chutzpah...the guy's got chutzpah.

"I don't want to be impolite, chaplain, but my religious beliefs are more in line with Dr. Weizman's."

"It's just..." he began when Mary Oakes, the charge nurse, entered the room.

"Excuse me, chaplain, but what are you doing here? You know how Dr. Weizman feels about you seeing his patients without his permission."

"I overheard your nurses saying how Mrs. Charles was upset about being here. I came in to help."

Mary turned to Edna. "Excuse us."

She escorted the chaplain into the corridor and closed the door. "This is deliberately provocative, chaplain and I don't like it. The last thing I want is to have Dr. Weizman on my case about you seeing his patients. He's made it clear to us that he doesn't want it. We respect his wishes and so should you."

"Listen, Mary. I'm just doing my job and neither you nor the esteemed Dr. Weizman should interfere."

"Look, chaplain. You've been helpful to us and to many patients, but do you really want to force yourself on patients and physicians who don't want your assistance?"

"It's that damned Weizman...he has it out for me, God knows why. I'm sick of tiptoeing around that man. Maybe it's time to bring this to a head."

"Don't take this personally, chaplain. It's not you. Before you came to Brier, we had chaplains of many denominations. We even had a rabbi. Jacob is not anti-chaplain, he's against anyone interacting with his patients without permission. Many patients, especially the elderly and the survivors in his practice, carry the emotional baggage of a lifetime. Jacob simply wants to protect them."

"I'm only trying to help but he won't let me."

"You're going to tell Jacob Weizman what's best for his patients? That's a laugh."

Mary stood, and headed for the door. "Be smart, chaplain. Find patients and physicians who want your help. If Jacob's patients need chaplain services, come through nursing or get Jacob's permission first."

"We'll see about that," said Carleton Dix. He turned and stumbled into a nurse's aide carrying a tray of food that bobbled and crashed on the floor.

That same afternoon, in Jacob's office, Zoe couldn't wait for the day to end. After the phone calls through the night, she'd managed only three hours of sleep and she was feeling it. Two of the four thick office charts had been on her desk for days, the others for at least two weeks. They needed letters and referral notes.

The intercom and Margaret's voice interrupted her musings. "Byron's on the line."

Zoe frowned then pushed the flashing button.

"Hey, Zoe. Just want to know when you'll be home tonight. I thought I'd take you to dinner."

"You know I had a bad night last night...or don't you remember?"

The line remained silent for a moment. "It was just a thought since I suspected you were going to have a bad day."

"I'm sorry." Zoe softened her voice. "I'm going to make quick afternoon rounds. I should be home at six thirty."

Zoe pushed the charts aside, grabbed her white coat, and started to leave.

When she reached the reception area, Margaret asked, "Did you do those dictations, Zoe?"

"I'm sorry, Margaret. Too much on my plate. I'll get to them tomorrow."

"Patients and referring docs are asking for those dictations, Zoe."

"I said I'll do them."

Chapter Thirty-Nine

The ringing phone echoed through the house as Jacob returned from work.

I can't get a break, he thought as he picked up the receiver.

"Jacob, it's Phyllis Rodman."

"What's up? How was the trip?"

"I'm sorry to bother you but we just stepped through the front door of our home after our flight from Japan, when Harry had a few seconds of chest pain and couldn't catch his breath."

"Call the ambulance and have them take him to Brier. I'll meet you there."

"An ambulance. Is that necessary? Can't we drive in?"

"Phyllis..." growled Jacob. "Just do as I say."

At fifty-eight, Harry Rodman served as Chairman of the Board of Education although he planned to retire soon. Phyllis, two years his junior, taught fifth grade. With the encouragement of their two grown children, they had accepted a summer teaching position in Japan...their first trip to the orient, their first real adventure of a lifetime.

Jacob stood under the overhang at the ER entrance daydreaming in the magic of the heavy rain. He loved the look and the smell of a fresh rain...a lifetime of memories flooded in. The downpour reminded Jacob of gazing through the barred barrack windows at Auschwitz. The flooding water ran off the hard ground and into the ditches under the electrified fences. Pure water ran down the partially open window. He reached out allowing the fresh drops to pool in his palm, and then retracted his hand and sipping of a world beyond this nightmare.

His reverie ended with the screech of the ambulance on arrival.

The transport gurney's shiny aluminum legs snapped in place as the EMTs slid Harry out of the ambulance and wheeled him into Treatment Room II. The oxygen tank rode next to him and connected to prongs that carried life into each nostril.

Harry grunted with each breath as he stared wide-eyed at Jacob.

When they transferred Harry to an ER bed, he grasped for Jacob's coat and gasped. "Help me, Jacob. I can't breathe. It kills me every time I take a deep breath...what's wrong with me?"

Jacob pulled out his stethoscope and moved the flat side of its head over Harry's chest and heart. "Where does it hurt?"

"Here," he pointed to the front lower rib cage on his right.

Jacob placed the stethoscope to the exact point indicated. "Take a deep breath."

Harry opened his mouth and started to inhale when he suddenly grimaced. "That kills me, Doc!"

At the deepest part of the breath, Jacob heard a loud rubbing sound and knew at once the diagnosis: Harry had thrown a clot from his lower extremities that moved into his lungs, a pulmonary embolus.

Harry tried another breath, but coughed uncontrollably as he brought up bright red blood.

"How long was that flight, Harry?"

"About twelve hours."

"Did you get up during the flight?"

"Once, to pee. Those damn seats are too small for a normal person, no less someone of my size. I could barely move, doc. I felt like a canned sardine."

"I'm going to run some tests, Harry, but the odds favor a clot to the lungs coming from your legs. We call that a pulmonary embolus."

Harry tried to sit up, but Jacob placed his hand on Harry's chest.

"How dangerous is that?"

"Small clots are bad enough. A large one can be life threatening. If the tests confirm my diagnosis, I'll give you a clot dissolving medication and start you on blood thinners to prevent more clots."

"Whatever you say, Doc." He hesitated. "You'll explain this to Phyllis...but please, Doc, don't scare her."

After the x-ray, lung scan, and a study of the deep veins in Harry's legs, Jacob talked with Phyllis. He tried to maintain his optimism, but would not mislead her about the seriousness of Harry's condition.

"This is a dangerous condition, Phyllis. I'm treating Harry aggressively and I'm asking our chief of cardiology, Sharon Brickman, to consult."

"You're scaring me, Jacob. Should I be scared?"

"Yes, at least for a while." He placed his wrinkled, age-spotted hand on her shoulder. "The first few hours are the most dangerous."

"I'm Dr. Brickman, and this is Ahmad Kadir," said Sharon as they entered Harry Rodman's room. "Dr. Kadir is a resident studying intensive care at UC San Francisco."

Ahmad bowed slightly, and with his Palestinian accent said, "So nice to meet you."

When Phyllis Rodman stared at Ahmad, her mind flashed on the images of suicide bombers she'd seen on TV. Embarrassed, she looked at the floor, saying nothing.

Harry grunted his greeting and extended a trembling hand.

Ahmad and Sharon examined Harry, and then put his x-ray up on the view box. "See this white area, Mrs. Rodman." She pointed to the right side of the film. "That's where the clot went into Mr. Rodman's lung."

Sharon sat in a chair opposite Phyllis. "Here's where we are. If he shows any signs of more clots or if he becomes unstable, we may have to do a pulmonary arteriogram to visualize the clots in his lungs, and go into something much more aggressive and a lot more dangerous."

They moved Harry to 614, one of the rooms in the step-down cardiac care unit where he'd be on the monitor while he received heparin, an anticoagulant. The laboratory would monitor how well his blood clotted.

Kate Planchette, Harry's nurse, approached the bedside and turned to Phyllis. "You must be jet-lagged, Mrs. Rodman. That long trip, and now this. Why don't you go home and rest. I'll call you at once if anything develops."

"Are you sure it's all right? I'm dead on my feet."

"It's fine."

Phyllis kissed Harry. "I'll see you in the morning, sweetheart."

Harry grunted something unintelligible, and then closed his eyes.

Luck is with me, I think, as I slip into Harry Rodman's room.

Not so for you, Harry. This time, we'll leave it to the fates.

Better make it quick.

Neither the beeping of the cardiac monitor nor the nurses coming and going disturb Harry's sound sleep.

I reach into my white coat and remove the syringe containing 300,000 units of heparin and flush it into his IV line.

With this massive dose of anticoagulant, Harry won't need to worry about a blood clot, now or ever and if I'm lucky again, Harry—you won't have to worry about anything.

Kate had seen Tommy Wells going in and out of Harry's room all evening to perform bedside clotting studies. He was due back in another thirty minutes when Kate entered the room. She pulled the sheet off Harry's arm to measure his blood pressure, and then stared. His arm and entire chest wall were purple. Blood oozed from venipuncture sites, the IV site, his nose, and mouth, and when she pulled his lids open, Harry's eyes bulged bright red.

My God, she thought. He's bleeding out!

Kate pushed the call button and when the ward clerk answered, she said, "Get Dr. Weizman stat, and have the lab come up to draw a blood count and to do another clotting study."

She tried to awaken Harry, but he failed to react. The right side of his mouth drooped and bloody saliva oozed out. When Tommy entered the room, Kate said, "Get a blood count stat and draw a clotting time."

Tommy looked at Harry. "This guy looks like shit."

"Tommy," she shouted, "keep that language to yourself."

"I'm sorry," he said inserting a test tube of blood into the automated device.

They waited...stared at the machine awaiting the tell-tale beep that indicated a result. After 10 minutes the machine alarmed and flashed: Infinite. Harry Rodman's protective clotting system lay in paralysis...he could bleed from anywhere.

Three minutes later, Zoe entered the room. "I was admitting another patient on the fifth floor. What's happening?"

Tommy studied the clotting device. "His clotting time is infinite. I've been doing clotting times every hour or so and they were in therapeutic range."

"What was his last clotting time?" asked Zoe.

"That's it. He can't clot at all."

Zoe did a rough calculation then gave Harry a dose of protamine to counteract the heparin. "I hope it's not too much or too little...each has its set of problems."

After Kate administered the dose, Zoe completed her examination. "The drooping mouth and the flaccid muscles says that Mr. Rodman has had a stroke. We need an emergency brain CT scan." Zoe paused. "I'd better call Jacob, and someone get me Mrs. Rodman's number."

"Should I call the chaplain?" asked Kate.

"Not a bad idea," said Zoe, "except ask him to leave before Mrs. Rodman gets here. She'll freak if she sees him."

Chapter Forty

Jacob had a sixth sense for trouble and it was sounding strong as he walked toward Harry Rodman's room that evening.

When Jacob arrived, Zoe saw his hair listing to one side and his bow tie askew.

He's too old for this, Zoe thought. He should be in bed.

Jacob pulled back the sheet to expose Harry and saw the bloodstained bed, the bruising and bleeding, and yelled, "What the hell happened?"

"He has an infinite clotting time, Jacob," said Sharon. "He's bleeding from everywhere and clinically he bled into his brain too."

"Oh, my God...how is he now?"

"Stroked out," said Zoe. "How much heparin did you order, Jacob?"

"I gave him a standard loading dose of 50 units/kg of body weight then a maintenance dose of 20 units/kg/hour."

"You adjusted that for his lean body mass?" asked Zoe.

"What are you talking about? I've been giving heparin for decades. Of course I adjusted the dose."

Jacob stared at Zoe and Sharon, trying to read their minds. "His clotting time following the large loading dose was in the therapeutic range and so were the first few follow up readings. I don't understand your questions and I resent your implications."

"Take it easy, Jacob," said Sharon. "We're trying to find out what went wrong."

Jacob stared at Zoe. "What are you doing here? I'm on call tonight."

"I was here anyway, so I decided to come up."

"Check my orders, Sharon, to your satisfaction..."

"That won't be necessary, Jacob."

"If the orders were appropriate," said Jacob, "then I see only two other possibilities: a dosing error or another process leading to a clotting problem like DIC (disseminated intravascular coagulation). The heparin may have been the wrong concentration or they diluted it improperly. Off hand, I don't see any reason for DIC."

"I talked with Kate Planchette and reviewed the set up of the heparin infusion; it's cookbook. Unless the heparin itself is mislabeled, I don't see that kind of error."

"Even if the Heparin infusion pump went bad and he got too much," said Jacob, "that wouldn't explain a massive overdosage."

Sharon plunked herself down in the easy chair in Harry's room and stared through the rain-streaked window. She turned to Jacob. "Maybe this isn't an accident, Jacob. Bad things are happening to patients around Brier, especially your patients: Lidocaine overdose, heroin overdose, and excuse me Jacob, the question of morphine overdose...and now this. Could Brier Hospital have its own serial killer?"

"That's absurd," said Zoe. "There's got to be some other explanation."

"You're not party to the detail of these cases, Zoe," said Sharon, "but the more I think about it, the more obvious seems the explanation."

On their way to view Harry's CT scan, Zoe turned to Jacob. "I'm sorry. I wasn't thinking straight. I was reaching for an explanation. I'd never..."

"Forget about it, Zoe. I know all too well the effects of stress and uncertainty on the human mind and its rationality."

"But, you've done so much for me...how can I have thought...?"

"Forget it."

The chief of radiology, Bernie Myers, stood before the high-resolution screen paging through slices of Harry Rodman's brain. "He's lucky, Jacob. It's a small frontal lobe bleed."

"The last thing I'd call this man," said Jacob, "is lucky."

"Well," said Bernie, "I've seen a lot worse. If Harry has no further bleeding, he might just pull through."

When they returned to Harry's room, Phyllis Rodman sat next to her husband, holding his hand and crying. Her daughter Carol stood at her side stroking her mother's hair.

Jacob entered the room. Phyllis rose and embraced him, tears running down her cheeks.

"My God, Jacob! What happened?"

"Something happened with his anticoagulant...I don't know what. His blood couldn't clot. He's bleeding everywhere, including, I'm afraid, into his brain."

"His brain?"

"We just looked at the brain scan. Thank God it's a small bleed. I think he'll recover, but it's going to be iffy for a while."

Carol turned to Jacob. "I thought he needed the blood thinner to prevent another clot to his lung."

"He does," said, Jacob, "but I see no way we can give him a blood thinner now. It might make the bleeding in his brain worse."

"What are you going to do, Jacob?" asked Phyllis. "You must do something."

"I'll talk with Sharon Brickman about putting a filter inside the large vein in the lower part of his abdomen (the inferior vena cava). That way, if more clots break off, we can catch them before they reach Harry's lungs."

"Whatever you think best, Jacob," said Phyllis. "We trust you. We've come this far with you. We might as well go all the way."

"I'll never have that kind of loyalty...that kind of respect," murmured Zoe. "The best of medicine will die with the departure of men like Jacob Weizman."

Jacob turned to leave. Carol caught him by the arm. "You don't know how this happened?"

"No," said Jacob, "but I'll find out!"

Chapter Forty-One

When Mary Oakes, the charge nurse on the fifth floor medical unit, looked at the skeletal Angelina Cass, she felt her eyes moisten then she flushed with anger.

This is a total waste of our time, she thought. We'll never get to her.

This was the sixth admission for this thirty-year-old woman in the last six months, each time for the same sequence of problems: anorexia nervosa, a severe anxiety disorder, with malnutrition and dehydration leading to multiple electrolyte abnormalities, often life threatening.

Mary pushed aside the standard blood pressure cuff at the bedside, too large for Angelina's twig-like arm, and grabbed the pediatric one. After she completed her assessment of the brooding, angry young woman, she saw Joanna Davis, Angelina's mother, in the hallway talking with Arnie Roth, her daughter's physician.

"What more can we do, Doctor? Angelina's seen dozens of shrinks, psychiatric social workers, and participated in three eating disorder inpatient programs. Nothing worked."

Arnie shook his head. "I don't know. Let's first get her out of trouble."

"I'm so sick of this," said Joanna. "I have a life too, you know."

"I'm sorry," Arnie replied. "I'll try to find another program after she's stable."

"I don't want her to have any visitors. Her friends are nearly as bad as she, and her son-of-a-bitch husband Milo, he'll only upset her more."

"I'll write the orders for no visitors."

When Arnie entered Angelina's room the next morning, her eyes bored into him. "It's you again, damn it. I told you I don't want your help."

"I don't think you're competent to make that decision, Angelina. You almost succeeded this time in killing yourself."

"It's my life," she snarled, pulling on her restraints. "I can do what the fuck I like with it. I want you to remove this stomach tube and IV. And get these damned restraints off me."

"Not a chance."

Angelina's eyes bulged as she strained to sit upright. "You fucking bastard! You can't do this to me. I'll sue the shit out of you and this damn hospital."

Arnie had the foresight to step back from Angelina's bed as a large wad of mucoid spit flew across the room landing on the wall.

He watched the thick saliva sliding downward. "I'll have the nurse give you something to calm you down. Maybe sometime soon we can talk about a future for you."

Arnie left the room. When the closed door muffled her profanity, he sighed with relief.

I'm getting too old for this crap!

The intruder ignored the large 'No Visitors' sign and entered Angelina's room.

Grabbing the end of the feeding tube, the intruder attached a large syringe and pushed in the thick, green fluid. After the third syringe-full, the intruder smiled, caressed Angelina's cheek.

With a shake of the head, the intruder departed.

At 4 a.m., the voice of Angelina Cass boomed through the intercom. "You got to help, my stomach is killing me."

"I'll send your nurse right in," said the ward clerk.

When Patti Sax, the night nurse, entered the room, Angelina was bent over clutching her stomach and retching. "I never felt this bad before...these cramps are killing me."

Patti wiped off the vomit, and then checked Angelina's vital signs. Except for a racing pulse, they were stable. She felt Angelina's abdomen which felt soft and wasn't tender.

"I'll call Dr. Roth."

Arnie listened to Patti's description. "It might be an ulcer or possibly pancreatitis. Give her a shot of Compazine and have the lab draw her morning bloods right now. Ask them to add an amylase and lipase to rule out pancreatitis. I'll be at Brier in a couple of hours. Call me if she gets worse."

When Arnie arrived for rounds, the morning nurse raced to meet him. "She won't wake up, Dr. Roth."

Angelina groaned when Arnie examined her, but except for deep breathing, he noted no other abnormalities. Back at the nursing station, Arnie turned to the ward clerk. "Where's today's lab?"

The ward clerk handed him the printout. "It just came up."

Arnie stared. He'd rarely seen so many abnormalities of a patient's chemistries with a pattern of too much acid in her blood.

Now I know why she's breathing that way.

"Transfer her to ICU stat. I want a set of blood gasses, a chest x-ray, a new set of electrolytes, and get Jack Byrnes to consult."

Two hours later, Arnie sat with Jack looking over Angelina's laboratory tests.

Jack stood. "Come with me, Arnie."

They walked to Angelina's bedside.

Jack looked at Arnie. "Turn off the lights."

"What's going on?" asked Arnie.

"Just turn them off." Jack grabbed a peculiar shaped lamp. When the room became dark, he shined the purple light on the bag of urine collected from the catheter in Angelina's bladder. At once, the urine glowed green.

"What the hell?" said Arnie.

"Somebody poisoned her," said Jack. "The chemistries, the pattern of electrolytes, the severity of the acid in her blood, and the green glow, says one word to me: antifreeze."

Arnie stared at Jack. "Antifreeze!"

"I sent out a sample to our reference lab, but we can't wait for the results. I think we need to pull out all the stops."

"Whatever," said Arnie.

"Where's her husband? I'd prefer him to sign the permit for dialysis."

"We called their home, but nobody answered."

"I'm starting an intravenous alcohol infusion, until I get the dialysis machine ready. The alcohol competes with antifreeze for its metabolism. That should help until we remove it."

"I have a few alcoholics who'll line up for that IV anytime," said Arnie.

"Once they get the whole picture, I don't think they will."

After four hours of dialysis and with the continued alcohol infusion, Angelina was in a cheery mood. With speech slurred, she giggled, "I really like you, Dr. Roth...you're my favorite doctor."

So that's what it takes, Arnie thought.

Chapter Forty-Two

It was noon with the sun lighting the cloud margins with shiny lace trim. When Marilyn and Sarah Hughes approached Brier Hospital in their Toyota Minivan, the police barricade surprised them. Marilyn rolled down her window.

"I'm sorry, ma'am, you'll need to turn around. The street's closed."

"What happened?"

"I'm sorry, ma'am, just move on."

Marilyn turned then pulled into a waiting area one block away. She dialed Bob's cell phone. "We're a block away. What's going on?"

"Somebody tried to kill one of our patients."

"Who? What?"

"I'll tell you about it later."

"Is it still okay if Sarah joins you for lunch?"

"Of course. Just let her off. She can walk in. I'll meet her in the ER."

Marilyn kissed Sarah. "Have a good time."

Sarah suddenly embraced her mother, holding on tight for thirty seconds. "I love you, Mom. I'm so sorry..."

Marilyn flushed with affection and felt the tears streak over her cheeks. "I love you too. Nothing can ever change that."

Sarah walked down the sunny street toward Brier. Media vans with their microwave dishes elevated were double-parked. Onlookers filled the streets and the plaza before the hospital. When Sarah approached the north ER entrance ramp, Carleton Dix stood smoking a cigarette.

Shit!

She altered her course to the opposite end of the ER ramp.

In an instant, their eyes locked. He hurled the cigarette to the pavement, crushed it with his heel, and moved to intercept her. Sarah increased her pace, but he crossed diagonally to stand in her path. She moved to pass by. Her heart pounded. "Excuse me, Padre."

He shifted, and again placed himself in her way. "I'd like a word with you, Sarah."

"I have nothing to say to you, now get out of my way."

"Don't you owe me an apology? You knew very well what you did, and how it would affect me. How could you do it?"

Sarah trembled as he came closer. Being in the same room would have been too much for her, but this...

She raised her hand in a stop gesture, and then took two steps back. "This is your own doing, Padre. I told you to leave me alone. I told you never to touch me, yet you did it anyway."

He looked toward the sky. "I was just trying to help you, Sarah. Your parents asked me to help."

"I don't need your help. I don't want your help. Do you finally get it?"

"Don't do this, Sarah. You're anything but naïve. You knew what the word 'touch' implies, yet you used it."

"You're right, Padre. I may be young and inexperienced, but I understand exactly what your looks and your touch meant. Don't deny it now that you've been busted."

The reverend's eyes narrowed and his lips tightened. "You're asking for trouble, Sarah. All of us have something to hide."

"I don't know what you're talking about."

"Oh, I think you do. Don't forget, Sarah, that you're placing your immortal soul in danger. Remember the Ninth Commandment: Thou shalt not bear false witness."

"Not to worry, Padre. The truth is my best defense."

Jacob Weizman's office was particularly busy this afternoon.

Margaret Cohen called Zoe over the intercom. "I have Peggy Weiss on the phone. She's asking for her lab results."

"Bring me her chart and tell her I'll speak with her later this afternoon when I get a break."

"I can bring the chart right in."

"No, that's okay. I'll call her later."

"It'll only take a second."

Zoe stared at Margaret. "Aren't you a little tired of the way Jacob indulges patients like Peggy Weiss? I am."

Margaret stared back at Zoe. "Indulgence is pejorative. I assure you that Jacob doesn't think that way about his patients. His attitude is what makes Jacob so beloved."

Zoe smiled, and then shook her head. "Of course you're right. Tell Peggy I'll call her back for sure."

"Yes, Doctor."

At three in the afternoon, Margaret knocked on Zoe's door. "Peggy called again. Please speak with her, Zoe. She's a wreck."

"I will."

Margaret hesitated a moment. "It's important. A few words is all it takes."

Zoe stared cold-eyed at Margaret. "I said I'll call."

Jacob and Margaret were getting ready to close up for the day when the answering service line to the office rang. Margaret looked at Jacob. "Should I take it?"

"Go ahead."

"Sorry to bother you, Margaret," said the operator, "but we have Peggy Weiss on the line. She's really upset. Can you talk to her?"

"Sure. Put her through."

"What's wrong with me?" cried Peggy. "It must be bad or Dr. Spelling wouldn't be avoiding me."

"Wait a sec, Peggy," Margaret said, putting the call on hold. She grabbed Peggy's chart and handed it to Jacob. "Please talk with Peggy Weiss, Zoe's patient. She's upset."

Jacob flipped through the chart, read the most recent note, and reviewed her new lab tests. He picked up the phone. "Dr. Weizman. Can I help you?"

"What's wrong with me, Doctor? How bad are they?"

"How bad are what?"

"My tests. It's cancer. I knew it. It's cancer," Peggy cried.

"Cancer? What are you talking about? I see no sign of cancer of any kind. Your tests are perfectly normal. Am I missing something?"

"It's just...I thought... When Dr. Spelling didn't call, I thought it was something bad."

"I looked over your chart, Mrs. Weiss..."

"Peggy...everyone calls me Peggy."

"Yes, Peggy. Dr. Spelling's last note and your tests say you're doing just fine. Maybe I can look deeper to find something for you to worry about."

Peggy laughed. "No, that's okay. I feel like such a fool going off like that."

"I don't know anyone who doesn't get a little anxious waiting for test results. It's natural to be concerned. Anything else?"

"No, Dr. Weizman. Now I see why people talk so kindly about you."

After Jacob set the phone down, Margaret placed her hand on Jacob's shoulder. "That was sweet of you, Jacob."

"Did Zoe try to reach Peggy today?"

"She said she'd try."

Later that same afternoon, Bruce Bryant stood behind his desk looking at the small crowd gathered within: members of the medical staff, hospital counsel, the police, and representative of the DA. Outside his street level window, people milled about and stared into his office.

"See what I have to put up with," Bruce said, as he lowered the blinds.

Ira Green, the chief of police studied Bruce. "What did you expect? You have a serial killer loose in Brier Hospital,"

"Wait a minute," said Al David, the hospital's attorney. "You're jumping to conclusions. One poisoning with antifreeze does not a serial killer make."

"Excuse me," said Jeremy Finch, an assistant DA, "I'm just getting up to speed, but this isn't the only case."

Al David turned to Bruce Bryant. "Nobody's proved that those other cases were anything but simple errors."

"Simple errors?" said Warren Davidson, the chief of medicine. "I care about this hospital as much as you do, Bruce, but let's not kid ourselves. Rory Calhoun and his narcotic overdose, Nathan Seigel, overdosed with Lidocaine, Harry Rodman, overdosed with heparin, and finally the antifreeze case. Must I draw you pictures?"

Jeremy Finch stood. "This is out of your hands, gentlemen. The DA's office has heard more than enough to begin a thorough investigation. I expect all of you to fully cooperate with Chief Green and the DA's investigators."

"If this hits the press," said Bruce, "it's going to kill us."

"It's too late, Bruce," said Warren. "And, I'd be careful in my choice of words."

Chapter Forty-Three

Jacob walked to Harry Rodman's room at Brier's Skilled Nursing Facility (SNF). After they placed the blood filter into his inferior vena cava, Harry had no further clots, but the frontal lobe bleed had caused neurological problems.

Phyllis sat at Harry's bedside and when Jacob entered, she rose and gave him a kiss on the cheek. "We're so glad to see you, Jacob. What's happening?"

"How am I doing?" Harry asked in a monotone, extending his hand.

Jacob sat next to Harry and addressed him deliberately. "You have injured part of your brain, Harry."

"What part?"

Jacob placed his hand over his forehead. "It's here in the frontal lobe. Damage here can produce dramatic or subtle changes. In your case, Harry, we find few signs of injury when we examine you."

Phyllis held Harry's hand. "He's different, more mellow. Is that a part of it?"

"Could be."

Jacob walked up to Harry. "I'm going to do a few tests...okay?"

"No problem, Doc. No needles, right?"

"No needles. I'm going to raise either one or two fingers. If I raise one, I want you to say two. If I raise two, I want you to say one. Got it?"

"Got it."

Jacob raised one finger.

"One," Harry said.

Phyllis paled.

Jacob repeated the instructions, and then tried again, raising two fingers.

"Two."

"You don't have to watch this, Phyllis."

"No, it's okay."

Jacob repeated his instructions then performed the finger test ten times. Harry got it wrong in all but one.

Harry blinked blandly and stared at Jacob. "What's wrong with me?"

"It's okay, Harry. It's just a mild injury. It should improve over time."

Phyllis sat wringing a handkerchief between her fingers. "How much time?"

"Months, I'd guess."

"One more test, Harry. I'm going to give you sixty seconds to name as many things as you can starting with the letter F, no proper nouns. Got it?"

Harry nodded.

Jacob looked at his watch. "Begin."

"Fish...friend...phone..." came slowly, then Harry paused.

Jacob stared at his watch. "Come on Harry, you have thirty seconds."

Harry stared ahead in silence. The seconds clicked back to zero.

Jacob caressed Harry's head. "It's okay. You'll get it."

Afterward, standing outside in the corridor, Jacob turned to Phyllis. "Don't be upset. Time is on our side. The brain has wonderful healing powers for this kind of injury."

"I miss him, Jacob," said Phyllis, "the old feistiness...the old Harry."

"I know. I'm sending him home tomorrow, but you two are going to be busy with physical and occupational therapy, and a series of neurological rehabilitation programs to whip his brain back to its old self."

"I read the papers and watch the news, Jacob. Was Harry's bleeding problem part of that?"

Jacob locked on Phyllis's eyes. "I'm not sure, but it's the only explanation that makes sense."

"Harry never hurt anyone in his life. Who could do such a thing to him, Jacob?"

"I wish I knew."

"I don't get it, Zoe," said Jacob when he returned to the office after lunch.

"Don't get what?"

"How someone could deliberately try to kill a sweet man like Harry Rodman. Even the SS in the camps had to dehumanize their victims before they killed."

"How sure are you that it was deliberate? Maybe it was an accident."

"I tried to believe that, but I have no doubt that these are cold-blooded acts of a serial killer, a psychopath who doesn't care who he injures or kills."

"What's going to happen?"

"The hospital and the police are investigating and the increased security should make our patients feel better. If you ask me, I think it's too little, too late."

"That's pretty pessimistic for you, Jacob."

"No really. He's going to get caught. Like all psychopaths, he's doomed to make a mistake…he needs to make a mistake…it's part of his disease. That's how it's going to end."

"The chaplain did what?" Lola shouted as she began her next session with Sarah.

"Don't get your britches on fire. I handled it."

"I haven't worn britches in seventy-five years." Lola paused. "He got angry?"

"He was pissed for sure. Maybe he can't tolerate sass in general, or perhaps it's just me."

"I don't trust the man," said Lola. "Approaching you, under these circumstances, suggests bad judgment at the least. I don't want you anywhere near that man."

"I tried to avoid him, but he was determined to get in my face."

"I'm proud of you," said Lola, "or maybe I should say you were, what's the term you girls use...oh yes...wicked."

"You're too much, Lola."

"I'll take that as a compliment. Not to worry, I'll talk with Jacob about the good chaplain."

Jacob and Lola sat in the den after dinner sipping Adega Velha, their favorite Portuguese brandy.

"You're preaching to the choir, Lola."

"If Dix had any common sense," said Lola, "he would have kept a mile away from Sarah. It's what we'd expect from a sociopath or maybe a narcissist who thinks he has the ultimate control over the world."

"Come on, Lola, don't people have to cross some line before you nail them with such specific diagnoses?"

"Of course. It's the difference between paranoia, varying from mild to severe and paranoid personality disorder or paranoid schizophrenia. We're just talking, but I'm sure something's wrong with that man."

"I agree. I thought, at first, that it was his self-righteous overconfidence, the arrogance of a man who thinks he's doing God's work. Maybe it's more complicated. Let's see what we can find out about chaplain Carleton Dix."

"Remember, Jacob, a person may need to be a little crazy to ascend to the chaplain's heights of religious zealotry."

"I'll accept the heights metaphor, if you include the fall."

Chapter Forty-Four

San Francisco Chronicle

Dateline, Berkeley, California

Berkeley Police are investigating the poisoning of a Brier Hospital patient. The hospital spokesman and the police refused to release any details. However, informed sources say that a patient, Angelina Cass, a thirty-year-old woman, received a near lethal dose of antifreeze. Sources say that after emergency treatment including kidney dialysis, she's recovering.

This is the latest of several patient misadventures, and unexplained deaths at Brier Hospital, previously thought of as one of the finest hospitals in the bay area.

Berkeley's Chief of Police, Ira Green, promises a thorough investigation.

Bruce Bryant held up the newspaper. "Look at this crap. Previously thought to be...It doesn't take long to destroy a reputation, does it?"

"I've briefed our public relations people," said Al David. "They'll use all the right words: Meeting the highest standards, the finest medical staff, the highest rating by the Joint Commission on Hospital Accreditation, and cite all our awards and achievements, but that will pale next to 'Killer stalks the halls of Brier Hospital'. Solving this, and doing it quickly, is our only hope."

"If this turns out to be the action of one of our employees or somebody on the staff," said Bruce, "we're twice screwed."

Ira Green sat behind his gray metal desk at police headquarters in Berkeley. "The phone's been ringing off the hook since this thing hit the front pages."

Detective Shelly Kahn studied her nails. "What did you expect, Ira? The hospital is a sanctuary, the one place people trust and can go to when they're sick and most vulnerable. The enemy should be disease, not a murderer."

"The mayor called, then the Attorney General. Please tell me you have something, Shelly."

"Nothing, chief. We'd have been incredibly lucky to have a lead at this stage of the investigation. Dr. Davidson asked the Quality Assurance Committee to review all the deaths in the last eighteen months with one question in mind: Were any of them murder?"

"What's the hospital doing?"

"Like most hospitals, Brier is pretty lax about security except in the pediatric area. Now, if anyone on the staff arrives without their picture ID, they send them home. Heightened security should discourage any further attempts, but if it's an inside job...?"

"I hope so, Shelly, but when you're dealing with this kind of sicko, you never know."

"Anything else, Chief?"

"You're heading this investigation, Shelly. I'll give you whatever resources you need. Just catch this son-of-a-bitch...and soon." He paused and looked up at Shelly. "Let's not forget the fundamentals."

"Fundamentals?"

"The fundamentals, such as who do you like, sight unseen, when a husband or wife is killed, and where was Angelina's husband Milo?"

"He was home, drunk."

"Alone?"

"So he says. I'll get on it, Chief."

Hospitals, like people, have personalities, and can't avoid the effects of the mayhem surrounding them. Brier Hospital, after years of struggling, had reached the point where its name spelled optimism, competence, compassion, and security. Now it spelled murder.

Before the San Francisco Chronicle article splashed gruesome details about the deaths at Brier, gatherings around the lounges and water coolers spread speculation and supposition like oil on a pond. Now, with increased security and the presence of many new faces, the staff felt like they were working in a fish bowl.

A group of nurses sat in the staff lounge sharing the afternoon newspaper.

"Every time I look over my shoulder," said Ginny Harrison, "I meet another pair of accusing eyes."

"In your case," Mary Oakes said, smiling, "that's perfectly appropriate."

"Now I know how you made your way to the top of nursing administration, Mary...ruthlessness."

Gail Sergeant, another senior nurse said, "Since this whole thing began, I've been having terrible nightmares. I suddenly awaken in a sweat, and look around my room making sure nobody's there."

"It's got to be someone on the staff," said Ginny, "but who?"

Mary shook her head. "It's difficult to believe that someone you work with, maybe a friend is a serial killer."

Ginny yawned from lack of sleep. "I don't know how long I can work under these circumstances."

"That's nothing," said Mary Oakes. "Imagine how you'd feel if you were a patient."

When Jacob slid his card through the reader at the hospital's rear entrance, the door lock clicked open and for the first time he faced a security guard.

"Excuse me, sir, but I need to check your ID."

Jacob smiled. "Andy? Didn't I deliver you, your brothers, and your little sister?"

"You sure did, Doc, and I'll never forgive you for bringing my sister into this world. She's a swift pain in the..."

Andy pointed to the surveillance camera overhead. "Sorry, Doc, but I can't make any exceptions."

Jacob pulled the card from his coat pocket and presented it to Andy.

"Thanks, Doc. Please pin it on your coat or wear it on a lanyard or your trip through Brier will be a slow one."

When Jacob made it to the doctor's lounge, Warren Davidson was chatting with Jack Byrnes. Jacob pulled up a chair. "It's like a war zone. I haven't seen so many uniforms in one place since Vienna."

"Everyone's running scared." said Warren.

"How goes your investigation?" Jack asked.

"We're not used to second guessing ourselves over the causes of death," said Warren. "Ninety-nine percent of the time, we know it's coming and exactly what happened. It's difficult to look at these cases, especially the ones dying of terminal illnesses and ask; could anything else be going on? I find it hard to be that suspicious."

"Did you find anything in my cases?" Jacob asked.

Warren opened his folder. "You did have many deaths, Jacob, but your patient population is much older. Let me mention a few names and get your response...did you expect the death or even in retrospect are you suspicious?"

"Shoot."

"Shannon Hogan?"

"Definitely unexpected and tragic, but we did an autopsy that showed nothing."

"It was a routine autopsy, Jacob, not a forensic one."

"Of course. We had no reason to expect foul play."

"P.J. Manning?"

"Expected, and a blessing. A horrible ALS death. Why would someone kill a person nearing death?"

"Joshua Friedman?"

"If you're going to hit me with Marion Krupp's bullshit on that case..."

"Easy, old timer," said Jack.

"Old timer, my ass. To answer your question, terminal esophageal cancer. Another expected death, not soon enough if you ask me."

"Nathan Seigel?"

"Now here you may have something. He definitely died as the result of Lidocaine toxicity, but we had no indication that it was deliberate."

"And finally, Harry Rodman?"

"Harry didn't die. Why include him?"

"He nearly died of a heparin overdose, Jacob. Could this have been deliberate?"

"God knows. Why would someone want to injure Harry? It makes no sense."

"It isn't like you, Jacob," said Warren, "to be having these kinds of problems with your patients."

Jacob reddened. "Are you accusing me of something, Warren?"

"Don't shoot the messenger, Jacob. I'm asking the same exact questions of every doc whose patient died or had some sort of adverse, unexpected event. Don't get paranoid on me."

"It's not paranoia when physicians and nurses question my practice, Warren, and when you give credence to malcontents like Marion Krupp."

Jacob turned to Jack. "Do you think I'm too old to practice, Jack? Am I delusional and don't recognize that I've outlasted my usefulness?"

"Don't do this, Jacob. While you don't have the public image of a young superstar, and while you sometimes become a bit contentious about anything, you can take care of my wife and me anytime. I trust you. You've been the best, and in my mind, you still are."

Chapter Forty-Five

Margaret Cohen came into Jacob's office after they finished for the day. "Do you have a moment, Jacob?"

"Sure, Maggie."

"No 'Maggie' today, Jacob. I have something...something important." She paused, her eyes beginning to fill.

"What is it, Margaret? Are you sick?"

"No, I'm as healthy as a horse." Her hands shook. She walked back from Jacob's desk and closed the door. "I want to talk with you about Zoe. I'm having problems with her."

"You were her biggest fan. What happened?"

"What happened was time and experience. She's lovely and charming and, no question, she's an asset to the practice..."

"I'm waiting for the 'but'."

"When she first came, she charmed everyone, including me. She's smart and her patients love her, but I don't think she really likes what she's doing, and its beginning to show. In addition, I have questions about her character."

"Go ahead."

"Maybe you spoiled me, Jacob," she paused in thought. "No, it's more fundamental than that. When you say something, I know you mean it. When you promise something, I know, barring death, that you'll do it. When you tell me something, I know it's the truth."

"You're holding me to too high a standard."

"Sure I am." She smiled. More serious now, she continued, "Let me give you a few examples. Do you remember the situation with Peggy Weiss?"

"Of course. What about it?"

"That's so typical of you. When you commit to someone, you view them through the lenses of a loving father."

"Mea culpa...you're right, of course. What's the point?"

"The point, Old Man, is that if anyone else treated one of our patients like Zoe treated Peggy, you'd be all over their case. With Zoe, you didn't even see the problem."

"That's petty stuff. She's busy and maybe doesn't manage her time well."

"You're a sweetheart, Jacob, and too loyal. I love you for it, but phone calls are important. Patients waiting for critical results, waiting to find out about their loved ones, needing a sympathetic ear...their physician's ear. It's cruel. You'd never do such a thing."

"What else?"

"Haven't you noticed that you're doing lots of referral notes and reports?"

"Yes?"

"We keep them away from Zoe. She promises, but never gets them done."

"What else?"

"I'm sorry, Jacob. I know you don't like to hear these things, but you need to know."

"You're right. Go ahead."

"This may be more symbolic than important, but it shows Zoe's attitude toward her patients. She sees patients with complicated problems too quickly. She's got to be cutting corners. For what...to find time to talk with her stockbroker?

"Often, I'll find her standing in the doorway of her office talking with her patient. She did it recently with Brenda Gomez. It's a clear message to her patients...get out, I'm through with you. The staff sees it and they resent it. She thinks she's so slick about it, but patients are beginning to recognize her disinterest. A few of Zoe's patients have requested to transfer their care to you. It's just wrong. It's not the way we treat patients in this office."

"Anything else?"

"Yes. When you consider what I've said so far, this is going to sound strange. At first, I thought Zoe was trying to be helpful, but now I'm not so sure."

"What is it?"

"She's sticking her nose into the business aspects of the practice, asking for financial information, billing procedures etc. The staff resents this as an intrusion."

"That seems appropriate to me, Margaret. If she's going to be a partner, she's entitled to know and have input into how we do business."

"Sure, but then she takes every opportunity to cull off your patients, like if you're late to the office or if you're delayed with a patient. Again, at first I thought she was trying to be helpful, but now I'm getting the feeling that she's trying to subvert you."

"All this is a little disturbing. I'll talk with her."

"Okay, but don't be her grandfather. If you want to help her, be tough. Find out what's really going on."

After Jacob and Lola cleared the dinner table that evening and loaded the dishwasher, Jacob paraphrased Margaret's observations.

"Have you noticed anything, Jacob?"

"Not really. You know me. Once I commit myself emotionally to someone, it's difficult for me to look behind the curtain of my own conviction."

"Nothing?"

"Well, nothing specific, except several times I felt that she questioned my judgment."

"Jacob, sweetheart, you were born arguing with physicians and nurses, you're an expert. Zoe questions something, yet you say nothing. Weren't you disappointed a little? Didn't she hurt your feelings?"

"When you talk about feelings, I get an irresistible impulse to head for the door. Anyway, it wasn't like that, it's just..."

"Like Zoe's the daughter you never had, and unlike our boys, she's the one who followed you into the profession." Lola smiled and then caressed Jacob's cheek. "Don't fight me on this. You know I'm right."

"I'm not fighting, but how would you like to live with a mind reader?"

"I'm not reading your mind, but when you've lived with someone for almost sixty years and if you're a shrink, well, you can't help yourself."

"You're too damn smart. Combine that with experience and charisma, you're a force."

"I hate the word 'charisma', it's sounds pretentious or ultra-religious, like charismatic."

Jacob patted Lola's hand. "Choose your own words, but patients love you. In the early days, I had little regard for psychiatry, but you made me a believer. You really help your patients. In my mind, that makes you a superstar."

Lola reddened. "Superstar? You're embarrassing me. You made me blush, you old fart."

Jacob put his arms around his wife, and thought Lola's the best thing that ever happened to me.

Lola wiped her eyes. "Now, where were we?"

"Zoe. We were talking about Zoe."

"Well, one thing for sure, I wouldn't dismiss anything Margaret has to say."

"I'm not. That's why we're having this discussion. I plan to talk with Zoe, and I thought, since you know her, you might have some insight."

"I don't keep myself in shrink mode all the time, but I did notice a few things that concerned me."

"Like what?"

"I'm going to mention some small things, trivial things, if you like, but perhaps these shine light into her personality. When we first met Zoe and Byron, she made sure to introduce him as 'professor', and then treated him with disdain."

"I never noticed."

"You probably didn't notice that you offended her when you failed to fuss over the wine they brought."

Jacob smiled. "I'm a terrible person."

"Remember the day I came to meet you for lunch?"

"Yes."

"Zoe and I chatted for a while and she confided that she wasn't all that happy with her marriage, wondering how we managed with our busy schedules. She told me about her passing interest in Jews for Jesus and Kabbalah."

"Bernie must have loved that."

"She knew he'd hate it, but made no attempt to hide it. I don't believe that she really understood how he felt about that, especially as a holocaust survivor."

"She's spoiled. Bernie said that he argued with Maury, his son, about giving her too much. Maybe she turned out to be a Jewish American Princess."

"I don't think so. Sure she's selfish and self-involved, but I see more."

Jacob stretched, and then shifted his position on the couch. "You've thought about this?"

"Yes. In my experience, there's a distinction between describing someone's personality characteristics and identifying them as psychopathology. Everyone can be selfish, paranoid, and a bit narcissistic, but that doesn't rise to the level of a psychiatric diagnosis. The threshold for diagnosis is disruption. When these characteristics lead to disruption of a life then we label them with a type of personality disorder."

"You think Zoe has a personality disorder?"

"I don't know, but I'm suspicious."

Jacob stared at the ceiling, shook his head, and then smiled. "Maybe you're right. I'm suspicious of any woman who doesn't appreciate her husband."

Chapter Forty-Six

My sessions with Sarah Hughes are going well, Lola thought. As if a weight lifted from her shoulders, Sarah progressed from depressed and withdrawn to lighthearted and optimistic. This morning, she bounded into Lola's office wearing shorts and a tank top. She virtually jumped into the soft easy chair across from Lola.

Lola smiled. "You look like you're in a good mood this morning."

"I feel great."

"Anything special happening?"

"No, but I'm finding joy in the simple things...the things that I dismissed before. Like last night, I went to dinner with the 'rents'. We talked and everything...no pressure...no lectures. It was terrific."

"Maybe they've learned something too." Lola rubbed her chin. "I'm a little out of touch, but when I hear the term 'rents' it sounds disdainful. Is it?"

"Maybe you're right, although I didn't mean it that way. It's the way kids talk about their parents, and most of the time it's not a compliment. I'll try to break the habit."

"How's it going at school?"

"You won't believe how cliquish school can be. Once I decided that hanging with my old friends was a bad idea, I took time to move into other groups, but with the clubs and the school newspaper, it's worked out okay."

"How did your old friends take it?"

"Those losers? They were pissed that I bailed on them, but I don't give a damn."

"What about Kelly Cowan? You guys were close."

Lola watched Sarah cross her arms in an embrace. It didn't take a psychotherapist to see the effect of that name on Sarah. The room suddenly grew colder. "I'm sorry, Sarah. Why are you upset at the mention of her name?"

"They talked to you about Kelly?"

"They, who?"

"My parents."

"Absolutely not. I told you I wouldn't talk with them behind your back. I knew about your friendship with Kelly from the girls in the program. They said you two were close."

"Yeah, until she went bonkers."

"You're sitting with a psychotherapist and you're criticizing a friend because she needed psychiatric help. I don't buy it, Sarah. What's going on?"

Sarah stood, and then walked to the window gazing out at the brick wall view. She clutched a lock of chestnut hair, twisting it repeatedly.

"Come on, Sarah. I get the message. If you start sucking on your thumb, I won't be able to stop myself from laughing."

Sarah returned to her chair, looked at her feet. "You can't talk to anyone about this, Lola. I'd die."

"Oh, please. You know that will never happen, and by the way, you're not going to tell me something I haven't heard a hundred times before."

Sarah raised her head and stared into Lola's eyes. "I'm a lesbian!"

Lola struggled to suppress her smile. "So, you're a lesbian. Big deal."

Sarah stared at Lola in surprise. "I mean, I think I'm a lesbian. Well, Kelly and me... you know."

"No, I'm afraid I don't know."

"We did it."

"Did what?"

"You know."

"You mean, do I know what lesbians do in their intimate moments? Of course, I do, but I don't know what you two did. Did you masturbate each other? Did you have oral sex? Did you?..."

"Enough," Sarah interrupted. "Nothing gross like that."

"You kissed?"

"Yes."

"You touched each other?"

"Yes."

"It felt good?"

"It felt great when we did it, but I felt awful after."

"Why?"

Sarah studied her feet. "Because it's wrong."

"Look at me, Sarah. Is it wrong in general or wrong for you?"

"I don't know. It feels wrong."

"I'll skip the big lecture. Many girls your age experiment with each other. For most, it's just that, experimentation. You may feel close to Kelly. You may love Kelly, but when you have your sexual fantasies, is it with boys or girls?"

"Boys."

"Who are you attracted to, boys, or girls?"

"Boys."

"I hate to tell you this, Sarah, but you're not a lesbian. You can throw away your 'lambda' tee shirts."

"Are you sure?"

"At this point in your life, I'm sure. Will you ever develop an interest in women or men and women, it's possible, but I doubt it. Whatever you do sexually, if the couple enjoys it, and nobody is injured or demeaned, it's okay by me."

They chatted for another twenty minutes, then Lola rose indicating the end of their session.

As they approached the door, Sarah embraced Lola. "Thank you. I feel so much better." After she released Lola, Sarah stood in thought. "When Carleton Dix found out about us, he told Kelly that she'd be writhing forever in the fires of Hell...that's part of what led to her breakdown, I think. It's difficult to believe that these vicious things could come from a man who lives his life by the tenets of the Bible. And, by the way, he also threatened to expose us."

"Jacob and I know, first hand, what those who subvert the Bible are capable of. If hell exists, Sarah, Carleton Dix and his ilk will find themselves right at home."

Chapter Forty-Seven

Jacob sat at the head of the table for the Quality Assurance meeting. "Is this really necessary?"

"I'm afraid so, Jacob," said Arnie Roth, the committee chairman.

"Are you going to give me a Miranda warning?"

Arnie, in spite of his decision to be all business, smiled. "You've reviewed physicians' practice and behavior before we had QA committees. It's an essential function for the medical staff. We all need to support it."

"You're right, of course," said Jacob, "but I'd like to know if this is pro-forma, following up on complaints, or does the committee have problems with the way I practice?"

"Both," said Warren Davidson, who'd come in his role as department chief. "The recent events at Brier have put us under additional pressure. We're looking at all adverse outcomes, especially unexpected deaths. A few of your patients fall into those categories."

Jacob shook his head in disbelief. "You want to know if I killed any of my patients. Should I call an attorney?"

"Don't get melodramatic on us, Jacob," said Warren. "We have some gripes with you...you know all about them, but nobody, except the bizarre Marion Krupp, thinks such a thing is possible."

Jacob stood. "Well, thank you gentlemen. I have work to do."

"Jacob, please," said Jack Byrnes. "Don't get sensitive in your old age. You know that everyone who watches you work only marvels at your abilities and experience."

Jacob shook his head, and then returned to his seat. He smiled. "See how easy it is to seduce me. Okay, let's have it."

Arnie opened his folder. "When we studied unexpected deaths or complications at Brier over the last eighteen months, among a few dozen, we came up with five of your cases: Shannon Hogan's death was a surprise to all, but we don't see evidence of foul play; P.J. Manning and Joshua Friedman were terminal. Note that I'm ignoring Marion Krupp's complaints."

"I appreciate that."

"Nathan Siegel and Harry Rodman are a different story. Both suffered complications of medications and Nathan Siegel died."

"You think I had something to do with their deaths?"

"Please, Jacob," said Warren. "We just want your help."

"It doesn't sound like it. You can't have it both ways. When I'm ultraconservative with medications, and ultra careful, you call me a therapeutic nihilist. Now your suggesting I've been careless with medications. Make up your minds."

"Are you going to help us or not?" said Arnie. "We can fight about philosophical differences in practice later."

"Of course I'll help," said Jacob.

"I'll ask you the same question I asked of the Siegel and the Rodman family," said Warren. "Do you know of any reason someone would set out to injure either patient?"

"No."

"Could someone be out to hurt you, Jacob, through your patients?"

Jacob adjusted his bow tie. "I can be annoying, for sure, but getting at me by hurting my patients, that's more than bizarre. I've had my run-ins with docs and a few nurses, but...no, I can't see it...sorry."

"Getting back to philosophical differences in using medications," said Warren, "it isn't merely a question of style."

Jacob studied Warren. "I'm not sure what you mean."

"Everyone respects you, Jacob, so when you take such an extreme position against medication, it makes us question our own practice. Nobody likes to think that they're wrong."

"That's not my intention," said Jacob as he stood. He cast his gaze on each member of the committee. "Look at this face. It's not pretty...hell, it never was an attractive face, but with the wrinkles, hopefully, comes an element of wisdom. I believe in an extraordinary level of wariness in prescribing medication and I'm equally skeptical about their effects. I practice the way I do because I believe in it, but I see that I've been a bad advocate for these principles by questioning the physician rather than the medication. That wasn't my intent."

"C'mon Jacob," said Jack, "controversy has been part and parcel of physician training forever. That's not the issue.

I see...we see great benefit in the use of the medications you disdain."

"Disdain isn't the right word, Jack. It's fear. Let me mention a few names: Fen-Phen, Propulsid, Vioxx, and DES among many. One study in the Journal of the American Medical Association showed that more than half of the dangerous side effects of drugs are detected only after they've been on the market for seven years or more."

"Medicine isn't perfect, Jacob," said Arnie.

"You're right, Arnie, but you're missing the point. In 2001, the drug companies used more than 600 lobbyists, outnumbering lawmakers. In 2002, they spent $22 million on campaign contributions and untold millions on advertising to the profession and directly to the public. Don't tell me they spent this much money without getting something in return."

The room remained silent.

Jacob scanned the room. "Let me ask you a question. Does anyone remember the name Frances Oldham Kelsey?"

"It sounds familiar," said Warren.

"It should. In 1960, Chemie Grünethal, a German Pharmaceutical firm, through an American company, applied to the FDA for approval of a drug. The approval wasn't expected to be controversial, but when it reached the desk of the FDA's newest reviewer, Frances Kelsey, she refused to clear it until she obtained better documentation of it effects and especially some reported neurologic effects. Despite increasing pressure, Kelsey held out for more toxicity studies until the effects of this medication on developing fetuses around the world became obvious.

In 1962, they awarded Kelsey the President's Award for Distinguished Federal Civilian Service for preventing thousands of deformities in the United States from the drug thalidomide."

Jacob stood, then headed for the door. He turned to face the group. "Do you know what would happen to a Frances Oldham Kelsey in today's FDA? They'd fire her ass."

Chapter Forty-Eight

Terry Wilcox leaned back in his office chair with his legs raised on the desk. He looked out the window at the falling South Dakota snow and sighed.

This sure ain't California.

The ringing phone shook him out of his reverie. "Wilcox Detective Agency," resounded his bass voice.

"Terrence, is that you?"

"Who wants to know?"

"It's Jacob Weizman. What's the matter, is business so bad you have to answer your own phone?"

"Hey, Doc, I was just thinking about warm California. It's sure great to hear your voice. Are you in town?"

"No, Terry. You know I never go north of latitude 37 degrees."

"The family really misses you, Doc. We've seen a few jokers in this town, but nothing the likes of you."

"You're too kind. How's Sally and the kids?"

"They're great, except they hate Sioux Falls, especially in winter. If I get the chance, we'll head back to the bay area in a flash."

"I was wondering if I could impose on you, Terry?"

"Impose away. We can never repay you for your help and especially your kindness and understanding."

"Do you work elsewhere than Sioux Falls?"

"Anywhere the money takes me, Doc. What can I do for you?"

"I need background information on someone who worked in Rapid City. Do you go that far?"

"Been there many times. What do you need?"

"I want to know about a man named Carleton Dix who had a ministry in Rapid City. I want to know all about him, and I'd like to know why he left."

"When was he there?"

"The mid nineties, I'd guess."

"How quickly do you need the information?"

"A few days would be okay. Can you do it?"

"I can have the basics in a day, but the dirt...I'm guessing you want the dirt, will take a little longer."

"I never thought of myself as being in the position of digging up dirt on anybody. It feels..."

"Slimy? Yeah, Doc, it's the nature of the business. Often when I get home, my first act is to head for a hot shower."

"What's it going to cost me, Terry?"

"It's on the house, Doc."

"I can't let you do that."

"You don't have a choice, but you can do one thing for us."

"Of course."

"Promise you'll live long enough for us to return to your practice."

"I'll do the best I can."

Just as Jacob placed the receiver into its cradle, Margaret knocked on his door, then entered.

"What's up?"

"I had to sign for this, Jacob. I hope it's all right."

She handed him the thick envelope and when he saw the return address, Malvin & Lutz, Attorneys at Law, he knew that he'd been served.

"This is just what I need."

"What is it?"

"Another damn lawsuit. We managed to practice for fifty years before I got my first malpractice suit. It's not because I'm perfect, I'm not. It's not because I don't make mistakes, I do, and it's not because tragedy hadn't hit our patients unexpectedly, it has."

"You may think that it's all luck, Jacob, but I know better. Our patients always knew, they were certain, that you were on their side and felt their losses almost as much as they did."

"Maybe. At first, I took each lawsuit personally. I refused to accept that any of my patients believed the things alleged in their complaints."

"They didn't and still don't," said Margaret. "It's money, greed or opportunistic trial lawyers. Don't take it personally."

"I don't know any other way to take it," he said, holding up that first fifteen-page complaint. "If any of this is true, they should have me on the first boat back to Austria."

Jacob stared at the envelope. He grabbed his cherry wood letter opener and pulled out the thick bundle of pages. He scanned the first few pages. "It's about Nathan Seigel, a wrongful death suit, from the plaintiff, the estate of Nathan Siegel and from his daughter Patricia Seigel Clark."

"I didn't know he had another daughter," said Margaret.

"Not one that he ever talked about."

"How many years did we treat him? How many times did you run into the hospital in the middle of the night? And, how often did Patricia Seigel call in to find out how her father was doing? It makes me sick to think that she's suing you now."

"Well, Margie, we're in good company. She's suing Brier Hospital, Sharon Brickman, Zoe Spelling, Ahmad Kadir, Kate Planchette, and my favorite 'one hundred unnamed physicians'. I think they simply listed all the names that appeared on any of his charts."

"Has Zoe been sued before?" asked Margaret.

"I don't think so. I hope this doesn't upset her too much. She needs to deal with this, it's part of medical practice today."

When Jacob brought the papers in for Zoe, she grabbed them. She studied each page, then placed it face down on her desk. After she finished the last page, she reddened. "What a load of crap."

"It's okay, Zoe. Don't tell me that you're a malpractice virgin?"

"No...I mean yes...I mean...I never saw Nathan during that last hospitalization. Why me? It's not right...I didn't do anything."

"Right or wrong, guilty or not guilty, responsible or not responsible, none of it has meaning in a medical malpractice case. You'd better get used to it."

Ida Rosenthal hated hospitals, the idea of hospitals, their smell, their uncertainty, their threat. Of the last three people she knew who were admitted to Brier Hospital, only one came home.

If she hadn't fallen, hitting her head and fracturing her hip, they'd have never gotten her past the Emergency Room doors. At the age of eighty, this was only her third stay in a hospital, each time before she returned home with a baby. Now, if she survived, she'd return home with a walker.

"All that security frightens the hell out of me," she said to her nurse. "I don't like to think about all that stuff in the newspapers about a serial killer."

"Don't worry, Mrs. Rosenthal," said the nurse. "Nobody can get near you who doesn't belong. Do you need anything for sleep?"

"A couple of codeine pills would be nice. They make that hip pain disappear."

Ida dozed into the early hours, waking every forty-five minutes to an hour. She'd look around wide-eyed then managed to fall asleep. When she last stared at the clock, the red LED's read 2:45 a.m. She must have nodded off because when she opened her eyes, she saw the dark shadow bent over in the corner of the room doing something.

Is this real or am I dreaming?

"Who's there?" she tried to say, shaking her head awake, but her mouth, lips and tongue were cotton dry.

"Desculpe-me, señora," came the thick, coarse voice.

"Who!

"What!

"Leave me alone!" she screamed as the shadow moved closer to the bed, then, "No...No...No!"

Suddenly the room flooded with intense overhead light as the nurse and the uniformed policeman entered.

"Yo no hice nada," screamed the middle-aged janitor, standing with his back against the wall, a plastic bag filled with garbage in one hand. "I didn't do nothin'."

"Don't move," ordered the policeman as he turned the janitor to face the wall. He quickly frisked him. "He's clean."

The nurse held Ida as she cowered in bed. "It's all right. He's just the janitor...it's all right, he won't hurt you."

Afterward, the policeman released the janitor and said to the nurse, "For Christ's sake, don't let these guys skulk around in the dark. With the tension around here, someone's going to get hurt."

Chapter Forty-Nine

I nod and smile, returning the friendly greetings in the corridors of Brier Hospital, hiding in plain sight.

Security is everywhere, an index of my recent successes. They're delusional if they think this will slow me from my work ahead.

It's amazing, I think. The opportunities to offer eternal salvation fall gratuitously at my feet. He's guiding me—that's enough.

I share with them the final release and the ecstasy of their last moments.

It's addictive. I need more.

When I walk through the Skilled Nursing Facility, my eyes fix on the name Harry Rodman, room 434, flashing brightly on the white board listing the patients' names.

The door to 434 is open as I pass by. Visitors surround Harry's bed.

I'm impatient, but not stupid.

We'll meet again, Harry...and very soon. I promise.

The box, gift-wrapped with pink flowers, sat on the roof of Sarah Hughes's car after school.

A secret admirer?

She smiled, then lifted and gently shook the box. It was light and rattled slightly.

Sarah sat in the driver's seat and placed the box on her lap, then began removing the wrapping, taking care to preserve the beautiful decorated paper, a habit inherited from her mother, Marilyn. She lifted the lid, then saw the green tissue paper wrapping. Lifting it, Sarah saw the bloody arm, a baby's bloody arm, then the legs and the head severed from the doll's body. She gasped, pushed open the door and threw up on the pavement.

Sarah reached Lola that evening at home. "I've got to see you."

"What kind of sick son-of-a-bitch sends you such a thing?" Jacob asked as he and Lola sat with a distraught Sarah.

"Carleton Dix," said Lola. "I wouldn't put it past him. He's just sick enough."

Lola rocked Sarah. "It's going to be all right, sweetheart. I know how upsetting this is, but it's just the reaction they intended. It's hate propaganda of the worst form, the vile voices of those who vindicate their beliefs by the violation of others."

Sarah trembled. "I thought it was a real baby."

"I'm taking this to the police," said Jacob. "Maybe their forensics lab can tell us who's responsible."

The next afternoon in the office, Margaret entered Jacob's consultation room. "I have Terrence Wilcox on the line. He says he needs to speak with you. Are he and his lovely family coming back to the bay area?"

"Not right now, but I think they've had enough of the South Dakota winters."

Jacob waited until Margaret left the room, then picked up the flashing line.

"That was quick," said Jacob.

"We're just getting into it, Jacob, but I'm seeing a lot of smoke rising over the Rapid City skyline, pardon the expression."

"Smoke?"

"Right now, all I have is rumor and innuendo, but I have a contact in the DA's office and we should have more information soon. This is what I know: Carleton Dix was a popular minister at First Rapid City United for five years. Then one day, the president of the church announced that Pastor Dix had left for personal reasons. When Sissy Preston, a fifteen-year-old girl, suddenly moved to San Diego to live with her aunt, the gossip remained about sexual abuse, pregnancy, and an abortion. The news flooded the town like a summer storm. Rumor had it, that the Pastor took a personal interest in several other young women. The Pennington County District Attorney interviewed several teenage girls."

"Can you get those records?"

"Not a chance. They're sealed, Jacob. Why all the interest in this character?"

"He's the director of Pastoral Care at Brier Hospital."

Terry's laugh made Jacob uncomfortable. "A hospital chaplain...great choice, Jacob. Great choice. The next thing you'll tell me is that he works with a group of teenage girls."

Zoe Spelling stood her dripping umbrella in the rack, then hung her raincoat on a hook in the vestibule, and sang out, "I'm home, Byron."

Without an answer, she moved into the kitchen and spread the mail over the table. "Byron?"

Zoe glanced at her watch, 7:30 p.m. Where's Byron?

Just then, she heard the beep of the answering machine that showed one message in a blinking LED window. She pressed play and heard Byron's voice: "I tried to reach you at the hospital, but I guess you didn't hear your page. I have a faculty meeting tonight that should keep me out until ten or eleven. See you later. Love ya."

All of a sudden he's having meetings of one sort or another.

Zoe hung up her suit and changed into shorts and a Cal Berkeley, Go Bears sweatshirt. She stared at Byron's side of the closet and his row of suits and thought, don't be ridiculous, Zoe...there's no reason to be suspicious.

She slid each suit on the support rack then started to leave. Before she reached the door, she changed her mind and returned to the nearest suit, his only Armani. Looking over her shoulder furtively, she placed her hand into each pocket and then the inside jacket pocket finding nothing.

Why are you doing this? What's the matter with you? This is stupid.

Compelled by forces she was unable to control, Zoe continued to search each suit in turn until she reached the next to last one where, in the breast pocket, she found a pack of matches. Palming it in her hand, she moved into the light of their bedroom where she saw the embossed "W.P.H." the Waterfront Plaza Hotel that overlooked Jack London Square.

Zoe felt flushed and a little dizzy as she sat on their bed studying the matchbook.

Don't do this, she thought...and whispered, "Byron, how could you do this to me?"

The clock read 10:45 p.m. when she heard their front door open.

When he entered their bedroom, she lay with her back to him. He whispered, "Are you awake?"

She kept her breathing regular as she listened to him change for bed, brush his teeth, then slide into bed beside her.

You won't get away with this, my love, she thought.

Sixty seconds later, she heard his regular breathing and irritating snore.

Chapter Fifty

When Shelly Kahn and a uniformed patrolman arrived at Milo and Angelina Cass's home, nobody answered the doorbell or their repeated knocks.

A passing neighbor pointed to the driveway. "I think he's in the back."

Shelly and the patrolman walked up the driveway toward the garage. They heard movement from within and when they entered, the tall thin man in overalls jerked up, banging his head on the raised hood.

"Shit!" he said, holding his head.

"Milo Cass?" asked Shelly.

"Who wants to know?"

Shelly pulled her coat away from her belt exposing her badge and her service revolver. "Shelly Kahn, Berkeley P.D., and this," she said signaling the officer to enter, is patrolman Hastings. "We'd like a word with you."

Milo wiped the grease from his hands, then sat on a stack of used tires. "Well, make it fast."

"Where were you the night Angelina got so sick?"

"Got sick," he cackled, "she's always sick."

"Don't play games with us, Milo."

"I was right here."

"Can you prove it?"

"Can you prove where you slept last night?"

Shelly continued, "It's common knowledge in the neighborhood that you and Angelina didn't get along."

"I wished them damn people would mind their own fucking business."

"Milo?"

"Shit yeah, we didn't get along. Big deal. I've had it with that bitch. Don't expect me to shed any tears over that loser. She's always in and out of the hospital and I'm plain sick of it."

"Since you don't have an alibi, I think we better continue this downtown."

"Now wait just a minute," he said pointing a grease-stained finger at Shelly. "I didn't want to say nothing, but I had company that night."

"Company?"

He wiped his face with a oil-stained rag. "You know...a lady friend."

"Does she have a name?"

"Misty...Candy...damned if I know. Met her in a bar in Oakland."

"What bar?"

"I don't like this shit. Maybe I need a lawyer," he said pacing and looking into the right rear corner of the garage.

Shelly's eyes followed his glance to a shelf on which stood an open container of antifreeze.

When Shelly's eyes returned to Milo's, he made a sudden sprint for the open door only to meet Hastings who grabbed him by his overalls. "You ain't goin' nowhere buddy."

"Cuff him," said Shelly, "and read him his rights."

"Got good news for you, chief."

"I could use it."

"We arrested Milo Cass for attempted murder this afternoon. Once he started talking, we couldn't shut him up. He hated Angelina and got the idea from a TV episode of E.R.. He snuck into her room and pushed three syringe-fulls of antifreeze into her feeding tube."

"Brier Hospital's going to give a great sigh of relief," said Ira.

Word of the arrest flashed through Brier.

"That's great news," Bruce Bryant said to Warren Davidson and Jack Byrnes. "Finally, we can get things back to normal."

Warren looked at Jack and shook his head. He turned back to Bruce. "You must be kidding. You think that Milo Cass, an auto mechanic, wandered through Brier Hospital, unseen. That he killed or tried to kill our patients with morphine, Lidocaine and heparin. That's pretty sophisticated stuff for someone without medical knowledge."

"You can learn anything on the Internet," said Bruce.

"Don't live in a dream world," said Jack. "We have an attempted murderer, but someone's out there a lot smarter and much more dangerous."

Tommy Wells walked toward Kelly's Bar, glancing down at his new black Adler slip-on shoes. Four hundred bucks. A few more with the habit of Morgan Ferris and I'll get that Porsche, he thought.

When Tommy rounded the corner, he came to a complete stop.

The Oakland Police cruiser sat in front of Kelly's bar, blue lights flashing. A moment later, Morgan Ferris, hands cuffed behind his back and a policeman on each arm, bent over to enter the police car's rear door.

As the officer placed his hand over Morgan's head to protect it, Morgan's eyes widened as they met with Tommy's.

Tommy turned and walked away. I'm screwed. They're going to want his supplier...he'll make a deal. I'm fucked.

One more score...a big one...right away, then I'm out of here.

Chapter Fifty-One

Jacob looked for an opportunity to sit and talk with Zoe. It was unlike him to procrastinate on anything, especially things that involved his practice or people he cared about. Jacob couldn't see much of himself in Zoe. In many ways they were polar opposites.

Maybe I've been projecting, one of Lola's favorite words, too much on Zoe as my legacy, the guardian for a sixty-year practice.

He watched her in the office and on rounds in the hospital. He read her notes with particular attention to her thoroughness. He made subtle inquiries of physicians who worked with her and patients she treated.

"She's great! A real asset to your practice, Jacob," said several physicians.

Questioning patients about Zoe was more difficult, no less interrogating them, but Jacob got a series of reactions: "I love Dr. Spelling, Doc...don't take it personally, but it's nice to have a woman physician for a change. Smart as hell, and great to look at, too. Good move, Doc. It's great knowing she's around. And, sometimes her mind seems elsewhere, Doc. Maybe she's overworked."

At the end of a busy afternoon, Jacob knocked on Zoe's office and stuck his head in. "I have a few things to do, then can we sit for a minute and talk?"

"Why sure, Jacob. Is anything wrong?"

"You drink decaf? I'll make a pot and meet you in the lounge."

"Decaf's fine."

Zoe listened to the 'goodnights', the 'see you in the mornings', as the last of the staff left for the day. She entered the lounge to the smell of freshly brewing coffee. She sat on the aging sofa, picked out a magazine, but only stared at the pages, unable to read. After a few minutes, she stood and paced, becoming agitated. Just when she decided to seek him out, Jacob arrived.

"Sorry to keep you waiting. I was on the phone with a patient about to lose it. It took me a while to bring her down."

"I don't know how you still have the patience for that after all these years."

"It's no different from looking at a throat or prescribing antibiotics, Zoe. It's giving patients what they need."

"What did you want to see me about?"

"Have a seat. I only want to take a few minutes to see how you're doing...how we're doing."

Zoe sat on the sofa's edge twisting a lock of hair. "Have I done something wrong? Is anyone complaining about me?"

"You're a sophisticated woman, Zoe. I don't expect perfection from myself or anyone else. You can bet that one time or another, the world will blame you for what you do right and praise you for what you did wrong. That's why Lola says the only critic that counts is the one in here. " He pointed at his head.

"I still don't know why we're having this conversation."

"People have noticed that you seem troubled. They don't know if it's personal or professional, and I'm not sure that it's any of my business."

"What people?" Zoe's face began burning.

"I'm not making this a matter of personality, Zoe. I've noticed, as have others, that something's affecting your work."

"My work. Who's complaining about my work?"

"How are things at home?"

"What's that got to do with anything?"

"God damn it, Zoe! I'm trying to help you. I don't want to be your shrink. I'm your partner and your friend. If that's not enough for you," Jacob said rising, "then goodnight."

Zoe choked over each breath. She reached for Jacob's arm. "No...don't...I'm sorry, it's just..."

"It's just what?"

"I only want to please you, and Lola too. You're the kind of person...the kind of doctor I've always wanted to be."

"You've heard the term 'feet of clay'? It's Biblical, you know."

"I know. It's from the Book of Daniel."

"You know your Bible," said Jacob then he continued, "I have my faults and like any thoughtful person, I want people to appreciate me as a real person, not as fantasy. I've made my mistakes...you've seen some yourself."

Jacob hesitated. "These are our observations: You make promises to staff and patients, then you don't keep them. You don't return patient phone calls. You slough off reports and letters to me...I really don't need the extra work, and your interest in your patients goes from disinterest to dismissive. You've got to know how I feel about that."

"That's unfair...I'm trying so hard..."

"I'm not sure that I want you to respond to these observations. The last thing I want you to do is go on the defensive. Something's going on with you, Zoe. I know it. People you work with know it, and I think you must know it too."

"Maybe I should resign."

Jacob ran his hand over his scalp. "That's great. You want to take the easy way out. For what? What's so terrible that you're unwilling or unable to work out some simple problems?"

Zoe's eyes focused on a point behind Jacob. With shoulders rolled forward and neck muscles taut, she looked like a spring stretched to its breaking point. "Jacob, I can't talk...If you only knew what I'm going through..."

"I'm trying to help you like a father."

"I know. Since we first met, I thought of you as a grandfather...no, a father is more accurate.

"If you can't talk to me, talk to Lola or have her refer you to someone who can help. We love you, Zoe. The last thing we want is to lose you."

Chapter Fifty-Two

Carleton Dix had finished his last counseling session of the day.

I'm sure glad that one's over, he thought. How much teenage whining I can take?

Carleton Dix's secretary came to his door. "I have a woman on the phone, chaplain. She refuses to identify herself."

"What's it about?"

"She says she's an old friend from up north."

"It's okay. I'll take the call."

He pushed the flashing line button. "Reverend Dix. How can I help you?"

"My, my, how formal. Is that the way to treat a special old friend?"

"My God...Rita, is it really you?"

"In the flesh, and it's good to hear those soothing tones again. It's been a while. We really miss you up here, especially on those cold winter nights. How are you doing in the land of Sodom and Gomorrah?"

"Saving souls...lots to save down here. I hope your call means you've decided to come here for a vacation. I would enjoy seeing you."

"I bet you would," she purred. "Sorry, but right now First Rapid City United couldn't survive without me. I have talents."

"I hope you're not employing those talents at work, Rita."

"No. I'm exploring other, less risky venues."

"Well, what can I do for you?"

"No reverend, it's what can I do for you. Is everything okay in Berkeley?"

"Why do you ask?"

"I'm afraid a private investigator, Terrence Wilcox from Sioux Falls, has managed to open old wounds with his questions about you and your interlude with us."

He felt a hollow cramp sensation in the pit of his stomach and began sweating. "What did you tell him?"

"Me, I told him nothing, but he had conversations with the president of the church, several elders, county social services, and with the police. I think, my friend, that old faucets leak, no matter how hard you try to tighten them."

Please, dear God, the chaplain thought, stunned into silence.

After a minute, Rita said, "Are you still there?"

"Yes, Rita. This is terrible news."

"Adios, chaplain. Give me a call sometime from wherever your travels take you."

When Byron Harwood pulled into the driveway, he was surprised to see Zoe's car. He checked his watch, 6:30 p.m. He couldn't remember her getting home before 8:00 p.m. in the last year. Byron grasped the knob to the door leading from the garage to the kitchen. It turned, but he had to push hard before it opened. Got to fix that damn door.

He lifted his nose in the hope that Zoe had prepared dinner, but sensed instead, cigarette smoke and trouble. "Zoe, I'm home," he yelled.

He put his briefcase on the kitchen table and walked through the house. After checking the upstairs bedroom and the den, he retraced his step. Through the patio windows, he saw rising wisps of cigarette smoke.

"Hey, sweetheart, didn't you hear me come in?"

Zoe took a long drag on her cigarette, and then looked away. "I'm sorry. What did you say?"

"I thought you stopped smoking."

"I did."

"You're home early. Is everything okay?"

She turned to face him. Her eyes were red, but cold. "Who is she?"

"What are you talking about?"

"Please, Byron. Don't insult my intelligence. Just tell me who she is."

"Please, Zoe," he said approaching her. He reached for her hand, but she jerked it away.

"Don't...don't touch me."

"Have you been drinking?"

"How could you do this to me? After all we've been through together. How could you?"

"This is absurd, Zoe. I won't know what you're thinking until you say it."

"Why is the wife the last one to know? Tell me about The Waterfront Plaza Hotel."

"I still don't know what you're talking about. What about the hotel?"

"I know you've been there with her. Why lie about it now?"

Byron's head was spinning. "Of course I know the hotel. We had dinner there once about a year ago, and I met Lynda, our accountant, there several weeks ago for lunch...a business lunch."

Zoe's eyes widened. "You thought I wouldn't notice the late meetings, the weekend retreats, and the trips out of town. I'm not an idiot!"

"Please calm down, Zoe. The neighbors will hear you."

"I don't give a shit...let them...let them know who you are, what you are."

"You're out of control. I'm calling Jacob."

"You're not calling anybody. Now get out before I call the police."

"Zoe, please. Don't do this. I've never thought of cheating on you...you must know that."

"I only know that I want you out of here, and I mean now."

Byron raised his hands in surrender, and then slowly backed away. "I'm leaving now. I'll be at the faculty club. I'll call you in the morning to see if you're okay."

Zoe stood. Her eyes blazed with rage. "Just shut up and get out."

Chapter Fifty-Three

Sarah Hughes tossed in bed, switching from one side to the other, unable to find a comfortable position. Beads of perspiration bloomed on her forehead and upper lip. She turned back the blanket, leaving only the top sheet.

She must have slept, because when she opened her eyes the red LEDs of the alarm clock were flashing 12:00...another power outage. Sarah reached for her pillow, and as she slid her left arm under its softness, it passed over something warm and slimy. She reached further under the pillow and felt something firm caught in a fold of the pillow case...what is that? Her hand grasped the object and when she turned on the bedside lamp, she saw the tiny fingers of the bloody severed hand. Sarah raised her blood soaked hands and heard an unearthly scream...it was coming from her.

"Wake up...wake up," cried Marilyn. "You're having a bad dream. Mama's here."

Sarah sobbed in her mother's arms. "It was horrible. The blood, it was everywhere...and the arm."

"It's okay," said Robert. "It was only a nightmare."

Sarah was still shaken when her alarm clock sounded the next morning. She showered and dressed, then noticed the flashing icon on her computer screen indicating new email. The first two were reminders from friends about their outing this weekend, the third was her Spanish word of the day, but the fourth labeled URGENT came from her own email address. That must be some sort of mistake.

When she opened the email, the words flashed on the screen in large red letters: LYING LIPS ARE AN ABOMINATION TO THE LORD (Proverbs XII, V.22), then near the bottom of the screen: HELL IS THE WRATH OF GOD—HIS HATE OF SIN (P.J. Bailey).

Sarah printed off a hard copy.

Who had access to my e-mail account, she thought. How had they discovered my password?

They think I'm a sociopath. That's a laugh.

He'll get caught, they say. That kind of lunatic pushes and pushes until he achieves his objective: to be caught...to be stopped.

The halls of Brier Hospital create a casino of discovery for my wagers, the fortuitous flings of life's fortunes. Chance rules, but my mission sets the odds.

I search for the names, the patients, their physicians and try to assess their karma.

The heightened security makes travel through Brier difficult, for most, but not for me.

I haven't forgotten you, Harry Rodman.

I look around.

The hallway is empty.

I start back for his room when the bathroom door opens and his wife returns to his bedside.

I keep walking.

Not to worry my friend. Your luck can't hold out forever. Nothing worthwhile comes easily.

We'll meet again soon.

"They want to do what?" cried Jacob.

Mark Whitson refused to meet Jacob's eyes. "The DA has ordered the exhumation of Shannon Hogan and P.J. Manning."

"That's absurd, and worse, it's cruel to families who have suffered enough. I won't have it."

"You don't have a choice. I think it's a long shot too, Jacob, but two of your cases, Nathan Seigel and Harry Rodman, are likely victims of this killer. Then we have Joshua Friedman."

"If you mention Marion Krupp and her bizarre charges..."

Mark shook his head. "Easy, Jacob, this has nothing to do with Marion. We went back over Joshua's blood and Jacob, the levels of morphine are way beyond what anyone would use to control pain in the most difficult terminal patient.

"Don't take this wrong, old friend," he continued, "but it's in your interest to clarify the precise causes of death in these patients. So far, seven deaths popped up in our screening, and Jacob, five of them belong to you."

Chapter Fifty-Four

Carleton Dix didn't hear it at first as he sat with his head down on his desk, eyes closed. The soft tapping, more urgent now, caught his attention. He raised his head, straightened his collar.

"Come in."

The door opened slowly and Kelly Cowan entered. She stared at the floor. "Do you have a few minutes, Reverend?"

"This isn't a good time, Kelly. Is it important?"

"No, it's all right." She turned for the door. Tears streamed down her cheeks.

He shook his head in frustration. "Come on, Kelly. It's okay. Let's sit for a moment and find out what's wrong."

She grabbed a tissue from his desk and blew her nose, then sat in the middle of the sofa, knees together and arms crossed.

He rolled his desk chair in front of her, then stood and locked the door. When he returned to his chair, he reached for her cheek and caressed it. "We won't be interrupted. Now, tell me what has you so upset?"

She held her face. "I know something's wrong and I want to help. You must let me help."

"I don't know what you're talking about."

"People are talking. They're looking at me funny. I think they know."

"Nobody knows anything. What happened between us is secret. I didn't tell anyone, did you?"

She blew her nose and wiped the tears gaining control. "Of course not. I love you. I want to be with you. Let's go away together."

"I'm sorry, Kelly, but that's not going to happen. I'm fond of you and thought our little get-togethers would help you. I tried to support you...as a friend."

"A friend?" she breathed deeply. "Friends don't do what we did. I was a virgin...I gave myself to you. You can't dismiss me this way."

"I'm not dismissing you, Kelly. I have great affection for you, but now's not the time for us to expand our relationship. I'm under pressure. Things are going on...things you know nothing about...things that can hurt both of us. If you care for me, the best way to show it is by trusting me."

She stood, then wrapped her arms around him. "I love you. I'll do anything you want me to do. I'll protect you in any way I can. Just love me a little in return."

He kissed her on the lips. "This is the kind of thing we must avoid for a while. A hint of impropriety could spell the end for me."

Carleton walked her to the door. "I'll call your cell when I have the chance."

After the door closed, Carleton returned to his desk thinking it's out of control. How long can I hold her off? Who's making these inquiries, and what do they want?

Jacob drove home for lunch. Edna Charles's Lincoln Navigator sat in the driveway.

Three salad bowls, heaped full, sat on the kitchen table. Lola and Edna, deep in conversation, didn't notice him until he coughed.

Lola smiled at Jacob. "Hey, look who's here."

"We tried to put her out of our misery when she visited at Brier," said Jacob, "but that's one tough old lady."

He bent over Edna and gave her a firm hug.

"Easy, Jacob. I'm not that tough."

"How are you feeling?"

"Is that a professional or a personal inquiry?"

"Your choice."

"You know, I really love what you and Brier Hospital do, but the place gives me the creeps."

She took a sip of iced tea. "It's not just that I'm old...who at our age doesn't think of where it will all end, it's something else.

"The first morning, when I awakened in the bright light streaming through my window. I felt spacey and had the urge to walk into the light...what a cliché. I shook my head, smiled and thought not yet, damn it, not yet.

"I remember the somber scenes in the movies when the safari comes into a hidden clearing filled with bones and ivory tusks, the skeletal remains of the elephants who, when it's their time, find the way to the elephants' burial ground. I've always found that image particularly poignant and sad. Whatever you say, Jacob, you won't find me plodding my way back to Brier when it's my time. You'll make sure that won't happen."

"Just make sure I outlive you, Edna."

Lola turned to Jacob. "Did Edna tell you about her visit by your favorite chaplain?"

"You have a mean streak, Lola," said Edna. "Let the poor man eat his lunch in peace."

Jacob plopped himself into a kitchen chair. "What visit?"

"It was no big deal. The man meant well, but religious dogma...if my hip wasn't broken, I'd have sprinted for the door."

"I told that guy to keep away from my patients. What's the matter with him?"

"I don't think he can help himself," said Lola. "He has the zeal of the true believer, and Jacob, my love, you are anathema to everything he cherishes. That's why you two get along so well."

"For most of my youth," said Jacob, "I embraced a live and let live philosophy, until the men in brown, the Nazis, convinced me otherwise. Nobody can separate ideas from behavior, that's what makes the religious fanatics dangerous."

"You're too hard on the man," said Edna. "He carries the burden of an evangelical imprimatur...serious business for a minister."

"That's why I keep away from the topic of religion," said Jacob. "Every time I open my mouth a wisecrack forces its way out. I've seen, first hand, how religion comforts people, and I have the greatest respect for those who have devoted their lives to helping others..."

"I'm waiting for the but..." said Lola.

"What I cannot stomach is evil cloaked in the vestments of religion, and in the case of the good chaplain, his incredible hypocrisy."

"What hypocrisy?"

"Later," said Jacob.

Chapter Fifty-Five

Jacob and Lola sat reading in their matching La-Z-Boy chairs when the doorbell rang.

"Get me my rifle," said Jacob, "just in case it's someone out to save our souls."

"Oh no you don't." Lola smiled. "Use the baseball bat. The last time, it took me a week to get the blood off the porch." She stood. "I'll get the door."

"No, it's all right...we're out of ammunition anyway."

Jacob switched on the porch light then peered through the peep hole and saw Byron Harwood, Zoe's husband. "Byron, what a surprise. Come in."

Byron's eyes moved wildly. His face was drawn and he hadn't shaved for several days.

"I'm sorry to bother you, Jacob," he stuttered. "I had to talk with somebody."

Lola joined them at the door. "It's okay. Come in. Sit. I'll make coffee."

They moved to the great room. Byron sat on the sofa. "Did Zoe speak to you?"

"No," said Jacob. "If anything, she's been quieter than usual. What happened?"

"I'm not really sure, but she believes that I'm having an affair." He paused, staring alternately at Jacob and Lola. "I'm not. I love Zoe and I've never been unfaithful."

Lola studied Byron. "She must have some reason to come to that conclusion."

"That's the weird part, Lola. Sure, I've been out at meetings lately and away several weekends, but it was all business and nothing but."

While Lola stared at Byron, Jacob formed the image of Lola as Superman with x-ray vision, as she pried into the soul of the man.

Byron looked up to meet her eyes. "And there was the matchbook."

"The matchbook?" Jacob asked.

"It was nothing. Just a matchbook from a hotel in Jack London Square. I was there for a business lunch with our accountant. To Zoe, it was proof positive of cheating."

"There must be more," said Lola.

"Nothing. She won't talk to me. She won't let me explain." His eyes filled with desperation. "You've got to talk to her, Jacob. She'll listen to you. She worships you."

"Jacob will talk with her tomorrow," said Lola. "We'll get to the bottom of this."

Just before noon the next day, Jacob stepped into Zoe's office, closing the door behind.

"Oh, Jacob. Is everything okay?"

"Byron came to see us last night."

Zoe tightened her lips. "I'm so sorry, Jacob. He shouldn't have done that. I apologize for involving you in our sordid little mess."

"Don't be sorry. If we can help, we want to."

"Nothing can help, Jacob. It's too late."

"You don't talk much about your personal life, Zoe. I respect that, but Byron...he's quite convincing. Lola and I believe him when he denies having an affair."

"It's not your problem, Jacob. You've said it yourself a thousand times: Nobody knows what goes on between a couple in the privacy of their home."

"Dismiss me if you will, but find somebody to help you two out."

"I'm not dismissing you...God, no. I'd never do that. But there are things...too many things..."

"I've offered Lola's services before, Zoe. Talk with her or have her make a referral. Lola's good at what she does. I know she can help."

"I'm sorry, Jacob. I'm just not that big on psychotherapists. Too much of it is a waste of time."

"I don't know what kind of shrinks you've dealt with before but I assure Lola is unique. Think about it."

Later that same afternoon, Margaret Cohen knocked on Jacob's door. "It's Bruce Bryant's office. He's having a meeting at 5:30 this afternoon. Can you make it?"

"Of course."

Jacob walked in light drizzle to Brier and entered the administration offices through the ornate portico. When he reached Bryant's office, the door was closed.

His secretary turned to Jacob. "Have a seat, Dr. Weizman. Mr. Bryant will be just a moment."

After five minutes, the door opened and Bruce appeared. "Dr. Weizman. Please join us."

It surprised Jacob to see Warren Davidson, Mark Whitson, Sharon Brickman, Ira Green, Jack Byrnes, and a young woman.

"I don't know if you know Ira Green, he's chief of the Berkeley P.D., and this is his investigator, Shelly Kahn."

"I know Ira like nobody does, I delivered him." Jacob turned to Warren. "What's going on?"

Bruce pointed to the chair next to Mark Whitson. "Have a seat, Doctor. You need to hear this."

"What is it, Mark?" Jacob asked.

Mark clutched a manila folder. "We have the autopsy results from the exhumation of Shannon Hogan and P.J. Manning. Both were murdered!"

"Murdered? That's insane," cried Jacob grabbing the arms of his chair to steady himself.

Warren leaned forward. "Are you all right?"

"I'm okay...I...I can't believe what I'm hearing. Are you sure, Mark?"

"You think I like telling you this? Your patients were killed. Murdered. Shannon Hogan with the muscle blocker acetylcholine, and P.J. Manning with insulin."

Jacob paled. "Oh my God. Shannon and P.J., I just can't believe it. What son-of-a bitch would do such a thing?"

"Jacob. Jacob. Think for a moment. It can't be coincidental that five of seven cases in your care were victims. Somebody is unhappy with you, and your patients are paying the price."

"Paying the price?" Jacob whispered. "Who hates me so much that they kill the innocent?"

"That's the million-dollar question," said Ira Green. "We need your help to find the answer."

When Marion Krupp returned home from work, it surprised her to see the family room empty.

"Abby," she called. "Mommy's home."

With no response, Marion rushed up the stairs to Abby's room where she found her asleep. She sat next to her daughter, placed her hand on the child's head and reflexly removed it.

She's on fire!

She shook her daughter. The little girl moaned, then gradually opened her eyes and smiled. "Mommy, you're home."

"What are you doing in bed, sweetheart?"

"I don't feel good, Mommy. I feel hot and my head hurts."

Marion, like most health professionals, mentally ran through a list of diagnoses, starting with the gravest first. Maybe it's meningitis or encephalitis. She called her pediatrician, Michael Butler, reported Abby's symptoms and fever of 102 degrees, and answered each question with a 'no'.

"It sounds like a virus, Marion. We're seeing a lot of it around. Let's watch her for a day or so. It's likely to pass."

Marion remained tense, but felt reassured. Two days passed and Abby wasn't any better.

Abby coughed repeatedly. "Mommy, my head hurts a lot and I have ringing in my ears."

A fine red rash had appeared on her abdomen, chest and her arm pits.

Must be that damn virus, Marion thought. Mike must be right.

On the third day, Abby became worse. Fever continued and was accompanied by chills and sweating that soaked her sheets. When Marion saw a black spot develop on one of Abby's fingers, she was at Mike Butler's office at once.

Mike Butler took one look at the child. "I don't like the looks of this, Marion. I'm going to admit her to the hospital."

Marion sat by Abby's bed. She grilled each physician for answers. Each 'we don't know' made her more desperate and more angry.

After two days in the hospital and an extensive workup, Abby's condition deteriorated. She developed more dark spots on her fingers, and she became confused and finally lapsed into a coma.

They called an infectious disease specialist, a dermatologist, and Jack Byrnes, director of the ICU.

"Let's call for an emergency Grand Rounds," said Jack. "Maybe somebody on the staff will have an idea."

Brier's main auditorium, seating two hundred, was full with standing room only. Mike Butler presented the case in exquisite detail. Jacob sat in the rear, listening and making notes to himself about things he needed to do later that day. While Mike presented the clinical findings, Jacob lifted his head from his pad.

Dozens of hands flew up for questions and suggestions. The staff suggested diagnoses from Anthrax to Toxic Shock Syndrome. Nothing fit. As the number of raised hands declined, Jacob stood.

"Any ideas, Jacob?" said Jack Byrnes.

"Tell me more about the rash. Does it involve her face?"

"No," said Mike.

"Does it involve her palms or soles?"

"No," said a more anxious Mike. "Jacob, please, if you have any idea…"

"You said she had a fever of 102.6, and pulse of 70, and signs of early gangrene."

All eyes remained on Jacob. He scanned the room. "It's typhus— epidemic or sporadic typhus. She needs to be on Tetracycline and Chloramphenicol, yesterday."

"Are you sure, Jacob?"

"Age has its advantages. I've seen most everything in sixty plus years of practice, but typhus and I go back to Auschwitz where it killed thousands. Mike, I know typhus. I know typhus too damn well. And, yes, I'm sure."

Mike Butler walked away from the podium and up to Abby's bedside where Marion was waiting. "It's typhus, Marion. I'm starting antibiotics immediately. She's young and has a great chance."

Abby's fever dropped in the first eight hours of treatment. By the second day, she opened her eyes, looked at her mother's drawn appearance and bloodshot eyes. "Are you okay, Mommy?"

Marion wept.

Mike Butler handed her this morning's laboratory results. "In case you have any questions about the diagnosis, look at the result I circled."

Marion looked at the sheet and saw, Antibodies to typhus greater than 1:2560, strongly positive!

Chapter Fifty-Six

Carleton Dix sat in his darkened den staring at the wall.

There's a name for someone who does the same thing repeatedly and expects different results: crazy...or just stupid. I've had it hard enough in the ultra-liberal Berkeley, but now I have Kelly Cowan, and someone digging into my past.

He turned on his computer and when he got to Google's web page, he typed in the name, Terrence Wilcox. Among the hundreds of hits, he found one entitled Berkeley Police Detective Terrence Wilcox Drug Bust. He opened the link to an article in the Oakland Tribune dated March 6, 1989. He skimmed the article about bogus triplicate prescription pads for narcotics stolen from the office of a Berkeley physician, Jacob Weizman.

Weizman...Weizman? Of course. I should have known. He's managed to transform our disagreements into a vicious vendetta against me. The manipulative bastard is trying to ruin me. If Weizman ever discovers what I've been doing, a change of address won't be enough this time. I can't let that happen.

Lola's mind focused on finishing the notes from her last patient, so she didn't hear the soft tapping on her door. When the tap became a knock, she said, "Yes. Come in already."

A girl, looking about fifteen, peered around the door. "Dr. Weizman? Can I speak with you for a moment?"

Girl-next-door type, Lola thought, but then noticed the multiple holes in her ears and one in her nose for body jewelry, now absent. She also noticed the characteristic discoloration over her right deltoid area...the telltale sign of tattoo removal.

"I'm sorry, young lady. Do you have an appointment?"

"No," she said, tears streaming down her cheeks, "I just thought..."

Lola stood and guided her to the sofa. "Please. Nothing could be so bad. Come in child, have a seat."

"Thank you, Doctor. I'm sorry. I'm not usually so rude. I'm Kelly Cowan."

"The Kelly Cowan? Sarah's friend?"

"Sarah talked about me? What did she say? We used to be so close...I mean as close as two friends can get."

Lola put on her knowing smile to provoke her. "I understand exactly."

"Exactly...what do you mean by exactly?" Kelly's voice rose an octave.

"I'm sorry, Kelly, but what my patients tell me, I hold in strict confidence. That's an unbreakable rule. Patients can tell me anything and know it will go no further."

"You can't say anything, even if it's about me?"

"Especially, if it's about you." Lola looked at her watch. "What can I do for you, Kelly?"

"I need to talk with you," she said crying again. "I need to talk with someone and all the girls say good things about you, Dr. Weizman."

"Please call me Lola. I'm sorry, Kelly, but I'm late for a meeting. Maybe your parents can call me for an appointment."

"God no, Lola. They can't know anything about this." She stood, walked to Lola's window, then stared at the brick wall. "I need to talk with you before it's too late...before anything else happens."

"Before what happens?"

Kelly kept her eyes on the floor as she whispered, "I'm having thoughts, disturbing thoughts."

"What kind of thoughts?"

"I'm feeling so bad...sometimes I don't know if the whole thing is worth it."

"You've thought about hurting yourself?"

Kelly, head still down, nodded.

Lola joined Kelly by the window. She turned Kelly around with both hands on her shoulders. "This is serious business, Ms. Cowan. If you're trying to bullshit me, it's not going to work."

Kelly stared back at Lola with empty eyes and an expressionless face.

Lola shook her. "Do you want my help or not?"

Kelly's lips parted, then she drifted to her right. Lola caught her head as she slipped to the floor.

Lola pushed the intercom. "I need an ambulance. I'm admitting a patient to the locked psychiatric ward at Brier Hospital."

"It's Lola for you, Jacob," said Margaret Cohen.

Jacob picked up the phone. "What's up doc?"

"I'm admitting Kelly Cowan to Brier Psych. I need someone to take a look at her medically."

"Is this Sarah's Kelly Cowan?"

"The one and only."

"What's wrong with her?"

"I'm not sure. It could be a reactive depression with suicidal ideation or she could be playing me."

"Why in the world would she try to play you?"

"Something's going on with this girl, and I'll discover what it is, one way or the other."

Pale green paint covered the walls of 2-West at Brier Hospital. A great choice for a psychiatry unit due to its calming, soothing effect, and if you believed it, for its healing powers.

Jacob joined Lola at the nursing station that same afternoon. "Medically, she looks fine to me. A bit catatonic, but I'll leave that up to you. I ran some routine tests, endocrine function, and of course, a drug screen."

"I don't think we're seeing the effects of drugs, Jacob."

"I'll leave her in your capable hands. See you tonight."

"I'm so tired," groaned Kelly Cowan in a monotone as Lola sat at her side. "I just want to sleep."

The nurses had placed Kelly alone in their four-bed ward. The neatly made beds, the empty bedside tables and night stands lent an eerie hollowness to the place and a slight echo as they conversed.

"We need to talk, Kelly, but not today. I'm giving you something mild to help you sleep. We'll get into this first thing in the morning."

"Do I have to have visitors? My mom's freaking and I don't want to see certain people."

"I'll tell the nurses you're not to have any visitors."

"I have a lot to tell you, Lola," Kelly whispered as her eyes closed.

"I'll see you in the morning."

Chapter Fifty-Seven

To the bitter disappointment of the Brier's administration, the hospital took on the atmosphere of a prison. It felt like the Medical Facility at Vacaville, California, the home of Charlie Manson and other notable serial killers, but without the barbed wire and security towers.

Besides uniformed guards at each entrance, new faces appeared throughout the hospital, especially on the wards.

Bruce Bryant sat with Ira Green. "How long can we keep this up?"

"Just give me the word and I'll pull my officers, but in my opinion that would be a mistake."

"Nobody will try anything in the face of such security," said Bruce.

"You're right. No normal person would."

"I don't have much choice, Ira," said Kevin Walters, the DA for Alameda County. "I'm forming a task force. The press is all over this and it won't end until we catch this son-of-a-bitch."

"Can't say I blame you or the press, Kevin, but four homicides and three attempted homicides at a community hospital will have CBS' 48 Hours or Geraldo Rivera At Large camping on our doorstep before you know it."

"I'm letting you run with this," said Kevin, "but I'm adding two top investigators from the DA's office." He caressed his chin in thought. "What do you think of the Jacob Weizman connection?"

"Five out of seven were his patients. You don't think Jacob had anything to do with this, do you?"

"Jacob Weizman delivered me," said Kevin. "I think he delivered more than half our family. Jacob's involvement in this is like believing that Santa Claus is a murderer or a pedophile."

Ira smiled. "I've always wondered why Santa likes to bounce all those little kiddies on his lap."

"You're a very sick man, chief."

All those years in Berkeley, and Jacob had never stepped inside police headquarters.

"Take it up with the city council!" the uniformed desk sergeant shouted at an angry middle-aged woman standing in front of his desk.

"I don't know why I bother. Berkeley P.D. isn't worth a damn!" she turned then departed.

The sergeant turned his attention to Jacob and stared a second in surprise. "Hey Doc. What are you doing here?"

"I'm here to see Chief Green."

"What the hell's going on at Brier?"

"That's the question, Sergeant."

"Just head up the stairs, Doc. It's the first office on the right."

Jacob entered through the frosted glass door. He introduced himself to the secretary, who said, "It'll be a minute, Dr. Weizman. Have a seat."

The door labeled Ira Green, Chief, opened and Kevin Walters stuck his head out. "Jacob. Come in."

The dingy office looked all business with wanted posters and notices of all types on the stuffed bulletin boards that overflowed onto the chipped walls. The slow turning ceiling fan had gray dust fibers on its trailing edges.

Ira Green pointed to a small table in the corner. "Come over here, Jacob."

Ira and Kevin sat on one side, Jacob on the other.

"Should I have my attorney with me?" Jacob asked, smiling.

Kevin smiled briefly in return then through tight lips began. "Jacob, we need your help."

"Anything."

"These killings, these attacks," Kevin asked, "they can't be random...they're personal, they involve you, Jacob, don't you think?"

"God, yes," said Jacob, "but I've been searching my mind for a reason...even an irrational one. I can't think of anything."

"You're a forceful outspoken person," said Ira. "I'd guess you've had your share of confrontations with docs and other members of the Brier staff."

"Life is conflict, chief, but such anger, such a grudge is way out of the norms of behavior that I think we're dealing with psychopathology of some sort, a serial killer mentality. I've dealt with many angry people, and even a few who fit into the categories of Antisocial Personality or Borderline Personality disorders...I try to avoid them at all cost."

"Rumor tells me that you've had your run-ins with nurses, physicians, and the chaplain," said Kevin.

"I live for a good argument, gentlemen. A good argument keeps you on your feet and encourages a sharp mind, but for the most part these are intellectual sport...hardly the kind of thing that leads to murder."

Ira looked at his notes. "We heard that things between you and the chaplain were getting hot and heavy."

"Hot and heavy describes Lola and me." Jacob smiled. "My hostility toward the chaplain is mostly philosophical, but..."

"What is it?" asked Kevin.

"I have my concerns about the chaplain, but I don't think it has anything to do with what's happening at Brier. I really can't talk about it...it involves confidences that aren't mine to break."

"Jacob, if you have anything, you must tell us," said Kevin.

"If I were in your position, Kevin, I'd take a trip through the Chaplain's past, and a good look at what he's doing with his TeenTalk group."

The clock read four in the afternoon when Thomas Wells wheeled his cart to the nurses' station and grabbed a handful of lab slips from the outbox labeled, Laboratory.

Mary Oakes smiled at Tommy. "Looks like they're keeping you busy. I see you everywhere."

"The whole system would collapse if I called in sick. Getting around is a little more difficult, but by now all the security guards know me." He hesitated a moment then leaned over to Mary. "Not too subtle, these 'new people' we're seeing throughout the hospital."

"Brier can't do much about it once they've acknowledged the risk. If they reduce security and someone else is injured or worse, the consequences for the hospital will be devastating."

When Tommy left work, he felt the door closing on this chapter of his life. He longed to be nameless and faceless as he checked the streets in front of his apartment and glanced into his rear view mirror as he searched for a parking space.

Chapter Fifty-Eight

When Jacob arrived home, Lola was asleep on the couch. He added water to the coffee maker and made a fresh pot of decaf Columbia Supremo.

Lola sat up and stretched. "That smells great. You can bring an old lady a cup."

Jacob carried both cups to the coffee table and sat beside Lola.

"How did it go with the police?"

"They really laid it out this time, and I can't disagree with their conclusion that these killings are aimed at me."

"It makes sense. We were too close to see it but when you look back at the cases, I don't see any other conclusion."

"It's not like we haven't experienced more than our share of evil, Lola, but here it's hidden. I don't know who or why."

"I don't know why either, but I'll bet that when they find the killer, his motives will be related to you in the most tangential way."

"You're assuming it's a man."

"It's almost always a white male, but women are on the march and account for 16 percent of serial killers. I don't want to sound sexist, but these killings feel like the kind of thing that comes from a man."

"Well, they're looking at anyone who might have it in for me but I'm finding it difficult to accept that premise."

"Talking about someone who isn't one of your biggest fans, tell me what you discovered about Carleton Dix."

"You remember Terrence Wilcox?"

"Of course. He's in the Midwest somewhere."

"South Dakota, Sioux Falls to be exact."

After Jacob finished paraphrasing Terrence's findings, Lola stood in anger. "My God, Jacob, the chaplain is a child molester, a regressed type of pedophile. Technically, it's ephebophilia but that's a mouthful and I'll stick with the more common term, pedophilia. That explains a lot, maybe more than you think. Sarah Hughes's instincts were right, and Kelly Cowan...?"

"I never liked the guy. Now I know why."

"It all fits. He fulfills the typical profile: a man over twenty-five and never married; he lives alone; and he has an excessive interest in children, in this case young girls. I'll bet you'll find that he rarely dates and has few friends...it all fits."

"Does he fit as a serial killer?"

"I've been around for a while and I've learned in practice that the only thing certain about human behavior is its uncertainty. Can a pedophile become violent? I don't doubt it, but I'd expect it only under two circumstances: First, if the person has a mixed diagnosis like an Antisocial Personality Disorder, or second, if he reacts with aggression to the threat of exposure."

"What should we do?"

"As a professional, I have an absolute obligation to report this to Child Protective Services. That's the easy part.

The hard part will be helping his victims, especially Kelly Cowan."

The next morning, when Lola came to see Kelly, she was asleep in bed. The nurses reported that she'd been up only once, to use the bathroom.

"I'm going to get a cup of coffee," said Lola. "Wake Kelly, get her breakfast, and I'll be back in an hour."

Lola spent the time in the medical staff library, reviewing several recent psychoanalytical review articles on pedophilia. When she returned to the ward, Kelly stood looking out the window. She smiled when Lola came and sat beside her.

"How are you feeling this morning?"

"I'm feeling great. I can't remember sleeping that long."

"I think you were physically and emotionally exhausted. Can we talk...are you up to it?"

"Of course, but first I'd like to apologize for my behavior. I should have handled it myself...my dad is big on self-help."

Lola rose, walked to the door of the room and closed it. Kelly coughed several times and began twisting a lock of her hair.

Lola recognized Kelly's anxiety. "It's okay. I'm here to help, and I assure you that you can't tell me something I haven't heard many times before."

"I don't know what you want me to say."

"I know all about Carleton Dix."

"Know what? I don't know what you're talking about."

"Please, let me help you. You did nothing wrong. It's not your fault."

Kelly turned her face away from the window, lowered her head and cried.

Lola placed her arm around Kelly's shoulder. "He's a sick man. He used you for his own satisfaction. You were vulnerable and he took advantage."

Kelly tuned to face Lola. Tears streaked down her face. "You don't know. You just don't know..."

"I know about him, and I know about you. Let me help."

"I'm in love with him. He's everything to me. He loves me, too. We're going to be together."

"No Kelly, he doesn't love you. He used you. I think you know that by now. You weren't the first, not by a long shot, but by God, if I have anything to do with it, you'll be the last."

Kelly lowered her face into Lola's lap and sobbed. After she cried herself out, she looked up at Lola. "There's more...much more...I'm so ashamed..."

"Let go of it, Kelly. I mean all of it."

"I just wanted to protect him."

"Protect him?"

"He was upset...under too much stress. I just wanted it to stop."

"Kelly, I don't know what you're talking about."

"The bloody doll...the phone calls...the emails...it was me. I did it to protect him. I'm so sorry. I didn't mean to hurt anyone, but I did...I hurt Sarah. How can anyone ever forgive me?"

Lola gasped in shock. Surprising her wasn't easy. Lola took a deep breath. "What you did was cruel, heartless, and let's face it, evil. I don't think you really knew what you were doing, but you did it, and you need to take responsibility. That's the first step in getting you well."

"Please, Lola...I don't want to see him hurt."

"Stop it, Kelly. Think about others he's injured. Think of the next girl that he's going to use and discard. Who's going to protect her, if we don't?"

Kelly looked up at the ceiling, tears continuing to flow.

Lola faced the girl. "Do you think you were the only one?"

"What are you talking about?"

"My experience and what I know about the chaplain, shouts for all to hear that he's been involved with others, many others."

Kelly crept back into bed, placed her head under the pillow, and shook with tears.

Chapter Fifty-Nine

Lola shook her head in surprise when Zoe called Monday night. "Can I come and talk with you?"

"Of course. Do you want to come here or meet me in the office?"

"Your office is better. I hate the thought of bringing my problems into Jacob's home."

Tuesday morning, and the streets were packed with students on their way to the UC campus. The Berkeley Woman's Health Clinic on Channing Way had its own parking. Thank God, Zoe thought as the guard showed her to an empty parking space.

Zoe wore jeans, a silk blouse, and her favorite pink Arista sunglasses. When she walked into Lola's office, she placed the glasses into a hard case, then in her purse. They shook hands and as Lola looked up to meet the eyes of the much taller woman, Zoe looked away.

"I don't know what I'm doing here. Jacob said you might help us...I find it difficult to reject anything he suggests."

"I'll tell you right from the start that it's part of Jacob's character to help. He can't be passive, but if you feel coerced, it's coming from within you."

"I just hate to disappoint him."

"How can I help you?"

"You can't."

Lola stood. "Well, that was quick. You have a nice day."

Zoe remained seated.

Lola returned to her chair, leaned back and relaxed her short legs. She knew that silence, an old ally for an experienced therapist, was oppressive to most patients. Lola watched Zoe shift in her chair, cross and uncross her long legs, and avoided eye contact.

" I know what's going on, Lola. I did a psychiatry rotation, you know."

"What do you think is going on?"

"Do you want the encyclopedic version of my life, or will the Cliff Notes do?"

"You have a strange idea of what I'm about. Have you ever seen a psychiatrist before?"

"Of course. Who hasn't?"

"Do you want to talk about it?"

"Most of them meant well, but how can you play the violin when you're tone deaf?"

"You mean your therapists were hard of hearing?" Lola tried to lighten the atmosphere.

"Deaf and dumb, too," came through clenched jaws.

"You don't think much of psychiatry?"

"Who does?"

"Jung said: 'Show me a sane man, and I will cure him for you.'" Lola looked for a reaction. Not even a grin.

"Why so angry, Zoe?"

"You've had a great life, Lola. Professional and personal achievements...more than anyone expects in this corrupt world."

"What was the sentinel event of your childhood?"

"Here it comes. Like the income tax man, sooner or later, the shrink appears." She hesitated, "Should I start in utero?"

"You're wasting both our times, Zoe. I have no hidden agenda. I have few illusions about psychiatry, but if I'm going to help you, I can't work in a vacuum. You must give me something."

Zoe looked up and to the left, searching her memories. "I really don't remember much from my childhood."

Lola sat in silence waiting for her to continue.

After five minutes of silence, Zoe stood and stared at Lola. "You're right. This is a total waste of our times."

When the clock approached three that same afternoon, Brier's halls were busy as the staff prepared for the p.m. shift. The white coated figure stood at Abby Cantor's bedside, grabbed the IV line, and prepared to inject the syringe filled with cranberry-colored fluid. Abby looked up and smiled.

The door burst open and a deep voice said, "Freeze...freeze," then pulled the syringe away violently as a line of red fluid sprayed across the white sheet.

"Did she get any?" said a female voice.

"I don't think so," said the uniformed officer who turned the white coated figure around slapping on the cuffs in one fluid movement.

Zoe Spelling struggled against the cuffs. "Get these off me now or you'll pay for this travesty."

Shelly Kahn stared at the officer then at Zoe, uncertain about what to say or do.

Shelly held up the red fluid-filled syringe. "What is this?"

"Get these damned cuffs off me."

"Not until you answer my questions, Doctor."

"Am I under arrest?"

"What's in this syringe?"

Zoe reddened and through clenched teeth. "I'd like to speak with my attorney."

An hour later, at Police Headquarters in downtown Berkeley, Ira Green pointed his especially long, bent-at-its-tip index finger, at Shelly Kahn. "What in hell did you do?"

"Wait a minute, Chief..."

"No, you wait, Shelly. Without cause, you cuffed and arrested Dr. Spelling, one of Brier's most respected physicians."

"Now hear me out, Ira," cried Shelly. "You know what it's like at Brier. Everyone waiting for the next murder. We didn't have a choice."

"Bullshit, Shelly. Have you forgotten everything we taught you about procedure?"

"One of our officers saw her draw up the red fluid and proceed to Mrs. Cantor's room. We had to act right away before it was too late."

"Too late? I love police heroics, Shelly. You saved Mrs. Cantor from the ravages of a vitamin B-12 injection."

"Vitamin B-12?"

"Vitamin B-12. Dr. Spelling gives Mrs. Cantor a shot of B-12 each week."

Shelly blushed, shrinking into a corner of the chair before Ira's desk. "Why didn't she tell us?"

"Maybe she didn't like being manhandled and cuffed in front of her own patient."

Ira looked toward his open door and saw Zoe, and a well-dressed man, her attorney, approaching.

The chief grabbed Shelly by the arm, pulling her into a standing position and whispered, "Apologize, damn it...apologize."

Shelly turned to Zoe. "I'm so sorry, Dr. Spelling..."

Zoe held her hand in the classical stop gesture. She leaned through the door and smiled. "Meet my attorney, Harwood Harrington, you'll be hearing from him soon. This fiasco is going to cost Brier Hospital and the Berkeley P.D. a bundle."

Chapter Sixty

Carleton Dix walked up to the psych ward nursing station. "I would like to see Kelly Cowan."

"I'm sorry, chaplain, but we're under strict orders: No visitors."

"But, I've counseled her. I can help."

"I'm sorry, sir. Dr. Weizman's orders."

Lola watched the encounter while sitting in the glass-enclosed dictation room across the hall. She rose, opened the door. "Why don't you join me, chaplain."

As Carleton walked across the hall, Lola turned to the ward clerk and whispered, "Get hospital security. Keep them out of view, but get them here, just in case."

"Will you be okay, Doctor?"

"I'll be fine."

When Carleton Dix entered the tiny room, he slumped into the chair across from Lola, keeping his eyes down.

"Chutzpah...Chutzpah, that's what you have, Reverend. Haven't you done enough?"

"I don't know what you're talking about. What has she told you?"

"Enough."

"She's a very disturbed young woman. You're an experienced psychotherapist, how can you believe anything she says?"

"My experience allows me to recognize the truth. If your acts weren't despicable enough, I'd laugh at your pathetic protestations."

"She's completely confused about my intentions. I just wanted to help the girl."

"Like you helped the girls in Rapid City?"

His eyes widened. "That was a complete misunderstanding."

"Very creative, chaplain. That might work, except we've seen the records. We know what you've done and what you're capable of doing. How can you live with yourself?"

"I..." He stood with fists tightened.

As Lola looked through the window for help, she saw the ward clerk talking with two security guards. When they walked toward the door, she raised her hand in the stop gesture.

Lola returned her gaze to the chaplain. "If you're a psychopath, you're also the world's greatest actor."

He blanched. "You don't know what it's like. To have urges you can't control. Do you think I like being this way?"

"You and your type...you mystify me and I don't mystify easily. It takes a particular kind of denial to make that extreme form of rationalization work."

"I never forced myself on anyone. I'm no rapist. I loved those girls, each and every one. They had problems. They needed my help."

"Isn't that step number three in the pedophile's defense manual..the step after denial and minimization?"

The chaplain clenched his teeth and growled, "You can't prove a thing. I'm sick of you and that senile husband of yours. I'll discuss this with Kelly's parents. They're in charge, not you."

"If you're stupid enough to try to talk with Mr. Cowan, make sure you're wearing a bullet proof vest."

Lola stood, walked to the door. "I'm a licensed health professional and I have an absolute duty to report any information I have about child abuse. If I were you, chaplain, I'd pack my bags."

Sharon Brickman, the director of the CCU, and Kate Planchette sat at the nursing station.

Kate watched as Ahmad Kadir walked away from the cardiac step-down unit. "I don't like the way he skulks around, Sharon. He often appears in places he doesn't belong."

"He's a resident, Kate, and part of his training is to review charts and examine as many patients as he can."

"I never thought of myself as a bigot, but like most others, I find it difficult to look at any Arab man without thinking, could he be a terrorist or a terrorist sympathizer. I'm not proud of that."

"Believe me, I know all about it. Ahmad has taken plenty of crap right here at Brier…probably more than you or I could take. Some idiot attacked him for no other reason than his appearance."

"It's more than that," Kate continued. "Maybe it's cultural. Maybe it's a byproduct of discrimination, but the guy creeps me out."

"Is that a technical term?"

"I'm a good nurse, Sharon, and in part, it's because I read my patients well. Body language reveals truth more often than you'd think. Dr. Kadir's body language says, watch out. It says that this is an angry, secretive, oppressed man, just the sort who comprises the suicide bombers in the middle east."

"I feel sorry for him. He's tried so hard to fit in, but if anything, he's shown nothing but restraint."

"I worry less about those whose emotions are overt. I may be reading between his shifty eyes, folded arms, turning of his body away, and touching of his face, but the message I'm getting is clear: Nothing is as it seems. Beware."

"Maybe that's how we'd react if we didn't feel accepted in a foreign country or worse, when we're reviled."

"Maybe so, Sharon, but my impressions of a person are rarely wrong, and I'm not about to ignore them."

Chapter Sixty-One

Zoe carried her lunch tray to the doctor's dining room table nearest the window. She wore a white coat over her yellow sundress.

As she placed her tray down on the table, Arnie Roth smiled. "I'd go your bail any time, Zoe. Just call."

She smiled seductively. "Right Arnie. All talk and no action."

"Handcuffs?" asked Jack Byrnes.

Zoe brushed back her hair. "Won't you guys ever get over your adolescent fantasies?"

Just then, Jacob arrived and pulled up the seat next to Zoe. He placed his cup of black coffee next to his brown bag lunch.

"Aren't you tired of a sandwich and coffee every day?" asked Arnie.

"Don't forget the apple," said Jacob. "Got to have one every day, although looking around it doesn't seem to be working."

"What's it like Jacob to be working with a felon?" asked Jack.

"It's not the felon that's the problem. It's the rest of you who are free to inflict misery on others. That worries me." Suddenly serious, Jacob looked around the table. "Think about it. This is what we've come to. We've reached the point of desperation where any one of us is suspect."

"He'll stop," said Arnie, "or he'll get caught."

"He?" Jacob asked. "Maybe you know something we don't."

"You got me," said Arnie. "I have a hard time thinking about women in that way ...maybe it's a good thing I'm not a cop."

When Sarah Hughes arrived for her session, Lola stood. "It's too nice to sit around inside. Let's go for a ride."

Sarah held on for dear life, smiling all the while, as Lola sped east in her red Honda with the top down. They passed through the Berkeley streets, then on to Interstate 880 heading south. They exited at Marina Boulevard in San Leandro, and finally parked at the boat basin.

They walked past the marina gates and the hundreds of boats of all types. When they reached the tip of land forming the port side entrance to the marina channel, they sat on a wooden bench facing west. They had a perfect view of arrivals and departures from the San Francisco International Airport.

Sarah took a deep breath. "I love it out here, especially the smell."

"Jacob and I sailed the bay for years until these damned arthritic hands made it too painful."

As Lola stared across the bay, Sarah had the sense that the trip and the setting were for a specific purpose.

Lola faced Sarah, holding her hands.

"What is it, Lola?"

"I must tell you something, and I'm not sure how you'll take it."

"It's not about you, is it? You're not sick or something?"

Lola smiled, then caressed Sarah's cheek. "That's sweet, no, I'm fine. You just reminded me why I keep working. It's people like you." Lola hesitated. "You've heard of the Dalai Lama?"

"Of course, but I really don't know much about him except for respect he's earned."

"Remind me to give you a copy of his Instructions for Life, his simple yet elegant way of stating the profound. One other thing he said was: Our prime purpose in life is to help others. And if you can't help them, at least don't hurt them."

Sarah stared at Lola. "Please. I'm stronger than you think."

"The bloody doll. The phone calls and the emails...they weren't from our good friend the chaplain. They came from Kelly Cowan."

Lola watched as Sarah leaned forward covering her face with both hands.

After nearly a minute, Lola asked, "Are you okay?"

Sarah lowered her hands. Tears streamed down her cheeks. "I understand, but Lola, that's not Kelly Cowan...that's Carleton Dix."

"Kelly wants to see you. She wants to explain...to apologize. Can you do that?"

"Of course. I don't know why, but I'm not angry. I'm not even disappointed, well maybe a little, but mostly, it's sad...just so sad."

"Exactly! Let me quote from The Instructions for Life. For Jacob and me, it's particularly poignant. The Dalai Lama said: Live a good, honorable life. Then when you get older and look back, you'll be able to enjoy it a second time."

When Lola and Sarah entered Kelly's room, they found her sitting by the window, staring at the garden below. She turned to meet her visitors with her shoulders rolled forward and her arms folded across her chest.

Sarah put her arm around her friend. "I understand. It's okay."

Kelly started to weep, then grasped Sarah's waist. "I'm so sorry, Sarah...how can I ever explain?"

"No, it's okay. I think I understand."

"I just wanted to protect him. I loved him. He said, he loved me too. How could I be so stupid?"

Lola stood. "I'll see you later," she said, approaching the door. "You'll be fine, both of you."

Chapter Sixty-Two

It can't go on this way, Tommy Wells thought.

He felt like a fugitive newly ensnared in the witness protection program. Unable to control his anxiety, he searched the eyes of those he encountered at the hospital for any sign of recognition that they were on to him.

I've got to do something and do it fast.

Tommy approached the fifth floor evening ward clerk. "I'm going to need a few more blood culture bottles. I have to draw Mrs. Colbert in 545."

"How many?"

"Two more."

"Visiting hours are now over," announced the PA system.

She headed into the medication room refrigerator and emerged with the tiny bottles partially filled with red fluid.

Tommy wheeled his laboratory cart through the now quiet hallway to room 545.

"Hey, Mrs. Colbert," said Tommy. "Got to get more blood cultures."

Leona Colbert was seventy-eight and had early Alzheimer's. "I'm not going to have any blood left," she complained. She looked up at Tommy. "I have bad veins." Her eyes filled. "Tommy, please don't hurt me."

"Fortunately, you have plenty of veins, and no, this won't hurt a bit."

Tommy exposed her left arm, felt for a vein in the fold, then painted the area with an iodine solution. He attached a syringe containing 25 mg of Demerol to a length of clear tubing ending in a butterfly needle. He pulled back, obtained a flush of dark venous blood, then injected the Demerol.

In seconds, she was unconscious. "That should take care of it. I'll be back in a minute."

Tommy chose this room because it was distant from the stairwell. He opened the door to the stairs, saw the fire alarm and pulled it down. He was halfway back down the corridor, standing in the doorway of 545 when the loudspeaker blared, "Mr. Red report to stairwell 5B."

When the nurses and ward clerk passed by, he walked rapidly toward the nurse's station and the medication room. It took but a moment to insert the key to his problems into the cabinet lock. He scooped the vials of morphine, Demerol, the containers of Oxycontin into his small Nike bag, and in less than thirty seconds, he was on his way back to 545.

Tommy was trembling and sweating profusely as he reentered Leona's room. He placed the Nike bag in the wire basket of his cart, returned to Leona and grabbed the syringe to complete drawing his blood cultures.

Suddenly, the door to Leona's bathroom opened and Tommy heard the strong male voice, "Step back from the bed and raise your hands."

Tommy's heart sank, and before he could utter a word, a huge uniformed policeman cuffed his hands behind him. Shelly Kahn and the night nursing supervisor exited the bathroom.

The nurse shook the unconscious Leona Colbert. "What did you give her?"

Tommy remained silent.

Shelly Kahn unzipped the Nike bag and spilled its contents onto the bed. "If you think you're in trouble now, you have no idea how bad it will get if something happens to this woman. What did you give her, damn it?"

"I'd like to talk with my lawyer."

"How many more are you going to kill?" Shelly wailed.

The image exploded in Tommy's head...how many more?

"Are you out of your fucking minds? You aren't going to blame them things on me." He hesitated, then continued, "It was Demerol, 25 milligrams. Just enough for a nice little nap."

Shelly nodded to the officer. "You have the right to remain silent..."

"I don't understand what the whole fuss is about," said Leona Colbert the next morning. "Last night I had the best sleep in twenty years."

The following morning headlines said it all:

Oakland Tribune,

Informed sources at the Berkeley Police Department disclosed the arrest of one Thomas Wells.

Mr. Wells, a laboratory technician, was taken into custody last night in possession of controlled substances that he allegedly removed from the hospital's narcotic cabinet.

Sources say Mr. Wells admitted giving a patient a potent narcotic for reasons open to speculation.

With the recent murders at Brier Hospital, authorities will be looking at Mr. Wells's activities in a new light.

That same morning, Shelly sat with Ira Green. "Great work, Shelly."

"Thanks chief."

"What put you on to him?"

"We knew he was dealing drugs. Heard it from one of his best customers looking for a deal. The other part...the murders, that was just good luck."

"Good luck usually means hard work. Are you sure this is our guy?"

"Wells was on our radar screen as a disgruntled employee. The staff had reported him on several occasions for inappropriate behavior, including being at the wrong place at the wrong time, especially the medication room. That part of it fits, but the others, the murders...I'm not so sure. He's a small time hustler for sure, but multiple murders?"

"I don't see how we can avoid the obvious, Shelly. He gave Demerol to a patient. He was all over the hospital and had free access to the patients drugged or killed. Have you checked his time cards and do they match with the killings?"

"They do, chief, but something doesn't feel right about the whole thing."

"It's enough for Kevin Walters, the DA. He's drawing up the indictments even as we speak."

Chapter Sixty-Three

I toss in bed, unable to sleep...a guilty conscience...I think not.

I hate to be so tired yet unable to sleep. The last thing I remember are the red numerals, the LEDs of my alarm clock...

Looking down, the air rises and lifts the flying form...a glider first, and then the transformation into an eagle caught in the updraft. The yellow-orange dome shines below as the specter arrives on the dais. Turning the pages of the ancient tome on the lectern, the words remains a blur.

The specter turns to the sound of shuffling feet and sees the black shadow passing between the fluted columns then through the heavy wooden door. The floor shakes as it slams. The intruder pulls on the rusted cast iron handle but the door is frozen. The sunlight, streaming through the curved-linteled window near the ceiling, blazes on the tight white coat and bloody hand prints.

The visitor tries to run but manages only slow motion through the thick black mud that gradually chokes movement as the descent into the quicksand begins. The specter struggles in despair, gasps for life's air but can't escape hell's traction.

I scream and awaken in a drenching sweat, my pulse racing.

Harry Rodman's progress under Jacob's relentless rehabilitation regimen was remarkable.

Just as Jacob entered the room at the Skilled Nursing Facility, Harry was beaming as he slammed his cards down. "Gin."

"This is your fault," she said standing to embrace Jacob. "He's beating me a third of the time."

"At least half," said Harry.

"I want to send you home, Harry, but before I do, I'm getting a series of psychological tests to see where you are."

Harry smiled. "I'm in Brier SNF."

"How close are you to your old self?" asked Jacob.

"Ask her."

Jacob turned to Phyllis and nodded.

"When you consider what he's been through...that has to have some effect but I think he's as good as ever, maybe a little better."

"Better? What was wrong with the old me?"

"Nothing, sweetheart. You were perfect."

"No, really," Jacob asked. "How so?"

"He's more easy going. Things don't trouble him like they did. It's not like any of those things bothered me before, he's just easier on himself now."

"The psychological effects of a near death experience have been studied," said Jacob. "You have avoided a troublesome complication, post-traumatic stress disorder and suffered...no learned is a better term, what's important in life."

"I hate the term near death," said Phyllis. "Are the police any closer to discovering who did this?"

"They arrested Tommy Wells."

"Tommy?" said Harry. "He was here...I mean he was with me that night, doing clotting times. What does Tommy have against me?"

Jacob shook his head. "It wasn't you, Harry. It may have been me."

"What does he have against you, Jacob?" asked Phyllis.

Jacob remembered Tommy's words, fucking kike, but said, "God knows."

Byron sat across from Zoe at their dining room table. "Please. We can't go on this way."

"That's why I asked you over. In spite of everything, I miss you, and I miss our lives together."

"I love you, Zoe. I'd never do anything to put that in jeopardy...you must believe me."

"I don't want to talk about it."

"I can't have you believing something that isn't true."

"Byron. I said that I don't want to talk about it. Maybe I was wrong. Let's just leave it at that. Okay?"

It's not okay, he thought, but at least it's a start.

"When can you move back?"

"I'll get my stuff. It's in the car."

"Good," she said with a smile he knew all too well. "Bring it up to our bedroom...you remember where it is, don't you?"

Chapter Sixty-Four

Margaret Cohen caught Jacob staring out the window at the rain. "What's wrong, Jacob? You haven't called me Maggie in days."

Jacob managed a small smile. "I'm not sleeping well and I think it's catching up with me."

"Why don't you go see Dr. Roth? You do believe in doctors, don't you?"

He squeezed her arm in affection. "Barely. I'm not kidding myself. I'm not superman. I should expect that these killings aimed at our patients would take its toll on me."

That evening, after dinner, Jacob repeated Margaret's concern.

"She loves you, sweetheart. She may have as many hours invested in you as I do, and I agree with her that maybe you're a bit depressed."

"Don't go shrink on me, Lola."

"That's a wife's evaluation, not a shrink's. When you have enough time, fortitude and cash, we can get into the darker aspects of your personality."

"Neither of us will live that long. I think I'll skip it."

"What's happening with Tommy Wells?"

"He's not talking. They have him cold on the drugs, but all the rest of it, who knows. He had opportunity, the means, but motive...who knows why he'd go this far? I find it hard to believe that it was all anti-Semitism. The killings feel more like the acts of a psychopath."

"It's possible," said Lola. "If the overt acts of those with Antisocial Personality Disorder, or Psychopath, don't get them in trouble, they're likely to lead to the highest achievements in our competitive culture. Narcissism, aggression, and lack of remorse, work well in business, politics, athletics, and for more than a few religious leaders. It's the triumph of ends over means and the win at all cost philosophy. Like those who say we get the leaders we deserve, we also get the world we deserve."

"You may be an intellectual cynic, Lola, but I choose to define you by what you do. In my book, that makes you a pussy cat."

When Jacob awakened, he knew something was wrong. He felt different. His back ached, and when he got up to go to the bathroom, his right foot slapped against the floor. He tried to extend the right foot. It wouldn't move. He tried the right big toe that remained immobile in spite of his commands.

"Lola. Come here," he shouted as he fell to the floor.

She rushed to his side. "What is it, Jacob?"

"I can't move my right foot or big toe."

"Could it be a stroke?"

"I don't think..."

"I'm calling an ambulance and Arnie Roth. He can meet us at Brier Emergency."

"This isn't necessary," he said, trying to sit up.

"Jacob Weizman. Stay put or you won't have to worry about any disease. I'll kill you!"

Like the arrival of a celebrity, Brier Emergency filled with those concerned about Jacob Weizman.

Arnie Roth stood next to Jacob. "How do you feel?"

"Foolish. It's nothing. Get me my clothes and let me out of here."

"You aren't going anywhere, Jacob. Not until I run some tests."

"Yes, Doctor."

"Use that ancient brain. Give me a Jacob Weizman history."

"I went to bed well and awakened with an ache in my back, a little discomfort in my right thigh, and a complete foot drop on the right. How are my reflexes?"

"Nothing in the ankle and a diminished knee jerk."

"That's a lumbar disc three and four lesion. It's got to be a disc compression on those nerves."

"I agree. I'm sending you over for an MRI scan."

Jacob paled. "I can't Arnie. Ever since the concentration camps, enclosed spaces drive me crazy."

"You and lots of others. You'll deal with it."

"You'll never get me into that damn tunnel without sedation, Arnie. Don't even try."

"Would you sedate a patient with an unexplained neurologic diagnosis?"

"If it was me, you bet I would because that's the only way I could get the information I need. With conscious sedation, I won't know what's happening and will be awake in minutes."

Jacob awakened in the icy cold MRI suite with Lola and Arnie at his side. "Nothing to it."

"You were right. It's an L3-L4 disc," said Arnie. "The neurologic defect is profound, Jacob. I'm calling in a neurosurgeon. We need to get pressure off those nerves ASAP."

Lola turned to Arnie. "What about conservative therapy?"

"It'll take a while to know whether it will work. The foot drop's likely to persist, and with this much pressure, he'll need surgery anyway."

Arnie looked between Lola and Jacob. "Do you want to hear what I think?"

"Yes?" said Jacob.

"It's your personality," said Arnie. "I can't see you lying around for a month or so waiting to see if this thing improves on its own."

"Good boy," said Jacob. "Get the neurosurgeon in here and let's get this over with."

Chapter Sixty-Five

The DA, Kevin Walters, sat with Ira Green at the chief's Berkeley office. "Wells won't talk."

"I don't blame him," said Ira. "If he's responsible for the killings at Brier, he has nothing to gain by cooperating. If we had enough evidence, he might agree to a plea to reduce his sentence."

"Now that our focus is on Tommy Wells, maybe it's time to re-interview everyone to try and place him at the scene."

"That's not the problem, Kevin. He was around. He had access to all the patients, he had the means, but what's his motive?"

"The thing with Dr. Weizman...his anti-Semitism."

"Can you make that work in court?"

"Not based on what we have so far. Dig into his life. Talk with his friends, family and let's see what comes up."

"What about our surveillance at Brier?" asked Ira. "The administration hates the prison-level security."

"Keep your people in place for a while. I'd hate for something to happen to another patient if we pulled out prematurely."

"Do you think we have our man, Kevin?"

"I don't believe in luck in this business. Until we catch the perpetrator in the act, with pictures or video, and can prove it all in court, I'll remain a skeptic."

Lola sat at Jacob's bedside. "You've hardly uttered a word."

"This is no time for major surgery. I know the odds. I know the complications and the rehabilitation that I'll need. I don't know if I'm up to it." He hesitated, then took her hand. "I'm just tired...too damn tired."

"It's appropriate to feel that way. Even for the indefatigable Jacob Weizman."

"I've lived a long life, a productive life, and in spite of our time in Europe, a fortunate one too."

"Jacob, don't be a pain in the ass."

"Looking out through my eyes, the view from within has never changed over the years. If I didn't have to look in the mirror or feel the aches and pains of an ageing body, my perspective on the world remained unchanged until this thing hit me."

"And now?"

"Everything's diminished. My senses seem muted...color, taste, smell and even my hearing."

"Jacob, you understand all of this. It's your circumstances and your mood that affects perception. Use that fantastic mind of yours to make sense of this."

"Intellectually, I understand, but you've worked with depression long enough to know that it's like trying to swim through thick mud, cut off from sensation, where the smallest thing is just too difficult.

"Do I understand this? Sure.

"Do I know it's transient and will get better? You bet.

"Does knowing these things make me feel better, Lola? No!"

Mickey Katz, Brier's top anesthesiologist, sat at Jacob's bedside. "By acclamation, Jacob, the staff's decided that general anesthesia is the way to go."

"Your polite way of saying that they want me unconscious during surgery. The only way to shut me up."

"Seriously, we can do it either way, spinal or general. It's up to you. You know the advantages and disadvantages as well as I."

"When I was young and brave, or young and foolish, I would have picked a spinal, but now, I'm fearful of the discomfort, the claustrophobic sensations, and yes the inane conversation of the surgeons and nurses as they cut me up."

"Okay. I'll keep you under, enough for the relaxation they need, but as light as possible."

"Promise me one thing."

"Yes?"

"Don't put a mask over my face until I'm under...just the thought of it frightens the hell out of me."

"No problem, Jacob."

Lola had to curtail the well-wishers, admitting family, close friends, Margaret Cohen, and Zoe.

Margaret was pale and tearful, and when Jacob saw her, he grasped her hand. "You're giving me something to worry about. What do you know that I don't?"

"Nothing, Jacob. I'm just frightened."

"I'll be fine. Don't worry. Take care of our patients, would you?"

"Of course. I'll see you afterward." Lola held his hand as the gurney burst through the door. She leaned over, kissed him on the lips. "You come back to me...promise."

"You're not getting rid of me so easily, Old Lady." He paused, then turned to his wife, his eyes welling. "You are the best thing that ever happened to me. I'm so lucky."

Lola watched as they loaded Jacob onto the gurney. They pushed him through the door, and when it closed behind them, she lowered her head into her hands and wept.

Chapter Sixty-Six

"This pain is killing me," groaned Jacob the next morning.

Lola held his hand. "The neurosurgeon found two fragments of extruded disk material in the vertebral canal. Both were pressing on your nerves. He removed them easily."

"It feels like my back is on fire. Where's my dope?"

"Right here," she said, handing him the PCA (Patient Controlled Analgesia) button. "Go to it."

Jacob pushed the button and within two minutes felt the relief of the potent narcotic.

"If I push this hard enough, maybe I can sleep through the next three or four days."

"Remember, sweetheart, you can push as hard or as frequently as you like, but they're locking you out so you can't overdose."

He grimaced and pushing the button again. "This place is no fun."

"I had to turn off the phone and put a large 'Do Not Disturb' sign at the door. You have quite a following."

"Maybe I did something right, after all?"

"You might say that."

"How's Zoe doing?"

"She's running around. You left her with too many patients in the hospital and Margaret says the office is jammed."

"I should be back to work in a few days."

"Right. Why don't you go in this afternoon?"

Lola studied Zoe as she came into Jacob's hospital room just after noon. "You look beat."

Zoe had her lab coat over a yellow sundress decorated with red flowers. "Margaret's putting off as many patients as she can, but with a practice full of octogenarians, that's difficult. It's your fault, Jacob, for keeping them alive."

"Keeping who alive?" Jacob asked.

"Your office patients, Jacob," said Zoe.

Jacob turned to Lola. "What is she talking about?"

"She's talking about how busy it's been in the office with you out of commission."

Jacob looked at Lola and shook his head in confusion.

Zoe stared at Lola, looking for an answer.

"It's probably a combination of stress and morphine," said Lola. "He's fine most of the time."

"Betty, Trudy, and Margaret send their regards," said Zoe.

"Trudy...Betty, do I know them?"

Zoe held Lola's hand. "Don't worry. A little thing like surgery won't keep Jacob Weizman down for long."

"I'm not worried."

"I've got to grab a bite before I run back to the office. I'll try to come back later, but I may not make it until tomorrow. Make sure you're getting enough sleep, Lola. We don't want both of you sick."

"Thank you for coming," said Lola.

Lola ate a thick rare steak at the bedside for dinner.

Jacob sipped on clear liquids and ate lime-green Jell-O cubes.

"It's time for me to go," said Lola. "Are you ready?"
"As ready as I'll ever be. I hope you're wrong."
"I hope so too."

It's been an hour since the loudspeakers announced the end to visiting hours. The corridors at Brier are silent except for the occasional nurse moving between patient and nurse's station.

I love the evening, especially this one. I've been lucky, very lucky but tonight with Jacob Weizman within my reach...well, it's more than I hoped for.

Thank you Lord.

His door is ajar, the room darkened.

I hear Jacob snoring, a soft flutter like wings beating in the distance. A soft haze of illumination from the nightlight disperses over his coarse features. He looks good in this light.

You've lived too long, old man...your time is now, and thank God, I can be the agent of your ascension.

I won't hesitate.

Nothing can stop me now.

I grasp Jacob's IV line, and clean the injection port with alcohol...a senseless thing to do in a man about to die, but it's hard to break old habits. I pull the syringe from my coat pocket and appraise it in the dim light. It could be water or salt solution but it's a massive dose of Insulin.

I look up in silent prayer...thank you Lord, and then insert the stainless steel needle into Jacob's IV port. I tremble with anticipation.

I shake Jacob's arm, then push the plunger flushing the medication into his body.

Jacob opens his eyes. As they widened with recognition, he says, "It's you. I don't believe it...Why?"

"Relax, Jacob. It'll be over in a minute."

Jacob begins to shake."I'm hungry."

"It's the insulin Jacob...500 units. Not even the venerable Jacob Weizman can survive 500 units of insulin intravenously. You're plain out of luck, you son-of-a-bitch."

Jacob closes his eyes and violently shakes, his bed rattling.

"Thank you, Jacob. It's been an experience. I'll never forget. The memory will keep me warm on cold nights.

As I turn for the door, the room floods with light.

Lola Weizman stood at the entrance with Shelly Kahn and a uniformed police officer.

"You're not going anywhere, Zoe," said Lola. "What have you done?"

"Whatever I've done, it's too late for your precious husband." She smiled. "By now what's left of his ancient brain has turned to mush. He's a vegetable," she rejoiced, laughing. "The brilliant Jacob Weizman is a vegetable."

"What kind of vegetable?" came the soft, Austrian-accented voice from the bed. "A leek...I always wanted to be a leek."

Zoe spun to face Jacob, her eyes wide with disbelief. "How?"

"Didn't you enjoy my acting, Zoe? The hunger. The shaking...not bad for an old-timer, although it really killed my back."

"How?" Zoe repeated.

Jacob lifted the covers."It was Lola's idea."

Zoe's eyes followed the clear plastic IV line. It moved up Jacob's arm and into a small plastic IV bag rather than his vein.

Shelly snapped the cuffs on Zoe. "A smart woman, that Lola. She protected her husband and gave us all the evidence we need to put you in jail where you belong."

Zoe lowered her head. Her shoulders shook. Tears ran from her eyes.

"By the way," Shelly continued, "I wouldn't plan on collecting from your false arrest suit against Brier Hospital and the Berkeley P.D."

The next morning, Warren Davidson, Arnie Roth, and Jack Byrnes sat at Jacob's bedside. Lola took a washcloth and wiped Jacob's face.

"How did you know, Jacob?" asked Warren.

"I didn't know. Not until the end. It was Lola."

"It killed me to keep my suspicions away from the old man," she said, "but Jacob may have the world's worst poker face. If Jacob knew, Zoe would have known. I've been a psychotherapist so long that I can't separate my person from my profession. That's what happens when your business is people and you must live with them too."

Arnie smiled. "Maybe we should be careful what we say around you."

"Maybe, but it won't work. Normal people don't act their lives, they live them. Anyway, Margaret Cohen, Jacob's office manager, was the first to take notice of Zoe's behavior. What she described and what Jacob and I saw, was an excellent example of the classic narcissistic personality."

"That's not exactly foreign in the medical community," said Warren.

"You're right, of course. Their psychopathology drives them to succeed, to uphold and maintain the front they've created for themselves. Well-compensated narcissists thrive in competitive environments where ruthlessness and the absence of a conscience guarantees success. I have nothing against narcissists...some of my best friends are a little narcissistic, but who'd like to live with one?"

"There must be more," said Jack.

"Much more, but no real smoking gun. Zoe was envious of Jacob, in retrospect, pathologically so."

"I've worked my entire life to earn the respect, and yes, the envy of others," said Jacob. "It's the psychopathology of the oppressed, of the survivor, the desire to prove that your longevity meant something. The drive to feel as good as, or better than, anyone else led me to what I've achieved in life, but at what cost?"

Lola grasped Jacob's hand. "You never had to prove anything to me. Maybe, for the first time at the age of eighty-eight, you'll see that you don't have to prove yourself to anyone, yourself included."

Lola continued. "Margaret noticed that life had become more complicated since Zoe's arrival. At first, she wrote it off as resistance to change or an unavoidable alteration in the office group dynamic. We talked about it and hoped that with time, we'd adjust.

"Then came the problems: Zoe's lying, her failure to carry her load, her inappropriate emotional distance from her patients, and her odd past religious affiliations. What pissed Margaret off the most was Zoe's searching for any opportunity to demean Jacob behind his back. Several docs saw this too, but didn't understand it. I hate to say this in front of you guys, but all that's pretty par for the course when you're dealing with humans."

"Cynical," said Jacob. "Very cynical."

"Or realistic," Lola responded. "Then came the real warning signs: Zoe's paranoia about an affair her husband wasn't having, and her discordant reaction to the deaths of Jacob's patients."

"Discordant reaction?" asked Warren.

"She was more upset about Jacob's reaction to the deaths, than to the deaths themselves."

"Still," said Warren, "Multiple murders?"

"Trust me," Lola began, "I don't have the entire psych profile but my guess is that Zoe was seething with anger and resentment, maybe expanding into the delusional or psychotic."

"You're not giving us the coming attractions for her trial, are you, Lola?" asked Arnie.

Lola scanned the faces. "What other defense does she have?"

Warren smiled. "I hear you're up for an Academy Award nomination, Jacob."

"Maybe I should sit down," said Jacob.

"Your performance that night," said Warren, "the confusion, the memory impairment . . . very convincing, I heard."

"Jacob was perfect," said Lola.

"Maybe too perfect," said Warren with a smile. "Are you sure it was an act?"

As Byron watched the Berkeley Police tow truck raise the front of Zoe's car to take it away, he saw again the disquieting faded bumper sticker: No Jesus, No Peace; Know Jesus; Know Peace.

I didn't understand how she embraced that sentiment, he thought. Now I'm more confused than ever.

Chapter Sixty-Seven

San Francisco Chronicle
    Dateline, Berkeley, California.

Chief Ira Green announced an arrest in the Brier Hospital murders.

Zoe Spelling, a family practitioner, was placed into custody yesterday on multiple counts of murder and attempted murder.

Dr. Spelling practiced for several years in the Berkeley community as the partner of Dr. Jacob Weizman .

No details are available regarding the causes of these alleged assaults.

The staff and the administration have given a collective sigh of relief at the arrest.

A nurse stuck her head into Jacob's room the next afternoon. "I have a Dr. Spelinsky on the line. Can I put him through?"

Jacob nodded, and when the phone rang, Lola picked up the hand piece. "We thought we'd be hearing from you, Bernie."

"My God, Lola. I had no idea."

"Pardon my French, Bernie, but you're full of shit."

"Lola, listen to me..."

"To more lies? I don't think so. You had to know something. We were your friends. You should have told us. We would have helped."

The line remained silent for a minute. "I'm an old man. I love Zoe. I thought she was better, or maybe I made myself believe that she was well."

Lola shook her head at Jacob. "I'm waiting, Bernie. Don't forget to whom you're talking. I've seen just about every form of psychopathology."

"It started when Zoe went to prep school in upstate New York. They sealed the records of her assaults on several girls and they referred her for psychiatric evaluation. Initially, since Zoe was so well compensated and functional, and so damn smart, they refused to make a diagnosis. Later, after extensive evaluation and treatment at The Menninger Clinic, Zoe received the diagnosis of Paranoid Schizophrenia, although her psychotic symptoms were transient at best. Later they labeled her as having a Borderline Personality Disorder."

"I know the problems of categorizing such patients," said Lola, "but what about her behavior?"

"I really don't know. If you think I may be blind to Zoe and her problems, you should see her parents. They don't have a clue."

"I don't believe she just came here and started her killing spree. You need to take a good look everywhere she worked. What you find may surprise you."

"I'm so sorry, Lola. Can I talk with Jacob?"

Lola handed the phone to Jacob.

"If I had known it would come to this, Jacob, I..."

"Bernie, damn it, you should have said something...anything. We would have been in this together and perhaps our patients would still be alive."

"You can't make me feel worse than I already do. I tried to live a good life, an honorable life. I tried to help others or at least not to hurt them. This will be my legacy."

"Don't worry about your legacy, Bernie. Worry about your conscience."

"I'm hearing a lot of holier than thou crap, Jacob. You're telling me everything was perfect with Zoe, that you had no inkling of a problem?"

"Bernie, please. She's your granddaughter, a graduate of Columbia University, College of Physicians and Surgeons with incredible recommendations, and who could resist hiring someone awarded Resident of the Year."

"Resident of the Year?"

"That's what she said."

"I know all about her achievements, but never heard of that one. I think she exaggerated."

"Exaggeration is nothing compared to all she's done."

"I'm so sorry," said Bernie.

"Look, we all make mistakes. We justify and rationalize our decisions to protect our frail egos. Could we have done better? Probably, but that doesn't change your responsibility one iota."

Later that day, Jacob saw Lola and Marion Krupp in heated conversation in the corridor outside his room. He heard the raised voices and saw the gesturing, the heads shaking yes and no. Finally, Lola nodded and Marion entered the room, Lola followed.

She walked up to Jacob and grasped his hand and smiled.

Jacob pulled his hand away. "What the hell."

Marion looked down. "I just want you to know that I was worried."

"That I wouldn't die?"

"Good one," she said, laughing.

Jacob stared at Lola who stood mute.

"I know we've had our differences, Jacob...is it okay if I call you Jacob?"

Jacob remained silent.

"I've had to do some soul searching," she continued. "I've been angry and bitter. The only thing that kept me from total destruction was Abby, my little girl."

When Marion leaned over to hug him, he turned away in discomfort.

This is like being hugged by Attila the Hun, he thought.

Marion grabbed Jacob's other hand. "We owe so much to you. I can never thank you enough."

"Marion, I'm overwhelmed by this incredible change in how you feel about me, but I don't understand it."

Marion turned to Lola. "He doesn't know?"

Lola shook her head, no.

"The little girl they presented at grand rounds, that was my Abby. You made the diagnosis of typhus. You saved her life, Jacob. I'll thank you every remaining day of my life."

Byron sat across the bulletproof glass waiting for Zoe to arrive. This was his first visit to a jail of any kind. The discordant pastiche of tattoos, do rags, dreadlocks, short skirts and tight tops mixed with the stench of the unwashed, guests and visitors, kept Byron ill at ease.

The steel door clanged open and Zoe appeared in institutional orange. The uniformed guard looked like a prison matron from a 50s movie. She released Zoe's chained wrists, and pulled her by the upper arm to the chair across from Byron. Zoe tried to shake her arm free, but the guard simply forced her into the chair.

Even with the too large orange jumpsuit, no makeup, and her hair a mess, Zoe looks great, Byron thought.

They picked up the phone handset in mirror-like synchrony.

"I wish you hadn't come," she rushed to say, staring behind him at the exit sign.

"How could I not come?"

Zoe's face lighted up with a broad smile as she stood and placed her hand on the glass.

Byron placed his hand on his side opposite hers.

"I love you," she said.

"I love you, too."

"Sit down...do not touch the glass," came the voice over the loudspeaker.

"I can't stand it in here, Byron. You must get me out."

"I have a call into Alan Hayes. He's the best criminal defense attorney in Northern California."

"I've never heard of him. Are you sure he's the best?"

"The guy hasn't lost a case in ten years. Isn't that good enough for you?"

Zoe paused and studied Byron. "Why are you looking at me that way?"

"What way?"

"You haven't asked me why? Don't you want to know?"

Byron turned away.

Zoe stared at him. "Byron?"

"You've formulated a rational explanation for serial killing. Justification for the murder of patients who placed their trust in you."

"You're upset. I know, but you must understand that I'm sick...there's no other explanation."

"Of course you're sick, but so sick that you couldn't stop...so sick that you were delusional...so sick that you didn't know right from wrong?" He paused. "Trust me, Zoe, you don't want me on the jury."

"Then why are you here?"

"What you did makes me ill...maybe somehow I should have known and stopped you."

Zoe laughed. "You? You're pathetic."

Byron reeled back from her vicious assault. "Was any of it real? What were we doing together all these years? What I'm doing now?"

"You're doing what you've always done, protecting me."

"No. No More. I'm done."

Zoe placed her palm on the glass and Byron placed his opposite. He closed his eyes while her warmth flooded his body.

"Do you think I choose to be this way? Look what it's gotten me. I've lost everything I love, you, my practice, my friends, and Jacob...Jacob more than anything, I've lost Jacob."

Byron shook his head in disbelief. "Zoe, you tried to murder him."

Zoe lowered her head and wept. Suddenly, she stopped crying, blotted her eyes with her sleeve then scanned the room. "Have Mr. Hayes get me out of here. I can't stand one more night, Byron. They're talking about me."

"Who's talking about you?"

"They are."

"Who are they?"

"The voices."

"You mean the other inmates."

"I don't know. I'm hearing them...the men. They want me. They're threatening to hurt me. I'm frightened, Byron. Please you must help me."

"I'll do what I can, but with the charges against you, bail may be impossible."

"Time," said the loudspeaker.

The guard approached, stood Zoe and replaced her cuffs and chains. As he led her away, Zoe turned. Tears ran down her cheeks as she mouthed, "Please... please."

Byron exited and turned to the guard at the door. "Is it possible to put my wife Zoe Spelling into a woman-only area of the jail?"

The guard stared at Byron. "Your wife's in the woman's section. Even the guards are women."

Chapter Sixty-Eight

Carleton Dix's car sat in his apartment's driveway. He'd filled it with his personal possessions. Inside, he gathered his laptop computer, his leather attaché case, and his father's King James Bible. His mind was a thousand miles away as he heard heavy feet echoing down the corridor.

Please, God, he thought, anyone but the police.

The footsteps stopped at his door. After ten seconds, he heard the sharp rap of something hard against his door. "Berkeley Police. Open up."

Dix scanned his apartment looking for an escape route.

"Open up. This is the Berkeley Police. We have a warrant for your arrest. We know you're in there. Open up now or we'll break in."

Dix moved in slow motion toward the door. He watched his hand reach slowly for the knob, heard the lock click, then stood back as the door swung open.

"I see you're going somewhere, chaplain," said the uniformed officer, his eyes moving around the room. "I'm officer Baños and this is my partner, officer Amelia Martin."

"What's this all about? I'm already late."

Amelia pulled the handcuffs from her belt. "You'll be later. We have a warrant for your arrest for unlawful sexual intercourse with a minor...otherwise known as statutory rape."

"This is ridiculous," said Dix, stepping backward.

Baños moved his massive frame toward the chaplain. "Don't make this more difficult for yourself, padre."

Dix lowered his head, turned his back to the officer, and like an experienced felon, placed his hands behind his back for the handcuffs.

"I see you're familiar with the procedure," said Amelia. "Good. You have the right to remain silent..."

Bruce Bryant, Brier's CEO, sat across the desk from Kevin Walters in his downtown office.

Bruce held up the Oakland Tribune's front page. "We're getting killed with negative publicity."

"Did you expect that the media would ignore three arrests of Brier Hospital employees?"

"Zoe Spelling was a physician on staff, and Carleton Dix was an independent contractor, neither were hospital employees."

"You think that distinction is going to make much of an impact on the front page or on television?"

"Where do you stand with these cases?"

"We've come to an agreement with Tommy Wells on the drug and narcotic charges. He'll be going away for ten years. Your chaplain won't take a chance with a jury, not with the testimony we have from Kelly Cowan and his previous history. Sooner or later, he'll agree to a plea."

"What about Zoe Spelling?"

"Dr. Spelling is a serial killer. We caught her in the act. Her only defense is a psychiatric one, which since the Dan White Case is unlikely to succeed in the State of California. She was smart enough to hire Alan Hayes. He's good, but nobody's good enough for this case. I'll be meeting him in a day or so."

"This is so unfair," said Bruce. "These individuals have smeared the reputation of a great hospital. We live and die by our public image."

"We can't change the facts, sir. Maybe they'll all plead out and you can get it off the front page. Otherwise, I'd prepare for another O.J. Simpson media fiasco."

Chapter Sixty-Nine

"You're out of your mind," said Lola as Jacob dressed that morning to return to work. "It's only been ten days."

"The office is going crazy with no physician all this time. My friends have been great covering for me, but I can't impose on them any more."

"You can't even sit for more than ten minutes."

Jacob grabbed his coat and hat. "I'll work standing. Feel free to come by and give us a hand, sweetie."

"Remember the uniformed guards in the woman's prison movies of the 50s," said Lola, "that's going to be me. Give me trouble, and it's solitary."

Jacob looked into the bright sunshine, brushed leaves off the windshield of his Volvo then sank with a smile into the driver's seat. The joy of simple things, he thought. He pulled into his space at the office, struggled out of the car and grabbed his bamboo fishing pole cane, a gift from a patient, and climbed the four steps into his office.

When he entered the rear business office space, he saw the banner strung across the wall, declaring, Welcome Back Doctor W. The staff stood and applauded.

"I'll kill you, Maggie," said Jacob, reddening as one by one, they hugged him.

Margaret held him by the arm. "Let me help you, Doctor."

Jacob pulled his arm away. "I have enough left, Maggie, to pull a trigger."

He worked for two hours. The pain made it impossible for him to sit for more than a few minutes. He stood behind his desk as he talked with his patients, writing notes, orders, and prescriptions. He pushed the intercom. "Who's next?"

"A break is next," said Margaret. "Per the doctor's orders."

Damn that Lola.

He rested on the couch in the lounge and dozed off for fifteen minutes, awakening refreshed. Jacob worked until noon when Lola arrived with a box lunch. They sat with Margaret in the lounge, eating.

"We were so worried, Jacob," said Margaret. "I know you hate sentimentality, but damn it, Old Man, we missed you."

Jacob smiled. "The office was more than a work place for me. I loved coming here every day. You, especially Margaret, and the staff too always made me feel at home."

Tears began to stream down Margaret's cheeks.

Jacob grasped her hand. "We're a great team...an aging one to be sure, but there's life left in all of us."

Margaret looked from Jacob to Lola. "Zoe's arrest shocked us. We had misgivings about her, but nothing that even hinted at violence."

Lola turned to Margaret. "In retrospect, Zoe had difficulties at work."

"Look, we saw a whole variety of problems with Zoe's behavior, lies, indifference to patients, and even her less than subtle comments against you, Jacob, but that's a long way from serial killer."

"She had everyone fooled, even the cynical psychotherapist in residence, although Lola was the first to put words to the thought."

"Every time I think about it...Shannon Hogan, P.J., Joshua Friedman, Nathan Siegel... they were family to us. We knew them, cared for them, and loved them. I never thought I had the capacity to kill, but Zoe...She's not going to get away with it, is she?"

"That depends on what you mean," said Lola. "The best she can anticipate is a long-term psychiatric hospitalization, but the courts frown on mental health defenses. I think she'll go to jail for a long time."

"I feel responsible," said Margaret.

"Join the club," said Jacob. "It's difficult to make the jump from a narcissistic personality, the world is crawling with them, including the staff at Brier, to a malignant narcissist capable of serial murder."

Alan Hayes sat behind his enormous walnut desk. "It's not going to be easy defending Dr. Spelling, Professor Harwood."

"Please call me Byron."

The attorney rose and walked toward the west-facing window of his 16th floor suite of offices in Emeryville. "Come, let's sit by the window.

"You had no idea that your wife was capable of these things?"

"I've used the word in my mind a thousand times, but have never said it out loud. I've researched the subject and I understand it as well as a layman can..."

"I'm waiting."

"Why do I suspect that you know what I'm going to say?"

Alan stared ahead in silence.

"Zoe's a narcissist, but until her arrest, I never knew that she had progressed into malignant narcissism."

"You're right, Byron. If you said anything other than narcissist, sociopath or borderline personality disorder, it would have surprised me. Unfortunately, I've had the pleasure of defending all three."

"We must do something."

"I'll have her examined by the best forensic psychiatrists I know."

"They'd better be good. Zoe's smart and manipulative."

"If smart and manipulative works for us, so much the better."

Byron rose and shook Alan's hand. "By the way, Zoe may be having auditory hallucinations in jail."

Alan smiled. "That's convenient."

Chapter Seventy

Alan Hayes arranged for a private room for his first meeting with Zoe. The guard removed the handcuffs from the waist chain and sat Zoe at the table across from her attorney.

Alan turned to the guard. "I want the cuffs and chains off."

"They stay," said the guard, sneering.

Alan reached for his yellow pad. " Play it your way, Officer. What's your name? Tell me the director's extension, please."

"That won't be necessary," said the guard removing the restraints.

"I'll knock on the door when we're through."

Zoe smiled and extended her hand. "Thank you."

Alan accepted the gift, noting the long graceful fingers and perfect red nails. The hand was warm as she squeezed his own in encouragement.

She's incredibly beautiful, he thought. Will that help or hurt?

"You must get me out of here. This place is driving me crazy."

"Not possible."

"What do you mean, not possible?"

"Don't be naïve, Dr. Spelling. This is a capital case, a death penalty case. They caught you in the act. You have no chance in hell of any judge granting you bail."

"I'm anything but naïve, Alan. May I call you Alan?"

"Of course."

"And, please call me Zoe," she said with a smile perfected to melt snow.

"All we can do is push for an early trial date, but I wouldn't advise it."

"Why not?"

"Delay favors the defense. In this case, we need to play all the odds."

"You should see the kind of people they have in here. They're barely human, and that includes the guards."

"If you're intelligent as you seem, you best keep those opinions to yourself. If you think this place is rough now, just get those people acting against you."

"Byron speaks so highly of you. Tell me what you want me to do."

"I'm going to have you examined by two experienced forensic psychiatrists."

"That's great."

"Be smart. These guys are pro's, Zoe, and just between you and me, their testimony is crucial to your defense."

Zoe patted his hand. "That sounds ominous.".

Alan pulled his hand away. "Just cooperate with them. I'm unhappy to report that you'll need to meet with prosecution psychiatrists as well."

"Don't you want to hear my side of the story?"

"As a matter of fact, I don't."

"Can you do anything about this place?"

"If anyone threatens you or if your safety is at issue, I can request isolation. You don't want that, I guarantee it. Use your charm, Zoe. Make friends of inmates and guards too, and things will get better."

"I guess I can hold my nose and take the plunge if I must."

"Do you need anything?"

"No. I'll get what I need from Byron."

"One other thing, Zoe."

"Yes?"

"Don't talk with anyone about your case. Anything you say in here will find its way to the DA's ear and into court. A jailhouse snitch could only make things worse."

Chapter Seventy-One

Marty Abrams practiced general psychiatry for twenty years before he first stepped into the witness box to give testimony in a case involving one of his own patients. While he had the requisite medium-full beard, sweater vest, and vocal tones that could calm a stage mother, it was how he communicated with the jury, meeting their eyes, one set at a time, that eventually made him a superstar forensic psychiatrist. When Marty talked, juries listened, and when they listened, they believed.

His associate, Trudy Kornblum, while incredibly intelligent, insightful and experienced, fulfilled the urban myth that physicians went into psychiatry to fix their own emotional failings. She had a facial tic and rarely made or held eye contact. Medium height, medium build, medium brown hair, she was the perfect undercover agent, a face no one remembered.

Marty talked. Trudy took notes, and both listened.

When the guard brought Zoe into the meeting room and removed her steel cuffs and chains, she walked to the table, smiled and offered her hand to Marty, then to Trudy.

Zoe sat gracefully at the table. "It's so nice to meet you. "She hesitated. "Really, it isn't so nice, but what else can I say?"

Marty introduced himself and his colleague. "Any greeting will work. You understand the purpose of these meetings?"

Zoe grasped the table's edge. "I may be mentally ill, but I'm not an idiot."

Both psychiatrists remained impassive.

She stared into two pairs of impassive eyes. "I'm sorry, but jail hasn't done much for my social skills."

"You're doing better than most," said Marty.

"I can't say that it thrills me to have you two probing my psyche. I've seen psychiatrists before, and although I felt the need for their assistance, the whole process is just too intrusive."

"Please understand, Dr. Spelling..."

"Call me Zoe, please."

"Our aims are forensic, to try to understand and make a jury appreciate the circumstances and factors that led you to do the things alleged in the charges against you. I know you have a sophisticated knowledge of psychiatry and an opinion of its value, but don't let that interfere with our business here."

"Do you really know how shitty most psychiatry is?"

Trudy looked into her lap and jotted several lines of notes.

"We understand the value and the limitations of our profession, Zoe, but it shouldn't surprise you if I said that you aren't the best candidate for psychotherapy."

Zoe turned to Trudy. "Don't you say anything?"

"Mostly not. Trudy's greatest skill is the analysis of all aspects of what you say, and how you say it. She reads non-verbal communications better than anyone I've ever seen."

"That makes me feel like a specimen under a microscope."

"A good analogy."

"It's creepy...she's creepy. I don't like this one bit."

"We're not here for your pleasure."

"Don't I know it."

"Here's the plan," Marty continued. "Please bear with it. We'll be meeting with you every day for three to four hours at a time. It'll take perhaps sixty hours."

"I don't think I have sixty hours of anything to tell you."

"That won't be a problem, I assure you."

"Let's begin with your childhood."

Zoe smirked. "Prenatal or postpartum?"

After the first meeting, Trudy turned to Marty. "She's a malignant narcissist. We may get little from her."

"You're wrong, Trudy. We'll get everything from her. None of it will benefit Zoe Spelling, but it will give Alan Hayes an accurate profile of his client. How much will be of use in court, who knows?"

The next morning, Marty and Trudy returned to meet with Zoe. He placed a thick medical record on the table as Zoe entered and sat opposite them. Zoe stared at her chart.

Marty placed his hand on the chart. "You had extensive psychiatric evaluation and treatment, some at the Menninger Clinic. We reviewed their records."

"You did what? All that is privileged information. You had no business...no business at all..."

"This isn't a game, Zoe. You signed for Alan a release of all your medical records. What was their diagnosis?"

"The world famous Menninger program couldn't decide."

"About what?"

"At first I was a high performing paranoid schizophrenic...that's a unique compliment, then I had a Borderline Personality Disorder. It was a bunch of crap."

"Were you having hallucinations?"

"You saw the records. Why bring it up again?"

"What kind of hallucinations?"

Zoe stood and walked to the small barred window and stared out. "Textbook auditory hallucinations of someone with paranoia."

Marty pointed to the chair. "Please return to your seat."

Zoe returned to the table but kept her eyes down.

"You were psychotic?"

"Yes."

"Did they recommend antipsychotic medications?"

Zoe reddened. "They were out of their own fucking minds to think I'd take any of that shit. I know what those drugs do. I may have my flaws, but what I have is unique unto myself. I couldn't let them destroy me."

Marty shook his head in dismay. "You call what you did to those girls, flaws? What you did at Brier Hospital just a minor imperfection on an otherwise normal personality? Give us a break, Zoe."

Marty stood, paced the room twice then returned to sit across from her. Trudy sat in the corner taking notes.

"Tell me about your grandfather," said Marty, "He was a major figure in your life, wasn't he?"

"You've got to be kidding."

"Don't be a pain in the ass. Tell me you haven't tried to understand what makes you tick. I'll bet you're as familiar with the literature on the personality disorders, especially narcissism, as I am."

"Maybe more so."

"Okay, but we find a world of difference between an intellectual understanding of psychopathology and knowing how to control its effects. Otherwise, you wouldn't be here."

"You call it psychopathology. I call it the results of a relentless campaign of destruction."

"Whose campaign?"

"Who do you think?"

"How far back to you want to go with your blame, Zoe? From your parents to your grandparents...all the way back to Adam and Eve? And, of course, you don't share any of the responsibility."

"I'm simply saying that if you take any girl with an oversensitive temperament and some intelligence, and subject her to overindulgence and overvaluation by parents who live their pathetic lives through their daughter, then superimpose unrealistic feedback and unpredictable care giving, you get a monster; you get a Zoe Spelling."

Tears streaked down Zoe's cheeks.

"You didn't give a damn about the people you killed," said Marty. "They might as well have been ants on the floor."

"No, it's not like that."

"Then what's it like?"

"It's difficult to explain. Each time I helped someone along, it was a mixture of pleasure and despondency. They were a means to an end, to get back at him."

"Who?"

"Jacob...no...my grandfather...no..."

"What did they do that was so terrible?"

"It's not what they did. It's what they are...their accomplishments, their old-world values of duty and sacrifice and their Y chromosomes. I hate their smell, a combination of mothballs and decay."

"Maybe you can't or won't control this, Zoe, but I doubt that you're so intellectually impoverished that you find comfort with the obscene euphemism, 'help them along'. You didn't help anyone along, Zoe, you murdered them."

"I prefer the former.."

Marty stood and nodded to Trudy who closed her notebook and grabbed her purse.

"I think we've heard enough for today. If you believe you're doing yourself any good by this charade, you're sicker than I thought. Alan rejected the consideration that you were incompetent to assist in your own defense. Maybe we should revisit that possibility."

"Incompetent?" Zoe screamed.

Marty raised his hand in the stop gesture. "I've heard enough. Think about it. We'll be back tomorrow."

As they reassembled their notes, Zoe stood. "I have a simple request."

"What?"

"I'd like to meet with Jacob, if you can arrange it."

"Why?"

"At the very least, I owe him an explanation. We were very close."

"I don't think that's a good idea," said Marty.

"I don't care what you think. I need to see him."

"I'll see what I can do."

Chapter Seventy-Two

Jack Byrnes sat at his utilitarian ICU desk with Ahmad standing at attention. "Are you sure this is what you want, Ahmad?"

He shook his head slowly. "It's not what I want. It's what I need to do."

"You realize that when you finish this program, you can write your own ticket just about anywhere in the country. Hospitals are screaming for physicians trained in intensive care."

"I know, Jack, but what the country is not prepared for is to accept people who look like me or my family. I have a hard enough time dealing with the anti-Arab prejudice in this country. I can't subject my wife and children to it."

"What will you do?"

"You may find this difficult to believe, but I've accepted a position at Al-Maqased Hospital in Jerusalem."

"Out of the frying pan and into the fire."

"No, Jack, you're wrong. At the professional level, at least, Israel may be the one place where an Arab like me can get a fair shake. I've talked with several friends who work at Al-Maqased. They need me and accept me even though I'm not a Muslim."

"Life isn't easy in Israel for Arabs, Jews, and I'm afraid, Christians too."

Ahmad smiled. "If you really want to understand, put on a dark beard and a kuffiyeh then walk around even an enlightened community like Berkeley. It will be a revelation. You'll love it when you get on an elevator at Brier Hospital and people either get off or move to one side to avoid getting close to you."

Zoe's trial was six weeks away.

Lola was between patients when the intercom sounded. "I have Dr. Martin Abrams on line two," said the clinic's receptionist.

"Hey, Lola, how are they hanging?" said Marty, laughing.

Lola smiled and gave it a beat. "Down to my waist when I'm standing and under my arm pits when I'm on my back. Still, is that any way to talk to your aging mentor?"

"I'm only doing what my elders taught. You're relaxed, aren't you?"

"Any more relaxed, I'd be in a coma. How's it going behind enemy lines, Doctor?"

"You know me. I serve the truth, only the truth. In Zoe's case, it's an ugly one."

"Tell me about it."

"I'd like you on a panel at the upcoming Northern California Psychotherapy meeting."

"What's the subject?"

"Teenage violence, Lola Right up your alley."

"I'll do it, if you send a limo. I'm not driving into the city again."

"You got it."

"Now, Marty, tell me why you called."

"After our meeting today with Zoe, she asked to meet with Jacob."

"Why?"

"You want to know what she said or what I think?"

"Just tell me what she said, Marty. I'll provide my own interpretation."

"Zoe said that she wanted to explain. That she and Jacob were close and he deserved an explanation."

"I smell the malignancy of her narcissism. Do you believe her?"

"I don't believe anything she says, Lola, and neither should you."

"Thanks Marty. I'll discuss it with Jacob."

The next morning, Lola and Jacob drove to the office. She popped her umbrella against the rain and took his arm as they climbed the back steps.

Jacob's office carried enough patients for two physicians, not one eighty-eight year old.

"You must get some help, Jacob."

"Sure. Look what happened the last time."

"I'm serious. Even the inimitable Jacob Weizman has his limits."

"Margaret's interviewing nurse practitioners. That should help until I find someone to replace Zoe. I have a group of internists and family practitioners to share my night call, so I'll survive."

"Talking about Zoe, I had a call yesterday from Marty Abrams."

"Isn't he the psychiatrist who works for Zoe's defense? He's not one of those anything-for-a-buck expert witnesses, is he?"

"No, Marty's the real deal. I was his mentor for a while when he was in training. The interface between psychiatry and the law is a mess. Marty's trying to interject the rationality of what we understand about mental health into the legal system, a ship straining against a tide of crime and overburdened with antiquated ideas, bias, the need for revenge, and opportunism of every sort."

"You mean he's a good guy?"

"Yes."

"What does he want?"

"Zoe asked to see you."

"Me? Why?"

"She wouldn't say, Jacob. I assume it's another of her manipulations."

Jacob shook his head. "I'm not going."

"It's up to you."

"You think I should go?"

"It's up to you."

"Give me a break, Lola. You're the therapist. What do you think?"

"I know you're not as tough as you pretend. I think you saw in Zoe the daughter that we never had, and the heir apparent for your medical practice. She hurt us enough. I don't see any reason to give her another shot."

"Don't you want the answers to the big questions, what happened and why?"

"She may not know, although I'm sure she'll come up with something creative and persuasive. I don't want you to be disappointed again."

"I'll think about it."

Jacob tossed in bed, unable to sleep. Then at two a.m., he drifted off.

The night light casts shadows against drawn curtains. I feel her presence behind and turn to see her beautiful face contorted in rage. Her blue eyes shine with an unearthly glow. She smiles as the syringe approaches my IV line. Why Zoe. Why?

Chapter Seventy-Three

The Toyota Landcruiser's windshield wipers barely kept up with the downpour. The pounding on his roof ceased as Marty Abrams entered the underground parking lot in Emeryville. He left his hat and raincoat in the car and took the elevator to Alan Hayes's office.

Alan sat behind his enormous desk. "How are your interviews going?"

"If jurors respond to Zoe the way we do, you have big problems."

"Tell me something I don't know."

"I'll tell you this: I've cared for or interviewed all types of psychiatric patients, criminals, and mass murderers. Often, while trying to understand them, I felt a degree of sympathy for the agony of their tortured souls. I feel none of that with Zoe. I always thought that it was the psychopath, devoid of empathy, that I feared the most, but a malignant narcissist like Zoe Spelling has made me reconsider. Like the psychopath, she feels nothing for her victims, but when you superimpose self-gratification, it reaches the obscene."

"You don't like her."

Marty laughed. "I love a perceptive lawyer. Psychiatrists, especially forensic ones, do their jobs better when they remain objective, strictly professional. Zoe's like the red, blue, and yellow leaves of the Bird-of-Paradise plant, beautiful, seductive, and deadly."

"Give me something I can use...anything."

"In reality, she's not competent to stand trial, but you'll never prove it to a judge."

"Let me decide, Marty. Tell me why."

"Her mental state makes it impossible for her to assist in her own defense. I know this requirement was designed to fit the overtly psychotic or the catatonic, but it's just as true in her case."

"Any suggestions?"

"We're finishing up our evaluation, but I don't think we'll learn anything that we don't already know. Maybe you can lay out the reality of the trial and its outcome so she'll agree to a plea bargain. She responds well to authority figures, and while you have the credentials and experience that may make her listen, she believes that, as she has through her entire life, she'll get away with it. We need something to shock her to the extent that she'll cooperate as we try to mitigate her sentencing."

"You haven't mentioned my favorite phrase, diminished capacity."

"I'll lay it out for you. You tell me whether or not you can make it work."

"Shoot."

"Malignant narcissists have emotional defense mechanisms that work to keep them out of trouble as long as things are going well in their lives and they feel no stress. Under the pressure of circumstances, especially if their self-esteem is threatened, they can easily become humiliated. This can progress to rage and ultimately, in some patients, to psychosis. This gives you two shots: While psychotic she was unable to control her impulses, the irresistible impulse defense, or two, while psychotic she didn't have the mens rea, the intent to commit the crime."

"You really are a forensic psychiatrist. I might try to make one of these things work if Zoe had committed a single act, but multiple ones, selecting victims, choosing poisons, picking the appropriate times...it'll never happen. I don't think we can find a judge who will allow us to present such a defense under these circumstances."

"Where does that leave us, Alan?"

"A deal. We need to make a deal. I'll work from my end, you work from yours. Mine will be a hell of a lot easier, I think."

Zoe beamed as the guard brought her into the interview room. She'd brushed her hair and wore just a trace of lipstick.

Marty smiled. "You look like you're in good spirits today."

"I do feel much better. Byron was in and we had a good talk. I think we can put our marriage back on track."

"We're just about through with our interviews. I've talked with Alan Hayes..."

"When can he get me out?"

Trudy Kornblum shook her head.

Zoe stared at Trudy. "I really can't stand that woman. We get on so well, Marty. Does she have to stay?"

"Zoe, understand something. You're not getting out. Not for a long time."

"That's what they say."

"Who says?"

"The voices. They say, 'you're going down, Zoe. Going down big time.'"

Trudy shook her head again.

Zoe stood. "Stop her. Make her stop."

"Alan and I agree, Zoe. You can never take the stand. The DA will crucify you. A Not Guilty by Reason of Insanity Defense won't work, especially now, in California. It all boils down to one thing. You'll have to accept a plea agreement."

"Jail?"

"Probably jail, hopefully a short sentence, and then a mental institution."

"If you think I'm going to accept that, you're the crazy one. I know what I did was wrong. I'm responsible, but I couldn't help myself...I couldn't stop."

Trudy rolled her eyes. "Oh, Please. You're living in a dream world."

"Get her out of here," Zoe screamed. "Get her out!"

"Trudy's not going anywhere."

Zoe stood and looked around the room then walked to the window and back. "I'm not going to fry...who said that?"

"Who said what?" asked Marty.

Zoe clenched her fists at her cheeks and again moving her eyes around the room. "The voices...it's the voices."

Marty reddened. "Would you just stop it!"

"Don't talk to me that way...you have no right to talk to me that way, and don't you dare use those tones."

"Zoe, please."

"Get out. I want you both out. You're fired!"

"We don't work for you, Zoe. We work for Alan Hayes."

"Not for long, you won't. I knew you two were too stupid to deal with me, and I was right." She walked to the door, banged on it with her fist and shouted, "Guard...guard. Take me back to my cell."

Outside, Marty and Trudy stood by their cars.

Marty turned to Trudy. "You've got to give her credit. She's incredibly consistent."

"She may think that she's putting on an act, that she's manipulating us, but she's not. She's delusional."

"So, she's finally conquered your skepticism, Trudy. She made you a believer. You think she's delusional."

"No, Marty," she laughed, "Delusional is a metaphor. I simply meant that she's made a serious mistake in judgment."

Chapter Seventy-Four

Zoe Spelling plopped into the chair across from Alan Hayes, arms symbolically locked across her chest.

"Besides your psychopathology," began Alan, "do you have a death wish too?"

Zoe's soft blue eyes turned a shade darker. "I've had it with those jokers. They're less than subtle in their probing of me, their willingness to judge me, and their overall stupidity. If you want to get into my head, you need someone a hell of a lot smarter."

"For an intelligent woman, Zoe, you are particularly obtuse. We don't need to get into your head. We know what's inside and it doesn't take the talents of a Marty Abrams to understand you. We read you like a book."

"Maybe you should not be defending me...you spend all your time on attack."

"Be my guest, Zoe. Just give me the word and I'm out of here. It will make my life much less complicated."

Zoe smiled and reached across the table and placed her hand on his. "I'm just upset. This place drives me crazy, and those two, especially that Trudy Kornblum, get under my skin."

"Just between you and me, Trudy is Marty's secret weapon. She always elicits useful revelations, she's perceptive as hell, and while you may from time to time fool someone like Marty, you'll never get past Trudy."

"Tell Marty I'm sorry."

After Marty and Trudy met with Zoe for ten hours more, the pair met with Alan and his associates.

"We all agree, do we not, that Zoe's only defense is a psychiatric one, namely Not Guilty by Reason of Mental Defect, specifically Diminished Capacity secondary to Malignant Narcissism."

"How will you get the judge to accept that defense?" asked Marty.

"We may need a hearing on it, but if I'm persuasive enough, he'll have to let us go with what is putatively our only defense."

Lola helped Jacob with his jacket as he prepared to meet with Zoe. "Will you be okay?"

"You're kidding, right?"

"I can't help it. Excuse an old woman who worries about her aging mate."

"It's a conversation, Lola. I'm not parachuting behind enemy lines."

"Why did you pick today to be particularly dense?" She paused. "You won't forget what I said about dealing with Zoe."

"No, I won't forget."

"Don't raise your level of expectations. She'll disappoint you."

He hugged Lola and smiled. "Have I forgotten to tell you how much I love you?"

"I like to hear it, but I know it whether or not you say the words. I remember it like it was yesterday, the day we left Auschwitz. Your hand warmed me, warmed my soul...I still feel the heat to this day."

"You're getting sentimental in your old age."

"And, you're not?"

Jacob kissed her, then walked to the old Volvo. He drove into Oakland and parked near Jefferson Square and walked to the Alameda County Jail. He heard the roar of nearby freeways and smelled the acerbic fumes of passing traffic.

Jacob had a visceral reaction to the towering white building with barred windows. Physically far removed from the look of a concentration camp, it still evoked painful memories. Its labyrinthine corridors, steel doors, monitoring cameras and surly uniformed guards reinforced his uneasiness.

Jacob jumped when the door slammed behind him as he entered the attorney's small meeting room. A steel table sat in the middle with one chair on each side. On the ceiling, he saw banks of cool fluorescent lights and registers emitting cold streams of air and carrying the distant murmur of men. The familiar murmur of caged men chilled him further.

Slamming doors echoed in the corridor as Zoe and her guard approached. The guard undid her shackles, placed her in the chair opposite Jacob and handcuffed her to the table. She straightened her orange coveralls that held the black stenciled letters, PRISONER, and half-smiled at Jacob.

"Thank you for coming."

Jacob said nothing. He turned away.

"Please, Jacob," she tried again, reddening.

"I'm here. What do you want?"

"How are you? Are your well? How's Lola?"

"Oh, please, Zoe, you don't give a damn about us...or anyone else."

Zoe's eyes filled. She reached into her coveralls for a tissue and blew her nose. "But I do, Jacob. This is difficult for me. Of all people, I thought you'd understand...maybe even forgive."

Jacob stared into her eyes. "You're not serious."

"I'm so sorry. You must know that I couldn't control myself."

"You're pathetic. Everything about you, everything you said, everything you did...they were all self-serving lies."

"Look at me, Jacob," she said, getting more agitated. "I never lied to you, Jacob, I could never lie to you."

"Your whole life is a lie right from the first day we met."

"I don't know what you're talking about."

"Resident of the Year, that award you claimed. That was a lie."

"I won that award. Ask grandpa. He saw it."

"I did, Zoe. You lied."

"He's old. He just doesn't remember."

"Just like Columbia University doesn't remember either?"

"I thought...I was so sure...what's wrong with me?"

Jacob looked away in disgust.

"What's the matter with you, Jacob? Why won't you look at me?"

Lola was right, he thought. She hates it when you don't look at her.

Jacob turned to face her. "You're the monster who murdered my patients...my friends... decent people of more value to the world than you'll ever be. You snuffed out their lives like they were nothing. You feel nothing except the humiliation of being caught. I don't think you're capable of remorse."

Jacob stood.

"Please, Jacob. Don't leave. I need your help."

"My help?"

"You only think you know me. You have no idea what I've been through, how I suffered. If anyone...just one of them did what they should, I wouldn't be here today."

Jacob looked again at the ceiling. "Who are you talking about?"

"My mother, my father, even Bernie. Then came the parade of counselors, psychiatrists, psychologists and advisors of every stripe. They failed me. Please, Jacob, don't you fail me, too."

She's unbelievable. Lola was right. It's easy to see the futility of treating her.

"How can you be so bright and at the same time be devoid of insight into your own behavior, Zoe? You never take responsibility for any of your actions. It's always someone's fault."

"I do take responsibility. I'm not trying to get off scot-free. I need treatment...I know I must pay for my actions, but spending the rest of my life in jail...that's too much."

"This won't do any good, Zoe, but try for a moment to put yourself in the place of those you killed."

Zoe clasped her hands together.

"These people weren't strangers. They wanted to live, had every right to live. You stole everything from them and their families."

"Don't forget P.J. and Joshua Friedman...I helped them...I ended their misery."

"Out of the kindness of your heart? You're so transparent it's laughable. Be sure, Zoe, that I'll do everything I can to insure that you go away for the rest of your life."

"You can't do that," she said, straining against her handcuffs.

Jacob stood to leave. "Watch me."

Zoe tried to stand but the steel cuffs held her in place. Her face blanched then crimsoned. "You're a vile, disgusting old man, Jacob. Your look...even your smell...makes me sick. I hate your paternalism and sanctimonious self-righteous attitude. More than anything, I hate your patronizing superiority. I have only one regret, that I failed to end your sorry life."

Jacob smiled. "Thank you, Zoe. You proved that even an old dog can learn his lesson. I plan to visit you in court and especially I'll make sure I'm there for your sentencing."

As he knocked on the steel door to leave, Zoe growled, "Don't underestimate me, Jacob. Others have and lived to regret it."

Jacob shook his head, and then departed.

Chapter Seventy-Five

The Wiley W. Manuel Superior Court for the County of Alameda sat near the 880 Freeway on Washington Street in Oakland.

Media vans surrounded the multilevel white courthouse with their microwave dishes raised for transmission.

Members of the public and the press filled all the seats in Judge Horace Kemper's court as Alan Hayes and his team entered. Zoe sat at the defense table, wearing a muted rose Prada suit with a form fitting skirt just above the knee and an ivory satin-silk blouse. She'd arranged her chestnut hair in a French roll.

She looks great, Alan thought.

After jury selection, Alan and Kevin Walters battled before the judge in the absence of the jury on the critical issue: Zoe's psychiatric defense.

Following eight days of testimony with multiple expert witnesses, the judge allowed Zoe's psychiatric defense with the comment, "It's your funeral, counselor."

The trial lasted six weeks with detailed presentation of forensics of the killings and the attempted murder, expert psychiatric witnesses galore, and Jacob and Lola's eyewitness testimony of her attempt to kill him with intravenous insulin.

Alan stood before the witness stand. "You knew Zoe well, Doctor?"

"I thought I did," said Jacob.

"Did you find her final attack on you surprising?"

"Not completely. Obviously we were suspicious enough to set a trap for her, but right up until the end, I hoped we were wrong."

"Why is that?"

"After reaching my late eighties, I thought I'd seen enough to recognize a severe psychiatric problem when I saw one."

"Objection," said Kevin Walters. "Dr. Weizman is not a psychiatrist."

"Let me rephrase," said Alan. "Have you cared for psychiatric patients over your many years of practice?"

"Yes, and since my wife is a practicing psychotherapist and I consulted on her cases, I've had much more exposure to psychiatric patients than the average family practitioner."

"Objection overruled," said the judge.

"Continue, Doctor," said Alan.

"Zoe was smart, beautiful, socially skillful...patients loved her. She came from a great family. Her grandfather was my partner in practice many years ago in New York. While I understand that psychiatric problems don't recognize class or intellectual differences, I just couldn't believe that Zoe was this ill."

"Your Honor. Please," said Kevin.

"Overruled. If Dr. Weizman oversteps his qualifications, I'll put a stop to it."

"Thank you, your Honor," said Alan

"Over time, you saw problems with her behavior?"

"Yes, but they were the ordinary problems one might see in working out relationships in any group. Issues of authority, responsibility, and professional concerns about practicing medicine."

"You were concerned about her skills as a physician?"

"Not at all. Zoe was well trained at one of the country's best programs in Family Practice. She had superior intelligence and knowledge."

"So what was the problem?"

"You've heard it from all the psychiatrists. Zoe is a narcissist, and working or living with one isn't easy. I don't think I can add anything more than you've heard already."

"In all the time you worked with Dr. Spelling, you didn't recognize a level of hatred she must have had for you that drove her to kill your patients and eventually compel her to try to kill you?"

Jacob shifted in his chair. "What I saw were the actions of a narcissist trying to assert herself at my expense. I thought of it as a stage in her maturing process. It wasn't necessary to question my judgment or subvert me in front of professional colleagues and nurses...that hurt. I expected that over time, we'd come to a working relationship that suited us both, and in any case, I wasn't going to live forever. None of that gave me a hint that she was capable of doing what she did."

"How do you feel about Zoe Spelling now?"

"At first I was shocked and then outraged at her despicable acts. She's responsible for multiple deaths and attempted murders, including mine. None of it makes any sense except in the context of mental illness, and right now all I can feel is a sense of sadness and the waste of valuable lives, Zoe's included."

"Your witness."

Kevin Walters approached. "Good morning, Dr. Weizman."

"Good morning."

"Zoe Spelling killed four of your patients and tried to kill two others, including you?"

"Yes."

"Is she responsible for these acts?"

"That's for the jury to decide."

"I'm asking if you, Dr. Weizman, hold Zoe Spelling responsible for her actions?"

"I object to that question, your Honor," said Alan. "Dr. Weizman is a victim of the defendant's actions, and as such, he cannot answer that question objectively."

"Dr. Weizman is not on the stand to give objective testimony," the judge said. "The jury understands that, but as a victim, they are entitled to his opinion."

"My wife and I survived the death camps where the Nazi's slaughtered millions of innocents. Those who participated in these heinous acts sought to escape personal responsibility, too...how could this be possible?

"The first step was to dehumanize the victims; Jews, gypsies, homosexuals, and the mentally ill...it's easier to kill those recognized as a lower form of life, like the killing of an insect. Even so, what allowed seemingly normal people to commit these acts. Some were psychopathic and could kill under any circumstances and without empathy. Some bought the state propaganda and acted, they believed, as patriots, to protect the state from evil, and some simply had no choice...kill or be killed."

"We're getting a bit off track here," said Alan.

"Can you answer Mr. Walters's question, Doctor?" asked the judge.

"Like prison camp murderers, I believe Zoe Spelling, as sick as she was, had a choice. She had lucid periods where she recognized that what she was doing was wrong, and she should have sought help. After we discovered that Zoe committed these murders, I felt an element of personal failure, and yes, sadness too. Now, I find her lacking in remorse and doing everything possible to avoid punishment. To answer your question, Mr. Walters, I hold Zoe Spelling personally responsible for these deaths and all the misery she created."

Chapter Seventy-Six

Alan Hayes faced the jury for his closing argument. They'd been attentive and he hoped a little sympathetic to Marty Abrams and his explanation of Zoe's mental disorder. Marty scrupulously refused to use narcissism to excuse her actions.

Alan faced the jury. "This is a tragic case in so many ways. Zoe Spelling senselessly took the lives of the innocent and made attempts on others." He paused, looking across the jury's faces.

Zoe sat at the defense table, head down.

"Then why am I standing before you?

"Mr. Walters, the DA, will tell you that these acts are a simple reflection of evil and that such loathsome acts require the harshest punishment. He will also tell you that Zoe Spelling is a physician who swore an oath to 'do no harm', but abused the trust placed in her by her patients, her colleagues, and even Brier Hospital itself. We agree.

"Mr. Walters will go on to say that Zoe Spelling doesn't deserve a degree of understanding. We disagree.

"When I finish, the DA may have little to say about that," Alan said, turning and smiling at Kevin Walters, "though I doubt it."

The jury smiled.

"I'd be the last one to tell you that all criminals, by their acts, are mentally ill. I've worked in criminal justice too long and this system, just like in the rest of the world, has proven unequivocally that evil does exist. Just open your morning paper or turn on the TV.

"The defense has one additional burden in trying to understand Zoe Spelling's actions; her mental disorder, narcissism, is unlikely to evoke sympathy. The schizophrenic holding his sign and babbling in the park about repentance and doomsday, the child seething with uncontrolled rage, and those whose lives are frozen by intractable depression, evoke both fear and compassion.

"Not so with the narcissist whose behavior stands in sharp opposition to our most cherished religious and cultural values such as love, forgiveness, the ten commandments, and especially the Golden Rule.

"Narcissism is named after the Greek God Narcissus who fell in love with his own reflection and died pining for the love he could never have. You've heard the phrase, 'a legend in her own mind'? That surely defines the narcissist who thinks the world revolves around her. Healthy narcissism exists in nearly everyone. It gives us a sense of our own value and leads us to be productive and creative.

"Zoe Spelling manifests characteristics of what we psychiatrists call malignant narcissism. You ladies and gentlemen of the jury understand these by now but let me reiterate because I have a point to make. Zoe Spelling is angry, resentful, envious, dishonest, and thinks she's entitled to special treatment. She exalts herself at the cost to others who she uses then discards. She suffers from persecutory delusions and above all fears exposure and humiliation."

"I've heard enough of this," screamed Zoe.

"Please control your client, Mr. Hayes."

"Yes, your Honor," he said as he returned to the table. Alan Hayes held Zoe's arm, whispering in her ear.

"It won't happen again," said Alan to the judge, but turned to the jury and continued, "Imagine someone in court saying those things about you, especially your defense attorney.

"Let me continue. Who would choose to be this way?"

Alan glanced at his yellow pad for effect, then smiled. "I ask for your indulgence for a moment for a little psych talk. Our best experts in the human mind have speculated that narcissists were born to parents unable to connect to them emotionally and thus they learned not to let another person become essential to them. Typically, they're treated like royalty or little gods and as a result they make the terrible choice not to love. They become complete unto themselves, not needing anything or anyone."

Alan returned his pad to the defense table. Zoe's head remained down.

He returned to the jury. "We sit today as witnesses to tragedy, multiple tragedies. We ask not for your forgiveness, but your understanding.

"As I prepared for my closing today, I found a quote from Jesus Christ...and no, for the skeptics we're not trying to bring Jesus on our side at the last moment. You judge the appropriateness of Jesus's saying: 'For everyone who exalts himself will be humbled, and he who humbles himself will be exalted.'

"Thank you, ladies and gentlemen for your attention."

Kevin Walters rose from the prosecution table and moved into his spot before the jury. Even in his pin-striped Armani suit, his informal folksiness came through.

"Alan Hayes is a great attorney, don't you think?"

Not expecting an answer, he continued, "Defending Dr. Zoe Spelling for murder and attempted murder is beyond his considerable skills. In the sanctity of a hospital, bound by everything we hold sacred to help and protect patients, this physician acted against the oath of her profession and the fundamental laws and values of our society."

Kevin Walters reviewed each case emphasizing the cruelty of the means employed by Zoe Spelling and the tragic loss of life.

"Here's what's uncontested: Zoe Spelling knows why she's here and has participated fully in her own defense. She knew right from wrong, but even under the increased scrutiny at Brier Hospital she continued her monstrous acts. What's left for the defense?

"First they trotted out the diminished capacity defense; her narcissism made her do it. That's the Dan White Twinkie defense and won't fly in this state where we believe in personal responsibility. Then they suggested that Dr. Spelling didn't have the mens rea. That's the lawyer's fancy term that suggests the absence of a guilty mind or the lack of intent to commit the crime.

"Let's look at that critically: Five separate events left four dead and one pushed to the brink of death and left with permanent disability.

"A guilty mind? She planned each murder in detail using her familiar face to move through the hospital, a predator in white. She picked exactly the right times to commit her heinous acts then disappeared into the night.

"You've heard much psychiatric testimony, but in the end, the determination of insanity is, under the law, a layman's decision, your decision."

Kevin walked back to his table, picked up a book and returned before the jury. "This is Sam Vaknin's book, Malignant Self Love: Narcissism Re-Visited. Let me quote a few characteristics that the defense attorney omitted: Narcissists' deeds are frequently overlooked; they only seek therapy when caught; they are often fully aware, cunning, premeditated and sometimes even enjoy every bit of it."

"Finally. I'm sure you're glad to hear that word," he paused, smiling, "hold Zoe Spelling responsible for these murderous acts. The one statement that appears in every description of the narcissist is that they always think they can get away with it."

Kevin paused to meet each juror's eyes. "Let me say it again...Zoe, in her narcissistic fantasy, thinks she'll get away with it. Prove Zoe Spelling wrong, and find her guilty on all counts. Thank you."

Chapter Seventy-Seven

As Lola and Jacob finished lunch, she turned to him. "How long has the jury been out?"

"They only had a few hours yesterday after the judge delivered his charge, so perhaps five or six hours."

"What does the DA think?"

"Kevin Walters believes that Zoe's refusal to negotiate a plea agreement is more proof of her narcissism and its associated denial. She's going away for a long time."

Jacob grasped Lola's wrinkled hand and brought it to his cheek. "This whole thing has been disappointing. Do you think you might have done something for her in therapy?"

"I always think I can help people, but narcissists may be the most difficult group to treat. They have little insight, won't admit that they need help, blame others and generally they are contemptuous of those wanting to help them. Will Zoe's confrontation with the reality of a long prison sentence make any difference? Who knows?"

"I just don't see how she can survive in prison."

"She won't have a choice."

"What about suicide?"

"Narcissists don't commit suicide. They love themselves too much."

The phone rang nearly simultaneously for the prosecution and the defense.

"The jury's back," said the clerk of the court.

The courtroom buzzed with excitement as they awaited the judge's arrival. Finally, the bailiff stood before the bench. "All rise." as judge Horace Kemper took his seat.

"Bring them in," intoned Kemper. "I'll not tolerate any outbursts."

After the jury took their seats, the judge turned toward the jury. "I understand you've reached a verdict. Will the foreman pass it on to the bailiff."

"The defendant will rise," said the judge. "How say you in the case of the County of Alameda against the defendant Zoe Spelling?"

The foreman, a thin, angular man in his sixties, held the verdict in shaky hands. "We find the defendant, Zoe Spelling, guilty on all charges."

After a few moments of shocked silence, the audience applauded.

Zoe sat with her head down.

"Remove the defendant," ordered the judge. "I will sentence her tomorrow at 10 a.m."

Judge Kemper gaveled the court into session the next morning. The judge glared at Zoe. "Zoe Spelling, pursuant to the jury verdict returned yesterday, finding you guilty on all counts of the indictment, I'm prepared to impose your sentence."

"Ms. Spelling, will you please come forward with counsel to the lectern."

Zoe, beautifully dressed as usual, walked with Alan Hayes before the judge.

"Do you have anything to say prior to sentencing?"

Zoe looked into the judge's eyes. "Yes, your Honor."

"Go ahead."

Zoe held her arms at her sides, squeezing her fists, her fingers turning white.

"I realize that anything I say now will come across as self-serving, but, at the moment, I'm rational enough to offer an explanation, not an excuse. God knows I didn't set out to be a killer. I went into the medicine to help others, but along the way something went wrong, terribly wrong.

"I don't understand how I could have done these things. I do remember the anger, the rage, the uncontrolled resentment and the sense that I couldn't control myself.

"Standing here convicted of these crimes, I wish that I'd embraced all those efforts to help me, to treat me. I just couldn't do it. I didn't trust anyone or anything. I wish I could turn back the clock and have prevented all the misery I've caused. For that, I'm truly sorry.

"Thank you, Your Honor."

Judge Kemper shifted in his chair adjusting his robe.

"I've been on the bench a long time, Ms. Spelling. Of all the killers who stood before me, you may be the worst, the most evil, the most contemptible. To most people, each life has value. To you, it means nothing.

"You are correct when you said that the court might consider your statements to be self-serving. I find them incredible, unbelievable, as I do your assertions of regret. I don't believe for one moment that you're sorry for anything except for getting caught.

"You placed yourself in a position of trust. You ignored your oath to do no harm and you betrayed those you pledged to help.

"You watched as Shannon Hogan struggled valiantly to live, then on the brink of recovery you killed her in the cruelest of ways, paralyzed, unable to move, to breathe, a witness to her own death.

"The fact that P.J. Manning and Joshua Friedman stood on death's door wasn't enough for you. You had to deprive them and their families of their last precious moments together.

"The murder of Nathan Seigel and the attempted murder of Rory Calhoun were as senseless as the rest. Did you smile as you injected them with lethal drugs?

"You nearly killed Harry Rodman and tried to kill your mentor, your friend, Jacob Weizman, all to satisfy your pathological envy."

Judge Kemper removed a handkerchief from his pocket and mopped his forehead.

"Intelligent and wealthy defendants pay smart lawyers and psychiatrists to come up with excuses, justifications for their evil acts. I'm pleased that this jury didn't buy it, and neither do I. If I had the power, Zoe Spelling, you would remain in jail, where you belong, for the remainder of your natural life."

Dateline, Oakland Tribune,

Dr. Zoe Spelling was found guilty in the murder of four and the attempted murder of two in the spectacular trial completed yesterday in Superior Court.

Judge Horace Kemper sentenced Dr. Spelling to a total of sixty years in prison.

Mr. Alan Hayes, the attorney for the defense, will appeal the harshness of the sentence.

Six months later, Jacob watched Lola reading a letter. "Another letter from Zoe?"

"We're real pen pals now."

"What's she up to?"

"What isn't she? Zoe's studying law and I think she will soon flood the justice system with her work. She still must deal with the civil wrongful death suits filed by her victims and their families.

"They offered her psychotherapy in prison, but she says their shrinks are a joke. She wants to know if we'll come visit."

Jacob shook his head. "I'll pass."

"Me too. I don't want to feed any delusions she's created for herself."

It was 9 a.m. when Jacob stepped into the bright morning sunlight. He'd spent four hours in the middle of the night with a sick patient. He was tired and anxious to get home for a few hours of sleep.

He walked down the emergency room ramp to the street level and the parking garage. As he waited at the crosswalk for the light to turn green, Jacob felt someone take his elbow. He turned to see a thirteen or fourteen-year-old girl smiling at him.

"Can I help you across the street, sir?"

Jacob felt himself flush with anger, then as he took a deep breath, he relaxed. He turned to the girl and smiled. "That would be lovely, young lady, just lovely."

When they reached the other side, Jacob put on his best grandfatherly smile. "Thank you. If you have a minute, I'd like to give you some advice."

About the Author

Dr Gold practiced internal medicine and nephrology (disease of the kidneys) for twenty-three years. He was an active participant in the hospital's quality assurance program that monitored physician performance. In addition, Dr. Gold served a chief of the department of medicine and family practice.

Dr. Gold retired and set sail with his wife, Dorlis and their cat, Furina. They cruised Mexico, Central America, and the Caribbean on a fifty-foot Sparkman and Stephens cutter. They sold the sailboat and cruised, Florida, the Bahamas, the United States east coast and Canada on a Nordic Tug,

They are back on land in beautiful Grass Valley, California with no ocean in sight.

Visit at: lawrencewgoldmd.com